Sacrificed

Courtney Farrell

Sacrificed

This book is dedicated to all the members of Fiction Foundry, my awesome critique group. Because of you, it's a much better story.

Chapter 1: Michelle

Mouthing Off to the Conclave

*D*on't screw this up, Michelle told herself. *Get so much as a scratch, and they'll never let you outside Institute walls again.* Her backpack leaned on the wall, ready to go, if Dillon would ever show up. She checked the time and flopped back on her bed with a groan.

Heavy footsteps bounded up the stairs. Michelle sat up, her blue eyes narrowed. "About time, Dillon. You're thirty minutes—"

Brian walked through the door instead, flashing a grin that rocked her world. "He's late? Might as well get used to it. Norms are never on time."

Brian hasn't been here since . . . that night . . . before I met Dillon. He looks so different. Despite Institute regulations, he hadn't cut his hair since his exile in the Warren. Loose blond locks brushed his broad shoulders. Between his scores and his mother's rank, he got away with a lot.

Michelle tried to stop staring and say something coherent. "So, you came to say goodbye? I'll only be gone a week."

Brian smirked. "What, and waste these brand-new camping clothes?"

Michelle's stomach did a flip. "Are you saying they're sending you? With me...and Dillon? Isn't that going to be..."

"Awkward?" Brian's smirk grew into a huge grin. "Oh, yeah."

Michelle felt like all the air had rushed out of the room. "How could they do that to us?"

"Apparently your mother isn't comfortable sending you off alone with your Norm boyfriend."

"Half Norm," Michelle corrected, making a sour face at her disturbingly hot ex.

"I'm not judging you. It's just kind of sudden, that's all. And I thought...you know... you and me, we were just getting started." Brian sat down on the bed, surprising Michelle with a kiss on the mouth that sent tingles through her lower belly.

"Mmm. Don't do that."

"Hey, relax." Brian gently turned her chin toward him, cupping her cheek in his hand. His brown eyes held her gaze. "I'm not mad. Go have your fun. Come on back when it's over."

"That's awfully Enhanced of you, Brian," Michelle whispered. "And I mean that. Look, I...I'm sorry my mother dumped this job on you. This is going to be weird for us both."

"Only if we let it."

Brian's fingers traced lightly over Michelle's hair. Without really meaning to, she tilted her head into his hand and closed her eyes.

He doesn't get it. The Enhanced swap partners all the time, but Norms bond for life. I can never break up with Dillon. It would kill him.

Brian leaned in close, letting his lips tickle her ear. "I know, you think you trapped yourself. But those backward rules don't apply to us. I'd never try and own you like he does. It's uncivilized."

His words echoed her secret thoughts. Michelle felt naked and tried to hide it with a joke. "Uncivilized? Look in the mirror. If we weren't leaving, the Conclave would send a barber to your house."

"You know I'm a wild man. But that's our secret." Brian slid a hand behind her head and stole another kiss. The doorbell rang from downstairs. He rolled his eyes. "Norm-boy's here."

"Don't call him that." Michelle jumped up and ran for the door.

Brian tagged along, annoying as a kid brother. He pranced down the hall, pretending to be her. "Ooo, I can't wait! Dillon's here from the slum, with his Norm family." He did a couple of limp-wristed pirouettes at the top of the stairs.

Michelle tried not to laugh, but failed. "Shut up." She delivered a perfect hip-check, low on Brian's center of gravity and timed to catch him in the air.

Brian stumbled, made a beautiful save, and came up grinning. He threw an arm around Michelle's waist. "If I go down, I'm taking you with me."

She spun out of his grip and bounced down the stairs, giggling. Her mother was already there, pacing the circular, dome-roofed foyer. When Victoria Atherton saw Brian with her daughter, she gave him a sweet smile and a nod of encouragement.

Michelle pursed her lips in warning. *Stay out of it, Mother.*

Victoria looked away, shoulders set in a hard line. She took a deep breath and opened the door. On the front porch of the Atherton mansion stood twenty wet and muddy Normals, huddled together to get out of the rain. Dillon towered over them, auburn ponytail dripping. His eyes lit up when he spotted Michelle.

"Welcome, everyone. Please come in," Victoria said, in a tone that made it clear she'd rather they didn't.

The Norms trooped in, squishing stinking mud all over the fine teak floor. Michelle coughed, eyes watering. The open sewers of the Warren had overflowed again, like they always did when it rained. Brian made a loud choking sound and headed for the kitchen alone.

A red-haired woman spoke from the back of the pack. "Shoes off, please."

The visitors cheerfully yanked off their muddy shoes and tossed them

2

into a corner, leaving brown smears all over the white wall. Michelle winced. A bearded Norm chuckled self-consciously. One toe stuck out of a hole in his sock.

Victoria didn't seem to notice anything except the petite red-haired woman. "My God, Alexa, it's really you. I feel like I've seen a ghost."

"Hello, Victoria." Dillon's mother picked her way between puddles with the unconscious grace of a dancer. Alexa's old jeans and blouse had seen better days, but her Enhanced ancestry was unmistakable. Years of borderline starvation had not marred her beauty.

Victoria kissed Dillon's mom on both cheeks. "How good to see you! It's been, what, twenty years?"

"Eighteen."

"I feel so awful about the way they treated you. We never knew you had a child out there," Victoria said.

"Really? Does this mean you're going to call off the assassins, Victoria? Now that you run the Conclave?"

Victoria took a step back. "The Augments…they're after you?"

Alexa let out an exasperated breath. "Of course they are. Until someone gives the order to stop them."

"I didn't know. I'm not sure it's an issue, since most of our Augments died in the plague, but there are survivors," Victoria murmured, flicking her wrist to activate her surgically implanted cell chip. Beams of colored light arced across her palm. She manipulated them with one polished nail, making the beams whirl. The lights winked out. "There. I ordered the program halted, just in case. Alexa, I am so sorry. I wasn't in command when that order was given."

Alexa pasted on a plastic smile. "Of course you weren't, Victoria. But look at you now, heading up the Conclave. I always knew you'd do well."

"Come in, dear, let's catch up. My daughter and your son—who ever saw that coming?" Victoria led her guests through the living room, into the giant kitchen, and out onto the covered deck, where servants were putting the finishing touches on a lavish buffet.

Michelle let the rest of the crowd go first. At the back of the group she got a few seconds alone with Dillon. "Assassins, huh? Nice icebreaker."

Dillon stifled a laugh. "My mom's pretty up-front, but that was blunt even for her."

Michelle led the way into the kitchen, but her steps faltered there. Out on the deck, Norms were already jostling elbows over the buffet. Servants had arranged fine china and silver at one end of the table, but the Normals didn't line up and take plates. They swarmed in from all sides, grabbing food with their hands. Michelle's great-grandfather, the founder of the Institute, stood there gritting his teeth.

"Is that your grandfather? Bet he's itchin' for a shotgun right about now," Dillon whispered, too loud for Enhanced ears. The silver-haired man turned his head, blue eyes twinkling in amusement.

"*Great*-grandfather," Michelle mouthed. "That's the Institute's founder, our top-ranked man, and he *heard* you. Can we flee, please?"

Dillon laughed and shook his head. "We'll be out of here soon enough. Bitter Springs is gonna be crazy."

"I was afraid of that."

"Don't worry. You'll be with me." He slid an arm around Michelle's waist, pulling her in for a kiss.

Heat stirred inside her at his scent, leather and musk and something wild she couldn't identify. It took all Michelle's self-control to put her hands on his chest and stop him. "Not now. My mother's watching."

Dillon ran his hands down her sides, lightly stroking Michelle's skin through her filmy summer blouse. "It's okay, we're bonded now. She'll get used to it."

"No she won't." Michelle captured his hands before they went any lower. "Seriously, Dillon. You never told me people tried to kill you."

"They were after my mom, not me. She told the Institute I died as a baby, remember?" Dillon shoved his hands in his pockets and looked away, red-gold brows low over his eyes. "Apparently you can't just resign from the Institute."

"Right. Enhanced genes are company property." Michelle peeked at Dillon's tiny, fragile-looking mother through the window. "What a nightmare. I wonder how she survived."

"She survived because we killed every assassin they sent against us. My mom did it, at first, when I was small. When I turned fourteen, I took on the job. My cheery little springtime ritual."

"Lovely." Michelle busied herself pouring a couple of glasses of juice over ice, mostly to keep up the pretense that everything was okay. She pressed a cold glass into Dillon's hand. "I don't know why I'm surprised. That's what they do to the culled children. Why should adults be any different?"

"My mother wasn't culled. She got sick of the bullshit and walked out."

"Um, I guess you should know, your mom already told me the truth about that. When she got pregnant by a..." Michelle looked down and forced the words out. "By a Norm, Doctor Salomon ordered her to have an abortion. She ran to save your life."

Dillon didn't answer, but his eyes turned a darker shade of blue. A storm roiled just under the surface. It made Michelle nervous. *Maybe I shouldn't have said that.*

The doorbell rang, and one of the servants opened it. Smartly suited men and women filed in, wrinkling their noses at the pile of muddy shoes.

Michelle grabbed Dillon's arm and tugged him toward the back door.

"Come on, let's find seats."

"What's your rush?"

"The Conclave is here," Michelle whispered over her shoulder. "They kind of put my teeth on edge. Especially the doctors."

Dillon peered around the corner before he followed Michelle outside onto the covered deck. "They don't look that scary to me. A little uptight, maybe."

Michelle took Dillon's arm and leaned in so she wouldn't be overheard. "Dillon, the Conclave runs the Institute eugenics program. Those people decide everything. Which kids grow up, and which ones die."

"Yeah?" Dillon squared his shoulders. "Well, they don't decide anything for me."

"Sure. Who do you think sent the Augments?"

"I thought Doctor Salomon did, and he's dead now. You're saying it was them? So it isn't over?"

Michelle shrugged. "Who knows?"

"Great. This is going to be a fun lunch." Dillon loaded up a plate with food, even though the Norms' dirty hands had touched just about everything.

Michelle couldn't eat. "Let's go out back, by the wall. As far away as we can get."

"But it's raining."

"I don't care."

"Dillon, Michelle!" Victoria waved from her seat beside Alexa. "Come sit with us."

Michelle sighed. Her mother sat at the head of a long table, with a dozen extra seats for the Conclave. Dillon moved toward an empty chair by his mom, but Michelle stopped him with a soft hand on his arm. "Sorry. We belong on the other end of the table. The low-ranking end."

The Conclave marched onto the covered deck in silence. *That's a bad sign,* Michelle thought. *They mean business. Are they here to cancel our trip?*

The Conclave members took their seats. Portly Doctor Williams stood in for Doctor Salomon, who had been exiled for engineering the plague that killed most of the Norms. The Founder should have been there, but he sat alone in the kitchen, talking on his surgically implanted cell phone.

Victoria began the meeting without him. "We're all grateful that Michelle and Dillon have agreed to visit Bitter Springs and assess post-plague conditions there. As we all know, getting trade routes open is our top priority."

"So it's about money, not charity," Dillon rumbled.

Michelle kicked his shin under the table.

"Correction," Victoria added, with a polite nod to Dillon. "As I should have said, my daughter's safety is really my top priority."

"So it is for us all," Doctor Williams chimed in. "Michelle represents a tremendous breakthrough in the breeding program—"

Victoria raised a hand to interrupt. "Thank you, Doctor. So, as I was saying, she'll need a significant security force. Nine of our Augments survived the plague. I move that we send five of them on the mission to Bitter Springs."

"No way," Dillon said. "If you make us march in there with armed men, you know what's gonna happen?"

The Conclave stared, aghast at his breach of protocol. Victoria merely raised an eyebrow.

Dillon didn't seem intimidated. "Best case scenario, people avoid us. More likely, they'll target us from windows. Look, we'll be fine if you just let us go in quietly and blend with the population."

Victoria spoke slowly. "Without Security? That's out of the question. My daughter is far too precious."

"Don't confuse it with love. They're only protecting the genes I carry," Michelle whispered to Dillon, knowing full well her mother would overhear. Everyone else did too. Michelle immediately regretted shooting off her mouth. The cold eyes of the Conclave tied her stomach in knots.

Dillon sipped his drink and leaned back, like people weren't staring daggers at him. "Mrs. Atherton, I'm going to level with you. My contract specifies that I contact local merchants, but people are not gonna talk to me with bodyguards breathing down my neck. We'll come back with nothing."

"That's ridiculous," Doctor Williams blustered.

"It is not," Alexa said. "Dillon's right, Victoria. Security sets them apart. It actually increases their risk."

The Conclave erupted in arguments. Everyone talked at once, and no one listened.

Dillon's voice boomed across them all. "The Warren is bad enough, but Bitter Springs is worse. A lot worse, 'cause the gangs there all have guns."

Michelle put her head in her hands. She hated to admit it, but she was starting to understand Doctor Salomon's objection to recruiting wild-borns. The knowledge made her feel a little sick inside, like she was buying into the system she'd raged against her whole life.

When the white-haired Founder stepped onto the deck, everyone fell silent. "This conversation is over. Michelle, you won't be going to Bitter Springs."

Her heart fell. "But—"

"Pay attention. We've lost communication with one of our northern military bases. I'm sending you and your team to make contact. Help with repairs if you can. If they need components you don't have on hand, we'll deliver them."

"Which base, G.G.?" Michelle asked, boldly using her great-grandfather's nickname in public.

"Iron Torr."

Michelle bit back a gasp. *Not Iron Torr. I swore I'd never go there again.* Even the memory of the arctic military base made her feel trapped.

The old man snapped his fingers to summon a servant. "Send them in now."

"Yes, sir." The uniformed Normal hurried into the house.

Only seconds later, Jeanette Morley stepped onto the deck in jeans and hiking boots—not her usual high heels and overpriced fashions. Her long blonde hair was pulled back in a simple ponytail. Todd shadowed his sister, looking ill at ease under the scrutiny of the Conclave. Side by side, the Morley siblings looked remarkably alike, but the delicate bone structure that gave Jeanette her ethereal beauty didn't work on a boy. Despite the Institute's grueling workout program, Todd's biceps weren't much bigger than his sister's.

The Founder turned his laser focus on the newly arrived teens. "Where's the rest of the team, Jeanette?"

"They're coming, sir," Jeanette said. "Sylvia is saying goodbye to her parents on the front porch, since they're only recruits."

"Recruits? That'd be a step up." The Founder cast an acid glance at the Norms, who were tucking biscuits into their pockets. "They might as well come on in and join the rest of these monkeys."

Sylvia Ramirez walked into the party just in time to hear that. Her wide-eyed gaze swept from the mud-spattered Norms at one table to the Conclave at the other, and she didn't say a word.

Michelle jumped up to hug her best friend, mainly to whisper without being too obvious. "I'm so glad you're coming too! Brian told me it was just him, Dillon, and me."

The tip of Sylvia's waist-length black braid swayed as she laughed. "And you fell for it?"

"Totally. I could just kill him. Plus, up in my room, he tried to—"

"Michelle," the Founder interrupted. "Get your gear. You're leaving immediately."

"Yes, sir." Michelle turned away and hurried up the white-carpeted stairs.

Dillon walked into her bedroom a few seconds later and shut the door with a snap. "We have a problem. They're insisting on sending Security."

Michelle shrugged. "Of course."

"And that makes it a lot more dangerous for all of us. So I want to give you the chance to cancel. Forget the money. It's too risky."

Michelle knew what it cost him to say that. With one hand, she reached up and stroked the chiseled line of his jaw. "Dillon, I appreciate the offer, I really do. But you're at the Institute now. They're in control, not us. We cancel if they say we cancel."

Dillon turned away without answering. Michelle felt bad for him. It wasn't like he had a choice. He'd bonded to her, and that couldn't be undone. She loved him too, but it wasn't the same. Without Dillon, she'd mourn. If he lost her, he'd probably waste away and die, like bereaved Normals so often did. The pair bonding instinct interfered with the Institute's selective breeding program, so the doctors had eliminated it. Michelle wondered what she was missing.

Maybe Dillon deserves more. I love him, I know I do. But can I love the way we were meant to, before the doctors robbed us of the ability?

Dillon paced Michelle's big bedroom. "Look, you know I like Sylvia and Jeanette. And Jeanette's nerdy brother seems okay too. What was his name again?"

"Todd."

"Right, Todd," Dillon nodded. "He's the genius you told me about, who helped you find your brother. I have no problem with him. It's the Augments that creep me out."

"They're not creepy once you get to know them," Michelle said, since she couldn't figure out how to bring up Brian. "And besides, they're on your side now."

"Not once they find out I'm a Norm."

"You're not a Norm, Dillon."

Dillon tensed, his thin, wiry muscles held rigid. He bit out his words. "Wild-born, then. Half-breed. Whatever."

Michelle put her arms around his neck and stood on tiptoe to murmur in his ear. "They will see you as Enhanced, and they'll follow your orders. Augments instinctively defer to the Enhanced."

Dillon curled a lip in disgust. "The doctors built them that way? To revere you? I didn't even know that was possible."

"It is." Michelle pressed a little closer, and he wrapped his arms around her waist. "So...if you told them to leave us alone for a while, they would."

That thought made Dillon smile, but it didn't last long. A light tapping came from the other side of the closed door. "Tell who to leave you alone? Me?"

"Seth!" Michelle pulled away from Dillon, silently cursing her brother's Enhanced hearing. Whispering didn't help around him, even through walls. She opened the door.

Seth walked in wearing a navy-blue Security jacket that gave him a military look. On his return from exile, Seth's unruly dark hair had been cropped short again, but he'd never be the same, not really. He was still thin, so his cheekbones stood out, and his night-blue eyes looked too big for his face.

Seth nodded politely to Dillon but spoke to his sister. "So, you're off. I wish I could go with you."

Michelle laughed. "You do not."

"Okay, then. I kind of wish I was going." Seth grinned. "As in, I'd like to go someplace, just not Iron Torr. But I've got Security to deal with. That's my excuse."

"So I get to go freeze my butt off in the Arctic, while you hang out with the Toklats."

"It's my job," Seth said, folding his arms. "The gang's replacing the Augments. That's a Conclave decision."

"I told Mom that was stupid. We'll never get rid of those criminals now."

Seth's lip twisted in a mocking smile, but he refused to be drawn into his sister's favorite argument. "I didn't come up here to talk about that." He looked away, as if searching for the right words. "Michelle, I know the Conclave harped on safety 'til you were sick of it, but they're right. This trip really is dangerous. Stick close to Brian. He's worth more in a fight than all your Augments put together."

Dillon's head snapped around.

Michelle winced. "Sorry, Dillon, I was going to tell you. The Conclave ordered Brian along. It wasn't his idea. Or mine."

Dillon didn't answer. Didn't change expression. *Not a good sign.*

Seth met his eyes. "Dillon. A word, if you don't mind?"

Seth left the room. Dillon clenched his jaw and followed him down the long hallway. Michelle took a few steps after them, but a subtle hand signal from her brother stopped her. *Oh, crap. What's he going to say?*

The young men moved away, almost out of earshot, and faced each other under framed oil paintings of Atherton ancestors. Seth had that relaxed, aristocratic posture that he always adopted when he wanted to dominate someone. It sent the message that he was in control, without even trying.

"Dillon, I need you to try very hard to understand something," Seth said. "My sister is no ordinary girl. She's the culmination of generations of effort. Selective breeding. Genetic engineering that, frankly, you're not equipped to comprehend. The risk involved, taking her into a place like the Warren--"

"How long were you in the Warren, Seth?" Dillon interrupted. "Three months? And that makes you an expert."

Seth growled an answer, too low to be heard.

Dillon's voice carried. "She'll be fine."

Michelle tensed, fingers gripping the door frame.

"I'm sure you understand how important it is for us to ensure that," Seth said cordially. Brian came around the corner and stood behind him, arms folded in silent backup. If a fight broke out, it would be two on one. Michelle's palms went damp. Her half-Norm boyfriend wouldn't have a chance.

Dillon muttered something Michelle didn't quite catch, but it didn't matter, since it mostly sounded like Norm swear words. Seth made a small flicking gesture, as though dismissing a servant, and turned away. Dillon flexed a shoulder, and for a split second, Michelle thought her boyfriend was going to blind-side her brother with a punch to the head.

Jeannette appeared on the stairs. "Break it up, boys, we're going now. Bye, Seth, see you next week."

Dillon shot Seth and Brian a final glare and followed Jeanette downstairs.

Michelle grabbed her pack and walked down the hall. Her brother wisely retreated to his room when he saw her coming, leaving her alone in the endless corridor. From the dark-framed portraits, the eyes of her ancestors watched her go by. They reminded her of Dillon's father. She didn't know much about him, only that Institute doctors tried to recruit him before Dillon was born, and they failed.

Alexa gave up everything for that man. And look what happened. He ended up with a bullet in the head. If he was anything like his son, I can see why.

Chapter 2: Michelle

Iron Torr

Inside the helicopter, white leather seats stood in a semicircle around a mahogany coffee table. A matching couch, just big enough for two, faced them. There'd be no privacy on this flight. Michelle boarded last. One empty seat remained, on the couch beside Dillon.

While the Augment pilot finished his pre-flight check, Jeanette reached out and slid a partition closed, separating them from the security guards on their straight-backed benches. She leaned back on her cushy armchair. "Awesome, they gave us the best helicopter. My father had this one converted from a military troop transport. The aft section's still mostly original."

The helicopter took off, leaving the Conclave behind. Michelle twisted to look out the window. Below, Institute bulldozers rumbled through the Warren, clearing away old ruins from the war. This had been impossible until last spring, when the plague struck. Norms once lived among the bombed-out buildings, in the shadows of shattered walls.

The aircraft swept north, over green fields. Todd snapped another door closed, sealing them off from the pilot and co-pilot. Engine noise suddenly quieted. "The passenger section's soundproofed."

"Nice." Brian grabbed some cold drinks from a built in mini-fridge. "Want one?" He handed a soda to Dillon like they were friends.

Everyone watched to see what Dillon would do, but he just thanked Brian and took the drink. Michelle knew what Brian was up to—he'd played this game since he was a kid. He loved to be overly friendly to people who hated him. It drove them nuts, and they could never do anything about it. Soon he'd be eating off Dillon's plate and following him to the bathroom so he could talk to him through the closed door. To Brian, being annoying was an art form. Michelle snickered.

Brian quirked a lip at her. "What's so funny?"

"I was just remembering how you stole Martin Williams' diary in fifth grade."

"Oh yeah. I took a red pen and corrected all the grammar and spelling in it," Brian said.

The Enhanced teens laughed, but Dillon just shook his head. "Bet he was pissed."

"It was great," Brian said. "I just looked at him, all sincere, and told him how friends do each other favors like that."

Dillon grinned. "Gods."

Michelle fixed Brian with a stern look. *He doesn't need to give Dillon yet another reason to hate him.* Brian smirked back, like he knew exactly why she suddenly remembered Martin Williams. *He's definitely up to no good.*

Michelle curled up on the leather couch, feeling small. "At least I'm going," she said in a low voice. "I thought they were going to stop me."

"Once we get there, you'll wish they had," Jeanette answered glumly.

Michelle caught Dillon's raised eyebrow, but she didn't want to talk about it. People needed time to deal with the bad news. *Iron Torr. Damn it! I swore I'd never go there again.*

Dillon seemed to sense her dark mood. He took her hand, and she leaned against his shoulder, staring into space. A tingle of energy sparked between their palms, flowing from Michelle's hand to his. Hazy images appeared in his mind and then snapped into painfully sharp focus. The sun seemed too bright, the whisper of the wind too loud. Needles on pine trees a mile away stood out in impossibly sharp detail. Iridescent waves of green and purple flashed across a fly's hairy little body before it buzzed away, transparent wings whirling in perfect synchrony.

Dillon gasped, and their mental connection broke. "Was--was that you, Michelle?"

Michelle gave him a secret smile. She touched the back of his hand with one finger and sent a single word. *Yes.*

Dillon jumped. "Gods! I heard that. In your voice, but inside my head."

Jeanette giggled. "I see you're still getting to know your new girlfriend, Dillon."

He stared. "You knew about this? Do all the Enhanced communicate this way?"

"We all know." Jeanette waved a forefinger, indicating their circle of teens. "But not all of us can do it. Todd and I carry the gene, and Michelle does too, obviously. Plus a few other people back home. But Dillon, it's essential that you keep your mouth shut about this. The Conclave doesn't know about our ability, and we need to keep it that way."

Dillon managed a nod. Shock made his mouth hang open. He took Michelle's hand again. Almost immediately, energy tickled between their palms.

There's a huge difference between us. You're pure-bred Enhanced, and I'm only a . . . Dillon stifled the thought, but Michelle heard it.

It's all right, love. You're perfect as you are. Want me to show you why we're all so apprehensive about this trip?

Dillon's transmitted thought came through, faint but clear. *Yes. Show me. I need to know.*

Okay. If you're still and quiet, I can share a memory with you. Brace yourself. This is Iron Torr.

Dillon watched through Michelle's eyes as she climbed an immense flight of stairs that twisted up the outside of a sleek modern tower of dark metal. The tower adjoined a much larger fortification that clung to the top of a rocky ridge. When Michelle turned her head to look around, Dillon saw a dark coniferous forest surrounding the base. A whitewater river rushed down a chasm below.

Two lines of black-uniformed Enhanced faced each other on the stairs. There must have been thousands of them, all standing at attention in perfect lines that spiraled up the endless staircase. Half had their backs to the wall, but those on the outside faced rigidly away from the precipice behind them. There was no handrail, so one step backward would mean certain death. Grant Atherton climbed the stairs between them. His broad back blocked the view ahead. Michelle's father set a punishing pace up the stairs, taking them two at a time. Beside him, his wife somehow kept up in her high heels. All eyes were on the family, measuring them, watching for weakness.

The barrier between Dillon and the memory faded, and he became Michelle. Her legs ached. The thin mountain air didn't carry enough oxygen, no matter how fast she sucked it in. She felt nauseous and faint, but she kept going, consciously keeping her head up. A younger version of Seth, fourteen or fifteen years old, kept pace beside her.

"Try and make it look easy," Victoria murmured over her shoulder at her children. Grant Atherton shushed his wife with a hiss.

An elevator door on the third landing stood open, but they weren't invited to use it. "They want to see what we're made of," Seth mouthed to his sister behind their father's back.

A child's cry startled them all. On the stairs below, a husky officer stood over a uniformed child of about seven. The little brown-haired girl clutched her elbow, backing away from the cane in her instructor's hand. A pale-faced boy beside her put a hand out to stop her from stepping over the edge. The officer spun his cane smartly and smacked the boy's wrist. The boy made only the slightest sound, a sudden, sharp intake of breath. The officer moved on down the line. The boy remained at attention, his back to the wind. Blood dripped slowly from his fingertips. Dillon felt faint at the sight, and it took him a moment to remember that the feeling was Michelle's.

Dillon felt the pain in his own chest as Michelle regulated her breathing, so no one would see her lungs heaving. Her muscles screamed for oxygen, and an altitude headache throbbed. Dillon found himself concentrating alongside her, as though he could help. Michelle's desperate thoughts whispered in his head. *Look relaxed. Don't show weakness.*

At the top of the tower, a man and a woman waited in cushioned chairs. An honor guard of officers stood on the small flat landing around them. The couple rose when the Atherton family approached, but only the man came forward to greet Grant.

The men ignored their wives completely as they conversed. Officers gathered around them, gradually pushing Victoria and her children back. The women and children waited in silence for a long time.

Michelle slipped between uniformed men to peek at their boss. Iron Torr's top-ranking man appeared to be in his mid-thirties, but he was Enhanced, so he could have been much older. He had a full head of blond hair and a handsome, chiseled profile, but his blue eyes were pale and cold. Something reptilian glittered in them, arrogant and unfeeling. She couldn't decipher the rank insignia on his uniform, but his black-and-white name tag bore one word: *Parker.*

Finally Victoria squeezed through the crowd and approached the man's raven-haired wife. Michelle followed her mother, marveling at these peoples' lack of manners. Parker's wife stood with her back turned to her guests, looking out at the dark forest. Her white-knuckled hands gripped the rail, like part of her wanted to vault it and plummet into the river below.

"Mary?" Victoria said. "How lovely to see you again."

The woman turned, and Michelle's mother recoiled slightly. "Oh, I'm sorry—" Victoria began, and then stopped as if she didn't know what to say.

"Quite all right," the woman said. "Mary Parker died in childbirth two weeks ago. I'm Brooke, Colonel Parker's new wife."

Michelle's eyes widened in shock. *Two weeks, and he's remarried already?*

The black-haired woman glanced nervously at her husband to see if he'd overheard her, and he had. Stress tightened the perfect features of Brooke's face. Grant Atherton made some polite remark of condolence, but Parker shrugged it off.

"I'm sure you'll have nothing but success with your beautiful new bride," Grant added heartily.

Parker's pale eyes flicked critically over his young wife, as if picking out flaws. "We'll see," he said shortly.

The memory faded. Dillon came back to the present. He glanced around the luxurious helicopter to get his bearings. Jeanette watched him curiously, but he ignored her.

Caning kids is bad enough, Dillon silently told Michelle. *But that's not what bothered me the most. The energy of the place . . . it's infused with fear.*

She squeezed his hand and tried to keep her next thought to herself. *Yeah. They're afraid for a reason.*

Below, green fields gave way to dark pine forests. Jeanette texted madly, a rainbow of colored light beaming over her hand. The lights slowly faded. "Out of service. Damn." Jeanette flicked her wrist in time with the word, powering down her surgically implanted cell chip.

"Get used to it," Todd said. "The system at Iron Torr is incompatible, so even if we get it working you won't be able to contact your army of minions. By the time we get back, they'll be following someone else."

Jeanette took her brother's ribbing with a smile. "I'm sure. Everyone will forget me in a week."

A few small towns crouched between craggy white-capped mountains. After a final refueling stop at a remote outpost, the landscape turned to wilderness. As the hours droned on, excitement turned to boredom, and people amused themselves with games.

By afternoon, only Dillon still stared out the window. "We must be almost there," he said. "We're flying really low now."

Michelle set down her game pad and joined him. "Look, there's a little village," she exclaimed. "How cute."

A circle of huts stood in a clearing. Smoke rose from their chimneys, and a herd of white goats grazed nearby. As the helicopter went overhead, brown clad figures dashed for the trees. Three men stopped at the edge of the forest and bent bows, aiming upward. With a stomach-churning lurch, the pilot took them abruptly higher.

"Gods," Dillon exclaimed. "They're shooting arrows at us!"

Sylvia gasped but Todd and Brian laughed. Dillon got in their faces about it. "What's gonna happen when we land? See how thick those woods are? They could shoot from cover and you'd never see what hit you."

"You know, he's right," Todd told Brian logically.

"Yeah, too bad I forgot my suit of armor," Brian said.

"That's enough, all of you," snapped Jeanette. "I don't care if you guys like each other or not. We're here now, and this is serious. We stick together. No more fighting."

Brian and Todd nodded, subsiding into silence.

"And you!" Jeanette turned on Dillon. "Lose the attitude. You don't know these military types. Their doctors make ours look all warm and fuzzy."

"Okay," Dillon said evenly, but he couldn't hide his irritated expression.

"Don't give me that look. Where we're going, it won't pay to advertise your feelings." Jeanette moved Michelle over with an impatient gesture and took the seat next to Dillon. She grabbed his shoulders and made him turn to face her. "Relax your facial muscles. Good. Now stay like that." She pinched his arm with her long fingernails.

Dillon slapped her hand off. "Ow! Quit it, Jeanette."

"I said stay like that. Even if it hurts. Let's try it again."

Jeanette coached Dillon mercilessly as they made their final approach to the base. The helicopter followed the course of a whitewater river up a hill, battling strong winds the whole way. Iron Torr sat high atop a ridge of dark stone. On the slope below the fortress, a landing strip had been blasted out of the mountain. A helicopter landing pad waited on top of the ridge, but no one was there. The pilot circled cautiously.

The intercom crackled to life with the Augment's voice. "I'm trying local com channels. Gettin' nothing."

"The place looks deserted," Michelle said.

"No, it's not." Brian pointed. "See? Some men are down there on the runway."

Two orange-vested men stood near the forested end of the runway. They waved in the helicopter with neon-orange plastic rods.

"I see 'em now, sir. Going in." Their pilot landed the helicopter precisely where he was told to. It sat there, blades whirling, as the engine powered down. The teens stood and began gathering their belongings.

"They're making us do the stairs again," Todd sighed, pulling on a jacket.

"Considering we're here to do them a favor, you'd think they could have let us land on top. Bastards." Brian grimaced. "One more time, up the wretched Torr."

"What's a Torr?" Dillon asked.

"It's an old word for tower, I think. They're all about tradition here." Brian rolled his eyes. "My mom sent me here when I was nine, for summer camp. More like boot camp. It sucked like you wouldn't believe."

"They made you climb that?" Dillon asked, bending to look out the window at the enormous Torr. "At nine?"

"Oh, that was just the warm-up," Brian said. "You should have been there for the sprints."

"I thought this place was supposed to be a fortress. Whose bright idea was it to put stairs on the *outside* of the tower?" Dillon shook his head.

"Good point," Brian said with a grin. "I never thought about it that way. I guess security's not a big issue, since the only other people around are natives."

"The stairs are ceremonial. The Torr only houses classrooms and living quarters. The real fortification is underground," Todd explained.

"Ceremonial?" Dillon's blue eyes went round. "What a waste of resources. That thing is huge."

"We don't care. We've got plenty of money. So we can treat our women to the luxuries they deserve." Brian's eyes lingered on Michelle and then went back to Dillon, making his point.

Dillon didn't take the bait. Brian turned away, looking a little disappointed.

"So, um, on the climb, who wants to go first?" Todd asked, way too casually.

"You do," Michelle said immediately, and Jeanette agreed.

Michelle could tell that bothered Todd, but it was the safest thing. They couldn't risk him falling behind and revealing his weakness. Constantly checking on him would be a dead giveaway too. It wasn't Todd's fault that the doctors who designed him focused more on academic ability than athletics.

When Dillon reached for his bags, Michelle stopped him. "If nobody mentions it, they'll probably send some lower ranks to bring up our stuff."

"Don't ask for help, or they'll say no," Jeanette added. "Just because they can. Just pile your gear at the edge of the runway, so they know what to take."

Dillon fingered a lightweight knife and started to slip it in into his boot, but Michelle shook her head. "Sorry. If they find a hidden weapon on you, they'll think you're an assassin."

"I wasn't planning on knifing anyone," Dillon said defensively. "Unless they really deserve it." He reluctantly left the knife behind.

Brian laughed too loud, pounding Dillon on the back. "That'd be at least half of 'em, and all the officers."

Michelle shot Brian an evil look. *He's being annoying on purpose. That's the last thing we need right now.*

The Augments insisted on leaving the helicopter first, so the teens stood aside. The pockmarked captain assembled his team. The Augments weren't identical, but they could have been brothers. All of them had the same coloring—brown hair, brown eyes, and brown skin, and similar features, like the doctors hadn't bothered to individualize them much. Their captain's scarred face marked him as a plague survivor. Augments were mildly enhanced, enough to make them good soldiers, but the doctors who designed them hadn't equipped them to resist a bioweapon. Nobody saw that one coming.

Michelle stepped outside into cool, pine-scented air and dumped her big pack in the grass beside Jeanette's. The smaller daypack got slung over her back. No telling how long it would be before their luggage got delivered. Below the runway, a river plunged off the mountain and arced into a chasm. A cloud of spray caught the light, casting rainbows. Wildflowers bloomed on the edge of the runway, nodding in the chilly wind that swept off the glaciers above.

No Enhanced lined the stairs. The place was deserted except for the orange-vested airfield attendants, who looked like Norms.

"Where is everybody?" Sylvia asked. Between the splashing of the waterfall and wind roaring through giant pines, her voice could barely be heard

Black metallic walls of the fortress loomed overhead, casting a dark shadow over the forest. The back of Michelle's neck tingled, but no faces showed themselves at the windows. "I don't know, but this is rude. Who sends Norms out to greet their guests while they wait inside?"

"It is rude. We're obviously from the Institute." Jeanette waved an irate hand at the Institute's DNA double helix logo on the side of the helicopter. "Somebody should be out here any second."

"What are you talking about? Somebody's out here now," Dillon said shortly. He pointed to the end of the runway, where the two orange-vested men stood in the long shadow of the tower. One of the Norms was a burly middle-aged man with a long black beard. His young partner looked enough like him to be a grown son.

"They're *Norms*, Dillon," Jeanette said, as though that explained everything.

Dillon bristled. "So?"

"So, I guess we might as well go talk to them," Jeanette said, airily ignoring his glare. The blonde tossed her windblown ponytail and ran lightly down the tarmac toward the waiting men. Two Augments sprinted to catch up with her.

"I want to hear what they say," Michelle told Dillon in a low voice, and she hurried after them.

When Michelle jogged up, Jeanette was already there, flashing her famous smile.

"Hi, I'm Jeanette Morley, from Institute Headquarters." The orange-vested men stared solemnly. When they didn't answer, Jeanette's smile slowly died. She switched to her talking-to-idiots voice. "And you are?"

The older man spoke slowly. "We are...here t' welcome y' to the Torr." He extended a hand to Jeanette, who took it gracefully.

The Norm didn't let go right away, but Michelle didn't blame him. She knew how men reacted to Jeanette. Her eyes fell briefly to Jeanette's hand, engulfed in the man's weathered one. The dirt under his nails contrasted oddly with his shiny clean vest. That bugged Michelle. *Institute employees have to clean up. Don't they make them do that here?*

Dillon touched Michelle's arm and twitched his chin toward the forest. Men weaved between the trees. In their brown and green clothes, they blended with the colors of the forest. The newcomers fanned out into a rough semi-circle as they approached. Once Michelle spotted the leaders, her sharp eyes quickly picked out more, half-hidden in the foliage.

"Oh, good. Look, Jeanette," Michelle said. When she pointed, the younger Norm winced. "Here are our hosts, finally."

"Um, Michelle?" Dillon grabbed her arm and tugged her back a couple of steps. "I've got a bad feeling about—"

"Down!" an Augment shouted, an instant before the Norms opened fire.

Arrows flew from hidden perches, high in the trees. Dillon threw Michelle into the nearest cover, a thorny gooseberry bush, and covered her body with his. He reflexively reached for his absent knife and swore. Around them, Augments snapped into a defensive formation, weapons drawn, and began cutting down archers.

The burly Norm seemed to think he had a hostage. He hooked an elbow around Jeanette's neck and dragged her close to shield him, but her slender arms were stronger than they looked. She yanked him into a shoulder throw and dropped him hard on the ground. A quick strike with her boot, and he lay still. With an Augment on each side, Jeanette bolted into the woods.

"We've got to move," Sylvia shouted from somewhere in the trees.

Michelle raised her head to shriek. "Go! Don't wait for us."

Sylvia and Todd took off, zigzagging madly through the forest. Bowstrings twanged and arrows sliced the air behind them. One Augment raced behind them, desperately trying to cover their retreat. His brothers burned ammunition wildly, blazing away at hidden enemies.

"This is our chance," Dillon cried. He grabbed Michelle by the hand.

With the pilot on their heels, Dillon and Michelle ran for the Torr. Arrows hissed past them. Michelle dove under the spreading branches of an old pine tree and flattened herself on her stomach. The tense, muscular shoulders of the men pressed against her on both sides. Fallen pine needles stabbed Michelle's palms, while low-hanging branches brushed her neck with sticky aromatic sap. She tried not to move.

"Guns're in the helicopter," Dillon gasped.

"There's a lot o' open ground between here an' there," the pockmarked pilot hissed back. "We won't make it. Damn it, I fell for it."

"None of us knew," Dillon muttered. "It was so easy. All they had to do was steal those vests."

"My fault, sir."

"Forget it," Dillon said. He put an arm over Michelle's back, shielding her head with one hand. "We've got to get her to the fortress. That's top priority. Over me. Over everything. Got it?"

"Yes, sir."

In a momentary lull between gunshots, Michelle heard footsteps circling around behind them. She turned to look, and the men got the message.

"You hear 'em?" the pilot mouthed.

Michelle mouthed her words on the slightest sigh of air. "Moving to circle us."

"We've got to make it to the Torr. It's our only chance," Dillon whispered, and the Augment pilot grunted assent.

"Michelle, I want you to run as hard as you can. Get to the stairs," Dillon said. "They'll open up when you get close to the door. Don't stop, no matter what happens."

A great weight settled over Michelle's heart. *I don't deserve this.* She shook her head. "We should all stay together."

"I'll only hold you up, miss," said the grizzled pilot. "But I got yer back. I promise."

From the look in his eye, he meant it. Michelle finally nodded. She listened and then silently pointed out the hidden men around them.

The Augment targeted the closest one. Gunfire rocked the chasm, drowning out the roar of the waterfall.

"Go!" Shoulder to shoulder, Michelle and Dillon exploded from their hiding places. An arrow whizzed past her ear, and she cried out. Fear made her body light. Skirting the airfield, they raced through the trees and arced uphill toward the base of the immense staircase. Loose rock shifted underfoot, making it hard to run. Cold, thin air burned her throat as she sucked it in. Behind her, men shouted from the woods. *They're closing in.*

Near the patch of open land between the woods and the base of the stairs, Michelle hesitated. A bearded face popped up from the bushes. Dillon swept a rock off the ground without slowing and hurled it from close range, splitting the man's forehead in a tremendous gash. Michelle froze, horrified, until Dillon grabbed her hand and pulled her into the bright sunshine. They ran across the rocky ground and pounded onto the metal stairs.

Michelle and Dillon spiraled up the tower and fled to the far side, where enemy arrows couldn't reach. Three turns up, at a small, flat landing, was the first door. *Three times through the arrows. And then we find out if they'll let us in.*

Michelle rounded the first bend at top speed, with Dillon right beside her. On the far side of the tower, they were safe for the moment. She crept up to the next turn and peered around it.

"Good, the pilot made it to the stairs," Michelle exclaimed.

"Yeah, but look behind him," Dillon said.

Archers gathered at the base of the staircase. They took aim and let their arrows fly. All but one of them missed. That one cut a bloody swath across the pilot's face and twisted away in the wind. The Augment dropped to one knee and gunned down the cluster of Norms, while others shot at him from the woods. He stood up and ran. Arrowheads rattled against the metal tower. Dillon and Michelle picked their moment and dashed around the bend. As they went higher, the accuracy of the archers diminished, but reinforcements must have arrived below. Scores of barbed arrowheads rattled off the tower and fell to the rocks below. The Augment pilot doggedly followed them up the stairs, stopping intermittently to fire at enemies hidden in the trees.

With a hiss and a thump, an arrow hit Michelle in the back. The barbed arrowhead slammed into her daypack, so it didn't penetrate to her skin, but the impact shocked her. She squealed, dropped to the stairs, and kept going on all fours, gripping the cold metal stairs with her hands.

Dillon gulped. "Are you all right?"

"Yeah. They're on all sides of the Torr now."

"Smart. That's what I would do."

They crawled onto the landing, hugging the shelter of the low stone wall around it, and found Todd already there, huddled with Sylvia in a corner. Two Augments knelt nearby, sniping at archers.

"Is anyone here?" Michelle asked.

Todd shook his head. "Seems deserted. We banged on the door, and the elevator's off."

"Maybe they're all dead," Michelle said.

Sylvia shot her a dark look and said something, but gunfire drowned her out.

The pilot appeared on the stairs behind them, blood streaming off his cut cheek. "Move," he snapped.

The four teens ran. The trip to the top was endless. Sweat soaked Michelle's shirt, and her hands and knees were rubbed raw from the rough edges of the stairs. Arrows fell short more often now, but someone below had a crossbow. Bolts clanged alarmingly from the metal tower. Michelle almost sobbed in relief when they came upon Jeanette and Brian on the next landing. Brian squeezed Michelle's shoulder briefly and then moved off to pound on the steel door. There was no sign of life inside the tower. A closed elevator stood nearby. Todd pressed the useless button, pulled out a multi-tool, and began prying off its cover. A couple of crossbow bolts smacked the wall in front of him, and he jumped back. That changed his mind about standing around fiddling with electronics, so Todd led the pack up the stairs again.

At the top of the tower, the circular platform stood deserted. Their guards swiveled their heads nervously, but the base was silent except for the call of a lone raven soaring on the cold wind. The Torr was immense, and far below, the tall pines looked tiny. Augments took up defensive positions around the walls, with two men covering the stairs. A closed steel door lead into a low building that flanked the tower. Michelle pounded on it with her fist, but no one came.

"Give it up," Brian whispered. "They've got to know we're here."

"If anyone's even in there, you mean."

Long moments passed. A few arrows arced toward them, but all of them fell back onto the rocks. Far away, tiny figures of Norms began to fade into the forest.

Michelle let out a shaky breath. "We're out of range. I think they realize we can shoot them easily if they come too far up the stairs. They're leaving."

Dillon leaned over the railing to peer down at the runway below. "There's still a bunch of 'em by the helicopter. Hey! They're taking our guns!"

"There's nothing we can do about it. Will you stop leaning over the wall, you're making me nervous." Michelle grabbed Dillon's arm and pulled him back from the edge. He teased her, faking a gasp and leaning over the rail again, while Brian laughed. *Great, it's two against one now.*

"How can you two joke at a time like this?" Michelle snapped, but that only made them laugh harder.

"Get down," the pilot ordered. "They got rifles now, and you're in range."

The boys immediately crouched down behind the low wall. Michelle left them alone and huddled in a corner with Sylvia, trying to get out of the bitter wind. Sweat cooled on her body, and she began to shiver.

More Norms appeared from the forest and unloaded the helicopter. A line of them disappeared into the trees, laden with loot. Michelle was too emotionally drained to care much, but when the natives figured out how to load the rifles, shots rang out. Whoops and hollers came from below while bullets whizzed past the tower. Michelle felt a wild urge to run, but there was nowhere to go. She shifted, ready to bolt. Sylvia grabbed her shoulder and dragged her down to the cold stone. Bullets smacked the tower above them, sending out little puffs of black dust. Finally, someone below shouted an order and the gunfire trailed off.

The sun slowly dropped behind the mountains and afternoon turned to gray twilight. Exhaustion took over, and Michelle's eyes closed. An explosion ripped through the air, startling her awake.

"Ah! The helicopter," Brian exclaimed.

"Oh, no." The pilot watched the fireball rise and then slumped, covering his face with one hand. His shoulders shook in silent sobs.

After a moment, Dillon crawled over and put a comforting hand on the man's shoulder. "I'm sorry."

The pilot looked as though a living thing had died. "She was…like, my baby, y'know?"

"I get that. She was beautiful," Dillon said softly.

"Yeah. It was an honor to fly her." The pilot gripped both of Dillon's hands. "Thank you, sir."

"You don't have t' call me sir," Dillon said. He dropped his eyes. "I'm… just a Warren kid."

The pilot gave him a bewildered look, but the man was past asking questions. He sank down on the rock platform and sat there, watching the column of smoke rise into the gray sky.

Jeanette knocked on the door every few minutes, becoming steadily more impatient. "I refuse to believe every last one of them moved out. Where would they go?"

When her hand wore out she switched to kicking it with her hiking boot, which rang the big steel door like a gong.

From inside, an irate male voice said, "Stop banging! We know you're here."

"Then open the Goddamn door," Jeanette snapped.

The door opened a crack. The muzzle of a shotgun emerged and tracked upward, targeting her face. Jeanette stood absolutely still, eyes wide.

In a moment she tried again, this time taking a more respectful tone. "We're from Institute Headquarters. We were attacked when we arrived. I need to speak to Colonel Parker right away."

"Wait here while we confirm that with the colonel," the man said. The shotgun withdrew, and the steel door slammed shut.

"Oh, nice," Jeanette huffed.

The door finally opened again, revealing three soldiers in forest green uniforms, not the dress blacks Michelle remembered. After perfunctorily disarming the Augments, the soldiers didn't speak again. They led the team down an endless maze of windowless hallways with gleaming tile floors and walls of huge stone blocks. Fumes from harsh cleansers filled the air, making Michelle's eyes water. At the end of a hall, two soldiers pulled a pair of double doors open to reveal a large dining room. Colonel Parker sat at the head of a long table, sharing a meal with his officers. He was exactly as Michelle remembered, as though no time had passed. Brooke, the colonel's wife, sat on his right, looking thin and frail.

Parker beckoned the teens to enter, but Iron Torr soldiers barred the Institute security guards from following them. "Wait outside."

"Like hell," snapped the pockmarked pilot, one hand falling to his empty holster. "We've got orders to stay with our charges, an' we plan on doing that. Over your bloody corpses, if necessary." The grizzled captain looked to Jeanette, and she nodded.

That triggered a standoff. The Institute team wouldn't enter without their guards, so they waited in the hall, coolly disregarding the colonel's imperious gestures. Jeanette leaned languidly on the wall, arms folded, while the pilot gazed at her, eyes lit with genetically engineered reverence. Blood dripped from his arm, staining the tile floor, but when Dillon tried to take a look at the wound the man waved him off. Dillon tried to argue the point, but a glare from Jeanette silenced him.

Michelle touched Dillon's arm. *"They're trying to see if they can push us around,"* she silently conveyed, and he nodded almost imperceptibly. *"Don't start anything. Our Augments are stressed to the limit. They'll lay down their lives if they think we're in danger."*

Minutes passed. Time seemed to stretch out, and Michelle's anxiety slowly built. Her heart began to flutter, warning of an impending panic attack. She closed her eyes and took deep breaths, desperate to calm herself. *I simply cannot afford to break down. Not here. Not in front of Parker.*

Sweat began to soak through Michelle's shirt, and her breath came faster. She was losing control. It wouldn't be long before some military type would notice. Todd glanced at her, concern in his blue eyes. He'd used his freaky mind trick to head off one of her panic attacks, back when Michelle and Sylvia had faced down the Conclave and won. With a conscious effort, she brought up the memory of the link, remembering what it felt like to look out her brother's eyes. Seth's calm confidence was inside her, somewhere, if she could only access it. She pictured her brother's face. Remembered how it felt to stand across from him in a circle with their friends, their minds linked. Seth's calm confidence had filled her then. Where was it now?

Colonel Parker made a magnanimous gesture, like an emperor bestowing his blessing on the poor. "They may enter, with their guards."

Michelle's mind raced. *I'm out of time! Get a grip.* She scrubbed her damp palms on her pants and scanned the dining room. The colonel and his cronies were stuffing their faces in self-satisfied comfort. *Jerks. They were perfectly willing to let us die out there. Why should I care what they think of me?* That thought broke the grip of the panic attack. Seth's confidence filled her. *Not his confidence. Mine. I'm done falling apart over every little thing.* Her heart slowed. She caught Todd's eye and gave him a tiny smile. *I'm okay now.*

Parker's soldiers stood aside while tense Augments marched in and took up positions along the walls of the dining room. The Institute team strode in after them. They slowed as they neared the colonel's chair, and Michelle suddenly realized they hadn't appointed a spokesperson. Everyone eyed the teens expectantly, but no one spoke.

She impulsively stepped forward. "I'm Michelle Atherton, from Institute headquarters. As I'm sure you're aware, communications are down, so our Conclave instructed us to contact you and offer assistance."

"Assistance? From a pretty little thing like you?" Colonel Parker said, triggering smirks from his officers. "Headquarters must be downright overwhelmed if they're sending us such…subordinates."

The Founder must have known that sending teenagers would annoy the hell out of the colonel. He did it on purpose. Damn you, G.G.

"Not at all, sir. I imagine the Founder simply saw your problem as a valuable exercise for students."

The colonel held Michelle in his icy gaze. She battled to keep her face impassive during the uncomfortable silence that followed.

Crap! I just implied that an issue the military can't solve is nothing but homework for Headquarters kids. Why can't I keep my mouth shut? Jeanette would have been better at this. Should I apologize?

She decided not to, and she sealed her lips. The silver-haired officer on Parker's left gave her a grudging nod of approval.

"We were attacked on arrival, and our helicopter was destroyed," Michelle added, biting her tongue to keep from blurting *since you didn't bother to help us.*

Parker nodded impatiently, making a get-on-with-it gesture with one hand. He obviously knew that already. "How many people did you lose?"

"None."

The colonel's men murmured among themselves, sounding impressed, so Michelle pushed her luck and made it sound easy. "They were just Normals, after all, and there were only, what, about fifty of them, do you think?" She glanced up at the pilot.

"Seventy-two, by my count, miss."

"Thank you, Captain."

Parker fell silent. His eyes traveled uneasily over the room. There were far fewer officers there than Michelle expected, just a few dozen at most, and a lot of empty chairs. Parker looked back at her, eyes narrowed. A slow chill spread down her limbs as Michelle realized that she'd just made an enemy. *The locals decimated his army, and I had to rub his nose in it.*

With an abrupt wave, Colonel Parker dismissed the officers at his table. Men and women grabbed their plates and took them when they left. Brooke Parker shifted in her seat as though she might go too, but she remained beside her husband.

"Sit down, children," the colonel said.

Stone-faced Enhanced teens took chairs at the colonel's table. Unfortunately Michelle got the seat right beside Parker. Nerves tingling, she waited to see what he would do.

"So, you're here to offer assistance, are you? I know exactly what you could help me with," Parker leered, right in front of his wife. His eyes roamed over Michelle's body while men snickered from the next table. Head down, Brooke nibbled halfheartedly at her food. Across the table, Dillon tensed but said nothing.

Michelle ignored the jibe. "Our orders are to provide replacement components and to aid in the repair process, if needed. We have a technical expert on hand as well," she added evenly, nodding at Todd.

"Oh, good, a technical expert," Parker repeated sarcastically. The colonel eyed Todd's bony shoulders, swallowed by his jacket. "You know, it takes more than brains to survive out here, boy."

Michelle stood up abruptly, and her friends followed suit. "If you don't need us, sir, we'll be on our way."

The Institute team turned to leave, and Jeanette's arm casually brushed hers. Michelle heard the desperate thought. *Yes, Jeanette, I know the woods are crawling with pissed-off Norms. I'm not keen on camping with them either. Wait and see what he does.*

"Oh, stay here. We'll put you to use," Parker conceded, making a graceful gesture of acquiescence. "But first, have some dinner." He pointed them to a buffet table.

Michelle breathed a secret sigh of relief. "Thank you, Colonel."

The teens lined up and picked up plates before they realized that the food had all been devoured. Only a few crusts of bread and the scrapings from serving dishes remained. They gathered what scraps they could, and when they returned to the table Colonel Parker was gone. He'd moved to another long table, where he sat conferring with his officers. Michelle caught the phrase, "leverage this asset," before Parker saw her watching him and turned away. Brooke remained at her place, hands limply in her lap. After a few failed attempts to engage her in conversation, Michelle gave up and left the woman alone. It didn't take long for them to finish eating.

Michelle subtly touched Jeanette's arm. *"Now what?"* she silently sent.

"If we try to walk out, I bet they'll send someone to show us to our quarters."

The Institute team headed for the door, followed closely by their Augments. The colonel intercepted them. A handsome boy of about seventeen hovered at his elbow.

"Slade will show you around the base," Colonel Parker said. Michelle nodded serenely. Parker moved off without another word, leaving the boy behind.

Slade made the rounds, introducing himself. His smile was genuine, and his almond eyes twinkled. He stood out here. Most of the people at Iron Torr were blondes or redheads, with a few pale-skinned brunettes. Slade's straight black hair, slanted eyes, and golden skin looked a lot like Brooke's.

As the institute team followed Slade out the door, Sylvia caught Michelle's eye and raised an appreciative eyebrow toward their guide. "He seems nice," Sylvia whispered. "Maybe he can answer some questions about this place." She winked and skipped up to the front of the group to walk beside their guide.

Michelle followed Jeanette's platinum-blonde ponytail down the hall. Behind her, Augments followed in silence except for the unified thuds of their boots on the tiles.

Brian fell in step beside Michelle as they walked. "Well played," he whispered.

"Are you being sarcastic again, Brian?"

"No, I mean it," he said. "Good job. You gave 'em hell."

"Yeah, and you did it with class," Todd agreed, coming up on her other side.

Michelle felt pleased and surprised by this, at least until Jeanette looked over her shoulder and shook her head.

"Don't be stupid, you guys. You can't humiliate a man like Parker and expect him to forget about it. Michelle, you made a serious mistake there."

Michelle flushed angrily. "If you're such an expert, why'd you let me deal with him all by myself, then?"

Up in front, Slade said something to Sylvia that caught their attention. "Sorry nobody met you at the airfield. We're locked down now, we've lost too many patrols to the insurgents."

"How many?" Sylvia asked.

Slade stopped, and they gathered silently around him. The black-haired boy glanced up and down the hallway before answering. "It's bad. We're down to about twenty percent of our original force. Nobody's allowed outside for any reason. Even to help you," he added apologetically. "The communications building got bombed. Radio, cell service, Internet— everything got hit, and all our repair crews come under fire."

"That's why he made an issue about an offer of assistance, from me, of all people," Michelle concluded. "I'm obviously no soldier."

"No, that was just the colonel being…the colonel. He's always like that. Don't take it personally," Slade told Michelle, meeting her eyes compassionately.

She gave him a grateful smile. Not everyone there was awful, after all.

"The thing is…" Slade hesitated. He waved a subtle finger at the walls, and the message was clear—someone could be listening.

Sylvia put an encouraging hand on his arm. "We won't say a word, we swear," she murmured, and her friends all whispered agreement.

"Okay, seriously, I'd get in major trouble for saying this, but you have to know. You offered to repair communications, and they'll expect you to do it. But you'll be shot at for sure, and my, um, I mean the colonel—won't send anyone out to support you."

The Institute kids shared appalled glances, but there were no furious outbursts, even from Dillon.

"Thanks for warning us," Sylvia managed, in a small voice.

"And if we refuse?" Michelle asked. "He'll throw us out?"

Slade nodded. "Probably. None of us would want him too, but, you know. He makes the rules."

The Institute team fell silent.

"Something else is weird too," Slade whispered. "We've fought the Norms on and off for years, but their attacks have changed. Their strategy is really well thought out now, hard to beat. We think they have some rebel Enhanced on their side."

"When did this start?" Sylvia asked him, and then shot a quick glance at Michelle.

"About a month ago, right after the plague ended."

Michelle looked up at Brian to find him staring at her. She didn't need to touch him to know they were thinking exactly the same thing. *There are no rebel Enhanced. This is my fault. I caused this when I augmented the Norms, trying to cure the plague. I made our enemies smarter.*

Slade motioned them down the hall again. "Come on, I'm supposed to give you the grand tour."

The exhausted teens groaned and followed him. Slade took them into Iron Torr's gleaming medical center first. "This is where our doctors design and implement genetic enhancements."

Technicians in white coats and latex gloves worked at lab benches that ran down the center of an enormous room. No one acknowledged the visitors' presence. For a place with so many people, the room seemed awfully quiet. It made Michelle uncomfortable. That feeling spiked into fear when Slade took them into a smaller room equipped with six reclining seats. A male nurse met them there, but he didn't look like any nurse Michelle had ever seen. The red-bearded man wore a nurse's scrubs, but he carried himself like a soldier.

"Take one of these and follow the instructions on the label," the big man rumbled, holding out a fistful of plastic-wrapped swabs.

"Why?" Dillon demanded, and not even Jeanette quashed him for that. The reclining seats had sturdy nylon straps to belt patients in, and their last experience with something like that had been a bad one.

"My orders are to take DNA samples from each of you."

"Why should you care about our DNA?" Dillon asked. "We're not sticking around to have babies."

The nurse refused to argue. He just turned to Slade, who nodded slightly in acknowledgement.

Slade sidled up to Dillon. "I'm sorry. They do this to all our visitors. If you don't comply with the mouth swab, he'll take a blood sample." Slade didn't exactly make a threat, but his dark eyes lingered over the straps on the chairs. The implication was clear—cooperate or be forced. Their Augments hovered in the doorway, strung tight and ready to explode.

"Either way, they win. Okay, gimme the swab," Dillon sighed.

Their Augment security captain signaled his men to relax. The nurse handed out the cotton swabs, instructing the teens to run them around the insides of their mouths. Michelle quietly submitted, even though the swabs were soaked in something that tasted salty and horrible. She didn't have anything to hide, but she worried about Dillon and Sylvia. *Will this test reveal their Unenhanced ancestry? Military doctors might not approve of recruits.*

"When do we get the results?" Sylvia asked.

"You don't get the results," the nurse told Sylvia. "My commanding officer does."

"Fine. Whatever." Sylvia whipped her long black braid over her shoulder as she turned away.

Next the nurse herded them over to a tall, narrow chamber lined with glowing multicolored lights, barely large enough for one person to stand in. The idea of being locked inside it made Michelle claustrophobic, and her palms began to sweat.

Dillon walked up to the doorway and peered inside. "What's this?"

"Imaging scanner," the nurse said shortly. "One at a time. Walk in, stand still. Wait until the door opens."

Dillon shrugged. "Okay." He began to take off his jacket.

The nurse shook his oversized head. "Don't bother. It sees through your clothes."

Jeanette and Sylvia shared a scandalized look. "Oh, lovely."

"One layer at a time, down to the bone," the man added.

"Ugh," Jeanette sniffed. "When you put it that way, it doesn't sound so sexy after all."

They escaped from the medical center as soon as they could. Out in the hall, Brian trapped Slade in a corner. "Hey, buddy, got any other surprises for us?"

Slade looked small with Brian looming over him. The wiry dark-haired boy shrank back, hands out in a placating gesture. "Sorry, I don't run this place."

Sylvia stepped between them and put a hand on Brian's chest. "Brian, stop it. It's not his fault."

Brian reluctantly backed off. Slade met Sylvia's eyes and squeezed her hand gratefully before he led them on through the base.

The tour seemed like it would never end, and Michelle was exhausted by the time they finally arrived at the guest quarters. Those consisted of two nearly bare rooms with three twin beds in each. The Augments got a dorm-style room with bunk beds, just across the hall.

"Good night," Slade smiled. He made the rounds with the guys, shaking every hand, and then he gave each girl a chaste hug. "We do a group workout every morning. Somebody will wake you in time for it."

Sylvia didn't say a word, but everyone knew she hoped it would be him.

After Slade left, Michelle wanted to go to sleep right away, but Dillon made waves by insisting on sleeping in her room. "Did anyone besides me notice that the bedroom doors don't lock?" he pointed out.

"It's a *fortress*, Dillon. We'll be fine," Jeanette protested.

Todd backed up his sister. "It's obvious. There's one room for girls, and another one for boys."

Dillon wouldn't give in. "After what Seth said? Forget it. I'm staying, so deal with it." He claimed the bed closest to the door and refused to move.

Michelle didn't join the argument, but she hated the focus on her safety. It made her feel like no one cared about the other girls at all. She leaned against a wall, arms folded, until Sylvia beckoned her over. The pair sat together on one of the beds, letting the argument go on without them.

"Michelle, I know you feel bad about this," Sylvia said softly. "But you really are important. You'll change everything at the Institute. How many deformed babies suffer and die behind the scenes? Eight? Ten, for every perfect child born? You're the first of us to ever breed true! Your kids will all be perfect, so the doctors can model new ones off them. Imagine … no more dead babies, no more grieving parents … that is, unless you get yourself killed."

"You sound just like my mother, word for word," Michelle muttered. "I bet she coached you." One look at Sylvia's flushed face told Michelle she was right.

"Fine," Jeanette announced from across the room, loud enough to interrupt. "I'll sleep with the boys. I don't care, as long as they don't snore. Just wake us if you…uh, hear anything." Jeanette followed her brother from the room without another word.

Sylvia and Dillon shared a significant glance, and Michelle caught it immediately. "What?"

Sylvia's normally cheery face looked deadly serious, and the truth was suddenly glaringly obvious.

Michelle still wanted her to say it out loud. "Sylvia, tell me why you're here."

Sylvia swallowed hard before she spoke. "The Founder sent us as . . . glorified Augments. We have orders too. The same as theirs. To die, if necessary, to protect you. We totally failed at that today. We all got separated, and you came in last, and I thought maybe..."

Sylvia's eyes fell on Michelle's daypack by the door. An arrow still protruded from it.

"That I'd died? Oh God," Michelle whispered. She curled on her bed, arms wrapped around her knees. "Jeanette too? Her, of all people?"

"Yes, her too," Sylvia said, sounding a little bit offended. She glanced at the wall between the rooms and lowered her voice. "Do you know that Mrs. Morley had eighteen pregnancies? Eighteen! And only Jeanette and Todd survived. Jeanette said in the meeting—"

"You had a meeting without me?" Michelle looked at Dillon. "So you were there too."

He nodded without a trace of guilt.

Sylvia's dark eyes shone with tears. "Jeanette said in the meeting that she'd rather die than have twenty babies and bury all but one or two of them."

Michelle felt sick at the thought. "As talented as she is, they'll breed her half to death."

Sylvia paused to wipe her teary face on her sleeve. "Don't you get it, Michelle? You represent Jeanette's hope for the future, too. She'll protect you with her life, if it comes to that. Either way she's just as dead."

"She really said that?"

"Yeah. In front of the whole Conclave. Mrs. Morley totally lost it, and you know how controlled she always is."

Michelle put her face in her hands. "And I brought you all into a war zone. I'm so sorry."

"The Conclave didn't know that when they sent us here," Sylvia said softly. "They thought you'd be safe with all these soldiers."

"I'm surprised my mother let me come here at all, war or no war."

"She had to," Dillon said. Both girls looked at him. "They're afraid they'll lose you from the program, like they lost my mom. Once she took up with my father, she never came back."

"Right," Sylvia nodded at him. "The Founder said if they treat you like a prisoner you'll run away, just like Alexa did with Dillon's dad. He made them agree to let you come."

"And now you're all in danger, because of me."

Dillon covered Michelle's hand with his. "It's dangerous in the Warren, too, so it doesn't matter to me where we are. So long as we're together."

After Dillon switched off the light, Michelle lay awake for a long time, worrying about tomorrow. *What will happen when the colonel orders us out to repair communications? If we refuse, Slade will pay for warning us.* She tossed and turned until Dillon reached across the dark space between their beds and took her hand.

In the morning, a knock at the door woke her. "Good morning," someone called from the hallway. The door popped open, and Slade stood there gaping at them.

"What?" Dillon growled aggressively, sitting up bare-chested in bed. His protective instincts kicked on automatically, even from a sound sleep. In the slum he came from, passive types got weeded out early.

"Oh, um, sorry," Slade scrambled for words, obviously not wanting to mention their sleeping arrangements. "I just came to tell you the morning workout begins in thirty minutes. Here are some uniforms you can borrow." He dropped three folded white karate uniforms on the foot of Dillon's bed, and then fumbled with the pile. "Wait, these are all girl sizes."

"Just leave 'em. We'll figure it out."

Slade hastily shuffled the uniforms and fled. He knocked on the next door, and the girls stifled giggles when Brian bellowed, "What!" and Slade had to go through the whole routine again.

The teens dressed fast and met their guide in the hall outside. Brian high-fived Dillon in the hall. "How'd ya sleep, my man?"

"With two of 'em? Not at all." Dillon grinned. "You?"

"Her brother was in there, you know, so we had to keep the lights off."

"Not funny!" Jeanette slapped Brian across the face and stormed away while Slade stared after her.

"Okay, I confess, it didn't happen, all right?" Brian shouted down the hall after her.

"What he meant to say was the lights were on the whole time," Dillon quipped.

Todd punched Dillon hard on the shoulder. "That's my sister!"

Dillon fled to Brian's side, where he stood rubbing his sore shoulder. "Ow. Okay, game over. You win. Really. I'm not laughing anymore."

Slade stood there staring in astonishment. He looked from one person to another, but he didn't say a word.

Dillon and Brian stuck together on the way to the gym, whispering jokes back and forth.

"What is with those two? Separated at birth?" Jeanette sniped. "Whatever damaged gene they share, I swear to God, I will find it, and I will eliminate it from the population."

Chapter 3: Michelle

The Surrogates

Everyone at Iron Torr assembled for the morning workout, even children as young as five years old. Neat lines of black belts filled the front of the vast gymnasium, with lower ranking colored belts behind them. Much of the gym remained empty, reminding Michelle of the missing patrols. The Institute kids hovered in the back of the room, not sure where to line up. Their borrowed uniforms came with the white belts of beginners, but all of them were black belts, except for Dillon.

An assistant instructor came over and took charge. "What's your rank?" he asked Brian.

"Third degree black."

The young man pulled out a spare black belt and added three stripes of yellow tape to it. Michelle was next. "Second degree." She took her black belt with its two stripes and changed out of the white one on the spot. Dillon didn't know how to answer the question.

"He's a third degree like me," Brian interrupted. He soon slipped out into the hall with Dillon, and Michelle knew why. Dillon didn't even know how to tie his belt properly. Michelle heaved an aggravated sigh. *Idiots. Everyone will be able to tell he's a beginner.*

The assistant instructor walked them to their places in line. Michelle, Sylvia, and Todd lined up below all the other second degree black belts, just to be polite. Brian stood a couple of rows closer to the front, next to Dillon. Jeanette's blonde head was barely visible, up with the other fourth degrees in the front row.

Their head instructor turned out to be sixth degree black belt, Colonel Mark Parker. Parker's wife Brooke stood at the top of the class. It was hard to believe that the woman could fight at all—she seemed like such a mouse. The class bowed first to the colonel, and then to the Iron Torr coat of arms hanging on the wall. Luckily classes there followed the same format as the ones at home, so Michelle kept up easily. She sleepwalked through the basics, spending most of her time watching Dillon. Surprisingly, he did okay, but basics were easy.

When the colonel began calling out more complicated jump-spin kicks, Michelle worried for Dillon. *Is he up there making a fool of himself?* She tried to look for him during a jump and bumped the man on her right. "Sorry," she whispered, and he gave her an irritated look. She vowed to ignore her boyfriend and start paying attention to her own business. After a grueling hour of kicks and punches, the colonel called a halt and ordered everyone to sit cross-legged on the floor.

"Class, before sparring begins, I have a special announcement. We have students visiting from Institute headquarters, and our doctors tell me one of them is truly outstanding." The colonel paused for effect.

Michelle wanted to sink into the floor. She dreaded the embarrassing announcement about the breakthrough for the breeding program. *I represent the doctors' triumph, the goal they worked a hundred years to achieve, blah, blah, blah.*

"Dillon Russell Freeman, please stand up," Colonel Parker announced, and Michelle had a private meltdown.

The DNA tests! They know he's a half breed, and they're going to humiliate him in front of everyone.

Dillon stood up, bowed to the colonel, and then to the class, while everyone applauded politely. Michelle realized she wasn't clapping when she caught a glance from the man beside her, and she belatedly joined in. Dillon kept his face expressionless, thanks to Jeanette's wicked little lesson in the helicopter.

"Let's begin the sparring portion of our class with Dillon Freeman against . . ." The colonel paused, scanning his front line. "Junior Master Sawyer."

A young man in the front row stood up. Light glinted off his white-blond head. The colonel clapped his hands twice, and everyone stood up and bowed out. The Institute kids gathered at the side of the main sparring ring. All around the gym, people donned sparring gear and paired up, but a good portion of the crowd remained around the main ring. They were eager to see this outstanding new student get his ass kicked by their best fighter. Michelle thought she might throw up.

"Get a grip," Todd whispered. He brushed against her in the crowd, and she felt a weird tingling sensation where he'd touched her arm. Her panic immediately eased. It bugged Michelle that Todd could control her like that. Still, she had to admit it helped, so she couldn't bitch. Much.

Junior Master Sawyer moved like a predator. He had a cruel set to his mouth, even while he relaxed ringside with his friends. He didn't seem worried about the fight at all. Michelle couldn't get near Dillon, and that was probably a good thing. She'd just make him nervous. Brian waited in his corner.

The colonel refereed the match himself. "Three two-minute rounds, full contact," he announced. Dillon and his opponent bowed to each other, and all hell broke loose. Dillon fought like a Norm on steroids, breaking every rule in the book. He gouged, grabbed, and pounded with knees and elbows. He even took a groin shot, but Sawyer dodged it. The crowd shouted angrily, but the colonel wouldn't stop the fight. He didn't even call a single foul.

Dillon tripped his opponent with an illegal leg kick, took him down hard on the mat and landed on top. The two men rolled, grappling for a control hold, but Dillon got it first. With a fast twist, he got Sawyer's arm behind his body and held it there, elbow locked. One sudden move would break the arm, but Sawyer refused to submit.

Dillon looked up at the colonel. "He won't tap out, sir. Where I come from that means I get to break his arm."

"Then do it."

"Yes, sir." Dillon leaned back and took a breath, ready to snap the bone, but Sawyer suddenly tapped three times on the mat with his free hand, signaling surrender. Dillon released him. Michelle sagged against Todd, who used all his power to reinforce her emotional control.

Sawyer rolled to his feet, furious. "He broke the rules, sir!"

"What rules? You guys fight by rules, seriously? Rules protect the weak," Dillon argued, loud enough to be heard around the gym. "What's your goal here? To protect the weak, or eliminate them?"

The room fell quiet, and everyone waited to see what the colonel would do. "The boy makes a point," he announced. "I'll take this under consideration."

Colonel Parker perfunctorily named Dillon the winner, and the crowd applauded feebly. People whispered worriedly about the colonel eliminating sparring rules. Life at Iron Torr was hard enough already.

Dillon made his way through the crowd to Michelle and kissed her in front of everyone. Men nudged each another and grinned, making it clear that public displays of affection were forbidden there. Black belts crowded around to shake Dillon's hand and welcome him to Iron Torr. Michelle let the higher ranks crowd her away from Dillon. She swallowed, suddenly aching with thirst. They all needed water, and there weren't any drinking fountains along the walls.

She spotted the assistant instructor at his table by the door. "Where do we get water around here?"

"Oh, you weren't issued water bottles. You can get some from the storage closet upstairs. Third door to the right of the bulkhead on the fourth floor. It's unlocked."

"Okay, thanks."

Michelle made it to the fourth floor before she realized she didn't understand the instructions. *What's a bulkhead? I should have asked!* She roamed the halls, trying every third door on the right of anything. Most of them were locked.

Four low stone stairs led up to another passageway. *Is that considered part of the fourth floor, or the fifth?* Michelle didn't know, but she went that way anyway. She didn't want to confess any failure to the men of Iron Torr, no matter how small. The faint sound of a baby crying came from somewhere up ahead. It went on and on, until she wondered if anyone was taking care of the infant at all. The frantic wails awakened some latent maternal instinct Michelle didn't know she had. She crept nervously toward the sound, certain she'd be disciplined if they caught her wandering around. A steep staircase stood at the end of the hall. From the sound, the baby must be upstairs. Michelle took a quick look around and then ran up the stairs. *I'll just pretend I didn't hear the directions right if they catch me.*

At the top of the stairs, a large window opened from the hallway into a well-lit room full of young women. A slant-eyed brunette with a long braid down her back paced before a sealed glass partition. Numbered cradles filled the chamber beyond, each one with an infant inside. The brunette approached Michelle, making a pleading gesture through the glass. Leaking breast milk spotted the front of the woman's shirt. With a pang of sympathy, Michelle realized that the crying baby must be hers.

Another Plexiglas window separated the cradle room from a deserted nurse's station. Michelle ducked inside the dimly lit office and closed the hall door behind her. A twinge of guilt reminded her of her thirsty friends, but this was more important. *The nurses must be at the workout along with everyone else. But why separate mothers from their babies? It's mean!*

Normal women and girls clustered at the window into the nursery, all talking at once. Michelle could barely hear them, a room away and through glass. The slant-eyed girl pointed to a button on the wall. Michelle pressed it, and the automated door between the women and their babies slid open. The mothers all rushed to the cradles and took their babies in their arms. The young brunette immediately carried her screaming infant to a rocking chair and began nursing it.

Another button activated the intercom. Frantic female voices filled the nurse's station. "Help us!"

"Let us go."

"Shhh," Michelle hissed. "We have to be quiet; I'm not supposed to be here. Why are you prisoners?"

"We don't know. We didn't do anything."

"I was comin' back from the river, haulin' water, and they shot me with that." A girl pointed at a blocky gray gun on the other side of the armored glass window. "It knocked me out."

Michelle lifted the gun off its hook and slid open the mechanism to reveal a long needle at the end of a vial of amber liquid. Her skin crawled, so she quickly put the thing back. "They tranquilized you, and you woke up here?"

The Normal girl nodded. "They got us pregnant, and they won't let us leave."

"They will," an older mother interrupted. "The mamas all go away.

When they wean their babies, that's it. They're gone." The woman shook her head, so streaks of silver caught the bright fluorescent light.

"Gone? Where?" Michelle asked, horrified.

"The mamas disappear, but they keep the babies." The woman shifted her infant with practiced hands, making Michelle feel certain the poor woman had other children, kids who missed their mother and wondered where she was.

Michelle suddenly had an idea, and she ran to the computer. The nurses had left it running with a file open. Numbers on the screen corresponded to the numbered cradles. She scrolled down. Each infant was listed by number, not name, and below that by coded genetic enhancements. These babies were Enhanced, but the mothers looked like Norms. Michelle stared through the bars, mystified. Then she checked the computer again, looking for something specific. She found it—the parentage of each child. Iron Torr used the same system as Institute Headquarters. The lion's share of a child's genome came from its parents, but other adults in the community donated certain special genes. The colonel's name appeared prominently on the list. Almost every kid carried at least a few of his genes, and one baby boy had all of them.

"A clone," Michelle breathed to herself. "That's a major breach of regulations! The Conclave would have a fit if they knew."

Michelle thought back, remembering every female she'd seen since she arrived. She hadn't noticed at first, but not one of them was pregnant. Enhanced women, especially high ranking ones, spent most of their lives pregnant and raising children. With a chill, Michelle realized that didn't happen there. At Iron Torr, mothers didn't carry their own babies. Instead, Parker's soldiers captured Normal women and transferred Enhanced embryos into their wombs. They used prisoners as surrogate mothers, and when they were finished, the women disappeared.

I doubt they get free rides back to their villages. Parker would choose the most efficient option. But why? Maybe the colonel was heartbroken when his wife died in childbirth, and decided not to risk any more women. No...he didn't seem that broken up about it, since he got remarried less than two weeks later. Pregnancy just takes female soldiers away from their duties.

Behind the bars, the surrogates cooed to their babies, their faces lit with love. *They don't know those aren't really their babies. They got pregnant and delivered them, but they're not even related.*

Michelle glanced at the clock. The workout would be ending soon. She didn't have time to separate the mothers from the babies and have them put all the infants back in their bassinets. Besides, most of them weren't finished feeding or changing diapers. She decided to run for it, and she dashed to the bars. "Please don't tell anyone I was here. I'll try to come back and help you!"

Michelle sprinted down to the fourth floor hall and noticed a door standing ajar near the top of the stone stairs. *The storage room.* Michelle grabbed some water bottles, filled them at a utility sink, and dashed back down the stairs to the gym. A crowd still filled the room, and she slipped in as unobtrusively as she could. Her friends were grateful for the water, and no one asked questions.

Slade came over to find them. "There's a one hour shower and rest break, and then I'll come get you for breakfast. Today you get to eat with us, so that'll be more fun than dinner was last night."

"Awesome, we get to eat with the cool people," Brian grinned.

Slade only gave Brian a strange look. He turned away and slid up to Sylvia. "Hey Sylvia, if you're not too tired, there's something amazing I'd love to show you."

"Really? Sure."

The two of them left the gym together while Jeanette and Todd giggled behind their backs. "Oooo! He has something to show her."

"I'll bet he does."

Dillon and Michelle walked back toward their room, leaving Jeanette and her brother behind. Dillon bounced down the hall, all fired up about his win in the sparring ring. "My mom trained me for years; she's a fourth degree, you know. I used to make money at the pit fights."

"I saw one of those street fights. Those are horrible!"

"Ha. Those are profitable." Dillon dropped his voice to a whisper, even though no one else was in the hall with them. "Hey, did you like my excuse? What, you guys have rules?"

"You knew they had rules."

Dillon laughed and lowered his voice before continuing. "I wasn't all that clear on what they were, so I blew 'em all off. But seriously, I hope you know I didn't really mean the part about eliminating the weak. It seemed like something the colonel might buy, so I threw it in."

"The scary thing is, he liked the idea."

Back at their dorm room, Dillon pulled Michelle inside and closed the door. "Wish it locked, but I have a solution." He leaned back against the door and drew Michelle against him. "We'll just lean on the door the whole time." Dillon kissed her until her knees went weak, but when he tried to pull her down on the bed, she resisted.

"Sylvia could come back any minute, and she'd walk in on us. Besides, we need showers."

"Great idea. The bathroom door locks."

"Dillon," Michelle squealed in mock protest. He easily lifted her off her feet and she wrapped her legs around him, giggling as he carried her across the room.

When Sylvia and Slade walked in, Michelle and Dillon were sitting on his bed in clean clothes while she combed the knots out of his wet hair. Sylvia invited Slade in, but the black-haired boy kept a nervous eye on Dillon.

"We rode the elevator up to the top of the tower, and the view from there is incredible," Sylvia enthused. "There are three waterfalls downriver, way far away. Slade says you can only spot them in the morning."

"That's 'cause the sun rises behind the Torr and lights them up," Slade explained, eyeing Dillon to see if he'd be irritated about this little outing.

Michelle suppressed a giggle. That joke from this morning really threw Slade. He seemed to take everything literally. *Does he really think Dillon's got Sylvia and me in his own little harem?*

Even so, Slade seemed jumpier than he ought to be. He flinched a little when Dillon casually asked him where their guards were. "Oh, they're out training with our security force. You know, just like you worked out with us, your guards are working out with ours."

"You need to run decisions like that past us first," Dillon instructed, sounding exactly like an officer himself.

After Slade left, Jeanette fumed about the missing Augments. "Yesterday you couldn't have pried them off us, and this morning they're just gone." The team waited around, but their Augments still hadn't reappeared by the time Slade arrived to walk them to the dining hall.

Even breakfast at Iron Torr managed to be weird. Teenagers and kids sat by rank, with Junior Master Sawyer at the head of a long table in front. Michelle and her friends took empty seats near the back. They hadn't even started on their meager bowls of oatmeal when Sawyer sent a boy over with a message.

"Excuse me, Mister Freeman? Junior Master Sawyer invites you to join him at the head table."

Dillon's eyes widened. "Just me?" He looked over at Michelle uncomfortably, and she touched his knee under the table.

"Go," she sent silently. *"See what you can find out."*

"Um, I don't know," Dillon said. "I thought Sawyer was pissed at me, after that fight."

"He was," the boy said evenly. "But he got over it. Sawyer's actually a pretty good guy."

"Okay, then. Thanks," Dillon said, and he followed the kid toward the front of the room. An open chair next to Sawyer awaited him. All the higher ranks politely stood up until he was seated. The top ranking table stood laden with omelets, sausages, pancakes, and juice. Michelle forced her eyes away and went back to her unsweetened oatmeal, feeling like a recruit.

Jeanette slid into Dillon's vacated spot to whisper with Michelle. "I thought they were messing with him, but it looks like they really mean it. Dillon's got something special. Do you know what it is?"

"No. I thought they were going to out him for being a half-breed," Michelle confessed.

"He's not a half-breed," Jeanette murmured. "Well, maybe he is. But he's still got one hell of a pedigree. His mother holds half the performance records at the Institute, or she would, if they hadn't erased her. Of course, the old notes are still archived, if you know where to look."

"You *hacked* the archives?" Despite her efforts, Michelle's eyebrows climbed toward her hairline.

Jeanette shook her head. "Todd did. I only helped a little. That kind of thing is out of my league."

"What did you find out about Dillon's Normal father?"

"He was a recruit, and a good one, from what I gather, but he never finalized his application to join the Institute. They were a few notations of discipline issues, and then he disappeared."

"Discipline issues? What did he do?" Michelle knew she sounded way too impressed, but she couldn't help it. The Morley kids stole more Institute secrets than anyone. People fully expected to see them running the Conclave someday.

Jeanette ducked the question. "It's sad, don't you think? If Dillon's father had completed the recruitment process, his son would be considered Enhanced, not half Normal. It's just a technicality."

The girls snuck glances at the top table, where Dillon feasted on sausages and eggs with the high-ranking teens. His long auburn hair and worn clothing made him stand out, but it looked like people liked him. At least the brunette at his elbow did. She couldn't take her eyes off him.

"Dillon's got to carry some special gene combination, and Iron Torr wants it," Jeanette murmured, her lips tickling Michelle's hair. "They're bending over backwards to recruit him."

Michelle couldn't hide her worry. "They might succeed. He's the lowest ranked man at the Institute, and he always will be. What's he got to lose?"

After the meal Dillon returned looking grim. "Meeting," he announced shortly. "Our room, right away."

Dillon caught up with Todd in the hallway. "We need to talk." The two boys walked ahead so Michelle couldn't hear them. *Whatever it is, it's bad.*

Dillon paced the small space in the dorm room, waiting for the Institute team to gather. When the last person arrived he motioned everyone up off the beds and shoved all three of them together. "We don't know who's listening," he mouthed. Everyone circled up on the beds, lying on their bellies with their heads together, before Dillon spoke again. "This is it. We're supposed to go out and repair the communications center today."

"Not without our guards, we don't," Jeanette hissed.

"Okay, we'll make that one of our conditions. We'll need their help anyway, to secure the area. So, the communications building is here," Dillon sketched with his finger on a bedspread, making an invisible picture. "It's on the bottom of the valley, and cliffs rise on both sides. If I was a rebel, I'd put men up here, and here, on the hillsides. They'd get a clear shot at people below, and there's good cover."

"So we need to go up there first and clean 'em out," Brian said grimly.

"Right."

"Wait a minute," Sylvia protested. "You don't seriously intend to risk your lives for Colonel Parker. Absolutely not!"

An argument broke out, with everyone talking at once.

"Can I just say one thing?" Michelle interrupted tentatively. She was a little surprised when everyone shut up. "We don't have a choice. We can do this our way, or they'll shove us out the door and tell our parents we died like heroes."

Michelle told them about the colonel's use of Norm women as surrogates. "It tells you a lot about the kind of man he is. People are just assets to him. He won't lose any sleep if some of us die."

"Except for you, Michelle. We can't afford to lose you," Jeanette said, like that was the end of it. "You're not going."

"I'm not a little girl, Jeanette," Michelle snapped.

Jeanette turned to Dillon, her most likely ally. "We're not risking her."

"Actually," Dillon closed his eyes tight while he took a deep breath. "We're short on people. The way the terrain is, I really need someone to guard the gulch, right above the communications building. We'll have eyes in all the high places, but the gulch is loaded with cover. If I wanted to stage an attack, I'd come in through there." Dillon rubbed the bridge of his nose as if his head hurt.

Michelle squeezed his hand gratefully, but his dismal expression let her know he was telling the truth. He wasn't doing her a favor.

"Todd and Jeanette can't repair equipment and watch their backs at the same time," Michelle pointed out.

"She's right," Todd said over his sister's wordless noise of frustration. "That's what Security's for. We need Michelle in the gulch."

Jeanette started to swear but a knock on the door startled her into silence. She jumped up to open it. The missing Augments waited outside. Jeanette beckoned the five men into the already crowded room and shut the door behind them. "Where the hell have you people been?"

The stricken look on the captain's face revealed how much Jeanette's word's stung. "I'm sorry, Miss Morley. We were out on patrol."

"Outside? On whose orders?" Michelle put in gently.

The captain met her eyes. "Yours, Colonel Parker said."

"Mine?" Michelle repeated. "I never said that! It's dangerous out there. I wouldn't risk your lives like that, for no reason."

The captain scowled. "I should have known, Miss Atherton. The *colonel*...." The Augment let his words trail off before he criticized one of the Enhanced, but his tone was clear enough.

"Good thing no one was hurt. I hope you're up for another walk in the woods, captain, because we're going out to repair communications."

The captain nodded shortly. "I got your back, miss."

Under the captain's worshipful gaze, a heavy weight settled in Michelle's chest. *I hope I don't disappoint him.*

Chapter 4: Michelle

Insurgents

Michelle crouched in the bushes outside Iron Torr. *I wish I was the tech savvy type. Then I'd be repairing communications with Jeanette and Todd, instead of running around the woods looking for armed men.* She gripped her rifle with sweaty hands and scanned the mountainside. The reality felt a lot scarier than she expected. Her eyes darted about, drawn by every leaf that fluttered in the wind.

"If you spot any insurgents, just signal their location and run like hell, okay? Don't engage them," Dillon begged, so softly she could barely hear him. "Promise me."

Michelle didn't trust her voice, so she only nodded. On Dillon's whispered countdown she got ready, and then exploded from cover and bounded up the mountain like a deer. Halfway up the hill she rolled under a ledge of red rock and lay there trembling. Behind her, the ledge sloped down to meet the ground, leaving the rear of the shelter in shadow. The air inside smelled vaguely skunky. Soft shuffling sounds came from the darkness, making the back of Michelle's neck prickle. She twisted to peer into the darkness behind her. A lump of dark-brown fur hissed, baring oversized white fangs. Biting back a cry, Michelle yanked her foot back. The first wolverine she'd ever seen left its den and ran off through the trees in a weird hunchbacked lope.

Michelle fought back her fear and tried to focus on her mission. Her job was to make sure the hillside was clear of enemies before Todd and Jeanette made their break across open ground to the communications building. From her spot on the hill, the bottom quarter of the Torr hung below her. Its dark stone seemed to absorb the light, leaving the surrounding forest in ashen twilight. A glint at the highest window caught her eye. Someone stood there with binoculars. Michelle shouldered her rifle and took a quick look through the scope. The colonel stood there, waiting to see how his chess game played out. Parker recoiled visibly when he spotted Michelle, lying on her belly in the dirt with her gun aimed right at him. He quickly lowered his binoculars and retreated.

Another flash of movement came from the door of the tower. *There goes Brian!* He covered ground with inhuman speed. Michelle anxiously scanned his path for enemies. Sylvia came out next, hunched over and running scared, like a dog with its tail between its legs. She quickly disappeared into the woods with her rifle strapped to her back. Brian reached his position on the ridge, and it was time to go. Michelle didn't want to. She felt like crawling back in the wolverine's hole and digging it even deeper. But she rolled out from under the ledge anyway and wiped her sweaty palms on her pants.

Keeping low, Michelle moved uphill toward a better vantage point. Her knees shook, but not enough to stop her. Something moved in the bushes. She dove for cover and cracked her knee hard on a rock. A sparrow flitted from the underbrush. Michelle got to her feet, feeling stupid, but she still couldn't shake the feeling that someone was watching her. Someone besides the colonel at the window. Someone armed with a stolen Institute rifle.

Michelle deliberately cultivated brave thoughts, trying to beat down the panic that threatened to send her screaming into the forest. *I'm the predator here. If you're out here, you murderous sons of bitches, I am going to find you.* All the while, a smaller, quieter voice whispered from the back of her mind. *Parker kidnaps their wives and their daughters. His doctors rape them and steal their babies. Sure we're on the right side here?*

Michelle knelt and set her rifle down to flex her cramping hands. She pressed cool fingers against her temples, soothing frayed nerves. When something rustled through a patch of devil's club on the hillside below, she snatched up her gun. Large, flat leaves shifted like water in the wake of a submerged shark. Against all her instincts, Michelle plunged into the thicket and hurried after it, resisting the impulse to grab the thorny stems for balance as she skidded down the muddy slope. Ahead, leaves shifted, moving toward the open ground on the far side of the thicket. The intruder was about to show himself. Michelle stopped. She raised her rifle with shaking hands. A thin gray coyote trotted across the hillside, head and tail held level. With a shuddering sigh, she lowered her rifle and let it go.

Michelle watched the slope, straining her patience, waiting for soldiers to show themselves. None did, but the back of her neck prickled and her tension grew. Undergrowth grew thickly in the damp forest, providing plenty of cover. *We need to get this over with.* Reluctantly, Michelle pulled a tiny signaling mirror from her pocket. Its steel case felt cold in her hand. She pinched it tight between her fingers and forced herself to wait.

The gulley smelled of wildflowers and pine. Birdsong gave the place a peaceful feel. Michelle finally opened the mirror and flashed a message to Dillon below. After a nail-biting wait, another signal came from Brian on the ridge, and then Sylvia flashed the final all-clear. A ground-floor door of the tower immediately flew open. Jeanette and Todd ran across the pavement, surrounded by loyal Augments. They were almost unrecognizable in helmets and black-matte body armor.

Dillon came out last and scrambled up the hillside just above the building. He'd taken the most dangerous job himself. Holding that spot was essential, but cover grew thinly at the edge of the forest. Michelle could see him, and that meant enemies could too.

The forest suddenly went silent. Not a single songbird chirped. Michelle's stomach clenched.

Movement in her peripheral vision snapped her head around. She sucked in a hissing breath. On her right, the lush green grass swayed with the passage of something moving uphill along the gulley. Michelle crept that way, following the rustling stems. *Hope it's a huge grizzly bear,* she thought, repressing an insane giggle.

She crept up the hillside, finally dropping to her belly. Particles of itchy grass stuck to her damp skin, but she didn't dare wipe them away. Ahead, a helmeted man cautiously rose up to scout around. Michelle flattened herself in the grass, sick with fear. *Oh my God! I already sent the signal, and I can't take it back. I can't warn Dillon!*

A patch of the man's forest green tunic was barely visible through the deep grass. It shifted as he turned to look behind him. Can he feel my eyes on him? Michelle tucked her chin and pressed her forehead against the earth. When she forced herself to peek again, he was gone. The sweat that beaded between her breasts carried the rancid stench of terror, but she crawled on. *I've got to find him before he fires on my friends. I have to kill him.*

A ridge of red rock overlooked the gulley. Michelle impulsively sprang to her feet and vaulted to the top. In a flash she located the man in the grass below. Aiming fast, she fired her weapon. He twisted and fell in a spray of blood. Gunshots echoed back from across the canyon, and a dozen soldiers rose from cover behind her. Michelle whirled and cried out. *It's a trap!*

Firing blindly, she took a flying leap off the rock. She landed well in the deep grass, took two big strides, and got tackled hard from behind. The rifle flew from her hand as she hit the ground, and then a man's big hand grabbed the back of her head and smashed her face down. In a flash of hot blood and pain, her lip split against the earth. Biting back sobs, Michelle arched her back and pushed against the grinding pressure of a knee on her back. Someone threw a heavy canvas tarp over her head. She thrashed, kicking frantically, as unseen hands wrapped her in the tarp, making it almost impossible to breathe. Men lifted her by her hands and feet, and she twisted so hard that they dropped her painfully on the rocks. A man swore in a Norm accent. Claustrophobic and panicking, Michelle tried to throw the tarp off and run. Someone clubbed her on the back of the head and she went down.

She held very still, face down, pretending to be unconscious. Her heart pounded in her ears. As a child, she'd done the same thing to end beatings from her father, but this was worse. The air inside the tarp smelled strange, leaving a weird chemical taste on her tongue. Her mind raced. *Why don't they just kill me? Are they about to?*

Gunfire erupted from Brian's position on the other side of the canyon. Michelle flinched, and that gave her away. The soldiers hit her again and twisted the roll of canvas, pinning her. One of them threw her over his shoulder. The lack of oxygen made her dizzy, and the jouncing of the man's fast stride made it hard to breathe. Before long she fainted.

***

Michelle awoke to someone splashing water on her face. Her head pounded, and she felt nauseous. She rolled over and dry heaved over a dirt floor.

"Ya damn near killed her, Wade," a woman snapped. "By the Gods, we're not gonna be like them. This is nothin' more than a girl."

In the background, a child cried. Flies buzzed around Michelle's mouth. They walked on her lips, tickling horribly, but she could hardly move.

A gruff male voice spoke, full of resentment. "That little girl killed three men, an' wounded another."

"No doubt on the orders o' some lordly man like yerself," the woman snorted.

Wade slammed the door on his way out. Michelle rolled over and tried to sit up, and the woman rushed to help her. "Ya poor dear! Can y' make it to the bed?"

The woman got one thick shoulder under Michelle's and half-carried her to a pallet against the wall. Beneath the Norm's generous padding of fat were muscles of steel. She brought a threadbare cloth, dampened it from an earthen jug, and began cleaning Michelle's face. "What a pretty one y' are," the woman cooed softly, as she would to a baby. "Nobody's gonna hurt ya now."

Michelle gazed blearily up at the woman's round face and dark, silver-streaked hair. Her square jaw spoke of strength, but the brown eyes looked kind. She had to be somebody's mother. The woman began to sing softly as she gently stroked Michelle's tangled curls. After a while Michelle slept, dreaming of Normal women singing lullabies to babies that weren't theirs.

She awoke in the cabin. Through the single small window, a few early stars twinkled faintly in an evening sky. Michelle struggled to sit up, but the effort made her bruised head pound, so she laid still and looked around. Nets full of root vegetables hung from the ceiling, and a fire crackled inside a pot-bellied stove. A barefoot child, five or six years old, stood in the doorway. The girl peered curiously at Michelle and then crept into the room, looking over her shoulder like she wasn't supposed to be in there. When Michelle turned her head, the girl froze for a second, staring with wide eyes.

"I'm not gonna hurt you," Michelle whispered.

The girl came up to the edge of the low pallet, moving with a bouncy confidence. Feathers and red ribbons had been braided into the child's dark hair, and she wore a hand-embroidered woolen vest. Someone obviously treasured her.

"That's not what my uncle says." The little girl raised her chin in a childish challenge. "He says you killed my Da."

"Oh." Michelle's eyes filled with tears. "I'm so sorry." She wondered which one he had been, but asking about him wouldn't help. She'd hardly gotten a look at any of them.

Tears streamed down her face, dampening the homespun pillowcase. *She's lost her father because of me. Will she starve, like fatherless kids in the Warren do?* A small hand on Michelle's arm made her look up.

"Ma says it's a war," the little girl whispered.

Michelle nodded, but didn't answer.

"She says there's good people on both sides, and bad ones too. What kind are you?"

"Once I would have said I'm one of the good guys. But now?" Michelle blew softly through her nose. "I don't even know anymore."

The little girl slipped off the bed and padded away, leaving Michelle certain that she'd said the wrong thing.

Michelle dozed and was awakened by the child wiggling around on the foot of the pallet. The girl sat in silence, playing with one of the bluebird feathers braised into her long brown hair, and then abruptly turned to Michelle. "If you weren't good, y' wouldn't cry 'bout killin' nobody. You can stay here, an' not go back to the scary tower."

At this unexpected kindness, Michelle lost control and began to sob.

"Aw." The little girl crawled over the blanket and patted Michelle's hair with one tiny hand.

The heavy-set woman burst into the room, surprising them both. "Kalie! What did you just say?"

The child tilted her chin up defiantly, but her lower lip trembled. "I tol' her she didn't hafta go back t' the scary tower."

"Gods, child! That's a bindin' offer. Y' can't take that back without years o' bad luck, an' times 'r hard enough." The woman hauled Kalie off the pallet by one arm and hurried her away.

Adults' voices came from the next room.

"Ya sure she made the offer?" a man asked.

The heavy-set woman answered. "She said it, by the Gods. I heard 'er myself."

The argument got carried outside. From the voices it sounded like more villagers were gathering, adding their opinions to the exchange. *They're distracted. It's never going to get any better than it is right now.* Michelle struggled off the low pallet. A stab of pain shot up her leg and took her breath away. Michelle bit her lip to stop from crying out. A homespun cloth bandage was wrapped around her lower leg. She had to know, so she laboriously undid the tight knots, leaning on the log wall for balance. She peeled the bloody bandage back, moaned at the sight, and tied it back in place, feeling ill.

A bullet grazed my leg. Weird, I don't remember being shot.

The single small window of the cabin looked out on old-growth forest. The trees were magnificent. At their bases, most were wider than the hut. Their tops disappeared into the dark blue sky. *It'll be night soon. Should I wait until then? Which way back to Iron Torr?* A peek out the door revealed a fire pit with a group of Norms around it. The villagers were deep in discussion, with the heavy-set woman in the thick of it.

"A life fer a life," the woman insisted, and that made up Michelle's mind. She darted out the door and made a break for the woods, but a pile of animal traps lay in a shadow against the wall. She tripped on a nearly invisible snare and went down with a crash. In a heartbeat a man grabbed her. Michelle screamed in terror, sobbing and thrashing. One weak kick struck the Norm in the chest, but it didn't stop him. Men came to his aid, grabbing her wrists and ankles in powerful grips. They flipped her face down and pinned her hands over her head.

Girls and women gathered around, making sympathetic sounds. "Stop it, yer scarin' 'er, Wade!"

"Bring 'er over here," the heavy-set woman ordered, so Wade swung Michelle into his arms and carried her to the fire. For a second she fixated on the open targets across his neck and face, but hesitated and missed the chance to strike. Wade set her gently down on a rustic wooden chair, and someone brought a stump to prop the injured leg on. Michelle wanted to run, but her head throbbed and her stomach clenched with nausea. She trembled in the chair, looking over the rebel band. They looked like a family or two at the most, with five or six adults and twice as many children and teenagers. Their faces were open and kind, not at all like the brutal insurgents she'd imagined.

"Heya, honey, I'm Molly," the heavy-set woman said, and Michelle weakly held out both hands for the double handclasp of the Norms. Around her, villagers smiled. One by one, they approached her, welcoming her. Molly handed her a chunk of brown bread, and a ponytailed teenage boy brought her a mug of tea.

What's happening? Why kidnap me, and then act like I'm a guest? One thing was clear—she was in no shape to run. Sitting by the fire seemed infinitely better than making another break for it and getting nabbed by Wade. Even a big male Norm would usually be no match for her, but her strength was gone. She felt shaky and sick. Michelle's hands trembled, sloshing tea over her grimy jeans. *What happened to the others? Am I the only survivor?* When people came by to chat she could hardly speak. Hours later, Norms drifted off to their huts, but Michelle still slumped by the fire.

The ponytailed teenage boy came over and sat beside her. Dark hair came halfway down his back, and his handsome face was browned by sun and wind. "Worst day o' yer life?" he asked with a wry smile, and Michelle nodded weakly. "Y'know why yer here, an' not dead in the woods?"

"No," Michelle whispered.

"A life fer a life, that's the rule. Yer people killed Molly's man, so she gets a life in return. It don't matter none who pulled the trigger. You're her daughter now, and she'll love ya like her own."

"That's insane."

"If ya'd rather reject the offer, jus' tell Wade. He won't like it, but he'll put a bullet in yer head."

Michelle shook her head hard, but that set it aching again. Her vision faded from the edges inward, but she could still see the boy's face.

"If ya stay, I'll be yer cousin. I'm Laird."

The ponytailed boy walked away. With a pang, Michelle watched him go. Then she shifted in her chair and felt the tug of a rope against her ankle. Someone had tied her to a tree. She bit her lip to keep from screaming.

Chapter 5: Dillon

Gunfight

Dillon felt way too exposed on the rocky slope above the communications building. He hunched down behind a boulder and scanned the hillside, the rifle heavy and unfamiliar in his hands. Dillon's guts twisted into a knot at the thought of Michelle on the mountain alone, but he forced the thought out of his mind. *Help her by doing your job*, he told himself. *Look for insurgents*. Below him, in the communications building, Jeanette and Todd made repairs while Augments watched their backs.

Near the top of the gulch, a flock of birds burst out of the bushes, sending high-pitched cries into the sky. Undergrowth grew thickly up there, in the constant dampness of the forest. Dillon watched the spot intently, nerves on edge, but nothing moved. Suddenly gunfire rocked the canyon, first from the gulch, and then from the ridge where Brian had gone. All hell broke loose, with Augments shouting and bullets kicking into the slope all around him. Shards of rock cut into Dillon's face as he threw himself to the ground. Blood from his face stained the sleeve of his jacket.

"Help! We need some help out here," Dillon shouted, but the doors of Iron Torr stayed closed.

Jeanette and Todd pounded across the hard-packed earth that surrounded the communications building and disappeared into the forest with their bodyguards. Dillon put his head down and ran for the trees. He stopped about fifty yards into the forest, at the base of a pine. Every tiny sound made him snap his head around. Something moved on the ridge, up high and to his right.

Heart racing, Dillon shouldered his rifle and peered through the scope. Five green-clad men made their way along the ridge, toting familiar-looking guns. *Institute issue, from our helicopter. Thieving bastards.*

Dillon targeted the Norms, and for the first time in his life, he pulled the trigger on a rifle. He expected it to make noise, but the ear-splitting volume made his whole body jerk. The butt of the rifle kicked hard into the wiry muscle of his shoulder, and his shots flew high. He kept trying. The Norms sprinted into the forest while Dillon's bullets chewed into tree trunks behind them. A gun cracked, alarmingly close. Instantly a bullet kicked up the dust only a few feet away. Dillon panicked and ran down the hill, stumbling blindly over rocks and fallen logs. A man shouted nearby. Dillon whirled, gun raised.

Sawyer stood there, empty handed, with a stocky, athletic looking blonde girl behind him. "Don't shoot! Hurry up, come with us. We've got to get you inside!"

Sawyer led them at a run around the outside of the fortress. Here, pine trees gave way to aspens, and the cover was poor. Snipers took shots at them as they ran. The girl let out a mad cry of elation as she leaped rocks and swerved between trees.

At the tower, Sawyer grabbed Dillon by the arm to stop him. "Here." A rectangular outline on the dark metal wall revealed a hidden door. Sawyer pounded out a fast pattern on the metal, and Slade jerked it open for them from inside.

Dillon tumbled into a corridor crowded with young people from Iron Torr, about half of them girls. "My friends need help," he gasped. "Quick, grab your weapons."

Behind their backs, the elevator door glided open with a hiss.

The stocky blonde girl didn't seem to notice. Leaves caught in her hair, and a wild light lit her eyes. "Let's do it," she cried. "Get the guns, Slade!"

"Britta," Slade snapped, too late.

A pair of officers stepped out of the elevator. "Outside? And planning to access weapons. All without authorization. We'll have to inform the colonel."

The teenagers from Iron Torr stood in silence, eyes down. Apparently arguing was useless here.

Dillon tried anyway. "We got shot at. They saved my life!"

The blue-eyed officer looked Dillon over, from his old boots to his patched winter jacket. "Whatever that was worth," he grunted.

"My friends are probably hurt, 'cause they tried to help you," Dillon snapped, chin up. "So get out there and back 'em up."

The officer ignored Dillon completely and turned to Slade. "Stand by, Lieutenant Parker. We'll see what your father has to say about this." The officers stepped into the elevator.

"Tell Parker to send out some help," Dillon shouted as the door closed. He paced the hall angrily, scattering teenagers from his path.

Slade leaned on the wall, eyes closed. His dark face twisted in anguish. Sawyer clapped him on the shoulder. "You didn't go out, Slade. We did."

"I helped," Slade muttered. He reached into a pocket, pulled out a brass key on a chain, and clenched it in his fist. "I never get away with lying to him. He always knows."

Britta draped herself across Slade's shoulder. "Baby, when you say it, you have to make *yourself* believe it, or it's no good."

Slade ignored her and gazed up at Sawyer instead. "What's going to happen now?"

Britta answered for him. "Confinement to quarters, if we're lucky." Her comment triggered laughter, quickly stifled.

"What the hell is funny?" Dillon asked, in a quiet, deadly tone. Everyone looked at him. "My friends are out there, and my woman—"

"His girlfriend, he means," Britta interrupted, giggling. "She's only, like, fifteen or something."

"Sixteen." With a few rapid strides, Dillon closed the distance between them. The blood on his face made him look savage. Britta narrowed her eyes and stood her ground.

"Enough." Sawyer put a rough hand on Britta's jacket, yanked her sideways, and straight-armed her away from Dillon. "Sorry, Dillon. Britta likes to start fights. Look, we're trying to help you here, but we operate under orders. All the weapons are locked in the armory, and we're not going anywhere unless we're part of an organized combat operation."

Footsteps sounded on the stairs. Everyone except Dillon snapped to attention.

Colonel Parker strolled in. "Well, at least someone understands how things run around here," he said sarcastically. "Well *done*, Mister Sawyer."

Dillon stepped up and looked Parker in the eye. "I expect a full-scale combat operation launched immediately to rescue my friends."

"You expect? Here, children like you follow orders." Parker laughed in Dillon's face and turned to the young man who had rescued him. "Sawyer."

"Sir!"

Parker's voice suddenly went gentle, like a concerned father. "Twenty years you've lived here, under my roof. And now you betray me. Tell me why."

Sawyer stared straight forward as he spoke. "It was no betrayal, Colonel. They were guests, sir, and they were trying to help us."

"Guests, trying to help us. That's a recapitulation of the facts." Parker's voice took on a dangerous edge. "Facts I already know. Slade? Talk to me."

Slade blinked rapidly, but his face remained stoic. His fists were empty now, the brass key hidden. "It's…what friends would do, sir."

Parker laughed harshly. The sound gave Dillon chills. *What, Parker's never had a friend?*

"Friends?" Parker repeated, raising one golden eyebrow. "With some kids you just met yesterday. Whose loyalties we aren't sure of, sent here by my oldest enemy."

Slade's eyes remained downcast. He didn't answer.

From the base of the stairs, Parker cast his cold gaze over the assembly of teens. "I don't know how many of you were directly involved, and how many were spectators. So you're all getting the same punishment. Twenty-four hours, confinement to quarters."

"You're locking us up? Wait a minute! What about my friends?" Dillon bellowed.

Parker made an irate gesture. The nearest officer twisted his body and punched Dillon as hard as he'd ever been hit, with an explosive uppercut to the chin. Dillon never saw it coming.

Chapter 6: Michelle

Slavery

Wade, the village headman, treated Michelle like a slave, a guest, or a daughter, depending on his mood. During the daylight hours, Michelle limped around the village on a leash, helping the women with chores, while armed men watched her with sidelong glances. Every evening the headman came into the hut to tie her up. Molly would fold her arms and stare at him in silent disapproval while Wade, bumbling and apologetic, secured a scratchy rope around Michelle's wrists and ankles.

As Laird promised, Molly threw herself wholeheartedly into her new role as Michelle's adopted mother. This mostly consisted of tutoring her in the womanly arts.

"Y' can't so much as roast a haunch o' venison?" Molly asked, shaking her head in dismay. An' ya can't spin or weave, even a little? What'd they teach ya at home, girl?"

"I'm decent at calculus and quantum physics, and last term I got through my physiology textbook in three days. Mostly 'cause I had to, since I let it go and got behind," Michelle said, suppressing a smile at Molly's bewildered expression.

"Well, dontcha worry." Molly squeezed Michelle's shoulder affectionately. "I won't let anybody say my daughter's slow in the head. I'll show ya everything, as many times as it takes."

Despite Molly's kindness, thoughts of escape obsessed Michelle. She held off, first because the bullet wound in her leg ached, and then because men guarded her in shifts. *It's not time yet. Heal up a little more, and then go,* Michelle told herself, trying to silence the voice in her head that told her she was stalling, too afraid to make the break. *It'll be a lot easier if I can get them to let me off the leash.*

With that in mind, Michelle made it her goal to win over the Norms. She kept at it with instant obedience and plenty of plastic smiles. Her leg healed quickly, but she left the bandage on, hoping they'd watch her less closely if they thought she couldn't run. Sometimes Michelle pictured herself attacking the unfortunate Norm who held her leash, but the villagers were a good-natured lot, and it just wasn't in her to punch a smiling face. As the days passed she felt increasingly torn, especially once she knew which children had mothers who were being held in Iron Torr.

To Michelle's surprise, Molly assigned her to join the crew of young women who cared for the motherless toddlers. Her kindly co-workers seemed embarrassed by the rope attached to Michelle's ankle, so they pointedly ignored it, as if it didn't exist. Michelle began to look forward to afternoons, when the Norms tethered her to a tree inside the low fence of the toddlers' play yard. She sat on the ground there, changing diapers and playing with the little kids, who used her as a human jungle gym. Michelle could match each child's features with one of the imprisoned mothers, and inside, she burned with anger at the colonel.

Laird's dark eyes followed Michelle as she moved about the camp with loads of wood or water, and he sometimes brought her a cup of water when she had a moment to rest. Wade endured days of relentless pleading from his son before he gave in and allowed Laird to take charge of Michelle's leash. Michelle wasn't sure that was a good idea, but she didn't object out loud. No one there would listen to her, anyway.

Laird took his time untying the knots that held Michelle's rope to a tree. She waited, becoming more and more uncomfortable, while the village women whispered. Their eyes prickled the back of her neck. Michelle stared down at Laird's strong, tanned hands, working methodically at the knots. *Uh-oh, he's getting ideas. I'm going to have to slap him down, and I really don't want to. Laird's about my only friend here, besides Molly.*

"There." Laird tied Michelle by one wrist, coiled the remainder of the rope, and slung it over his arm. "Now you can go with me on hunts, an' help haul back the meat."

"Hunts? In the woods? Just you and me?"

Laird looked up, and his eyes met hers. "Don't flatter yerself. It ain't like that. You're kinda like my sister, see? So, no offense, but …eeeyuck."

Michelle flushed. Norms were a lot more perceptive than she thought they'd be. "Um, okay. Good. Yuck to you, too."

Laird smirked. "Come on, girl." He gave a mischievous tug at the leash.

Michelle was tempted to grab the rope and pull back, but a sideways glance showed her that more than a few men had readied their bows. Those guys wouldn't get the joke. *Besides, I can easily get away once we're alone.*

"Fine." She got to her feet and followed her so-called cousin into the woods.

Michelle's spirits soared as they took to a trail through meadows crowded with yellow wildflowers. Laird wrapped the overlong rope around his waist and tied it off, leaving his hands free to wield his weapons.

"What, no gun?" Michelle eyed the handmade bow and quiver on his Laird's back. In one hand, he gripped a long spear. "I know you guys have rifles, so don't try and hide it."

"I'm not hidin' anything," Laird said shortly. "Rifles 're fer war, an' ammunition's limited. My Da says we still gotta hunt like we always did."

Michelle raised her chin. "You do everything Wade tells you to?"

The boy only shrugged. "Yep."

After that, Laird laid claim to the narrow trail, forcing Michelle onto the overgrown shoulder. She took a bit too long to get over a rough patch, got yanked by the rope, tripped, and went down. Laird laughed at her.

"Oh, you think that's funny?" Michelle asked, playfully taking hold of the rope. She gave it a good yank and pulled the Norm down with her. They both scrambled to their feet and took off into a running tug-of-war, giggling the whole way. The game ended abruptly when they flushed a herd of young deer out of the aspens.

Laird let an arrow fly, and then another. Both shots missed. He swore. "Quit pullin' on the rope!"

"I wasn't. Come on, we can catch 'em." Michelle dashed a few yards with the Norm in tow, but quickly realized he couldn't keep up. "Laird, just cut me loose for a minute. Let me borrow that spear."

"No way." Still gasping for breath, Laird switched hands with the spear, trying to keep Michelle from grabbing it.

Michelle let him tug her to a halt. "Come on, Laird. Think of the meat. The children need protein. It'll stunt their growth if you raise 'em on nothing but bread and fruit."

Laird shook his head, his eyes on the disappearing herd. "I promised my Da."

Michelle took Laird's arm and made him look at her. "Cut me loose. I can easily get us a deer. I swear I'll come back. We'll throw a feast for the whole village."

"If ya run off, they'll beat me within an inch o' my life."

"Laird, I already swore I wouldn't," Michelle cried. "I gave you my word."

The dark-haired Norm hesitated. Then he reached a hand into his back pocket, pulled out a handmade obsidian knife, and began sawing at the tough rope. Michelle fidgeted impatiently as the deer disappeared into the trees. When the last strands finally parted, she blurted, "Thanks," snatched Laird's spear from his hand in one lightning motion, and bolted.

With no intention of returning.

Michelle chased the herd to the top of the ridge, ducked a few feet down the other side, and let them go. A flick of her wrist activated her surgically implanted cell chip so a dull red light glowed through her skin. That told her the chip was still working, but the thing was as useless there as it had been back at camp. *Aw, crap. I figured as much.*

Michelle turned in all directions, scouring the landscape for something familiar. The Torr should have stood sentinel over that wilderness, but the enormous black tower had simply vanished. Forest of aspen and pine reached to a horizon of craggy, snowcapped mountains, and nothing looked at all familiar.

Behind the ridge, the tiny figure of Laird labored toward her like an insect, arms and legs pumping furiously. Evading him would be easy. Michelle's acute sense of direction told her exactly where the village was, so she decided to make a wide circle around it and look for landmarks. *Iron Torr must be on the other side of the village, off to the east.* With one last guilty glance back at Laird, she bounded down the hill and vanished into the forest.

Three hours later, Michelle collapsed on a rocky ridge. She'd circled the village, and even made a few promising side trips, but she hadn't seen the colonel's tower. The wild, beautiful landscape had her completely mystified.

Where the hell is Iron Torr? It doesn't make sense. After the fight, the Norms carried me to their village. So why's it so hard to find my way back? They couldn't have carried me that far.

Movement on a faraway plain caught her eye. It was Laird, stumbling dejectedly along her trail. *Ha! The boy's a tracker, that's for sure.* Michelle sat up, poised to move either toward the Norm, or away from him. *I have a spear. I could hunt, wander around out here for a while, and maybe find my way back to Dillon.*

The afternoon sun sank lower in the sky and began to lose its warmth. The wind made an eerie sound as it sifted through the pines. Michelle didn't like the idea of sleeping out there alone with wolves and bears and whatever else lived in those mountains. Far away, Laird's tiny figure faltered, sank to the ground and lay there, unmoving. *He's given up.* From here, he looked small, weak, and very alone. *Aw, hell. I can't just leave him like that. What if there really are bears?* Michelle got up and trudged slowly back toward her friend.

When she got back to the spot where Laird had fallen, he was gone.

Michelle's breath caught in her throat. "Laird?" She circled the shrubby glen at a run, but he was nowhere to be seen. "Laird!"

Then she spotted the smooth print of his moccasin, heading back toward the village. Relief flooded her. *I thought he got eaten or something. He's just on his way home.* Michelle followed the Norm for a few miles, until something more enticing got her attention. Scores of tiny, cloven-hooved prints crossed the trail. Michelle's stomach growled. *Mmm. Deer.*

She stalked the herd onto a west-facing slope, where they'd bedded down to bask in the last rays of late afternoon sun, and picked out her target, a soft-eyed weanling. Michelle hefted the spear in one hand, considered throwing it, and decided to hang onto it instead. In a spray of gravel, she sprang from her hiding place. The deer bounded away, but before they'd gone a quarter mile, Michelle caught them. With a savage motion, she ran the smallest one through.

"Sorry, little deer, sorry," Michelle murmured, dropping to her knees. She touched its still-warm body and bit her tongue at the sight of bright blood coursing over the prickly buff hide. Her lip twisted. It was the first animal she'd ever killed, and she felt no pride, only pity and revulsion.

She hefted the body and set off with its damp weight on her shoulders, once again following Laird's trail. As the sun fell behind the mountains, Michelle entered a large grove of old aspen trees. The sky had turned a deep, rich shade of blue that cast the forest in a mysterious light. Heart-shaped aspen leaves rustled softly, as though nature spirits hid among them, whispering constantly to one another.

Laird sat against one of the white-barked trunks, eyes closed. Tears streaked his dusty face. He looked up when he heard her coming and struggled to his feet. "Michelle! I never thought I'd see ya again."

Michelle glanced awkwardly at Laird's teary face. She didn't know what to say. Even five-year-olds at the Institute knew not to cry in front of other people, and that boy had to be at least sixteen. Wordlessly, she dumped the stiffening body of the deer at his feet. It landed in the grass with a sickening thud.

Laird made a face at the carcass. "Yer supposed to gut it. Makes it lighter, an' the meat keeps better."

"Really? You'd carry it like that, all bloody and gross?"

Laird gave a weak laugh. "Yer such a girl. Here, roll it over, I'll do it for ya." He tiredly dropped to his knees beside the carcass and went to work with the stone knife.

Michelle sat beside him in silence, tasting her bitter disappointment. *Here I am, right back where I started. I need to get back to Dillon and our friends. What if some of them are hurt?*

"Look, Michelle, I'm…I'm sorry," Laird finally said, without looking up. His bloody hand sawed patiently at deer hide, splitting the carcass open across the belly. "I should've thought better of ya. I know, y' gave me yer word."

Michelle shrugged. "It's okay. You didn't need to try and keep up."

"I didn't keep up," Laird muttered darkly. "I cut a lot o' corners, when I could tell where you were goin'."

"Yeah, well, you look like hell anyway." Michelle softened the comment with a smile.

"This is nothin' next t' what I'd look like if I went back without you."

Michelle didn't answer. Laird kept on working. He didn't seem to mind the blood and guts. After a while he looked up, nodded at the spear in her hand, and flashed a brief grin. "Made it myself. Flies straight, eh?"

"I didn't throw it," Michelle admitted. "That's too hard. I just ran him down and stabbed him."

"You *ran down* a deer?" Laird repeated, eyes wide.

Michelle squirmed, suddenly sorry she shot off her mouth. "Um, yeah. Not that everybody needs to know that. People think I'm enough of a freak as it is."

"Yer not a freak."

"Yes I am," Michelle erupted. "I'm stuck here, tied up all the time, and nobody even cares how much it hurts!" She held out both hands, showing him the raw, red circles ringing her wrists. Angry tears filled her eyes. "Do you have any idea how it feels not to even be able to get up and pee at night?"

The way Laird gaped made it clear that she'd broken some Norm taboo, saying that, but Michelle didn't care. She turned her back to him, pulled her knees in, and hid her face in her arms.

In a minute, something softly hit the grass beside her. A coil of rope lay there, with the obsidian knife on top. Michelle reached out and traced the handle of the knife with her fingertips.

Laird's dark eyes looked pained. "Nobody likes keepin' prisoners anyway. We ain't...like that. Not usually, anyway. So go if ya wanna go. Or come on home an' be family." He wiped his hands on the grass and hauled himself to his feet.

Michelle sat very still in the grass, eyes on the spear. It was still well within her reach. Twilight slowly fell over the grove.

"The venison's yours," Laird said. He paused, but she didn't answer. After an awkward silence, he turned and walked away.

He hadn't gone far when Michelle grabbed the spear, slung the bloody carcass over her shoulders, and followed him. A light breeze cooled the tears on her cheeks.

***

Three days later, Michelle and Laird hiked in step along a trail. With one hand up to block the light from the sinking sun, she scanned the floodplain for game. Her other hand gripped the spear Laird had made for her—the first weapon she'd been officially allowed since her capture. Wade didn't know she'd been borrowing Laird's spear, and sometimes his bow too, so the headman sent guards to keep an eye on her. Of course, she wasn't supposed to know about that. Laird carefully said nothing, but, from the tension in his jaw, he knew. Men shadowed them, moving through the trees like wolves.

Michelle was irritated enough to deliberately point them out. "We've got company." She waved at the nearest pair, who skulked along about fifty yards to the right. The Norms straightened up, shrugged sheepishly at Laird, and started walking in the open.

Determined to ignore her escorts, Michelle stooped to point out some unfamiliar tracks made by tiny cloven hooves. "Laird, look. That's not deer or elk."

Laird bent over the tracks. "Bighorn sheep. Good eatin', but way way too hard t' catch. You mostly find 'em up high on the cliffs."

"I'll see if I can get us one." Before Laird could protest, Michelle loped off, aiming for a spiky spine of rock that jutted into the sky. Predictably, Wade's goons tried to follow her. She poured on the speed until they fell behind.

Near the top of a pinnacle of rock, Michelle bowed her head and let the tears flow. She missed Dillon intensely. *He's not the only one that's bonded. If I can't find him, I'll never be the same.* She closed her eyes and reached out with her mind, trying to reach him. All she heard was the wind, which never stopped blowing there. A sudden idea changed her focus, and she reached out for Jeanette instead. For an instant she imagined she felt a flicker of a connection, but then it was gone. Encouraged, she tried again. No luck.

Michelle had been hunting farther afield each day, taking advantage of the fact that no one could keep up. The Norms had no idea how long she could run, and she always went farther than they thought she did. As long as she came back with food, they didn't know she spent most of her time scouting. *They're good people, but I'd be gone already if I knew which way to go.*

Michelle scanned the crags for bighorn sheep, but nothing moved up there except a swarm of hyperactive picas. The little rodents chased each other across the sheer cliffs, oblivious to their frequent near-death experiences. She stood on stiff legs, shivering a little in the cooling air, and headed down. Far below, a big buck grazed in a gully she'd never explored. Not bothering to stalk it, Michelle hurtled down the hill, over rocks and logs. The buck flipped its tail up in alarm, showing the white underside, and took off in great springing bounds. She pursued it single-mindedly, heedless of the risk. One bad step here could mean a broken ankle, and no one knew where she was. In the headlong rush down the hill, she forgot her pain over Dillon and the life she'd lost.

The buck ran into the woods, but Michelle gained on him. A hard ten minutes later, she spotted him standing in some willows, blowing through flared nostrils. He carried a wicked rack of antlers, wider than she was tall. *This would feed the village for days.* Michelle sprinted hard, readying the spear in her right hand, but the buck bounded down a steep slope and disappeared. She followed but lost control on the hillside. Loose rock slipped underfoot, and she skidded downhill, sliding on her butt. When she regained her feet, the powerful animal was already swimming across a fast-flowing river. The current swept him downstream, and Michelle let him go.

She stared up the rushing river. To the east, three waterfalls cascaded down the cliff, lit by the afternoon sun behind her. *I've seen this river before. It flows past Iron Torr. I know exactly where I am! Iron Torr stands behind those waterfalls. It's got to be fifty miles away. How the hell did I get here?*

She stood there a long time, trying to piece together disjointed memories. *Nothing makes sense. They have no vehicles, not even horse-drawn carts. They couldn't have carried me this far, unless they kept me knocked out for a week. It didn't feel like that long, but how would I know?*

A look at the sky told her it was time to move on, and she walked slowly back toward the trail, where Laird would be waiting with Wade's men. After an hour she pressed reluctantly into a tired run. Molly would expect them back for the evening meal. In summer nightfall came late, but getting lost among those giant trees would be easy, even in daylight.

Tonight I'll pilfer some food and something warm to wear, and then I've got to go back. Hope everyone's okay back at the Torr. And I really hope Laird won't follow me there.

Michelle found Laird and the guards dozing under a tree, and they all walked back to the village together. Happy shouts greeted their return to the village. Men huddled by the fire, sharing mead. As a hunter, Laird didn't have to cut up the meat, so he joined them.

Molly hurried out to hug Michelle and take the two rabbits she'd bagged on the way home. "We've been eatin' like kings since ya joined us, daughter!"

Inside the hut, Molly poured warm water into a basin for Michelle to wash in. Then she brought out a surprise—a newly woven shirt and a handmade black vest, embroidered just like Kalie's. Molly sat Michelle down, brushed out her golden brown hair and braided it with silver beads and tiny black feathers.

"There," the Norm woman said when Michelle finished dressing. "Now y' look like somebody loves ya. An' I do." She hugged Michelle against her ample bosom, making her feel precious.

Questions rose to Michelle's lips, but she couldn't ask them. They would ruin everything.

Chapter 7: Dillon

Pink Drink

Dillon awoke when someone tossed him onto a bed. He rolled over, moaning. The cuts on his face stung, and his jaw throbbed with every heartbeat. He didn't care about any of that. *Michelle's out there! What the hell happened? Is she dead, or gunshot and bleeding? Gods, please let them find her and bring her in.*

A couple of girls cooed over him. One of them, a beautiful brunette with long, straight hair, sat down on the bed by Dillon's head.

"Come here, honey." The girl gently lifted Dillon's head and shoulders and slid under him, cradling his head between her large, firm breasts.

"Here, Dillon, drink this," a familiar voice said. Britta stood before him, but she'd changed into a silky white dress, slit daringly low in front. She pushed a cup into his face, filled with a lumpy pink liquid.

Dillon's throat felt raw with thirst, but the liquid smelled nauseating, all sickly sweet and medicinal. "Ugh." He pushed the cup away, spilling some of the goopy pink stuff down his shirt. "That's gross. Don't you have any water?"

"Sure, I'll get you some water. After you drink your medicine. It'll make you feel better," the brunette said. She took the cup from Britta and held it to Dillon's lips. "Come on, love, do it for me."

Dillon took a big gulp and almost spat out the contents, but that wasn't the slum he grew up in. Ornate wall hangings covered the stone walls, and the bed he lay on had a clean white bedspread. Soft, deep carpets hid the cold stone foundation beneath. People obviously didn't spit on the floor there. With an effort, he swallowed. A weird, cold sensation spread outward from his stomach.

"Good job, sweetie," the brunette murmured. Her silky hair brushed Dillon's face. "Have a little more."

Dillon took another mouthful of the viscous liquid, which didn't taste quite as bad that time. *Is my tongue going numb? Whoa, look at this place. Look at her!*

Dillon turned his head, and the brunette giggled. He got an eyeful of her curves, up close, through her transparent gown. "Um, sorry."

"Sorry?" the girl repeated. "Don't be. I'm not."

People giggled from around an ornate hookah on a little table by the wall. Aromatic hash smoke drifted toward the ceiling. Dillon struggled to sit up, but that made him dizzy, so he let the pretty girl pull him back down. This time she got a leg around him, so he rested on her hips when he leaned back against her. Delicious sensations of happiness and relaxation began to tingle through his body. *Mmm. This is so...damn... comfortable.*

Boys and girls flopped over curtained beds and the huge pillows that lay scattered over the floor. Everyone wore soft, colorful clothes, not the uniforms he'd always seen them in, and the girls' dresses...if you could call them that ...were sexy like nothing he'd ever seen. The gauzy material didn't hide much, and the sight of their lush curves drove Dillon crazy. Nowhere else were women so beautiful, so exotic, so...available. Music throbbed from everywhere at once, and it made his head spin.

The brunette stroked Dillon's hair and offered him another sip of the pink liquid. He took some, just to make her happy, and then a little more. Things seemed confusing. *Guess I got hit hard. I had some problem, but what was it?*

Dillon captured the elusive thought. "Outside. We need to go out." For some reason that made people laugh.

"Oh, no, lover, it's cold out there," the girl said sweetly, feeding him another sip of pink liquid. "Stay here with me. We're going to party."

"Yep, for another twenty-three hours and thirty-one minutes," Slade called cheerfully from the next room. That place looked like a boys' dormitory, but the door stood open between it and the girls' room.

Dillon made a major effort to sit up, so the dark-haired girl helped him. "Where are we?" he asked, looking around. The beds were curtained in rich jewel tones, giving the room an exotic feel.

"Girls' dorm," Britta said, tipping her head upside down to look at Dillon from her spot on a big floor cushion. She put a well-muscled leg straight up, pointing her toe at the ceiling. "We're confined to quarters, *suffering.*" One hand gestured dramatically over her head. "With no food, except for what we've stashed, just in case, and no men, except for the ones who *somehow* got in through there." She twirled a languid hand at the open door.

Slade came in jingling a ring of keys. "I never cause trouble. I've just got this problem with being locked out of places. Especially places full of girls like these."

"He's had that key since eighth grade," Britta said, giggling.

"Seventh." Slade flopped down next to Britta and nuzzled her nipple through her sheer dress. "When I noticed how the girls were separated from us by just...one...lock."

"And maybe a little cloth," Sawyer added, reaching down to tickle the damp spot on the front of Britta's dress.

"Mmm. Not for long, if you two keep that up," Britta purred. She offered Sawyer a bottle of wine.

Dillon hazily registered the fact that he should have been shocked, but he wasn't. The whole scene felt like some wild dream.

Sawyer lifted the bottle to his lips, swallowed a few mouthfuls, and kissed the redheaded girl next to him. Then he handed her the bottle. The redhead drank and kissed the person next to her, who, to Dillon's amazement, was another girl. No one seemed to think anything of it. The bottle made its rounds and ended up in the hand of a lean, blond-haired guy, about nineteen. He drank and then turned to Dillon, who squirmed uncomfortably.

"Um, no offense," Dillon told him apologetically. "I'm about as high as I've ever been in my life, but--"

The pretty brunette took the bottle out of the guy's hand. "No worries, Tai. But I think Dillon's saying you're not his type. You are mine, though."

"Mine too," said a boy across the room. Tai gave him a fragile smile.

"See, everyone loves Tai," the brunette said. She drank, set the bottle down on a nightstand, and wrapped her arms around Dillon's neck. He forgot all about the people in the room.

"I...don't even know your name," Dillon said. Forming words was an effort, but the rest of his body seemed to work just fine. Better than fine. He was on fire. Whatever that drink was, he liked it.

"I'm Marcia," the brunette whispered, and she pressed her lips to his.

Dillon lost control in a wave of desire. He flipped up Marcia's short skirt, ran his hands along her hips, and abruptly lifted her so she straddled him.

"Whohoo," people cheered. "Gotta love the pink drink."

"Pink drink, pink drink!"

"It does that to everybody."

The room suddenly felt stifling, and Dillon's throat burned with thirst. He let Marcia go, but she stayed on his lap, laughing. Dillon pulled his jacket and shirt off, amid cheers, and took the bottle of wine off the table. He tipped it and drank deeply.

"Oh." Dillon shoved the bottle away, suddenly nauseous. Marcia barely caught it before red wine went all over the bed.

"Whooaa," teens chorused. "Pink drink does *that* to everybody too."

"Did I forget to tell you?" Slade said, laughing. "Never mix it with alcohol."

Dillon swallowed hard, dumped Marcia on her back, and stood up unsteadily.

"Eeuw, get him to the bathroom, hurry," Britta squealed.

Sawyer bounded over, got a shoulder under Dillon, and half-dragged him down the hall. "This way. Now try hard and don't throw up."

Dillon shot him a bleary look and didn't answer.

"Seriously. You've gotta keep your medicine down, and besides, if you don't throw up, the sick feeling passes. If you do…like I did once…it, um, doesn't."

Dillon stood still, fighting down the urge to vomit. As quickly as the feeling came, it passed.

"Better?" Marcia asked, coming into the large bathroom behind Sawyer. "No more wine for you. Stick to this." She handed Dillon the last of his pink drink, and he downed it in one gulp. The nausea instantly disappeared, and ecstasy filled him.

The room was amazing, with showers in a semicircle and a huge stainless steel hot tub in the middle. Boys and girls streamed in, and there was plenty of room for everyone.

"Oh, yeah," Britta said. Her white dress hit the floor. "It's hot tub time."

Dillon's vision began to rotate slowly around him. "Whoa," he mumbled dizzily, took a few staggering steps backward, and almost fell.

Britta jumped in to steady him. "Oh, oh. Here he goes. Phase two, my favorite."

"Mine, too," Marcia giggled, bending down to unbuckle the strap of her high heel.

"What?" Dillon mumbled.

Marcia stepped out of her shoes and helped Britta walk him to a bench. Dillon's world turned into a kaleidoscope of moving colors, images of gorgeous girls, and strange, unfamiliar music. Somehow he ended up naked in the hot tub, surrounded by people, but he didn't remember getting in. Girls were everywhere, and they were all he could think about. Lucid moments visited him at odd intervals, and he looked around with the strangest feeling, like he was forgetting something important. Then Marcia, or…someone…pulled Dillon onto on a pile of pillows, and he forgot all about it.

Many hours later, Dillon stretched out across the pillows with a couple of girls. He traced his fingers down the redhead's spine, making her shiver.

Sawyer relaxed, bare-chested, on a nearby cushion. He put his thickly muscled arms over his head, stretched, and then reached over to squeeze Dillon's shoulder.

"Hey, little brother. Welcome to the family. This… is Iron Torr."

Chapter 8: Dillon

Phase Three

Dillon awoke in the morning with a start. Paranoia kicked on instinctively. *Where the hell am I?* Bits and pieces of the party came back as he looked around the opulent room. All around him, half-naked girls slept on floor cushions. Marcia was nowhere to be seen. Dillon lay still, expecting to feel hung over, but instead he got a mixture of odd sensations. Something weird had happened to his sense of touch. He rubbed a few fibers of the carpet between his fingers. Its texture captivated him. He tried to focus, but his mind felt cloudy.

Voices spoke low in the hall outside, so quietly that Dillon shouldn't have been able to hear them. One of them sounded familiar. It tugged at him, forcing him to listen.

"Was twenty-four hours enough?"

Someone else answered, almost inaudibly, with a vague affirmative.

"Did he have a good time?"

Dillon recognized the voice with a shock. *Parker!* For some reason, he felt certain that the colonel was talking about him. *Gods. Why would he care?*

"Yeah," someone answered. The voice was hard to identify, husky with sleep and smoke.

"So…how many?" Parker asked.

"How many what? Girls?" The husky voice tightened with obvious embarrassment. "I don't know, I was…um, busy. Four? Maybe five."

"Good. Don't let him get attached to any one person. Remember, we want him loyal to the whole community."

"Yes, sir."

Dillon listened to the slow rush of blood through his veins while the conversation receded into dream. His heart seemed to beat too slowly, but it pounded in his ears. After a while, he forced himself upright and focused hazily on the only other conscious person in the room. "Hey, Sawyer."

Sawyer stood at a counter, making coffee. He came over, his big hand wrapped around a steaming mug. "Want some?"

Dillon shook his head. "No. There's this thing going on. I feel weird, like…I can't explain it."

Sawyer crossed his long legs and lowered himself to the floor without spilling a drop from his overflowing mug. "We call that phase three."

"What!"

"Easy, Dillon. Let me explain. That pink drink—it's more than a party in a cup," Sawyer said. "It's something our doctors are working on."

Dillon sat up straight and shook back his long hair, which had somehow come loose from its ponytail. "You did something to me?"

"I didn't. The doctors did." Sawyer held him in a calm, steady gaze. "Think of it as a gift, Dillon."

Dillon's eyes kept snapping in to focus on tiny details—a lock of Sawyer's yellow hair, or the cream swirling in his mug. Logic told him he should be upset, but his enforced state of calm wouldn't allow it. "What did they do?"

"The drink—it contains activators. A bunch of your enhanced genes weren't being transcribed," Sawyer said.

At Dillon's blank look, Sawyer tried again. "That means some of your genetic enhancements were latent...you know, shut down. That happens a lot, which is why most of us have been dosed with the pink stuff at least once."

"I thought it was...I don't know...medicine, and then...whoa. I've never felt like that before," Dillon breathed, looking down at the sleeping redhead. "What a night."

Sawyer cocked his head in a good-natured way. "Still high, eh? Are you following me at all?"

With an effort, Dillon pulled his eyes away from the beautiful girl. "Still high, yeah. But I'm listening."

"The pink drink has activator proteins, to jump-start your enhancements, plus some opium and synthetic painkillers. The activators aren't pleasant on their own." Sawyer sipped his coffee thoughtfully. "This should have been done for you years ago. What's with the doctors at Headquarters, anyway?"

A few of Dillon's memories stirred, enough to warn him. *They don't know I'm a half-breed who should have been drowned at birth.*

Paranoia prodded Dillon into changing the subject. "Things feel different, now, like I'm super-sensitive. And I hear better, too, I think. But I've got this annoying thing going on, where little details jump out at me."

"Like they get magnified all of a sudden? Excellent, that happened to me, too," Sawyer whooped, clapping his hands in delight. The red-haired girl shot him an annoyed look through one slitted eye. Sawyer didn't bother to lower his voice, but he stroked the girl's hair to placate her. She cuddled against his thigh and closed her eyes again. "It's okay, Dillon. You'll learn to control it. With those abilities, you'll be one hell of a tracker. You could be a ranger like me and Tai."

"Another ranger?" Slade yawned, strolling in from the boys' dorm. "Good. We could use him. I wish they'd finish up with the training already and turn us loose on those insurgents."

A few more crucial pieces of Dillon's memory fell into place, and a wave of guilt overwhelmed him. *Gods. Michelle! How could I forget all about her?*

"I'm going after them," Dillon growled. "With or without you."

"Really?" Slade smirked. "Naked?"

Dillon looked around, but his clothes and boots were gone. "Where the hell are my jeans?"

"Relax," Slade said, pouring himself a cup of coffee. "Lower ranks came to pick up the wash."

"That reminds me. I've got presents for my new baby brother." Sawyer rolled to his feet and strode to a cabinet in the boys' dorm. He pulled out a duffel bag and tossed it to Dillon. "Let me know if those don't fit."

The bag held a forest green uniform, socks, a pair of lightweight, flexible boots, and a small sack of toiletries. Dillon dressed fast, considering that standing on one leg to put on pants was a lot more challenging than usual. He paused at the door. "Going with me?"

Sawyer still leaned on the counter, sipping his coffee. He grinned at Slade. "That's pretty good motivation for the morning after a pink drink. Usually people are ridiculously relaxed for a couple of days afterward, no matter what happens."

"Yep." Slade nodded. "He's gonna be a hard charger."

Dillon twisted the doorknob. It was locked. "Aagh!"

"Relax, Dillon. We've got almost an hour before they let us out," Slade said. "We'd better use it to get this place cleaned up in case they inspect us."

Sawyer leaned back on the counter and laughed. "Like I'm cleaning. Let's get some of the lower ranks in here."

An hour later, Dillon marched down an interior staircase at Iron Torr, working hard to stay in line. His missteps made embarrassing counterpoints to the unified rhythm of booted feet. When he lost his balance and bumped the boy in front of him, Marcia tugged him back into line with a businesslike hand. She looked older with the makeup scrubbed from her face and her hair pulled back in a bun. In uniform, the whole group morphed into something purposeful and unfamiliar. Though no officers were in sight, no one spoke. The girls' giggles and smoldering glances had vanished without a trace. Not a single person so much as cracked a smile.

When the lead student opened a door into a large enclosed courtyard, bright sunlight sent pain stabbing through Dillon's head. He blocked the light with a hand and blinked his tearing eyes. Black walls rose up on all sides, with the Torr itself dominating one corner. A running track followed the boxy perimeter of the walls, and a wicked obstacle course filled the interior. Apparently the courtyard was all they had for outdoor training at Iron Torr, now that insurgents infested the forest.

Without being told to, the teenagers split into four orderly lines at the gate of the track. Sawyer pointed Dillon to the back of the nearest line.

Dillon set his jaw and refused to move. "Where's Parker?" People in the lines stared and shifted their feet impatiently, but he didn't care.

Sawyer folded his arms and looked down at Dillon. "I know this is tough on you, with your friends missing, but you're more likely to get help if you show some respect."

Dillon deliberately mirrored Sawyer's gesture. "Fine. Where's *Colonel* Parker, then?"

A faint smile touched the corner of Sawyer's lip as he turned away. "Right behind you."

Oh, great. Dillon turned his head too fast, which set off an annoying set of phase three visual effects. The weave of Parker's nylon workout jacket jumped into crystal-clear focus, followed by a disturbingly close view of the pulse fluttering at the man's throat. Dillon struggled to form a coherent sentence, but failed, so he said nothing. One at a time, the lines of runners took off, leaving him alone with the colonel.

"Dillon." Parker flashed an unexpectedly compassionate smile and beckoned Dillon over. "Come with me. Let's talk about our plan to rescue your friends."

Dillon numbly followed the colonel onto the track. *Parker just said exactly what you wanted him to say. Don't piss him off now.*

Parker set off at an easy jog. Dillon pushed his sluggish body into a run and tried to keep up.

"Exercise helps with phase three," Parker said as they fell into step together. "Or so our doctors tell me. I never required the treatment myself."

"You really missed out," Dillon blurted without thinking, and belatedly added, "Um, sir."

To Dillon's relief, the colonel laughed. "That's what I hear."

The track was level, with a rubbery surface that should have made it perfect for running, but Dillon had to concentrate just to avoid falling on his face. The patch in front of him seemed to breathe like a living thing, rising and falling under his feet. The disconcerting hallucination diminished as he ran.

"I sent out rangers to track your girl," Parker said abruptly. "They think the insurgents took her alive."

"Alive," Dillon gasped. Relief and a set of new worries flooded him. "Why didn't you bring me along?"

Parker gave Dillon a sideways look, like the answer should have been obvious. Gradually, the colonel lengthened his strides. Dillon stayed with him, but just barely. They lapped the track three times at a breakneck pace while the burn in his legs and lungs grew. *I can't keep going much longer.*

"Up for a short sprint?" Parker asked.

Damn. He's not even breathing hard.

The colonel took off. Dillon gasped for air and forced his aching legs to greater speed, but he was nowhere near good enough. Parker easily left him behind. Nausea clenched Dillon's stomach, but he stubbornly refused to quit.

He's making a point. I'm a half breed, and I can't keep up. Better men have to do my work for me.

In a few minutes, Parker lapped him and came up behind. "Okay, let's walk it off."

Dillon bent over, gasping, while a line of runners flew lightly past him. The cold wind stung his face. When he forced himself upright, Parker put an arm around his shoulders and guided him off the track. Dillon couldn't meet his eyes.

"You did all right there, son," Parker said, as they crunched slowly along the gravel path that edged the track. "Most people can't even walk straight the morning after a treatment."

"Oh, sure."

Parker clapped Dillon gently on the shoulder. "I wouldn't tell you that you did well if it wasn't true. Really. Ask anyone."

Dillon gave him a disgruntled look and didn't answer.

"Don't worry. It takes time for latent enhancements to kick in, and when they do, your speed and coordination will improve." Parker led the way toward a stack of bleachers that climbed one of the dark metal walls. White-coated men and women crowded the lower benches, bent over clipboards and laptops. One of the white-coats gave Parker the thumbs-up, followed by a complicated series of gestures Dillon didn't follow.

Parker waved in acknowledgement, and the doctor sat down. "That was your score, Dillon. Baseline, plus a bonus for it being the day after treatment. You just set a record for your age group."

"Bullshit, *sir*. I got my ass kicked. I'm not stupid."

Fury darkened the colonel's face. Kicking gravel, Parker turned off the path and strode rapidly into the obstacle course. Dillon hesitated, and then hurried after him. He caught up in the shadow of a huge wooden wall. Dillon stared up at the immense obstacle. Judging from the scuff marks on its surface, the kids there could do it. *There's no way I'd make it over that without help.*

Parker spun to face him. "You did not fail," he spat. "You just think you did, because they raised you to be a loser."

Dillon shrank back, feeling like a kid in the Warren, threatened by a bigger boy over a coveted apple core or a scrap of bread. *It's been a long time since I've lost a fight. But against this guy, I wouldn't have a chance.*

"I should burn Headquarters to the ground for doing this to you," Parker said. "Starting with the Founder. Preferably alive."

None of that made sense to Dillon, but it was chilling anyway. *Burning people alive? The guy's a nut. Try and keep him focused.*

With an effort, Dillon raised his chin and took a step forward. "I've got to try and help my friends, sir. If I can't keep up with your people, I'll travel alone."

"Goddamn it," Parker erupted. All around the arena, heads turned their way. Dillon took a nervous step back. "Wait, Dillon. You don't understand." The colonel ran both hands over his damp blond hair, like his head hurt. "This isn't your fault."

Parker sank down onto the cold ground in the shadow of the wooden wall. "Come here. Let me explain."

Dillon sat beside the colonel, carefully staying out of arm's reach. Dead grass prickled his palms while cold from the earth seeped through his legs and butt, slowly chilling his body.

Parker put his head in his hands. "It kills me to see you this way."

Dillon wasn't sure he heard him right. "What way?"

Parker looked up and his hands dropped limply into his lap. "Half starved. Denied even the most rudimentary medical care. Obviously neglected. Alexa was the top-scoring female of her generation. And this is how they treat her firstborn son?"

Dillon stared in shock. His mother's name sounded alien on Parker's lips, a reminder of a faraway world of hunger and fear. *Alexa. He said Alexa. He knows Mom?*

"My sister made some mistakes," Parker said, staring away across the arena. "But making her child pay the price? That's inexcusable."

Dillon sat in silence, staring blindly into the distance while Parker's words sank in. *He's…Mom's brother. My uncle. Gods, I thought this couldn't get any weirder.*

Parker shifted on the frozen grass to face him. "Dillon, I know you were all fired up to chase the insurgents. And you're probably furious with me for stopping you."

"You bet I am! If you hadn't doped me up, I'd already be gone." Dillon glared, and to his surprise, Parker looked away first.

"You know what would have happened if I'd let you go? Even if I'd sent a couple of patrols with you?"

"What?"

"You would have been killed. The insurgents laid traps, like they always do. My men found them and diffused them. Still, I know how you must have felt, and I'm sorry." Parker glanced quickly around. No one was near, but he lowered his voice anyway. "Their tactics have changed, Dillon. I think the Normals are harboring some traitors…Enhanced defectors. They don't stage simple raids anymore."

Dillon tried to school his expression, so it wouldn't be clear that he already knew. They sat in silence while the wind cooled the sweat on his body. He began to shiver. Parker pulled off his own jacket and tossed it to him. The name *Parker* was printed on back in bold black letters. The colonel motioned

Dillon to put it on. "It's okay, I'm not cold. Besides, it has your name on it."

Dillon glanced up in surprise.

"If you'd been raised among us, you would've been a Parker too. I should have tried harder to find you. I just didn't know how bad it was until I saw the doctors' report. Enhancements, left latent, like no one cared. Long-term malnutrition. Broken bones, left alone to set however they could." Parker's face crumpled, and he covered his mouth with a hand.

"Hey, that arm got splinted," Dillon put in defensively.

"By who?"

"The healer. Um, a Norm healer, in the Warren."

Parker winced. "You poor boy. Alexa's son, and they let a Normal treat you? In the slum."

Dillon nodded, biting his tongue to keep from blurting, *Of course they did, I lived there.*

"I tried to contact my sister, but I couldn't find her. Every communication got returned, marked 'person unknown.' Like anyone could forget her." Parker shook his head sadly. "I meant to bring you both here, where you belong. You should've grown up alongside Slade, like brothers."

Dillon didn't know what to say to that.

"You can call me Uncle Mark," Parker went on. "But just so the other kids don't resent you, keep it for when we're in private. Slade calls me Dad, but only when we're alone. Otherwise say *sir*, like everybody else."

"Right," Dillon said, studying Parker's profile. *He does kind of look like Mom. The same nose.* "Okay, Uncle Mark."

"Good. Now back to business," Parker said, his pale eyes flashing. "We're going to get your friends back and incinerate those damned insurgents, so this never happens again. The doctors tell me those newly activated genes of yours should be fully expressed in about two weeks. If you train hard, you'll be ready to go with us."

Hope bloomed in Dillon's chest. "I can go?"

Parker grinned. "If you can shoot straight by then. Our best operative reported that the insurgents are holding Michelle in a village about eighty miles from here. We'll rescue her first. Then we'll take back the others."

"Yes!"

The colonel stood up and pulled Dillon to his feet. "I should have been here for you before, and I wasn't. But from now on, I'll make it right. I promise."

The colonel stuck out a hand for the single-hand handshake of the Enhanced, and then he pulled Dillon in and hugged him like a son. At first Dillon stood stiffly, but then he surrendered and hugged the man back. *It's all right. He's my uncle. We're family.*

***

Two weeks later, Dillon stretched luxuriously on his uncle's leather sofa, replete with the delicious dinner he'd just eaten. He gazed at the fine oil paintings on the walls while rain lashed the black glass of the tower window. Dillon didn't mind the weather. It made the plush room seem even cozier. Back in the Warren, rainy days meant leaking roofs, overflowing sewers, and stinking mud everywhere.

"This is the life." Dillon grinned at Slade, who sipped a glass of wine from a recliner by the fire, a book open on his knee.

Slade quirked a lip, trying not to laugh. "It's home. All that's missing is your mother, but we'll bring her here by solstice. Now that we know where to find her."

"But..." Dillon fell silent, unwilling to confide too much about his clan in the Warren. "We're, um, responsible for a lot of people."

"What, like servants, you mean? Bring them too, there's plenty of work to do."

"Servants?" Dillon almost laughed, but Slade was totally serious, he could tell. "No, they're kind of like... family retainers. Practically members of the family. My mother definitely runs the place. But the Norms aren't big on following orders."

Slade smirked. "Neither are you, but you're learning."

"This is one order I don't mind. Show up every night at Uncle Mark's for second dinner. Hang out with the family, and stuff myself on the best food I've ever eaten."

"You already look better," Slade observed. "Your ribs don't stick out anymore, and you're keeping up okay on the obstacle course, aren't you? But that won't stop my father from raining hellfire on Headquarters for starving you."

"I'd rather he didn't make an issue of it," Dillon said. He lowered his voice, glancing at the open door into his uncle's huge bedroom. "It'll just make it harder for me to get along with Michelle's family. I walked on eggshells around them before, but now that her mother heads the Conclave..."

"Oh, I get it." Slade leaned forward and set down his wine. "They've got rank, and you aren't good enough."

Dillon nodded awkwardly. "Yeah, that's it."

"Bastards. Well, don't believe them, Dillon. Look at this." Slade paced over to Parker's desk and rifled through his father's papers. He pulled one out of a pile and shoved it in Dillon's hand.

Dillon sat up to read it. It was a simple bar graph, labeled with test scores and percentiles. "Wow. Ninety-two, ninety-five... and a ninety-nine on unarmed combat. Not bad, eh?"

"Ninety-nine!" Slade grinned. "That's only 'cause you cheat."

"I do. Rules are for the weak," Dillon said cheerfully. His face fell as he read farther down the page. "Ouch, look at my score in marksmanship. I never shot a gun 'til I came here."

Slade dropped onto the couch beside Dillon and peered at the graph. "What'd you get? Eighty? What are you complaining about? You train for two weeks, and only twenty percent of us can beat you. As far as I'm concerned, Michelle's mother can bend over and kiss your lily-white ass."

The boys laughed, but then Parker's voice cracked from the other room, killing the conversation. "He has a right to take back what was taken from him!"

"The girl isn't his *property*, Mark," Brooke snapped. "But that's not the point. Every psychologist at the Torr agrees with me. This is a very sensitive time for him, with all those latent enhancements activated at once. What were you thinking? That should have been done gradually, over a year or more."

Dillon winced. "They're fighting about me."

Slade nodded, making a shushing gesture.

"Your mom sure acts different at home," Dillon whispered, more quietly this time.

"He's her commanding officer," Slade hissed back. "But only in public. She insisted on putting that in the contract when they got married. Pissed him off, but he signed."

Dillon opened his mouth to ask a question, but he didn't get the chance. Slade jumped up, ran the test scores back to the desk, and slid a few papers sideways to bury them. He hurried back to the sofa and sat down by Dillon.

Dillon tipped his head toward the front door.

Slade shook his head. *"Too late,"* he mouthed.

Parker marched into the living room, his wife on his heels. Tension made corded muscles stand out from the sides of his neck. "Don't question my orders, Brooke."

Brooke tossed her long black hair. "There's no *question* about it. You were wrong. If you traumatize him now, he may never recover."

Parker's wife came over and sat on the ottoman across from Dillon. She wore a calf length dress in a rich shade of burgundy, the neckline set off by a gold pendant that dropped enticingly out of view. It made a man want to lean forward and see where it went. Dillon couldn't help noticing how the soft dress clung to her body and shifted when she crossed her legs.

Brooke instantly derailed those thoughts with her maternal tone. "Dillon, it's important that you avoid stress and violence until your nervous system completely stabilizes. I understand that you love your girlfriend, and you want to help get her back. But that's not a good idea right now."

"Michelle isn't my girlfriend," Dillon said, and immediately regretted it. "She's more of...a wife, I guess. Where I come from, we don't have that distinction. It's all or nothing. I'm committed to her, at any rate."

"How sweet," Brooke said. "Isn't it, Mark? And she's only sixteen."

Parker only grunted, like "sweet" wasn't in his vocabulary.

Dillon caught Slade's raised eyebrow out of the corner of his eye and quashed it with a glare. *Okay, I slipped up, bad, at the pink drink party. With, Gods, I don't even know how many girls. A Warren woman would kill me for that, but the Enhanced swap partners all the time. Maybe Michelle will understand. Hopefully. If I ever have the balls to tell her, once she gets back. But what if she decides we have an open relationship? Brian would be all over her.*

"Dillon," Parker snapped, jerking him out of his thoughts.

"Sir?"

"We leave tomorrow at sunset. You're going." The colonel shot his wife a murderous look and stalked out of the room.

Chapter 9: Michelle

Raiders

Strangers filled the village, and more arrived every few minutes. Michelle hadn't had time to meet any of them. Her hands were raw from hard work, but she was almost done. A mountain of firewood waited at the edge of the clearing, along with more food than the village could eat in a month. That fit right in with her plan for escape. When Molly wasn't looking, Michelle slipped inside and hid a few loaves of bread under her own thin pallet. *They'll still be edible, even if I squash them flat.*

Men stood four deep around the fire, drinking and talking together. Behind them, on the big stump that served as outdoor table, a longbow lay unattended, along with a quiver fat with arrows. Michelle sauntered by, nerves on edge, and casually picked them up. No one said a word. With a few furtive glances around, she ducked behind a hut and kicked the bow and arrows under some bushes. *I'm out of here, tonight!*

Molly came around the corner and stopped suddenly, startled to see Michelle there. "What're you doing?"

Michelle froze. "Um, thinking about heading out for more wood."

"We've got more than enough, dearie. Come on inside, time to change fer the party."

Once Michelle had bathed and dressed, Molly insisted on rubbing her chapped hands with animal fat, which smelled rancid but felt great. Michelle stepped out of the hut with Molly on her heels and took a startled step back. The whole clan crowded around the door, visitors and all. The Norms burst into laughter at the surprised look on Michelle's face, and then gave her a cheer.

"The party's fer you, daughter," Molly beamed.

Laird laughed at Michelle's surprised face. "Ha! Gotcha! What'd ya think all the food was for?"

Michelle blushed. "I knew it was a party…just not, you know, *my* party."

Wade came over and took her arm in a fatherly way. He still made Michelle nervous, even though he'd been nothing but kind since he tackled her on her first night there.

"No worries, girl," he drawled. "This is a special day. Everybody's here t'meet ya. This is yer clan." Wade led her around, introducing her as, "My niece, Me-Shelle." His Norm accent made her name sound exotic and beautiful, and crowds of young men stared admiringly.

Finally Laird rescued her, and they sat down on a huge fallen log at the edge of the forest. "A little much, eh?" he asked perceptively.

"Yeah. I feel like everyone's staring at me."

"They are."

Michelle giggled at that. "Can't you at least lie to me?" she joked, but Laird looked serious.

"I can't do that. Yer family."

Darkness fell softly over the forest, and owls hooted from invisible places in the canopy above. Michelle and her cousin fell into a companionable silence.

A knot of young men clustered on the other side of the clearing, talking in low voices. "She's a beauty all right," a black-haired one said to his friend, stealing a glance her way.

"No doubt, but she ain't single, I'll wager."

That has to be his younger brother, Michelle thought. *They look a lot alike.* She turned her head away so they wouldn't see her watching them.

"Justin, her feathers are black, every one of 'em."

Michelle glanced at Laird to see if he was catching this, but he just stared across the clearing with a dreamy look. Norms probably couldn't hear that well. She hadn't known feather color meant anything. They were just decorations to her. She suddenly remembered seeing Molly take the white feathers out of her own hair, replace them with gray ones, and store the originals in a wooden box. *White must mean you're married, and gray is for widows. The single white feather? I don't know.*

"I tell ya, brother, she's got a bonded look about 'er. She ain't given nobody so much as a glance since we got 'ere. She's got 'erself a man."

"She ain't married yet."

"Right. So we better get a move on, before he gets back!" The men laughed loudly and went off to refill their cups.

Michelle's heart ached for Dillon, and her eyes filled with tears. *I miss him so much; even Norms can see it all over me.*

Laird bumped her elbow gently. "Heya. No sad thoughts. This is a happy day." He pulled her up by the hand and took her back to the table by the fire, where he poured her a cup of mead.

Molly pounced on them in a heartbeat. She snatched the cup back and poured half of it back into the bottle. "Y' can have this much, an' no more."

The mead tasted sweet and strong, and it made a comforting warmth going down. Soon Michelle cheered up and began laughing and talking with the visiting teenagers. A pretty blonde girl named Maya had black feathers in her braid too, but a single long feather at the bottom was white.

"Oh, you've got a white one," Michelle commented, hoping to discover what that meant.

"Fer now, anyway," the girl joked. "If 'e works out. If not..." She flicked her finger in the air. "Off with him."

The kids laughed. A tall dark-haired boy came over and slipped his arm around the blonde. He whispered something to Maya, making her giggle, and when he looked up Michelle almost spit out her mead.

"Slade!"

"Heya, Michelle." Slade smiled and held out both hands for a Norm-style greeting. Michelle suddenly wanted to break his arm, but she didn't know why. Instead she took his hands and smiled back, hiding her feelings like a true Institute girl. *What's he doing here?*

"Whatcha been up to, Slade?" Michelle asked casually, looking him up and down. "Roughing it?"

Slade dressed like a mountain man, with boots, rugged woolen pants, and a quilted homespun shirt. His hair wasn't long enough to tie into a ponytail, but someone had clipped a long braided leather ornament into it so it hung down his back. The single white feather at the bottom matched Maya's exactly. He almost passed as a Norm, but not to Michelle's eye.

With an effort, she kept her expression relaxed and friendly. Back at Iron Torr, Slade's charm had seemed a little too rehearsed, but she could forgive him for that. That place was insane. Still, seeing him here gave her a chill she didn't understand.

"I think I'll help Molly bring over some more wood from the woodpile," Slade said, catching Michelle's eye. She followed him out of the firelight and began gathering an armload of wood. Maya watched them, but she didn't follow.

"What are you doing here?" Michelle hissed.

"When we heard gunfire, I ran outside to try and help. Some Norms caught me. If I hadn't gotten adopted, I'd be dead already."

Michelle had a million questions, but they couldn't stay over there in the shadows. She spent one second alone with a guy, and it got everyone's attention. All around the camp, eyes flicked from her to the white feather on Slade's braid and back again.

"Michelle, what do you know about the others?"

"Nothing! Are they—" She swallowed and made herself say it. "Are they alive?"

Slade shrugged. "I tried asking, but it didn't go over well. I don't recommend it."

As Michelle lugged her wood back to the fire circle, Molly intercepted her, taking some logs off the top. "Don'tcha do that, dearie. You do enough work around here. Go enjoy yerself."

A cheer from the teens caught her attention. Men carried drums up to the fire and started setting up to play. "Wade made an exception, jus' fer you," Laird told her.

"What?"

"Drumming's not usually allowed, on account o' the hostilities. Noise is a risk."

That worried Michelle, but everyone else seemed fine with it. The party kicked into high gear, and all the men wanted a chance to dance with her. Orange flames leaped against the dark sky, turning the village into a safe haven against the wilderness. Dancing was fun for a while, but Michelle soon got tired of it, and she didn't mind when Molly came to get her. The woman chaperoned her into the hut, cheerily shooing away the most persistent admirers.

"Ya shined tonight! Jus' beautiful," Molly said proudly as she tucked Michelle in. "G'night, my dear, I love ya."

"Thank you, Molly." Michelle wormed under the covers, still in her daytime clothes, like a Norm. "I love you, too."

Molly sometimes treated her like a little kid, but Michelle tolerated it just to be nice. Besides, it felt comforting. It had been years since anyone mothered her like that. *I'll leave tomorrow. One more day won't matter. I'm too tired now, and besides, people are all over the place.* Michelle rolled over and stuck a hand under the pallet to reassure herself that the hidden bread was still there.

Chapter 10: Dillon

Unhinged

No moon lit the night, and a blanket of clouds cloaked the stars. Parker's soldiers cut the engines of the zodiacs and drifted the last miles down the river in silence, using oars to navigate around boulders and sunken logs. The damp night air carried a faint whiff of wood smoke, probably from some hidden insurgent camp. Dillon sat in the bow, where the spray was worst, but he hardly felt the cold over the adrenaline that pounded through his veins. Soon they'd reach the camp where Michelle was held prisoner. Countless times he'd imagined her tied up, fondled by rough hands, or locked, injured and bleeding, in some fetid cage. The thoughts filled him with rage. Dillon shifted on his seat. *I'll kill them. I'll kill every last one of them. And then I'll take her home to the Torr, where she'll be safe.*

The bow ground onto the sandy shore, and Dillon leaped out first. He helped tether the inflatable craft, hoping desperately that he wouldn't be among those selected to guard the boat. The colonel put a hand on his shoulder and spoke low in his ear. "You're with me."

"Good." Dillon took the moment to ask the question that had been plaguing him. "Where's Slade? I thought he was going with us, sir."

"He's already there, at the insurgent camp. He went in alone to gather intelligence."

"Alone?" Cold tingles shot down Dillon's limbs at the thought. "Gods. That took balls."

Parker met his eyes and nodded.

Dillon understood. *He doesn't hand out compliments easily, and that was a big one. Slade volunteered to help get Michelle back. He did it for me. As gruff as he is sometimes, Uncle Mark helped too. He risked his firstborn son for me. And for Michelle.* A huge weight of gratitude settled over Dillon's heart. He blinked rapidly, glad for the darkness that hid his face.

Dillon fell into line and moved through the dark forest as quietly as possible. A few miles in, Parker called a halt under an immense pine. The spreading branches blocked every ray of starlight, leaving the men standing in abject blackness. Dillon's imagination turned each creak of a branch into the footfall of an enemy. He stared into the shadows and forced himself to stand still like the disciplined soldiers around him.

"Final orders," Parker muttered. "Patrols one and two, engage and destroy any fighting men, including any associated young males who may have become radicalized. Patrol three, eliminate the future of this scourge. Target breeding females first, offspring second. We're going to nip this problem in the bud."

All around Dillon, men quietly chorused, "Yes, sir," but he didn't join in.

"Sir?" Dillon asked tentatively. "Are you really telling us to kill little kids?"

Parker looked right at him, turned his back, and walked away. His men followed, moving almost silently over the damp forest floor. Dillon's stomach twisted, and sour acid rose in his throat. In a moment, he followed them. *I can't let this happen. Gods! What the hell am I going to do?*

Too soon, they reached the village. Sounds of laughter and drumming carried clearly through the night air. *It sounds like home.* Parker cocked his head and listened a moment, and then shook his head in disgust. Soldiers took up positions around the village. Dillon thought they probably wouldn't attack until the villagers went to bed. He waited with them for hours, listening to joyful sounds while dew soaked his uniform and dampened his skin. A few droplets trickled down the back of his neck, setting him quivering.

Dillon thought up a thousand different plans to avoid bloodshed. *I could shout an alarm, or fire on these soldiers, even if some of them are friends. What if I shot Uncle Mark? No, he's got bodyguards. I'd be gunned down.* He finally settled on a plan and crept toward his uncle. No one was supposed to move, of course. Disapproval radiated silently from the men.

A twig snapped loudly under Dillon's knee as he knelt before the dark shape that loomed in the shadows. "Uncle M—um, I mean, Colonel Parker, sir."

Parker's hand rose up in slow motion, and Dillon thought he was about to be slapped. By starlight, the colonel made an unmistakable "sit-down-and-shut-up" gesture.

Dillon clenched his jaw and stayed where he was. "Sir, let me slip in there by myself. I can find Michelle and release her, and we'll get out of here without anyone getting hurt."

The colonel's hand came up again, and this time it wrapped across Dillon's face, digging in iron fingertips like claws. One inhumanly strong finger pressed painfully at the corner of his eye until flashes of false light stabbed the darkness. Dillon grabbed Parker's wrist with both hands and pulled, stomach muscles rigid with effort, but his uncle's arm felt like steel. He couldn't move it at all. Somehow Dillon felt certain that if he cried out he'd be killed. *Don't make a sound, don't, don't…*

Parker slowly forced Dillon's face down to the ground and held him there, still crushing his skull. A soft gurgle escaped Dillon's lips, and Parker instantly let go. Dillon curled at his uncle's feet, clutching his head with both hands to suppress a wild impulse to scream. *Don't make noise, or both sides will fire on you. Both sides, both sides...*

On the forest floor, Dillon's head began to gently rise and fall as though the planet itself were breathing beneath him. He opened his eyes in wonder. There, in the darkness, things that should have been invisible weren't. Ancient trees rode the waves, up and down, softly flexing their branches with the motion. Ferns beckoned him with their fronds, daring him to run. *Brooke was right. Phase three is back. I'm losing my mind.*

Dillon curled on the forest floor, listening to children's squeals and the sound of their running feet circling the camp. Just inside the ring of firelight, people danced to the beat of unseen drums. *This is evil! I'm not going along with it. I'd rather die. Michelle wouldn't want kids killed, even to break her free. She'd rather die too. I know it.*

A sharp tug on Dillon's jacket told him to get up. He got shakily to his feet, feeling as unsteady as he'd been the morning after the pink drink, and he took deep breaths to stay in control. Around him, soldiers readied their rifles. Dillon let them pass him, so he'd come up behind, a traitor in their midst. Someone patted his back.

"Come on, little brother," a man whispered. "Let's go get your girl."

Through his haze, Dillon recognized Sawyer's voice, but even that took a moment to register. Sawyer's strong hand towed Dillon forward. Ahead, soldiers broke into a run, sweeping around the village. Some hellish incendiary device arced through the darkness to explode on the roof of a hut. Dillon flinched.

"Go!" Parker hissed.

Sawyer let go of Dillon's jacket and bounded ahead, a hunting hound unleashed. Men shouted and children shrieked, but through the sound, Dillon heard Michelle's girlish voice, high with fear. "Hold your fire! That's an order!"

Parker scoffed under his breath. Then he seemed to notice that Dillon was still beside him. "Wake up, Dillon. Move in. Remember your orders."

Orders. To murder children. Dillon ducked his head into the shadows to hide his eyes. He left Parker in the trees and made his way forward, toward Michelle's voice.

Sawyer's voice came from the darkness, calm and sure. "Stay down, Miss Atherton. We'll take you back to the Torr when it's over."

"Sawyer, bring her over here," Dillon shouted. He sprang forward, but a wild-eyed Norm leaped around the corner of a hut and blocked him. The man was armed only with a hatchet. Dillon sidestepped and clubbed the man down with the butt of his rifle. In the dark, impossibly bright red blood bloomed from the man's head and spread across the ground, more blood than a man's body could rightly hold.

This isn't real, it's not real, it's a hallucination. But it didn't matter. Nausea overcame him, and Dillon lurched ahead into the village, just to get away.

The sound of Michelle's voice snapped his head around. "They're shooting at *children*, Laird!"

"Michelle," Dillon cried over the sound of gunfire. "Where are you?"

He dashed toward her voice, but she was gone. Then something came unhinged in Dillon's mind. He rampaged through the nightmare, madly searching for Michelle, for children, for the soldiers who came to kill them. The panicked Norms he brushed aside, but Dillon gunned down soldiers from Iron Torr, especially the ones that targeted kids. Norms and soldiers scattered into the forest, and some fell, but Dillon didn't stop until he stumbled across a familiar figure, lying face down in the central clearing. The man's helmet was tilted back, far enough that a bit of yellow hair caught the light from a burning hut.

Dillon knelt down at the man's side. All the fight left him. "Oh, no. Gods, no. Sawyer."

Sawyer's neck was twisted at an odd angle, too far sideways and broken that way. His rifle was gone. Dillon wept over the body, letting the fighting go on around him, while Sawyer's face slowly stretched to monstrous proportions. *It's not real,* Dillon told himself. *Sawyer's dead. Don't...don't do this to him.* Suddenly Sawyer's eyes popped open, glowing orange in the firelight. Dillon recoiled, a moan gurgling from his throat. When he looked again, Sawyer was back to normal, still dead, eyes closed and neck twisted. Dillon gently touched the face of his friend. Then he stood up and ran.

"Michelle," Dillon bellowed, but he couldn't hear himself scream over the explosions in his head. He crashed through the forest, no longer certain if the fires that burned all around him were real.

Chapter 11: Michelle

Defecting

Something woke Michelle. She opened her eyes in the dark. *Something's wrong!* Her heart pounded. The only sound was Kalie's soft breathing from the pallet against the opposite wall. Molly slept alone in the room she'd once shared with her husband. Michelle kicked off her covers and tiptoed across the room in her socks. A twig cracked outside. Men whispered.

Michelle slipped into Molly's darkened room and woke her. "Molly! I think someone's outside."

"Lotsa people are. All the visitors're sleepin' over, hon."

"No, I mean…they sound like men."

"Doggin' around outside? Let 'em. They won't bother ya till mornin'. Go on back t'bed."

Michelle backed off, frustrated, and then said what she meant to say. "Molly, they sound like *Enhanced* men."

Molly sat up as an explosion ripped through the camp. People screamed, and loud gunfire sent pain stabbing through Michelle's eardrums. From the other room, Kalie shrieked. Molly ran to her child as Michelle dashed outside into darkness. Faint starlight revealed the silhouettes of armed men all around the camp. Norms fled into the dark forest, but some didn't make it that far.

"Hold your fire! That's an order!" Michelle bellowed, but it didn't work at all. A familiar-looking soldier stepped into the clearing in a forest green Iron Torr uniform. He looked at Michelle, and a flash of recognition crossed his face. She recognized him too. *That's the guy who sparred Dillon. Sawyer, that's his name. Arrogant son of a bitch.*

Sawyer took two quick strides toward her, all business. "Stay down, Miss Atherton. We'll take you back to the Torr when it's over." Molly and her little girl dashed past in the darkness, and the young man raised his rifle to fire.

"No," Michelle screamed, slapping the gun aside. She kicked hard for his groin, but only hit him a glancing blow. Sawyer swore and pivoted the butt of his rifle to strike her. Reflex took over. She spun on one foot and hook-kicked him under the chin as hard as she could. Something crunched under her heel. The man went limp and collapsed. Michelle bent over him and lifted his gun with shaking hands.

Laird appeared out of the shadows, startling her. "Gods, Michelle! I think ya killed 'im."

"They're shooting at *children*, Laird!"

"Shhh. Get inside!" Her cousin pulled her back to the hut. "Quick, get yer boots on."

Laird rapidly circled the cabin, throwing things in a knapsack, while Michelle laced up her boots. Molly and little Kalie had disappeared. *I hope they're safe in the forest somewhere.* Michelle looked around the hut, but she owned almost nothing. She handed Laird the bag of bread, and, in a moment of sentiment, slipped on the black embroidered vest Molly had made for her. Then she slung the stolen rifle over her shoulder.

Laird made for the door, but Michelle stopped him. "Don't. They'll see your outline against the firelight."

She squeezed out the tiny back window and fished out the hidden bow and quiver while she waited for Laird to catch up. Together they ran for the trees. Behind them, low crackling sounds built to a roar of hot air as the burning hut caught fire in earnest. Her cousin stumbled twice, and Michelle realized that Norm eyes could hardly see in the smoky darkness. She turned back to help just as gunfire erupted behind them.

Michelle threw herself to the ground. After a breathless moment, she crawled over and found Laird face down in the dirt. "Are you okay?"

"I guess."

The soft sounds of boots approached. "Shh!"

The teens lay still and held their breath as soldiers thumped past them in the dark. Not far away, someone's scream rent the air. A Norm sobbed and begged for his life as soldiers yanked him from his hiding place. A single shot rang out, and then silence. Michelle trembled, burying her face in the grass to stifle her panicked gasps. An eternity later, the soldiers moved on.

"Come on," Michelle hissed. She seized Laird's arm and helped him to his feet. "Trust me? I can see just fine."

Michelle dragged her cousin through the woods at a run, weaving through the trees. Bent over and half-blind, Laird followed, clinging to Michelle's hand with desperate strength. The branches she bent sprang back to whip him in the face, but Laird barely grunted. Only the tang of his sweat gave away his terror.

An hour later, they were still on the move. "Lemme jus' rest for a minute," Laird whispered. "My knees 're shakin'."

Around them, old growth forest had given way to a tangled mass of young trees and bushes. The land dropped down to a swamp where patches of open water glinted in the moonlight, and then climbed on the other side to a shelf of sandstone, a darker shade of black against the horizon.

"I think I know where we are. There's a meetin' place. Y'know, in case of emergency. That way, on the side of the cliff." Laird pointed.

"Okay. Let's rest a minute, and then head up there." Michelle sagged tiredly onto a fallen log, but a writhing mass of slugs moved under her hand.

She squealed and jumped up.

"Shhh! Gods, Michelle. Yer such a girl."

Michelle didn't answer. She stared rigidly into the darkness, listening for pursuers.

Laird seemed to think he'd hurt her feelings. "I'm sorry, cousin," he whispered. "C'mon now."

"Forget it," she muttered, shaking her hand as though slugs clung to it. "I just hope the soldiers didn't hear me."

Laird fell silent. The only sound was the breeze sighing through giant pines.

The Norm sat down on the log, ignoring the slugs, and searched her eyes by starlight. "I saw ya take out that soldier. Without a weapon, y' just...broke his neck." The Norm paused, and then quirked the corner of his mouth at her. "An' yer scared o' bugs."

"Laird, forget the bugs. The important thing is, I'm just a girl. If I can do that, imagine the men of my clan. Enhanced men are faster than I am. Stronger. And a whole lot meaner. I'm not trying to scare you, but you need to know what we're dealing with."

"I know. I've watched 'em kill my friends." Laird sounded defeated. "They're smart too, wicked smart. We'll be lucky to survive till morning."

Michelle kept her voice low and even to hide her fear. "That's why we have to keep moving."

Laird stood up, and they slogged on through the dark.

Ahead, tiny broken branches bled aromatic sap. Michelle stopped and sniffed the air. A few scuff marks marred the ground. *People came through here recently.*

"Laird, is there an alternate meeting place? Someplace to go if you can't make it to the first one?"

He nodded. "Why?"

"If everyone heads to one place, they'll track us there. I'm sure of it."

"How d'ya know?"

Michelle answered without taking her eyes off the trail. "I could track them myself, so trained rangers can too. Probably a whole lot faster than me. We can't help the clan if we get caught along with them."

Her mind raced. *Maybe if we find the clan and then lie in wait for the Enhanced who come after them...*

"This other place, it's farther," Laird whispered. "But well hidden. We gotta follow the river west."

"Okay." She took Laird's hand and tugged him into a run again.

By morning, Michelle half-carried the Normal boy, walking beside him with one of his arms around her neck. It took all Laird's strength to stay on his feet and whisper directions. The sky in the east turned a brilliant dark blue, and the sun hovered just below the horizon. *We're running out of time.* Michelle stopped, getting ready to sling her cousin over her shoulders like a dead deer.

"There," Laird whispered hoarsely, pointing at a narrow crack in a canyon wall. Several sets of footprints led into it. Weak with relief, Michelle backed after Laird into the sanctuary, sweeping their prints away with a bit of brush. Inside, a tiny stream ran through a grassy clearing, and trees made a thick canopy overhead. On one end of the meadow stood a red sandstone outcropping. Michelle collapsed beside her cousin in the grass, back and legs aching.

"Slade?" Maya popped out from under a ledge and dashed toward them, but stopped in disappointment when she saw Laird instead. She turned away to hide her tear-streaked face and went back into the hole without another word. The black-haired brothers, Justin and Marcus, came out to see who had arrived. Michelle thought the younger one was Justin, but she wasn't sure, and under the circumstances, she didn't really care.

"Is this everyone?" she asked.

The older brother nodded. "There's only the three of us. Five now, with you."

"Sleep now, if you can," she told them. "We have to be on the move again soon."

Before Laird fell asleep, Michelle pestered him for directions to the primary meeting place, the cave high on a cliff. Then she climbed to the top of a big pine, getting sticky, fragrant sap all over her hands. She sat on the highest branch that would hold her, gripping the trunk with her thighs. The whole tree swayed in the wind. From there, the dark Torr bulged from the mountain like a tumor. *It's even farther away than I thought. How did the Norms get me all the way to their village?* For a second, Michelle considered the possibility that Wade had discovered teleportation, but she dismissed it with a bitter laugh.

In the morning sun, the Norms' meeting place could be seen for miles. *This one's safer, but they felt more secure up high.* Michelle's sharp eyes picked out movement around the cave entrance. People were sitting around outside. *Stupid Norms! They need my help.*

Michelle climbed down from the tree, swearing all the way. *The Enhanced will undoubtedly find the cave, but how long would that take? With helicopters and thermal imaging technology, a day at the most. Probably only hours.* Laird's voice echoed in her memory. *They're smart, wicked smart.*

She let the other kids sleep while she stared into space, forcing her mind to focus past her stomach-twisting dread. A final trip up the tree confirmed her fears. Almost too far away for even her eyes to see, specks moved through the forest. *It's a patrol. Parker's soldiers have spotted the cave!*

She woke the others and ruthlessly dragged them outside while they complained. "Already?"

"But I'm tired."

"Parker found the cave, and soldiers are heading that way," Michelle said.

That woke up the Norms. Their dismayed voices cut her off.

"Quiet," Michelle snapped. "We don't have much time. You want to defend your clan? I'm going to need your help."

The black-haired brothers, Justin and Marcus, could shoot, so she handed them the longbow and quiver. They had their own bows already, but the new one was finer. While they argued over it, Michelle ripped up the loaves of bread she'd brought and handed out pieces. She gave the last chunk to Maya, saving none for herself.

The Normal girl crouched over a crude map she had drawn in the dirt with a stick. Maya looked pale, but clearly she hadn't given up hope yet. "Slade's gotta be right here, at the cave," Maya said, poking at the map.

Michelle nodded sympathetically, but privately, she doubted it. *Slade showed up right before the attack on the village. He was obviously spying. When the bullets started flying, he ran. He's probably back at Iron Torr right now, taking a hot shower.* Michelle pushed her anger away and stood up. The teens looked up at her with hope in their eyes. It felt like a heavy burden. "All right, here's the plan," she began. "We catch the soldiers in the canyon on their way up to the cave. If we shoot one or two of them, they'll probably turn back. They won't waste men attacking the cave when they can just call in a helicopter and blow it up with a missile."

Anguished howls interrupted her. Michelle turned her eyes to the younger of the two brothers, who had somehow wrested the bow away from his bigger sibling. "Don't confront them directly. Okay? Um…"

"Justin," the boy supplied.

"Justin. Hide and snipe, you know what I mean? Shoot to wound them, not to kill."

"Bullshit. Kill 'em all," Marcus growled.

Michelle shot him a level stare. "There's no point in rescuing a dead man, Marcus. We want them to call in a ride for their injured, and the nearest place for a helicopter to land is here." Michelle bent to point at a spot on Maya's map, and the boys nodded. They knew the land better than she did.

Marcus shook his head disparagingly, even though he clearly didn't grasp the plan. "That makes no sense."

"Men are on their way to kill your families right now," Michelle cried, finally letting her anguish show. "So let's stop them. And maybe burn a helicopter while we're at it."

Side conversations broke out. Marcus postured, threatening Parker, but his brother Justin stood quietly, jaw tense.

Michelle roamed among the Norms, shooting down objections. "A simple attack won't work. They're better armed than we are. We have to set them up, see?"

The Norms didn't see, but they argued anyway. Finally Laird screamed at them all. "Shut up! Can't you see that they're smarter than you are? An' so is she!"

The kids fell silent, and Michelle took the opportunity to make a point. "They wear body armor, so only take head shots."

The boys nodded solemnly.

"Hit 'em and then run like hell. Leave them alone on the way to the kill zone." Michelle met each person's eyes, making sure they got the point. "They'll have to wait here for their ride, since it's the only meadow for miles. That's where we attack. They'll be in the open, and we'll hide in the trees. But if we don't get the pilot before he takes off again, everyone at the cave will die."

"What if we do?" Justin asked.

"If we do kill the pilot, you mean? They'll send more helicopters, of course, and they'll still blow up the cave." Michelle turned away to avoid Maya's stricken look. "But at least we'll have time to move the clan into the forest."

While the Norms got their boots on, Michelle paced. *We wasted too much time talking. Are these kids fast enough get to the ambush point before the Enhanced do? The biggest problem is the helicopter pilot. He could blow up the cave on his own if I let him get away, and he'll be well protected. And what if he hits the cave first, and then stops to pick up the wounded soldiers?*

***

The first part of Michelle's plan went perfectly. Justin put an arrow in a soldier's eye, and the man's screams echoed off the cliffs. Two more were put out of action carrying the wounded one, leaving a dozen who could fight. Someone barked an order, and Parker's soldiers changed course for the meadow. The Norm archers faded silently into the woods and ran.

"You're too slow," Michelle hissed, shoving Marcus up a rocky slope with a hand on his back. "We need to get there before them so we have time to hide."

Frustrated half out of her mind, Michelle took to chasing the laggards, smacking them in the back of the head. By the time they got to the clearing, the Norms feared her more than they did the soldiers. They got into position, hidden in thick undergrowth, and waited. Time stretched out until Michelle was certain she'd made a mistake. She was about to round everyone up and get out of there when Parker's platoon straggled into the clearing. Two more men had arrow wounds, and one talked into a cell phone. Michelle swore softly. *Lovely. Todd and Jeanette repaired communications.*

"Who the hell shot them?" Michelle mouthed to Marcus, who shrugged. From a distance, a helicopter thrummed its approach. "Remember," she whispered. "Wait 'til they're all clustered together."

Marcus nodded, but he kept an arrow nocked anyway.

"Here I go. Don't shoot till I do!" Michelle slung her rifle on her back and sprinted toward the men, making sure she made some spectacular leaps along the way. *They have to recognize me as Enhanced.*

"Help me," she screamed. "Take me back to Iron Torr!"

The men whirled, startled, but they held their fire. "I'm so glad to see you," Michelle cried.

"It's all right, Miss Atherton, the bird'll be here in a second, and we'll be off."

"Thank you so much!" She felt embarrassed for overacting, but if everything went well, those soldiers would never live to tell the story.

The helicopter appeared over a ridge. Thrumming loudly, it landed in the meadow. Michelle tried to follow the men inside, but they wanted her to go first. She hesitated.

The captain pushed past to speak to the pilot. "There's a nest of 'em up on the cliffs. We've got to burn 'em out before we go."

"Yes, sir."

"Lieutenant Parker. Get up here and help us locate the rebel base."

"Sir!" A young man ran past. He tried to avert his face, but Michelle saw him. Someone else did too.

"Slade," Maya screamed. She left her hiding place and ran toward him, clutching Justin's old bow. "Slade!"

A soldier turned and saw Maya. He hesitated, waiting for instructions. "Lieutenant? You know her?"

Slade looked at Maya with a strange, frozen look on his face. He began to put out a hand to her, but then turned his back and got in the helicopter. The soldier shrugged, put his rifle to his shoulder, and gunned the girl down. She fell dead not far from Michelle's feet. Slade turned deathly pale, but he said nothing. The white feather still blew from his hair. On the ground, Maya's white feather twisted feebly in the breeze, flecked with blood.

Staring at Maya's still form, Michelle felt faint, then nauseous. She gulped, trying not to vomit. *Slade let that girl die! And she loved him.*

After a moment of shocked silence, arrows whistled through the air. Two of Parker's men went down screaming while soldiers fired randomly into the trees. They couldn't see their attackers. Michelle jumped into the helicopter, but as much as she wanted to murder Slade, she only had one target in mind—the pilot. She swung her rifle around and got a shot off, but a soldier grabbed the barrel and wrenched it away. Enhanced men swarmed her, and she had no chance. Someone punched her hard in the stomach, and the men all held her down as one of them stabbed her thigh with a hypodermic needle. Michelle fell paralyzed onto the floor of the helicopter. She saw and heard everything, but she couldn't move. The soldiers cursed her viciously, but when they kicked her, she felt no pain. Trapped in a numb, useless body, she couldn't even cry.

Their captain stopped his men from doing more. "Let the colonel deal with her."

The pilot took off despite the bullet wound in his shoulder, and Michelle waited for the horrifying attack on the refugees in the cave. It didn't happen.

"I'm losing too much blood, sir," the pilot yelled. "I need to make sure you get back to base."

"Proceed to Iron Torr."

Chapter 12: Dillon

Bear's Clan

The morning after the nightmarish attack on the Norm village, Dillon woke alone on the bank of a little stream. Earth gradually rose and fell as the planet breathed beneath him. The sensation triggered a bittersweet memory of his mother. Leafy branches shifted in the wind, so spots of sunshine twirled on the forest floor. Beams of light stabbed his eyes. Wrapping his arms around his head didn't help. A flock of tiny birds chirped from the trees above. Dillon clenched his jaw against their high-pitched cries, but the creatures were relentless. Their beady black eyes measured him as they chattered endlessly amongst themselves. Finally, eons later, the flock ruled against him. Dillon knew they had—he heard the words in their repetitive little song. *Killed his own kind, his own kind. His own kind, his own kind.*

"What the hell was I supposed to do?" Dillon howled. The flock burst into flight. Their black shapes fragmented against the sky until they broke to dust and the specks blew away in the wind. *What kind is my own kind? I don't even know anymore.*

Dillon sat up and hugged his knees to his chest to stop their trembling. The sun had risen high enough to offer a little warmth, but his uniform was damp. Small cuts covered the backs of his hands, relics of his mad run through the dark forest. His left shin was badly bruised, and a cut stung one cheek. The tough Iron Torr uniform had done its job, protecting him from the worst of it, but he still wanted to burn the thing.

"I am not one of them," Dillon whispered to himself, tearing at the Iron Torr logo on his sleeve so savagely that he broke a nail to the quick. "Parker's a monster, whether he's my uncle or not."

The black embroidered patch, an outline of a forbidding tower against the sky, mutely resisted. Blood seeped sullenly from the base of the broken fingernail. *There's no way I can go back to the Torr now that I turned against them. Sawyer's dead. And Michelle…she was so close, and now she's gone.*

Maybe Parker's not my uncle. Maybe he lied. Dillon wanted to believe it was all a lie, that they could never be related, but the colonel's perfect profile was clear in his mind. *He looks a lot like Mom. She knows him…knows what he's like. Mom wouldn't ask her brother for help, so she raised me in the Warren, where we were hungry all the time. She knew!*

Tears streamed down Dillon's face. He clambered to his feet. Deep green leaves whirled around him in a dizzying carousel. He staggered and almost fell. Dillon threw his head back and bellowed at the sky like a madman. "Parker! I will not be like you! I will not be like you!"

"Glad t' hear it," said a man's voice, deep and calm, speaking from some hidden place.

Dillon jumped. He slapped for his rifle and abruptly realized it was gone. *I had it last night. Someone took it.* Anger flashed through him and set the trees to dancing. Dillon took deep breaths until the visions subsided. Large trees settled quietly back into the earth, but the unruly willows kept on slashing at each other with their spindly branches. They grew thickly around him, providing plenty of cover for the stalker.

Dillon spun in place, searching the undergrowth, but the speaker was well hidden. "Who are you?"

"Funny, that's just what we was askin' about you," a woman said, stepping lightly from the trees. Her slender figure made her look like a girl, but time and weather had cast a web of wrinkles around her eyes. With the morning light behind her silver-shot hair, she looked like one of those images of the Goddess devout Norms painted on walls in the Warren.

Dillon scrubbed at his tear-stained face with a sleeve. Shame made his neck feel hot.

"Elsie," a man said from somewhere deep in the willows. He sounded like a Norm. "Be careful, now."

"Stay put, Bear," Elsie said. She wrinkled her nose mischievously at Dillon. "He'd better stay put. One look at his ugly face, and brave men run."

Dillon smiled a little at that, and the woman smiled back. He took a shuddering breath and relaxed a little.

Elsie slowly pulled a leather bag from her back. "I'll wager you could use some breakfast. There's bread inside, an' the last o' the honeycomb. Come on, now, don't be shy."

Dillon's stomach growled. He sat beside the woman on a mossy log and accepted a chunk of bread, dripping with wildflower honey so clear it was almost white. When he looked up, an enormous man stood at the edge of the forest, wearing a rough homespun tunic and heavy leather boots.

Dillon tensed.

Before he could stand up, Elsie put a hand on his arm. "That there's my husband. Bear, sit down, would ya? Yer scarin' the boy."

Bear shrugged and settled himself onto the forest floor. Even in a sitting position, the man was nearly as tall as his little wife. When he smiled, his teeth barely showed behind his thick, dark beard, but the edges of his dark eyes crinkled with good humor.

"Good. Stay down there, like the dog that you are," Elsie teased, tossing her husband a chunk of bread. He caught it deftly in one hand.

The Norms let Dillon eat in silence. The hallucinations slowly subsided until the breathing of the planet was a subtle motion, hard to discern unless he looked for it. When he finished, Dillon walked across the clearing and stood over Bear. The big man started to stand up.

Elsie's sharp intake of breath was the only sound.

"It's all right," Dillon told the woman over his shoulder as her huge husband clambered slowly to his feet. "I'm not crazy. Not usually, anyway. I had a bad reaction to this, um, medicine, they gave me, and last night, I think I lost my mind in the fighting. But I'm better now."

"War-torn," Elsie whispered, nodding like she'd seen this before. "It's a wound y' can't see. Some men are jumpy fer the rest o' their days."

Dillon knew what she meant, but he didn't try to tell her that this was far worse.

When he offered Bear the double handclasp of the Warren, Dillon's hands almost disappeared inside the larger man's. "I'm Dillon Freeman." He met the Norm's eyes levelly, without shame. "Half-breed."

"Blessed Goddess," Elsie breathed from behind him. "I've heard o' people like you, but only in legend."

"Freeman." Bear spoke slowly. "I saw ya last night. Y' made a hard choice. You got no family now."

Dillon swallowed hard, fumbled for words, and found none. All he could do was make a pained gesture of acknowledgement.

"Y' made the right choice," Bear said, gripping his arm. "An' we owe ya a debt o' gratitude. I'd be proud to welcome ya into my clan. If you'll have us."

Tears sprang to Dillon's eyes. After a long moment of silence, he choked out a few words. "I...I will."

"Good." Elsie put a gentle hand on her husband's arm. "Let's get this boy home."

Before setting out, the Norms went back into the trees to gather their gear. Dillon followed them into the willows. When Bear slung Dillon's rifle over his shoulder, Dillon snapped out a hand and seized the barrel.

Bear wrapped his big hand around it and hung on. Tension spiked between them. "Y' gonna shoot me, boy?"

"Um, no," Dillon stammered, but he didn't let go.

"Then you don't need it right now." Bear put his free hand on Dillon's shoulder and gave it a gentle squeeze. "Let me carry it for ya."

"It still belongs t' you, son," Elsie murmured. "But it's a burden."

After last night, Dillon understood that in a way he never had before. He abruptly released his grip on the weapon and followed Bear and Elsie into the forest.

***

Bear and Elsie moved Dillon into their big canvas tent, even though all the other teenage boys had tents of their own. The couple tended to him patiently as he healed. Despite their efforts, one or the other of them occasionally startled him with some quick motion, and Dillon sprang to his feet on hair-trigger reflexes, primed for a fight. He tried not to frighten the rest of the clan, but everyone gave him a wide berth. Days blended into a week, or maybe two. He wasn't counting.

Elsie always seemed happier when they camped near willows. Dillon didn't tell her that the whipping of their branches warned him when an episode threatened, giving him time to run into the woods before the hallucinations hit in force. Dillon especially hated the way Elsie cringed when he shouted. She never understood that he wasn't yelling at her. Afterwards, when he calmed down, she crept back into their tent and rocked him like a child. Dillon drowned in guilt. He wanted to tell her that he couldn't help it, that the sounds of faraway gunshots maddened him, but at those times he had trouble forming words. It didn't matter. Elsie shushed him anyway.

One evening, after a particularly bad outburst, Dillon caught Bear and his wife staring at him like a monster had somehow inserted itself into their home. "I'm sorry," he muttered, turning over a piece of broken crockery in his hands. "I'll go ahead and go in the morning."

"None o' that talk now." Elsie put a bowl of stew in front of him, in shining newly-fired pottery. "I never liked that plate anyway. An' yer place is here."

Dillon shook his head and refused to eat. "I should be out looking for Michelle."

"Michelle?" Elsie repeated. She looked at her husband. "He had a woman?"

"First I saw, he was with his platoon. All men." Bear ran his thick fingers through Dillon's long hair and inspected the ends. That won him a disturbed stare from Dillon. Bear looked back, completely unembarrassed. "So. Did she have a white feather?"

"Did…Michelle… have a white feather?" Dillon slowly repeated the words, completely bewildered. "Um, not that I know of."

The Norms suppressed smiles at that, but Dillon didn't see why.

"That don't matter, Bear. They might have some other tradition," Elsie said. "Dillon, did she, um, choose you? Over all the other boys?"

Behind his wife's back, Bear brought his fists to his hipbones in a suggestive motion. Dillon burst out laughing.

Elsie turned on her husband in mock anger. "You, mind yer manners! I should change yer name to Dog. Bad Dog."

Their spotted mutt flattened his ears and stared up at Elsie. Elsie petted the dog while it wiggled under her hands, tail whirling. "I'm not talkin' about you. You're a good boy."

Dillon grinned for the first time in ages. "You're asking if Michelle and me are bonded. Yeah, we are. Since earlier this summer."

"Aw, Bear, I remember the summer we bonded," Elsie said fondly, gazing up at her husband.

"So do I." Bear raised his eyebrows a couple of times and made the lewd gesture again. His wife playfully pelted him with a few blueberries before he ducked out of the tent, laughing. Their spotted dog followed him, tail held high.

Bear's voice boomed through the canvas wall. "Get out here, Freeman. We got visitors."

Dillon felt well enough to hang around at the edge of the group while the men talked, but Bear hauled him into the circle and introduced him to the visitors. "This is my son, Dillon Freeman."

Dillon gave the newcomers a curt nod and sat. One of them was a tall, middle-aged guy called Wade. The ponytailed teenager with him was Laird. He might have been Wade's son, but Dillon didn't bother to ask. Bear's words were still sinking in. *My son, Dillon Freeman? That's weird. Weirder if he means it.*

The meeting began. Dillon remained silent until it was obvious that the Norms were warming up to do something stupid. Ridiculously, lethally stupid.

"We've had good luck puttin' traps outside the tower," Wade said. "I want you young guys to go out there on the dark o' the moon and set up some more."

"The colonel already thinks you're morons," Dillon snapped. "You aiming to prove him right?"

Everyone looked at him at once.

Wade rolled his eyes. "What do you know?"

"I know he's smarter than you'll ever be. You can't use the same trick on him over and over." Dillon let out an exasperated huff of air. "They've probably got traps of their own set, in case you come back."

"I dunno," Wade said. He looked at Bear, eyebrows raised in an unspoken question.

"When's the last time anyone was there?" Bear asked.

Wade chewed his lip thoughtfully. "Not quite a month ago. When we went to… um…pick up my niece."

"See?" Dillon cut in. "It's been a while. Every approach to the place has got to be a death trap by now. We need to try something new."

"All right, then. What?" Bear asked.

"I've got an idea," Dillon mused. "But it's risky. You know how the military's been kidnapping young women? They're using them as surrogate mothers."

"Using them as what?" Laird asked.

"Surrogate mothers," Dillon repeated. "That means they get them pregnant with babies that aren't theirs."

Laird made a revolted face. "What's the point o' that?"

"Pregnancy takes female soldiers away from their duties," Dillon said. "So they make Normal women carry their infants for them."

Wade shook his head dismissively. "That's not even possible."

"Wade, they're smarter than you, remember? They can do things you can't." Dillon leaned forward, ignoring Wade's scowl. "So, we offer them something they can't refuse. A group of pretty girls, camping all alone...except for the armed men hiding all around them."

The Norms quietly absorbed this, giving Dillon a few seconds to entertain a host of second thoughts. Guilt welled inside him at the idea of taking up arms against his uncle.

Wade finally spoke. "Who's gonna be the bait?"

Dillon shrugged. "Ask for volunteers. I'll be in the trees with a gun."

"This might work," Wade said. "They could sing and drum, make themselves real obvious out there. We ought t' send a few elders along too, or it might look like a trap."

"Now you're thinking." Dillon gave Wade an encouraging nod. "Can you round up five or ten good-looking girls for bait?"

"That, we got," Bear said. He looked across the clearing and raised his voice. "Hey, Tina, come 'ere fer a second."

A pretty brunette of about seventeen left her spinning and came over. Her hair was done in tiny braids, each tipped with a silver bead and a tiny black feather. They jingled when she tossed her head.

"Tina, this is Dillon," Bear said.

"I know who he is." Tina folded her arms and stared at Dillon, motionless except for the little muscle behind her jaw that popped when she clenched her teeth.

"He's got a plan, but he'll need yer help. And yer friends', too," Bear added.

Tina said nothing. She just stood there, watching Dillon like he was a venomous snake.

Dillon stood up and gave her his best smile. "So, Tina. How far are you willing to go to protect your clan?"

"I'd die for them," Tina spat.

"You don't win a war by dying," Dillon said in a patient tone. "It's better if the *other* side does the dying."

Tina gave him the kind of withering look that only a beautiful girl can do really well. She'd clearly mastered it.

"All right, then," Bear interrupted. "You two, go on. Take a walk or somethin'. Work out a plan. Talk t' the other girls. Come on back later and tell us about it."

Dillon looked at Tina and shrugged. She tossed her jingling braids and walked away, shoulders set in a rigid line. As Dillon followed her out of the clearing, he looked over his shoulder at Bear and got the leer he expected. *Great. Now he's throwing girls at me. I won't mind using this one for bait.*

Chapter 13: Michelle

The Longest Night

By the time Michelle could twitch, she'd been locked in a darkened prison cell for hours. Groaning, she peeled her face off the sticky vinyl mattress. Her jeans and flannel shirt were gone, replaced by a zippered one-piece coverall. The reality of that sank in with a chill. *While I was knocked out, some pervert stripped me and changed my clothes. Hope that's all he did.*

Michelle's head pounded, and her bruised body ached. She tried to escape into sleep, but lumpy foam beads inside the mattress crackled whenever she stirred, waking her. Finally she gave up the attempt and sat there rehearsing her story. It wasn't quite ready when someone flicked on the light. Colonel Parker stood there, cool and distant, just beyond the bars of her cell.

Michelle struggled off the bed and limped to him. "Sir, I want to apologize for accidentally discharging my weapon in the helicopter. It was inexcusable, especially considering how brave those men were to rescue me."

The colonel didn't speak. He just stared at her with those cold eyes. *He's waiting for me to lose my nerve and blurt out something stupid.*

"Is the pilot going to be all right?" Michelle held a hand through the bars. *If I have to melt his brain to get out of here, I will.* But Parker wouldn't take her hand, and she couldn't reach him.

"My squadron leader tells me that your assault on the pilot was intentional," he said coldly.

"Of course it wasn't," she cried, gripping the bars. "Why would I attack my own rescuer?"

Colonel Parker scrutinized her until she felt naked. "Why, indeed?"

Parker paced the aisle in front of the cell like he was the one in the cage. His movements were unconsciously graceful, both fluid and predatory. Michelle anxiously watched him, resisting the impulse to back away. She despised the colonel, but the animal part of her recognized him as a flawlessly enhanced male, virile and deadly. The man really was unbelievably handsome, even with those reptilian eyes.

As though he read her mind, Parker suddenly whirled and took two long strides toward her. Michelle flushed and hated herself for it, but she refused to look down. He held her with his eyes. They were his only flaw—too pale, too glittery, but somehow still beautiful. Michelle wanted to reach for his hand, to control him, but she only gripped the bars harder. The colonel's ice blue eyes moved over her form, leaving her tingling.

"You're far too beautiful to damage," he finally said. "No matter what you've done."

Michelle felt a wave of relief, but then he turned and walked away, leaving her alone in the dark. She fell back on the bed, sobbing.

Michelle remained there for the next two or three days. She couldn't tell how long it had been because the lights in the cell never came on. Disgusting dried algae pellets filled a bin at one end of the cell, so no one came to feed her. Feeling her way around, she discovered that, besides the food trough, there were only three other things in there—a tiny sink, a toilet, and the bed.

She tortured herself worrying about everyone she cared about. *Did Molly and Kalie survive? Where are Dillon and our friends?* She even tried tapping into the minds of nearby people, but she only felt their emotions, with no specific thoughts at all. Michelle only learned one thing. The people of Iron Torr were afraid—more afraid than they'd ever been.

The next time Michelle saw human beings, they all wore white coats. She hid her eyes from the stabbing glare of the overhead lights and peeked between her fingers. The technicians, two men and one frighteningly large woman, brought along a wheeled gurney outfitted with thick nylon straps. Michelle considered fighting, but she changed her mind. It seemed best to appear cooperative. She let the big bulldog-faced woman strap her to the gurney, even though that made her heart pound in fear.

"What's going on?" Michelle asked anxiously, staring up at their rigid, expressionless faces. "Where are you taking me?"

None of them responded. They rolled her down endless corridors, into an elevator, and out again. The gurney passed down another hall and through a doorway, where it stopped. The bulldog woman released the straps.

Michelle scrambled off the stretcher and found herself in prison with the surrogate mothers. "Wait! You can't leave me here. My parents are on the Conclave!"

The impassive guards took their gurney and left. The door locked behind them with a hollow boom.

Women stared from all directions. They all wore matching one-piece coveralls, just like hers. She'd been dumped in a small living area containing a single couch and some rocking chairs. Next to that was a central chamber full of numbered cradles, with a windowed nurses' station at the far end. The partition between the surrogates and the nursery stood open. Women moved back and forth in there, feeding infants and changing diapers.

Michelle stormed past the cradles to the nurses' station. She knocked on the armored glass window. "Hey, I don't belong here! Open this door right now."

A dumpy middle-aged nurse stood up. The woman said something to a colleague, but her voice was too muffled to hear through the window. Michelle banged until one of them pressed a button. The intercom crackled on. "Settle down, Twenty-four, or we'll sedate you."

"Go ahead and try it!"

The nurse took the tranquilizer gun off the wall and slid open the mechanism. When Michelle saw the long needle, she burst into tears. The nurse sat back down with a satisfied smile.

"It's good t' cry, honey," said a young mother with a long dark braid. "Let it out."

That bit of sympathy unraveled Michelle's self-control, and she began to sob. The young woman hugged her, bringing her infant into the embrace. She took Michelle over to the couch and sat with her. "I'm Sage. Welcome to our little clan."

Sage had the stocky build, dark slanted eyes, and prominent cheekbones of the northern indigenous tribes. She looked nothing like the baby in her arms. The infant, a lively little boy a few months old, had wispy white-blond hair and round blue eyes, a few shades paler than normal.

"Sage," Michelle asked tentatively. "How did you get here?"

The girl sighed and looked down, making Michelle feel like she made a mistake by asking. "It was my fault, really."

"Hardly," Michelle spat. "There's no excuse for what they're doing."

"I went along on a raid," the young brunette admitted. "All my brothers were goin', my cousins, and…this one man." Sage's fingers lightly stroked the remains of a white feather that was still carefully attached to the bottom of her braid. "So I went too. Not 'cause I wanted t' wage war, but I loved 'em. I loved 'em all."

Sage's eyes filled with tears, and Michelle knew that some or all of those men had died. She didn't ask. "I understand completely. I could see myself doing the same thing if Dillon and my brother were going off to war."

"Dillon? That's yer man?"

Michelle nodded sadly.

Sage smiled, obviously trying to cheer Michelle up. "What's he like?"

"Big, with red-gold hair. Funny and nice to me, but some of the men are scared of him. He likes to fight."

"Sounds perfect," Sage said. "Where is he now?"

"Free in the forest, I hope. I don't know."

"I'm sure he is." Sage reached out to pat Michelle's arm. "When I got caught I thought they was gonna kill me. But instead they gave me little Hunter here." Sage looked fondly at the baby on her lap. "I don't know why, but it's a blessing."

Even at a few months old, Sage's baby had enough strength to bounce on his tiny legs as his surrogate mother balanced him on her lap. The infant's ice-blue eyes seemed oddly familiar, until Michelle pictured them on the colonel. Hunter had clearly been sired by Mark Parker. Michelle scanned the room. *One baby here is Parker's clone...and I bet this is it. The Conclave would go ballistic if they knew.*

"He's adorable, Sage."

"Thanks! But he's gonna cause me problems back home." Sage lowered her voice in an uncomfortable way. "My man ain't gonna understand, and the boy looks nothin' like 'im."

"Tell him you were raped."

Sage winced and shook her head. "Not really. They gave me a shot, an' it made me sleep. A couple of months later, I knew I was pregnant."

"It's still rape, even if doctors knock you out to do it." Michelle felt tempted to explain the embryo transfer process and tell Sage that this baby wasn't even hers, but she didn't. The young mother cooed and laughed with her baby, and she celebrated when he gave her a tiny, toothless smile.

Why tell her, and rob the poor woman of the one thing that gives her joy? Upsetting her boyfriend is the least of her worries. She'll never see him again.

Three nurses entered the room, interrupting the conversation. The dumpy middle-aged one stayed back to guard the door. All of the attendants were women. Michelle looked them over appraisingly. None of them looked tough at all. She felt certain she could take any one of them, and probably all three at once.

"Number twenty-four," a young nurse with an electronic pad called out. No one responded. Finally, huffing in annoyance, the woman came up to Michelle and got in her face. "You are number twenty-four," she explained slowly, pointing to a number on the sleeve of the prison uniform. "When I call number twenty-four, you," she pointed a finger at Michelle's face for emphasis, "get up." With those words, the young woman pulled Michelle irritatingly off the couch. "And come to me." The nurse pantomimed that too, backing up and tugging her prisoner forward.

This is how we come off to Norms? How embarrassing. No wonder they hate us.

"Thank you for that exceedingly clear explanation," Michelle said, shaking the woman's hand off her wrist.

The other nurses giggled. "Don't you know who she is?" they whispered to their colleague, as though Michelle couldn't hear. "That's Michelle Atherton, top-ranked student at Headquarters."

"Well, she's got her hair done like a Norm," the young nurse said defensively. "Why's she here?"

"Take a look at this." The nurses left the room and locked Michelle and the Norm women in again. They all clustered around the computer at once. Michelle folded her arms, considering murder.

The dumpy nurse set a capped syringe on a tray and pressed the intercom button. "Stand by, Twenty-four. I still need to check your hormone levels."

Michelle immediately turned her back and walked away. *Hormone levels? They're planning to get me pregnant! Not without a fight.*

Someone stood in the hallway, looking in through the window. He tapped on the glass.

"Slade, you backstabber," Michelle screamed, startling the mothers and babies around her. One infant began to wail.

Slade took a reflexive step away even though he stood on the other side of an armored glass window. His voice sounded muffled. "Michelle, I'm sorry. You don't understand."

"I understand you betrayed a girl who loved you. That's all I need to know."

Slade stood there looking anguished. He wore his forest green uniform again, with no beads or feathers in his hair.

"Where's your white feather now?" Michelle shrieked. "Did you throw it away like garbage, like you threw away Maya?"

A tear streaked Slade's face, and he turned and ran.

A nurse stood up, one hand on the dart gun, and hit the intercom button. "Calm down, Twenty-four. This is your final warning."

Michelle collapsed onto the couch and sobbed while Norm women gathered around her, stroking her hair. Finally the oldest Norm mother brought a cute baby girl and set her on Michelle's lap. Michelle stopped crying and hugged the infant, stroking her soft baby hair. The women exchanged little smiles and nods, clearly happy this tactic worked. Michelle felt amazed by them all. *How can they stay so full of love in a place like this?*

***

By afternoon, Michelle restlessly paced the enclosure. Those rooms were designed for Norms. She could escape in at least three different ways, but the real problem would be getting out of the fortress. Not to mention evading capture on the trip to the village. Even that didn't seem like the best plan. *I don't want to live in a stone-age hut for the rest of my life. What I need to do is find my friends and get back to the Institute. If only I could contact the Conclave and get some help!* She considered sneaking into the Communications building, but it would be under guard. Michelle decided to stay put until she figured out what to do.

That night the nurses made the surrogates put all the babies in the bassinets, and they locked the armored glass partition between them. The women weren't allowed to handle their infants unsupervised, which Michelle thought was ridiculous. The mothers and babies were separated during morning workouts too, when all the nurses were gone.

Different nurses arrived for the night shift, and they handed out thin sleeping mats and a single blanket to each prisoner. A heavily pregnant teenager got the couch, and everyone else bedded down on the floor. Michelle ended up between Sage and the oldest mother, whose name was

Olivia. The nurses shut out the overhead lights, but Michelle couldn't sleep on the hard floor. The worn foam mats hardly helped at all. Her mind raced. *What's going to happen tomorrow? Are they going to get me pregnant? Will they ever let me leave?*

Near her feet, a pregnant girl rolled over, grunting with the effort. Michelle yanked her own mat out from under her hips and passed it over. "Here, take this and double up. You need it worse than I do."

The Normal girl touched her lips to Michelle in silent thanks.

Michelle wrapped herself in her blanket again and stretched out on the cold tile floor. Hours later, she fell asleep. A whirring noise woke her. She sat up as the glass partition into the nursery slid open. A dark figure stood in the hall. The surrogates began to awaken too. The women peered into the nurses' station and found it dark. A few mothers slipped into the nursery to check on their babies. Michelle haunted the armored glass wall between their room and the hallway, trying to get a look at the man outside. He entered the nurses' station and fiddled with some controls. In a moment, the door of their prison opened.

"Michelle," someone whispered, and it took her a second to realize it was Slade. Under the circumstances, she didn't scream at him. The two of them just stared each other down across the darkened room. Behind him were the shadowy forms of two night-shift nurses, paralyzed in their chairs. Slade had rotated the chairs so they stared into the corner, but she knew from experience that the drug let them see and hear.

I need to know if there are guards outside. Slade might be setting me up. A botched escape attempt will destroy any chance of the colonel forgiving me.

Michelle held out her right hand as if for a handshake, and Slade took it. She forced her way into his mind, experiencing his shock and outrage at the invasion. Sorrow and confusion masked the information she wanted. Finally one clear thought emerged from Slade's mind. *I took a risk to free you. Are you going to leave or not?*

Michelle sent a reply, trying to make the thought a powerful one, strong enough to be a compulsion. Then she dropped Slade's hand and ran. Behind her, he fell to his knees, both hands clutching his head.

Michelle darted downstairs and peered around a corner. Two guards stood on either side of the exterior door. She retreated back up the stairs again. The darkened doorway of a classroom yawned on the left side of the hall. Inside the deserted room, a single window faced the shadowy staircase that spiraled up the outside of the tower. Michelle rattled it in its frame, but the tough material only flexed under her frantic hands. *Agh! It doesn't open! Armored glass, I should have known. It doesn't matter. I can't get the mothers and babies out a window anyway, and I can't leave them here.*

Michelle caught up with Slade and the surrogate mothers in the hallway. A few sleepy infants fussed fitfully. Their whimpers sounded loud in the darkened corridor.

"Slade!"

"You're on your own, Michelle," Slade hissed. "I have the authority to move the women, if they're, uh, summoned, but I can't move you. I'd get in huge trouble for that."

"Not my problem." Michelle could think of only one reason those girls would be summoned. *Figures. Slade's the scumbag who delivers them to their rapists.*

Even in the dark, the venom in Slade's glare made Michelle flinch. She fought to keep her voice low. "So, what assurance do I have that you'll get these women out, along with their babies?"

Slade shook his head. "I'll get the women out, but the kids stay here."

"No deal. Guess I'll scream for the guards then. I'm already a prisoner, I've got nothing to lose." Michelle took a deep breath.

"No, no, don't! Okay, they can keep the babies, just shut the hell up. You're being way too loud."

"If we split up now, how do I get out of here?"

"There's an elevator at the end of the hall. Enter the code 6266. It'll take you up to the top. From there you'll have access to all the floors, even the restricted ones. Go down to the third floor and take the outside stairs from there."

Michelle grabbed Slade's forearm and gripped it. "Are you really going to help these women get home?"

Slade slapped her hand off. "Read my mind if you don't believe me, you crazy bitch." He entered the code on the wall-mounted keypad. The elevator doors opened immediately. "Here's the elevator—now go!" He pushed Michelle in, and, despite her misgivings, she went.

The frightened surrogates watched her until the doors closed. Michelle backed into a corner and wrapped her arms around herself as the lift took her higher. Every little sound made her twitch. *Why do I have to go up before I can go down? Is he sending me into a trap? Maybe it'll open into some creepy laboratory, or a jail cell.*

The elevator stopped with a bump. The doors opened into a sumptuous room decorated in a masculine style, all dark wood and fine leather furniture. An oil painting graced the wall, a tall ship tossed about on a black sea. Delectable smells of food filled the air, making Michelle's mouth water. Somewhere, a cork popped. Laughter and the sounds of intimate conversation came from inside.

Then a man spoke. "Oh, good. Sounds like Slade's back." His voice was unmistakable.

Parker! Oh, God. I'm in his apartment!

Michelle ducked into a corner of the elevator and stabbed at the third floor button.

A man's heavy footsteps approached. "What's the holdup, Slade?"

Parker asked. "Dinner's on. We made your favorite."

Just as Parker's shadow fell across the elevator, the doors hissed closed. As the elevator started down, Michelle was overcome by a wild fit of giggles. *Psycho Mark Parker cooks with his wife? I never imagined.*

That time, when the doors opened, Michelle was ready. She shot out of the elevator and dodged a couple of surprised guards. Men snatched at her as she slammed the outer door open and dashed outside onto a small, exposed landing with no guard rail.

"Hey! What're you doing?" A green-uniformed soldier snagged her sleeve.

Michelle jerked it away. The thin fabric of the prison uniform ripped, and she lost her balance. Screaming, she plummeted over the edge.

Michelle tumbled down the steep slope beneath the Torr in an avalanche of loose rock. At the bottom, she struggled to her feet, knees and palms dripping blood. The river thundered past, only a few strides away, sending cold spray into her face. On the hillside above, men shouted. Their flashlight beams split the night.

The sound of crying babies came from the darkness as Norm women fled with infants that weren't theirs. Michelle suddenly started having second thoughts. *Forget it. Those kids are better off.*

Slade's voice cut across the chaos. "Hold your fire. Don't risk the infants! Guards, to me."

Slade was delaying the pursuit, just as she told him to, but it wouldn't be long before patrols arrived. Not far down the bank squatted a low boathouse. Michelle tried the door and found it locked. A keypad on the wall glinted in the moonlight. With bloody fingers, she entered the only code she knew— 6266. The lock opened with a soft beep.

Michelle slipped inside and rammed the rusted deadbolt home. Several inflatable zodiac boats floated tethered in their slips, but she wasn't sure how to drive one. Plus, the engine noise would give her away. The last space bore a neatly lettered sign—*Private. For Colonel Parker's use only.* A sleek yellow kayak waited there.

Michelle threw on a raincoat with Parker's name on it and grabbed a paddle. The narrow boat tipped horribly as she got in and tightened the spray skirt around her middle. A little wooden gate freed the kayak into the river. The boat moved slowly at first, then faster, while Michelle's apprehension grew. Her heart raced. Black canyon walls loomed overhead, blotting out the stars. The river picked up speed as it shot between them. Michelle tried to steer, but her shredded palms hurt and she had no clue how to handle a kayak. She hit a bump, got a face full of water, and then the prow took an unexpected twist to the left. Churning whitewater swept the little boat downstream, sideways and out of control. Michelle paddled madly, palms on fire, and felt a wave of elation when she got the nose pointed downstream.

Freezing spray soaked her hair, but she didn't care. Her triumphant yell was lost in the roar of the river.

The crescent moon gave barely enough light to steer by. The ache in Michelle's arms spread to her wrists and back, but she stayed on the river all night. Soon, huge trees on the banks eclipsed everything, even the light from the moon. She floated on until the sky turned gray with the threat of sunrise.

Michelle started to beach the kayak, but thought better of it and let it float downstream alone. *Maybe that'll throw them off when they come after me.* She climbed the bank, walking on rocks to avoid leaving footprints, and ran for the forest. No helicopters buzzed overhead, and no zodiacs raced down the river after her. She tiredly wondered why.

Instinctively, she kept under the canopy, feeling safer among the old trees. Royal blue light brightened the eastern sky, enough to outline the canyon walls. The only familiar cliffs stood upriver. Michelle swore under her breath. *I've gone too far. It'll be a long walk back to the village.*

A few wisps of smoke rose above the trees. *There's another village! Maybe some clan members live there.* Michelle hiked that way, but as she neared the circle of huts, she hesitated. *What if they take me for an enemy?* Feeling stupid for overreacting, she hid in the bushes and watched. The village could have been Molly's. All the buildings stood in the same places, and the fire pit was an exact duplicate, with the same tripod and cast iron pot. She crept closer. A pile of animal traps lay against a wall, right where Wade stored his. But this village was a different one, miles away. *Weird. Maybe Norms just aren't that creative. They're creatures of habit.*

Michelle snuck up to the hut that would have been Molly's, feeling homesick and disoriented. People muttered inside, but she needed to find out more about them before showing herself. She crawled up to the wall under the window and lay still in the shadows, listening.

"Ya damn near killed her, Wade," a woman snapped. In the background, a child cried. Flies buzzed softly. "By the Gods! We're not gonna be like them. This is nothin' more than a girl."

Bile rose in Michelle's throat, but she didn't dare move. She knew what the man would say next.

"That little girl killed three men, an' wounded another."

"No doubt on the orders o' some lordly man like yerself."

Wade left on cue, slamming the door on his way out.

Molly's voice came from inside the hut. "Ya poor dear! Can y' make it to the bed?"

Michelle held still, afraid that Wade would hear her breathe. *This is how they gain our loyalty, and use us against our own people. I must have enhanced the hell out of these Norms. They're brilliant.*

"What a pretty one y' are," Molly cooed to her prisoner. "Nobody's gonna hurt ya now."

Michelle ached inside. *It was all a lie. They never really loved me. And I killed for them!*

In time, Molly came outside. Wade's whisper carried from the front of the hut. "Wait...and... go."

Light footsteps entered the room. Kalie's voice sounded high and clear. "Uncle says you're the one who killed my Da."

Michelle wanted to run into the forest and scream, but she waited, clenching blades of grass in her fists. She had to know who was in there.

"I don't know." The young woman's voice sounded sick and weak. "I shot at some men just to survive, but I don't know if I hit anyone. If one of them was your father, I'm really sorry."

That's Jeanette! They drugged her with whatever they put on the inside of the tarp.

Wade's heavy footsteps came around the side of the building, so Michelle scrambled away, hugging the walls. She slid under some ferns just before Wade walked past and strode into the woods. About twenty yards in, he stopped and pulled a bright yellow object out of his pocket.

A handheld radio? So their stone-age lifestyle is phony too.

The radio crackled and a distorted voice came out.

"Yeah, we're doin' it tonight," Wade said into the radio. "We're bringin' all the teams together."

Wade listened to whatever his companion said, but Michelle couldn't make it out over the static.

"We just got 'er last night. We picked off her guards, an' she was still a bitch t' catch. She stayed out there alone fer weeks." Wade paused to listen. "I know, but we're outta time. If the others trust us, she will too."

He shook his head, as though his companion could see him. "Nope, we lost that one. Damn shame too, it took real good on her. Justin says she shot a helicopter pilot!" Wade laughed. "Told ya it would. Okay, see ya tonight. Party time."

Michelle crouched in the ferns, stunned by the whole thing, while Wade inexplicably waded into a copse of thorny devil's club that guarded a shelf of red rock. Pressing the spiny stems aside with a boot, he revealed the hidden mouth of a den. The curved bow of a zodiac was barely visible inside.

Wade bent to tuck his radio into a compartment in the boat and then carefully backed up, letting the wide, flat leaves fall back to hide the den again.

Michelle's fingers dug into the cold ground. *The whole village is a set, and I thought it was real.* She let her forehead sink onto her hands and lay there for a minute, willing the ache in her heart to disappear. *I just want to go home.* Then, nimble as a cat, she uncoiled, sprang for the mouth of the den, and dove inside.

The stolen zodiac even smelled like Iron Torr. The faint, pervasive odor was unmistakable in the cramped, musty space—a blend of plastic, harsh chemical cleansers, and fear.

So that's how they got me here. They stole this boat from Iron Torr. That took guts.

A compartment near the front of the boat held a sheathed knife, some rope, a lantern, and what she was after—the bright yellow radio. Michelle grabbed it and froze. It wasn't a radio at all. *This is high tech, but old, from before the war. Kind of like a radio, but based on quantum entangled electrons. It's worth a fortune. Bet the Norms didn't know that when they stole it.*

She experimentally thumbed the red button. A voice crackled from the device, too loud in the small space. "Wade? That you, Wade? Bear here, go ahead."

Michelle fumbled frantically for the volume control, accidentally bumped the old-fashioned wheel, and changed the frequency instead. For the briefest moment, another voice came out, a familiar one, one that could solve all her problems. Her heart leaped.

Was that G.G.? Could it be?

Carefully, she rolled the dial until the voice came in faint but clear. It wasn't her great-grandfather, after all. Michelle's shoulders slumped.

"You've got a lot of nerve, acting as though you sent an aid team to our rescue." Colonel Parker's voice was instantly recognizable. His tone made Michelle glad she wasn't in the room with him. His words sounded clipped, with danger buried beneath, and not too deeply at that. "While in fact, a bunch of juveniles insinuated themselves behind my walls, then carried out your plan. I'll admit, their acting was brilliant. I took them for spoiled children at first."

"I designed no plan against you, Mark. Their orders were simple, to repair communications, nothing more."

Michelle's clenched a fist. *Yes! That's my great-grandfather, talking to the crazy colonel. In a few hours Institute helicopters will be here to rescue us. G.G. loves me. He'll move heaven and earth to get me back.*

"Then explain the actions they took against my people, in a direct violation of my authority as the ranking military officer of this district," the colonel spat.

"What actions?" Great-Grandfather was starting to sound irate. "What the hell are you talking about?"

"Don't pretend you don't know, old man. I've got twenty-two soldiers down, either dead or injured too badly for duty. And at least one of them was gunned down by your very own spawn."

"Michelle?" The Founder sounded stunned. "Michelle…shot a man?"

The colonel laughed harshly. "What, you didn't think she had it in her?"

"Oh, no," Great-Grandfather said. "That's not it at all. She's done this kind of thing before, but," the old man barked out a short laugh, and muttered, "only to Normals."

Michelle's mouth twisted in an involuntary expression of horror. *G.G. had to go and tell Parker about that?* A memory flooded her mind. *A Normal girl, fighting off multiple attackers, just plain lucky that Michelle and her friends were looking over the wall into the slum that day...It wasn't murder—anyone would have done the same.* She forced her attention back to the present.

"You trained them on Normals? How very brutal," the colonel purred. "But such a clever idea. Kids, too young to arouse suspicion, and yet, so well trained. My compliments."

G.G. snorted. "That's not what I meant! I don't know what went on there, but they're not assassins, Mark."

"I hope you know Michelle's unique mutations won't stop me from having her executed when I find her. After my doctors surgically remove her ovaries, of course," the colonel said.

A sick twist of fear spiraled up Michelle's chest and lodged itself somewhere behind her breastbone.

"Yes, that's regrettable," the Founder answered evenly. "But one doesn't take a king without sacrificing a few pawns."

Michelle went rigid with shock. Her world crumbled.

"You'd just throw her away? I don't believe it," Parker scoffed.

"As you're so fond of pointing out, I am an old man, Colonel. I've had hundreds of children. After a few centuries, a man gains perspective on that kind of thing. Look at it this way. I invested six of our offspring, and I took twenty-two of yours. If it ends today, I'm already ahead."

"It won't end today."

The line went dead. Michelle powered off the communicator and lay in the darkness alone.

Chapter 14: Dillon

A Baited Trap

Sunshine beamed down on a flower-filled meadow. Dillon sat cross-legged on the grass, the focal point in a circle of teenage girls and young women. Most of them were beauties, and Dillon was the only man there. Under the circumstances, he couldn't enjoy it much.

"Dillon, tell them what you told me," Tina said. "About my little sister and the other missing girls."

Dillon tried to talk but his throat tightened up. He managed to choke out a few words. "They...aren't coming back."

Tina only waited a couple of heartbeats before she got impatient and told the story herself. "The same thing happens to all the missing girls. Creepy doctors get them pregnant with more of those...those..."

"Enhanced," Dillon supplied.

"Enhanced babies. They're transferred from women who think they're too *perfect*," Tina spat the word, "for pregnancy."

"Eeuw," a girl murmured. "They can do that?"

"That is jus' wrong," another girl said, shaking her head.

Dillon interrupted the cross talk. "After the babies are born, they don't need the mothers any more. We don't know for sure, but we think they probably kill them."

A collective gasp rose up from the circle of women. A few of the younger ones began to cry.

Dillon squirmed under the pressure of a dozen pairs of eyes. *They're expecting me to have all the answers, and I don't.* "I've got a plan, though. It's scary as hell, but if you help me, we might be able make it work."

"Scary as hell?" Tina repeated, with a trace of her old abrasive manner.

Dillon wilted under the women's dubious stares. "Well, um, yeah. This might be kind of half-baked, but it's all I can think of. I have two ideas, and they both start the same way. A bunch of girls, all alone in the woods—except for the men hiding all around them."

"Oh, shit!" Tina exclaimed. "We're the bait."

Dillon nodded. "Yeah. So, like I said, we can do this one of two ways. The first way's less scary, but also less likely to be successful."

"Just tell us what it is, Dillon," Tina snapped.

"Okay. I need you girls to go off in the woods. Light a big fire. Sing and drum, make yourselves real obvious out there. I'm betting Enhanced soldiers will show up and try to grab you." Dillon waited for the moans to die down before continuing. "They'll dart you from the trees with tranquilizer guns. If you get hit, you'll pass out. Then they haul you off. We can try and prevent that, shooting 'em as they arrive. But they'll scatter and run, and it'll be hard to see them in the dark. Besides, they have night-vision goggles and fully automatic rifles, and we don't. A bunch of us could die."

"Probably will, you mean. What's your other plan?" Tina asked. "Because I don't care what it is, I'll take it. Just about anything would be better than that."

Dillon winced. "My other plan is…we let them dart you."

All the girls cried out at once. "What! Why?"

"A man's a lot easier to catch with a girl over his shoulder."

Tina swore. "I hate you, Dillon."

"Yeah, I know. Sorry." Dillon got to his feet, shoulders slumped. "You don't have to do this, you know. Talk it over. Find me once you decide."

Tina spoke slowly through clenched jaws, her words clipped. "Sit down. I already decided. I'll take the fucking dart."

***

Dillon set the trap as close to Iron Torr as he dared without making it obvious that they were trying to lure the soldiers out. It took most of the day to find the perfect spot, a flat patch of ground ringed with trees. A rocky ridge a few miles away made a good meeting place in case people got separated in the fighting.

Tina and five other girls volunteered to bait the trap. They hiked in early, taking a detour to avoid the Torr, and set up a few small tents. The women moved restlessly about, gathering wood for a giant fire. This blaze would burn on a flat bed of rock for maximum visibility.

As the sun sank low and the inevitable evening breeze began, three old women hobbled into the camp. Teen boys followed them, carrying their packs. Wade ran over and took the lead crone's elbow to help her over a rough patch of ground.

The old lady slapped his hand off. "I can walk, damn it!"

Dillon turned away to hide his smile and caught Tina smiling too. "I guess I'm not the only one who's nervous," he said.

Tina's beaded braids jingled as she shook her head. "Stella's always like that." She moved to Dillon's elbow and lowered her voice. "Um, Dillon? Got a second?"

"Sure."

A rare flash of vulnerability crossed Tina's pretty face. "It's about my sister. Soldiers took her about eight months ago, so the baby should be born soon. If what you said is true, they'll let her live a couple more months after that. Any chance we can get her out in time?"

Dillon stared over Tina's head at the dark shape of Iron Torr, rising above the forest. *Getting someone out of there would be practically impossible.* "There's always a chance. Let's get through tonight first, if we can. Then we'll talk about it."

Tina gave him a shaky nod. "Okay. Um, one more thing? Tonight, when they grab me…if you can't see us in the dark…just take the shot. Seriously. Even if you hit me. I can't stand the thought of going inside that tower. I'd rather be dead. Promise me."

"Okay," Dillon managed. "I promise."

A tear tracked down Tina's face. Before Dillon knew it, his hand was on her cheek, gently wiping it away. The Normal girl buried her face in his tunic and shook with silent sobs. Dillon slid an arm around her narrow waist and pulled her body against his. A primal thrill surged through him when she didn't pull away. Her braids slid between his fingers, wild and exotic. Pressed close, the effect she had on him would be hard to hide, but it didn't matter. They could both die tonight. Tina gazed up at him with smoldering eyes, and Dillon knew she felt the same way. He didn't let her go until his men gathered at a polite distance, awaiting orders.

Dillon posted snipers in the trees around the fire circle, and more along the best path back to Iron Torr. On his instructions, men scooped out shallow nests, just big enough to lie down in. They got in position and waited while women tossed blankets over the top and hid them under apron-loads of dead leaves, moss, and pine cones.

"Add lots of dirt," Dillon told the girls. "Use damp earth if you can. The soldiers have infrared goggles—they sense body heat. That's how they've been finding you in the dark."

Night came quickly, like it always did whenever Dillon dreaded it. One by one, men disappeared up trees and under camouflage. The girls and old women went back to the fire circle to prepare for some mysterious ritual.

Tina saw Dillon standing alone and came over. "You're the last one. I'll help you get hidden."

Dillon chose a spot at the edge of the circle and scraped out what looked far too much like a shallow grave. Together he and Tina gathered loose stuff from the forest floor and piled it by the hole.

"You ready?" Tina whispered.

"No." Dillon stepped into the grave anyway and sank to the ground, rifle tucked tight against his left hip. The arctic soil immediately began sapping heat from his body, and he shivered.

Tina knelt beside him and spread an old wool blanket over his feet and legs. Her lips moved in a whispered prayer.

Dillon knew he had to lie down, but he had trouble doing it. "Tina, I feel like I'm dying. I…I'm being buried alive."

"You are, in a way," Tina murmured, pushing damp earth over Dillon's legs. "But you'll be reborn. That's what this ritual is about. Maidens and crones. Death and rebirth. The circle is unbroken."

Dillon stared into the golden light of the fire circle. Girls in long, colorful skirts moved around the circle, lighting incense and placing statues of gods and goddesses on a central altar. Stella, the elderly priestess, seemed to feel his gaze. She turned and looked right at him with bright, birdlike eyes. In the firelight her face seemed to flicker, old and young and old again. *Maidens and crones. Death and rebirth.* Dillon forced his gaze away.

"Dillon, no man has ever seen this rite. It is one of the women's mysteries. You must never speak of it," Tina whispered.

With one gentle hand on his chest, she pushed him down. Trembling, he succumbed. The canopy of the forest spread out above him, fading to gray-green in the dying light.

Tina bent over him just long enough to press her lips against his, warm and sweet. "Tonight, I'll die too. But I know you'll bring me back."

Pressure on Dillon's body grew as Tina buried him, feet and legs first, moving up to his chest, and then, horrifyingly, his neck. When the suffocating blanket went over his head Dillon thought he'd surely scream. Fine soil sifted through the wool, coating his face and getting up his nose. He gritted his teeth, squeezed his eyes shut, and lay still, fingers on the butt of his rifle. Last of all, Tina placed a few lightweight pine boughs over Dillon's head, so he could peek through them as he emerged. Her soft footsteps grew fainter as she walked away.

Wind softly rustled the aspen trees above his grave. A faraway flock of birds chirped as they settled in for the night. Dillon flinched when a drum sounded, deep and slow. In a moment, more drums joined in. Tina began to sing, and her high, clear voice sent chills up his spine. The haunting, beautiful melody was a familiar one, one he was surprised to hear so far from home. He'd heard it too often during the plague in the Warren. It was a death song.

When that song ended, Stella's voice rose in an ancient chant. Girls joined in. Magic began to thrum through earth and air. Dillon felt the soft vibrations of women's feet, all dancing in unison. He pictured them hand in hand, circling, achingly beautiful in the firelight. Waiting to die.

And be reborn, Dillon reminded himself. *If I do my job right.*

Hours passed while the rocky ground grew more uncomfortable beneath Dillon's body. Women continued to drum and sing around the fire.

Uncle Mark keeps his window open at night, if it's not raining. He's got to be able to hear them. Will he come?

Stella's voice rose in one final shout and then went silent. Drums tailed off until the last rhythm died. Soon the soft clinks of spoons in bowls told him the girls were eating dinner. Someone laughed, a high, nervous sound.

Then Dillon heard the soft thud of a boot on loam. *They're coming. Oh*

Gods. Is Uncle Mark with them?

Dillon froze, praying the girls would stop talking so he could hear. His heart began to pound, and he regulated his breathing, hoping Enhanced ears hadn't already heard it. *Crunch.* Someone stepped on a pinecone and then froze. In a moment, slow footfalls began again. Dillon's right hand found the wool blanket near his face and gripped it.

Wait. Let them fire.

Tranquilizer guns went off all around, but the sounds were mere pops compared to the mountain-rocking booms of automatic weapons fire. Darts hissed through the air. Women screamed. Nauseating thuds marked the spots where their bodies hit the ground. A few girls panicked and bolted into the night.

"Run 'em down," an officer bellowed.

Booted feet pounded past his hiding place, and it took all Dillon's will not to move. One by one, tranquilizer darts slammed into their targets, and the women's cries subsided into silence.

Unable to stand it anymore, Dillon tugged the blanket off his face. Fragrant pine needles prickled his cheeks as he blinked dirt from his eyes. The moon stood directly overhead, shining brightly enough to let trees cast faint shadows. One shadow detached itself from the rest and moved toward the downed women. As it neared Dillon's position, the shape resolved itself into a black-uniformed soldier. No longer trying to keep quiet, the man strode over to join his squad. With rustles and grunts, soldiers hefted unconscious girls onto their shoulders.

Dillon clutched his rifle in one hand and the blanket in the other, ready to spring. Above his head, aspen branches shifted fretfully, leaving faint luminous trails against the sky. The earth began to rise and fall beneath him, as if he lay on a boat that floated on a calm sea. *Oh, no. Not now. Focus.*

A line of men thumped past, steps heavy with the extra weight of their prisoners. Tiny jingles carried through the damp night air—the silver beads on Tina's braids. Dillon exploded from the ground, only a few strides away, and fired from a sitting position, instantly cutting the legs from under three soldiers. Men screamed. Comatose girls tumbled to the ground and lay still among writhing soldiers.

Arrows jetted from the trees while Norms fired captured guns wildly into the dark. Enhanced soldiers dumped their prisoners, took cover, and began picking archers from the trees. An injured man bellowed as he fell from his perch. Another one dropped from a big pine, eerily silent.

Dillon rolled under a bush and fired from his belly, killing a soldier but missing the man behind him. That man dropped his gun and raised his hands over his head. Dillon rose to his feet, rifle leveled, and walked closer. The soldier was young, slim, and blond-haired—not that his short hair showed under his helmet. But Dillon knew it was there.

"Tai."

"Dillon," Tai answered softly. His hands stayed over his head, immobile.

Behind Tai, willows raised their branches in cheerful imitation. Dillon frowned at them, and the branches drooped dejectedly.

Tai peered at him. "Uh, you okay, there?"

"No," Dillon said. "Come to think of it, I'm not. Not at all. You?"

Tai didn't move his hands, but he quirked his lip and gave a slight shake of the head. "Nope."

Dillon gestured toward a gap in the trees with the barrel of his gun. "Get out of here."

Tai didn't waste any time. He dropped his hands and backed into the shadows. His voice came from the darkness. "Thanks, Dillon. Good luck."

Tai turned and ran. Someone pounded after him and a rifle cracked. "Wooo! Got him," a Norm voice yelled. Abrupt gunfire silenced the man's triumphant shout.

Nausea set Dillon's stomach roiling. He hauled Tina's unconscious body into a fireman's carry and ran deeper into the forest. Bushes waved their branches at him. Crunching and tearing, enormous trees rose from the earth and walked the land. Dillon leaped their exposed roots. He clung to the girl's warmth, the only thing real in the world, and kept moving. When his strength gave out, he tugged her limp form into the bushes and collapsed beside her.

Beneath them, the breathing of the planet became a panicked gasping. The ground heaved up and down, bruising the back of Dillon's head. Willows wrapped their branches around him, cradling him against the onslaught. Dillon pulled the comatose girl against his chest, shielding her in his arms as he rode out the storm. He looked up at the stars just in time to see them disappear as leaves wove themselves over him.

Chapter 15: Michelle

White Feathers

Michelle hid for hours before she got the nerve to walk into the fake village. She sat by the edge of the fire pit, watching ash swirl in the breeze.

A few minutes later, Molly bustled out of the hut, drying her hands on a rough cloth. "I've still gotta make bread and gather firewood before everybody gets here," she told Wade over her shoulder. Suddenly she looked up and saw Michelle. For a split second her expression was priceless—shock, dismay, and guilt all rolled into one.

"Hi Mom, I'm home." Michelle didn't smile. She didn't get up.

Molly snapped into character and rushed over. "Oh, honey! Where've y' been, daughter?"

Michelle burst into tears. She wanted it all to be real, but it wasn't.

Wade hurried over too, pasting that familiar fatherly smile over his shocked face. "Ya poor girl, y' must've had a helluva time. Thank the Gods yer back."

Michelle didn't make any accusations. She wanted to see what Wade would say about her showing up at the wrong village, forty miles from where she was supposed to be. It turned out he didn't say anything at all. *Yeah, let's all pretend this is the other village. Or are there half a dozen of them? Do you ever lose track of which one you're in, because they all look alike?*

Instead of helping with dinner preparations like she usually did, Michelle just sat there and watched everyone. If it hadn't been so heartbreaking, she would have enjoyed watching the actors' faces when they arrived to find her on the wrong set. She knew about half of them. Apparently they didn't have enough people to create an entirely separate cast for each fake village.

A surprising number of people suddenly decided to go collect firewood with Wade and Molly. They huddled in the forest just out of earshot, whispering madly. They must have come to an agreement, because when they came back they all treated her like a returning hero. Her return was a "miracle," and surprise, they'd decided to throw a party that night, just for her.

Across the clearing, Wade sidled up beside Molly. "Wanna bring 'er out now, or later?" He glanced meaningfully at the hut.

"Now, I guess." Molly clearly didn't like the way this was going.

Michelle stared into the fire so they wouldn't guess she could hear them.

In a couple of minutes, Wade came back, carrying Jeanette in his arms. Molly hovered around, doing her mother hen routine. They settled Jeanette at the fire and lovingly tucked a blanket around her.

"I'll get you girls some dinner just as soon as it's ready," Molly said sweetly, and she hurried off.

"Michelle, you're here!"

"Are you all right, Jeanette?"

"No, I feel awful."

"That's because…" Michelle looked over to see Wade watching them intently. She took Jeanette's hand and sent a message. *None of this is real. It's like a movie set. They're trying to gain our loyalty and use us against the other Enhanced.*

"I feel weird." Jeanette slouched in her chair, head lolling from Wade's knockout potion. "Nothing seems real. It's like a movie set, only I'm in the movie, you know?"

Michelle sighed. "Don't worry about it."

Jeanette shifted her bandaged leg and winced.

"Funny, I got hurt in the same place," Michelle said. "What happened? Did you get shot?"

"I guess. I don't remember."

That's no coincidence. They made sure we couldn't run away.

Shouts came from the edge of the forest. Michelle left Jeanette dreaming by the fire and went to see what the excitement was all about.

"Clansmen 're here, " Wade grinned. "Let's go an' meet 'em!"

Michelle ran ahead, following the sounds of whooping and laughter. Sylvia arrived with her Norm family in tow, and from the other direction came Brian and his crew. The two groups mingled just outside the village. Michelle ran down and joined the group hug.

"Michelle, I'm so excited you're here," Sylvia exclaimed. "I was so worried, but my clan is awesome. You're going to love them."

"Yeah, we're going to need to talk about that," Michelle murmured, but no one paid any attention.

Brian caught Michelle up in his arms. He didn't even speak; he just buried his face in her hair and held her for a long time. As she melted against his chest, some buried anxiety inside her finally let go. They'd known each other since they were babies, and everything about him made her feel at home. When Michelle finally met his eyes she caught a wave of emotion, and it shocked her. Too much flowed past to make sense of it all, but she got that her thing with Dillon tore him up a lot worse than he let on, and she knew he thought she'd died. *I'm so sorry. Sorry that your new clan is a farce too.*

"Not your fault," Brian whispered in answer to her unspoken thought.

In that moment, Michelle's heart overflowed with love. Brian felt it too, and it made him smile.

Todd's arrival created another outburst of cheering and celebration, and then they all went up to the village together. Torches burned around the perimeter, giving the place a festive atmosphere. People hung around them, and no matter how hard Michelle tried, she couldn't get her friends away from the Norms.

"Jeanette is here, but she's not feeling well. She's dizzy and nauseous, and her leg is injured," Michelle tried.

"Did she…um, just arrive?" Todd asked meaningfully, and Michelle nodded. *At least someone's paying attention.*

Michelle watched the party with new eyes, seeing everyone play their parts. Some of the jokes seemed scripted, making her wonder if she read too much into every little thing. Laird and the brothers, Justin and Marcus, made a big deal over her, but when they filled her cup to the top with mead, Molly didn't say a word.

Wade took Michelle and the other girls aside. "The last group's arrivin' now, and I want to warn ya," he said seriously. "They got a young fella with 'em that's just plain dangerous. Don't get me wrong—we need him— especially with the hostilities goin' on. He's worth ten men in a fight. Jus' leave him be, girls. Okay?"

"Sure, Uncle Wade," Michelle agreed. "Thanks for letting us know."

Wade walked away, and Sylvia said, "Look, here they come. Which one do you think he is?"

"That one," Michelle pointed at a tall hooded man who shuffled along in the center of a pack of Norms. "It's got to be."

The Norms moved slowly into the village. Even from a distance the girls could see that people were deferential to the hooded man. His clansmen seated him in the best spot by the fire, upwind of the smoke, and brought him food and drink.

"They treat him like he's Colonel Parker or something," Sylvia laughed.

"Like we need another one of those." Michelle rolled her eyes. "Come on, let's see who's there." The girls strolled past, but they took a wide berth around the fire circle.

"Wade won't take it well if he warns us away from some nutcase and we run right up to the guy," Michelle murmured.

If Dillon's not with this group, it doesn't mean he's dead, Michelle thought desperately. *Maybe he's out in the woods somewhere. Look how long it took them to catch Jeanette.*

They slowed just outside the firelight while she scanned faces in the crowd. The big guy slumped in a chair with his hood up, refusing to talk to anyone.

Laird popped out of the crowd, gnawing on a meaty bone. "Heya, cousin. Come an' get some food before it's all gone."

"Sylvia, meet my cousin—" Michelle started to say, but a crash from the fireside interrupted her. The guy with the bad attitude stood up suddenly, knocking over a small table laden with food and drinks. He didn't care; he just bulled through the crowd, shoving people aside. The man moved away, out of the circle of firelight.

"Somebody needs to leash that animal," Michelle said, way too loud.

At the sound of her voice, he turned.

"Dillon!" Michelle squealed.

He ran toward her, and a couple of Norms leaped protectively between them. Dillon swatted one aside as Michelle sidestepped the other. When he reached her, Dillon took her in his arms and lifted her off her feet. Wade lost his mind, shouting and hanging on Dillon's arm.

"Uncle Wade, stop it," Michelle cried loud enough to be heard across the village. "This is Dillon, he's …"

Wade stopped, staring. "He's yer man? That one? Oh, Gods!" He let go of Dillon while his clansmen laughed. Some guy patted Wade's back and refilled his cup of mead.

Dillon kissed Michelle on the lips in front of everyone, making Molly jokingly threaten him with a big stick.

"Dillon, they don't do that sort of thing in public here," Michelle whispered.

"I don't consider myself bound by Norm customs," he growled, and he wasn't kidding.

"Molly's gonna be pissed," Michelle giggled, but Dillon picked her up and carried her into the woods anyway.

"That'n needs a white feather," someone shouted, and the party went on without them.

Dillon didn't put her down right away, and Michelle began to feel nervous. Something seemed different about him, and it took her a moment to figure out what it was. He smelled different, and not in the way guys do when they need a shower. He'd been in a state of fury for so long that his body chemistry had changed. The most primitive part of her brain identified those pheromones and sent warning signals that made her heart pound. She wiggled uncomfortably against his shoulder, but he didn't seem to notice. He kept on walking into the forest with long strides.

The sounds of the party were faint behind them when he set Michelle down in the moss under a huge old tree. He crushed her against him and kissed her hard, scaring her a little. A little frightened sound escaped her when he took her down on the bed of moss, but Dillon didn't stop. He'd never been so aggressive and demanding.

Afterward, he stroked her cheek with unexpected tenderness. "Gods, Michelle, I love you so much."

An hour later, they walked back into the village together. Men stared enviously while their wives frowned in disapproval. One pretty Normal girl openly glared. With a whispered apology, Dillon slipped away and said a few words to the girl, who only tossed her beaded braids and walked away. Michelle didn't care who Dillon talked to. All her friends were together again. She bounced over to join them by the fire.

Jeanette sat up and stared when she saw Michelle coming. "Oh. My. God. What are you wearing?"

Michelle grinned, showing off her loose cotton coverall. "It's my prison uniform. See, I'm number twenty-four. And check it out; it goes with this!" She picked up the colonel's raincoat, turning it so everyone could read the name on back.

The boys cheered and hung it in a tree like a trophy. Wade and Molly gathered to stare, along with the other clan leaders.

Molly pinched Michelle's thin cotton suit between her thumb and forefinger. "It's real," she murmured to Wade.

"By the Gods," Wade said loudly. "You escaped, an' came back to us. It's a blessed day."

Tears flowed down Molly's face. "Yer not wearin' that another minute," she announced. "C'mon, I got somethin' for ya."

She took Michelle back to their hut, and Michelle had to remind herself that she'd never set foot in there before. From the inside, it was almost impossible to tell the difference.

"I made ya these. It was gonna be a surprise," Molly said. "An' then, those soldiers came..." her voice trailed off, and she sniffled. Michelle tried to look touched. *What an actress. Too bad the soldiers are real, and she's not.*

Molly opened a box and pulled out a soft gray skirt and a homespun white peasant blouse. It went with a pretty embroidered belt. She helped Michelle out of the prison uniform, and she exclaimed when she saw the embroidered vest underneath, "Ya saved it!"

Michelle only nodded. It wasn't the same to her now, but she couldn't say that.

"Don'tcha look sad, darlin'. Yer home now. Run along an' have fun."

"Thanks, Molly."

Michelle ran back to her friends. "Okay, Jeanette." She twirled in front of Jeanette's chair, showing off the new outfit. "Better now?"

"That's kind of cute," Jeanette responded in a slightly stoned voice. "But the blouse goes off the shoulder, so you show some cleavage." Jeanette tugged Michelle's blouse down, making her blush. "Tell me you're not wearing it with field boots."

"It's all I've got."

"See? We have arrived in hell." Jeanette slurred her words a little, and the boys laughed.

"She's not drinking," Sylvia put in protectively. "I'm giving her water."

"It's that knockout stuff," Michelle whispered. "Did they wrap you in a tarp when they caught you?"

"Yeah," the others whispered, nodding.

"It was all over the inside. Didn't you smell it? Listen, we need to talk. I learned a lot of scary things," Michelle whispered, but she couldn't say any more. Molly and Wade stood over them, banging on the cast iron cauldron with a stick to get the crowd's attention.

"As y'all know, I run a respectable house," Molly announced loudly. "An' if this sort o' thing is goin' on…" She gestured meaningfully at Michelle and Dillon, and people sniggered. "We need t' make it official."

Norms applauded, and Wade stepped forward. "Seein' as how she ain't got a Da, I'm gonna do the formalities." He held up two white feathers attached to beaded leather strings.

A thrill went through Michelle. She didn't care if the whole village was a sham or not. This felt real to her. She checked with Dillon, and he smiled at her, eyes shining.

Wade stood before them with the feathers in his hand. "Does anyone object t' these two young people bein' promised t' one another?"

The question was obviously rhetorical, but Brian astonished everyone by standing up. "Yeah, I do." He rolled his thick shoulders in an unspoken challenge.

I can't let this turn into a fight. "I'm sorry, Brian, but—" Michelle began.

"You're sixteen," Brian interrupted. "Sixteen's too young to be engaged, and that's what this is. Feathers or diamonds, it doesn't matter. They mean the same thing."

Despite the chill, Brian only wore a homespun vest, showing his big arms and a section of flat, hard abs that disappeared under the low waistband of his jeans. Firelight glinted off his pale hair, turning it bronze. Michelle sat frozen, staring up at the kid she'd known since babyhood. Somehow, when she wasn't paying attention, he'd morphed into a demigod. *Designed by his mother, the famous Catherine Halstead. Good God, did she know how magnificent he'd be?*

Dillon glanced sideways at the slack-jawed look on Michelle's face, and he started to stand up. Bear grabbed his neck from behind and yanked him down again. "No ya don't, Freeman."

Michelle cringed, expecting the men to clash before she could get out of the way. When Brian noticed, his brown eyes went soft. He took a few steps closer, reached out, and touched a fingertip to hers. Emotions flooded her, alien testosterone-fueled urges for violence blended with love, wild lust, and a deep, loyal friendship that would last a lifetime. Michelle's eyes met his, pupils huge, and she couldn't hide a thing. With a trace of his old smirk, Brian sent a wave of ecstasy through their connection so powerful she almost slid off her log seat. Michelle had to close her eyes.

"Now you see why I object," Brian rumbled, low and gentle for Michelle's ears, and then again, louder, for the crowd. "Yeah. I object. I probably always will." He turned his back and walked off into the darkness.

"Well, if he objects, then I do too," Justin shouted drunkenly.

"Me too!" his brother Marcus yelled, laughing. Men Michelle didn't even know joined in, shouting protests and making claims of undying love. It was only a joke to them, but her eyes filled with tears. Wade took the feathers and left without a word.

The party ended on that low note. Molly helped Jeanette back into the hut, leaving Dillon and Michelle alone.

"I'm sorry, Dillon."

Dillon answered without looking at her. "You didn't do anything wrong. Neither did he, actually. According to tradition, he had every right to speak."

Michelle let her long hair fall forward to veil her face. *According to tradition, I'm pretty sure he crossed a line. Big time. Dillon doesn't know about it, or he wouldn't still be sitting here.* She shifted her thighs, still tingling from what Brian did to her. *Thanks a lot, Brian. Right in front of everyone.*

After she got Jeanette tucked in, Molly came back to the fire and squatted down beside them. "I'm sorry, hon. But y' gotta understand. We live all together here, an' if there's trouble, it upsets everybody. Ya can't be promised until that young man agrees."

Michelle nodded. Her tears had given way to anger, and she wanted to go have it out with Brian. Or maybe make love to him. She couldn't decide. He'd disappeared though, along with most of the other party guests.

"Maybe he'll take an interest in Jeanette, or that pretty dark-haired girl," Molly said.

"Sylvia."

"Right. Leave 'em alone together, things'll work themselves out. You can sit here fer a bit, but ya hafta come inside soon," Molly added over her shoulder as she walked away.

Michelle whispered to Dillon, "They were going to let us share a bed, but Brian ruined everything."

"Let us?" Dillon stood up suddenly. "I'm not asking for permission." He grabbed his cloak and pulled her toward the forest by the hand.

Michelle resisted. "It's damp out there, we'll freeze."

"Okay, then. I won't let you be cold," Dillon answered, but his voice sounded distant. He angrily kicked the wooden chairs away from the fire, clearing a space, and laid his cloak on the dirt.

"This is gonna makes waves, Dillon."

"Like I care. C'mere." Dillon wrapped Michelle in his cloak and held her hard against his chest.

She tried to relax, but the smell of danger was all over him. Later, Wade trudged outside to check on them. Michelle sighed in relief when he retreated back into a hut, muttering unhappily. Wade didn't like what he saw, but he wasn't dumb enough to cross Dillon.

Good call, Uncle Wade.

It wasn't quite morning when Michelle woke up. *Dillon still doesn't know how the Norms manipulated us. I need to tell him, and I can't risk being overheard.*

"Hey, wake up. Come with me, okay?" Michelle slipped out of the village with Dillon right behind her. They stopped in a tiny clearing where crumbling logs lay in lush beds of ferns, shadowed by immense trees.

"You find the perfect spot?" Dillon asked, wrapping his arms around her from behind.

"We need to talk in private," she tried, but he wasn't really listening. He kissed the nape of her neck, tickling the tiny hairs there with his tongue.

"In private, yeah. This blouse is so sexy on you." He tugged the hem of it out from beneath the beaded belt, and Michelle gave up on talking.

Sunlight filled the clearing by the time Dillon could listen to anything rational. They lounged together in the meadow while Michelle told him everything, including the truth about shooting the helicopter pilot and getting thrown in jail with the surrogate mothers. She even reminded him that she caused it all by enhancing the Norms in a botched attempt to cure the plague.

"You were trying to help people," he said, reaching up to tuck his cloak around her bare shoulders. "Making them smarter isn't a crime."

She stretched out on her stomach and spoke without opening her eyes. "Oh yes, it is."

"Right, I should have guessed. It is, at the Institute." He sighed. "So who knows about this besides you?"

"Brian."

"Great. Exactly how pissed is he?"

Michelle shrugged.

"It's gonna be okay." Dillon stroked her back softly with his fingertips as he spoke. "We won't be going back to Iron Torr, that's for sure. How far would you say it is back to the Institute?"

"About two thousand miles."

Dillon sighed. "Long walk. And there's a huge mountain range between here and there."

"So we either spend a year walking home, or we stay here," Michelle said.

"Sure. With a bunch of psycho-genius Norms, killing our own kind."

At that, Michelle pushed herself up on her elbows and gave him a concerned look. Dillon held out his palm, and she rolled over on her side to press hers against it. His thoughts were too chaotic to make much sense, but she saw bloody scenes of combat. The Norms had already used Dillon to kill his own kind.

He let go almost immediately and stretched out on his back beside her, staring up blankly at the leafy branches. "Michelle, you know what the worst thing is?"

"What?"

"Once I lost you, it didn't matter which side I was on."

Tears welled in Michelle's eyes. "That's not true," she murmured. "You're a good man. You made a choice...you made the right choice."

Michelle pressed her palm over his heart, but she couldn't touch these wounds. They ran too deep. She put her arms around him and tried to heal him the only way she knew how.

Chapter 16: Michelle

Hard Choices

Breakfast was over by the time Michelle and Dillon returned.

"Where've ya been, cousin?" Laird smirked.

"Hunting," Michelle lied.

"An' ya came home with nothin'? Maybe that's 'cause ya forgot yer spear," Laird teased, but he made sure to quit before Dillon got mad. All the Norms tiptoed around him.

"Got one I can borrow?" Michelle called after Laird as he walked away. "I left mine…" She almost blurted *at the other village.* "Um, someplace."

"I'll see what I got." Laird came back with two bows and a quiver full of arrows. He sat down with Dillon and Michelle by the fire, but when he saw Brian coming, he suddenly found a job to do somewhere else. Brian sat on the opposite side of the circle, but said nothing.

Michelle hated uncomfortable silences. "Hey, Brian. We're going hunting."

"Fine. So go."

"All of us. Including you. Can you round up Todd and the girls?"

Brian got up and walked away without a word. Michelle wasn't even sure he meant to do what she asked until he came back with their friends. Except for Jeanette, they all carried longbows and quivers full of arrows. Michelle didn't care; she only wanted to get them out of the village so they could talk.

Molly and Wade jumped up at the sight of all the Enhanced teens leaving at once.

"Bye, going hunting," Michelle called. "We'll be back by dinner time."

"You kids don't hafta do that," Wade tried. He trailed them but everyone kept walking.

"Sure we do, Uncle Wade," Michelle said cheerily. "You have no idea how much these boys eat!"

Behind them, Wade and Justin sat on a log, hurriedly tying their boots. "Good luck keeping up, Norms," Sylvia said softly. The teens broke into giggles as they ran.

After only a mile, Jeanette's injury forced her to stop. The boys led the way into the best hiding pace they could find, a chokecherry thicket. By the time Michelle joined them in the shady grove, Brian and Dillon were already locked in a battle of wills, glaring at each other.

"Stop it," Michelle said. "We have more important problems. Join hands."

The boys both knew what was coming, and they didn't want to be linked, even from opposite sides of the circle.

Michelle sighed. "Please, you two, just do it." She composed her thoughts so she'd make sense. Then she took hold of Sylvia's hand on one side and Jeanette's on the other, and silently she told her story.

Afterward, tears ran down Sylvia's face. "They separated us on purpose, so we'd bond to them. And I bought it, totally."

"Did your village look like this one?" Michelle asked Sylvia.

"Exactly." Sylvia wiped her cheeks. "You know what really hurts? I thought they really loved me. I know I loved them. I still do."

"I have to admit, their plan was brilliant," Jeanette said. "It worked on all of you. But they never should have made the villages identical. That's what tipped you off."

Michelle nodded. "That and the script. I overheard them when I escaped from the Torr and wandered into the wrong village. They said the exact same things to me as they did to you."

"They memorized lines?" Jeanette repeated disdainfully. "That's stupid."

"They're only Norms, Jeanette," Michelle said softly.

Todd wasn't surprised. "I knew something strange was going on. Their words and their thoughts didn't always match."

Brian laughed harshly, making all their eyes turn his way. "Nice going, Miss Atherton," he said sarcastically. "Tactical genius was rare among savages, but you fixed that for us."

"Brian, you bastard!" Michelle scanned the faces around her, but no one looked at all surprised. "You told everyone? After you promised you'd keep my secret."

"I didn't say anything."

"Liar. You obviously did." Michelle turned to the others. "I swear it was an accident. Brian and I raided Salomon's lab that night the Norms broke into the Institute. I released one of the doctor's viruses, as a vector, you know, carrying Enhanced genes. I thought it would cure the plague, not kill more people."

Jeanette put a calming hand on her back. "Relax, Michelle. The Conclave can't cull you now. Besides, Brian didn't tell us that you enhanced the Norms."

Michelle glanced at Dillon, and he shook his head slightly. *He didn't talk either.* "Why's it public knowledge, then?"

"It's not public. Only the six of us know," Jeanette said.

Michelle glared.

"Okay, okay," Jeanette said. "Not that it's any of your business, but a few days ago, Brian and I, um, linked." She flushed at Michelle's raised eyebrow. "Mentally, I mean."

"Whatever. Do what you want."

"So I found out then, and then Todd lifted it off me, and he accidentally told Sylvia, when they were...um, touching, I guess." Jeanette glanced sideways at Sylvia's outraged expression and backpedaled. "I don't know, I wasn't there. And apparently you told Dillon yourself, so that part wasn't my fault."

Michelle folded her arms and stared angrily out into the forest.

"Maybe the enhancement could be reversed," Brian suggested coolly. "If the Conclave knew, or the doctors at Iron Torr."

"Brian, don't you dare," Jeanette exclaimed. "I'm not going to let you endanger Michelle over a trivial case of teenage angst."

"Trivial? Sample it, I dare you. See for yourself." Brian held out a hand to Jeanette.

Jeanette unexpectedly took his hand, and Michelle scrambled out of the bushes as fast as she could. *She could hate me after this.*

People followed her out, leaving Jeanette and Brian alone. Michelle prowled the forest for an hour before she dared to go back. Jeanette sat alone, crying under a tree. Michelle signaled Dillon to wait at a distance, and she went over and gave her friend a hug.

"Michelle, I feel like such an idiot. He totally knows how I feel about him, and he doesn't care. I tried to hide it, but we were linked, and...."

Michelle nodded sympathetically but said nothing.

"He loves you, Michelle, and he's like...like...." Jeanette broke down and sobbed, but part of what she tried to say sparked out of her skin where her arm touched Michelle's. Michelle tried to shield herself, but the emotions came through. Even secondhand, Brian's pain was unbearable. Michelle wanted to run after him and hug him, somehow make this all okay.

"Don't," Jeanette whispered. "That'll just make it worse."

"Jeanette, do you think he'll turn me in for how I altered the Norms?"

"I don't know. If he does, deny it. Blame Salomon."

After a moment, Jeanette spoke again. "I don't think he will, Michelle. He's angry and hurt, but I can't imagine him doing that."

Michelle stood up, glancing at Dillon, who still waited for her in the forest. "Look, I've got to go. We're supposed to be hunting, remember? We should bring something back."

"You're going to kill an animal? That's disgusting. Can't you find some berries?"

"You can't feed men on nothing but berries, Jeanette—they'll starve. And there's not much to eat in the village. If Brian comes back, keep him with you, okay? I don't want us all to get separated again."

Michelle and Dillon went off with the others, leaving Jeanette there waiting for Brian. They bagged a couple of quail, and then Todd made an incredible shot that took down a little doe. The girls cheered, and he smiled proudly.

When they returned to the chokecherry copse, Brian and Jeanette were still there, leaning on a tree with their eyes closed. Only their fingertips touched. The hunters waited for them in silence. When the connection broke, everyone walked back to the village together.

At the edge of the clearing, Michelle found an ugly surprise—Slade. She stormed up to him, ready to kick him in the balls. "What the hell are you doing here? You've got a lot of gall, coming back here after what you did!"

Brian and Dillon caught her by the arms and held her back. Slade backed off, but he didn't leave. He was dressed as a Norm again, with the braided leather piece in his hair. The white feather had been replaced with a gray one.

Michelle struggled like mad, cursing furiously. "You're wearing a mourning feather. That makes me sick! You could have saved Maya if you wanted to."

Slade shook his head, looking ill, and said nothing.

Sylvia got between them. "What's wrong with you, Michelle? Stop it!"

"Okay. Fine. I'm done." Michelle relaxed, and the guys let her go. She exploded forward and side-kicked Slade in the stomach. He fell on the ground, gasping, while men ran out of the huts.

"Freeman," bellowed a big brown-bearded man. "I tol' ya, no fightin'!" The man charged over, moving fast for a guy with a big gut. He crowded Dillon, who just looked at him innocently. Michelle noticed that Dillon didn't blame it on her. No one else did, either, if you didn't count Sylvia's glare.

"I'm all right now, Bear," Dillon said. "See? I'm calm, happy—I've got my girl back." He put his arm around Michelle while Bear looked him over.

"Good. Stay that way," Bear said shortly. He nodded politely to Michelle and then turned around and walked off.

Wade and a bunch of other men clustered outside a hut. "He's calm now, 'e says," Bear told them sarcastically.

The men laughed. "What's that mean? Slade ain't dead, so that counts?"

Slade struggled to his feet and limped back toward the fire circle. No one moved to help him.

"Look how easy they're being on us," Michelle whispered to Dillon. "They don't want to run us off."

The teens walked into the village, with Todd carrying the dead deer over his shoulders. Wade hurried over to help. "Me an' Laird'll take it from here, Todd. Hunters don't have t' help with butcherin'. We'll portion out the meat an' make sure folks know it's from you."

The Enhanced boys strolled over to relax at the main fire circle, while the girls dutifully followed Molly to her little cooking fire. That irked Michelle, especially since she brought home meat almost every day, like any man. Normal women weren't hunters, so this complicated Wade's life. He'd solved the problem by dubbing Michelle's hunting a "hobby" that didn't get her out of women's work. She gritted her teeth and tried not to complain.

That day, Molly wouldn't let anyone help. "Soup's on. Don't you lift a finger, everything's coming along fine."

"Really? Thanks, Molly." The girls walked away.

"See? I told you they're being easy on us," Michelle muttered. "Molly always makes me cook."

Tiny gurgles and cries came from the fire circle. Sylvia's face lit up. "Babies!"

The three girls hurried to the big fire circle in the central clearing. Surrogate mothers gathered there, holding infants that weren't theirs. Slade and Dillon sat among them, side by side.

Sage jumped up to hug Michelle. "You're free! Come sit with us. Tell us everything."

Michelle hesitated. She didn't want to be anywhere near Slade, but he wasn't moving. Sage noticed and fell silent.

"Michelle, at least talk to me," Slade pleaded.

Surrounded by infants, Michelle wasn't about to start a fight, so she gave Slade a chilly look and ignored him.

Dillon poked the fire with a stick. "It's only fair to hear him out."

Michelle reluctantly took a seat. "Okay, *Lieutenant* Parker. Talk if you want to talk. Why don't you start by telling me how you got all of them," she waved a hand at the surrogates, "over fifty miles from the Torr in just two days."

"I hid them the first night, and then I ...I betrayed my father. I stole one of his zodiacs, and I sabotaged the other one. That left him with nothing, since the Norms stole our third boat last year."

"You betray everyone eventually, Slade. Whose side are you on? Your own?"

"I could ask you the same thing. "

Michelle tossed her head and looked away, eyes narrowed. The surrogates whispered to each other and then tactfully took their babies and walked off.

"Michelle, nothing you see here is real," Slade whispered. "It's a ruse, designed to gain your loyalty."

"I know all that. I'm not stupid!"

"The thing with Maya...it was fake too. They made her do it."

"I don't doubt it." Michelle pressed her lips together in a hard line. "But however it started, she loved you at the end. And you let her die."

Slade put his head in his hands. "I didn't think they'd shoot her."

Michelle bit back an angry retort and just watched him, reminding herself that Slade was Colonel Parker's son. He wasn't stupid either. *What if all this is an act?*

"I can never go back now, after I helped steal the babies," Slade whispered. "My father will kill me."

"I'm sure he would. Half those kids are his. He sent you out here in the first place, didn't he?"

"He made me spy on the rebels, and they used Maya to try and turn me."

"Did it work?" Michelle asked bluntly.

Slade didn't answer. He fixed her with a hard look, and then he got up and walked away.

Sylvia came over and took his seat. "Don't piss him off."

"Why not?"

Sylvia's gentle gaze followed Slade through the village. "It isn't his fault. Imagine how hard it must be to be the son of a man like Parker. You ought to have some sympathy for that, considering how horrible your father was."

Michelle shrugged. "Any sympathy I may have had for Slade evaporated the day he let Maya die."

Sylvia persisted. "Plus, if you make an enemy of him, he could run home and tell them where we are. My clan could be killed."

"They're not your family, Sylvia," Michelle snapped, but she shut her mouth when Wade came out of a hut, followed by a group of grim-looking men.

"Hey, Freeman," Wade called, taking an unusually respectful tone. "Wanna join us fer a minute? We'd appreciate yer take on somethin'."

As Dillon stood up and began to follow Wade into the hut, Todd appeared on the edge on the clearing. The skinny blond-haired boy weaved a little as he walked.

Michelle swore softly. "Look at your brother, Jeanette. He's been drinking."

Todd wandered through the camp, managing to bump into practically everyone on his way to the fire circle. "Sorry, Wade." He grinned sheepishly, spun off and immediately bounced off Bear. "Oh, sorry."

The big Norm punched Todd on the shoulder. "Watch where yer goin', boy."

Bear, Wade, and Dillon disappeared into a hut, and the rest of the men trailed after them.

"Something's going on," Jeanette said, tracking them with her eyes.

Todd hopped nimbly over the stump beside Sylvia's, and then sat on it. All traces of his weaving walk were gone. Michelle got it and started to giggle.

Todd leaned forward and whispered. "I only got flashes, but from what I gather, they're planning an attack on Iron Torr. They want Dillon involved."

Sylvia curled up like she wanted to disappear. "Us too?"

Todd nodded. "Just don't say anything yet; they don't think we know."

Michelle waited for Dillon to come out of the hut, and when he finally did, they gathered their friends and went into the woods so they wouldn't be overheard. They all sat together on the grass. In some cryptic male peace offering, Dillon walked around the circle and deliberately took the spot next to Brian.

"Dillon, what did they say to you?" Sylvia demanded.

"The Norms are planning a combat operation. It starts in a couple of weeks, once the other clans arrive. And guess who they want to lead the troops?" Dillon looked around the circle to gauge their reaction.

"What troops?" Michelle interrupted. "They have, like, twenty guys."

Dillon shook his head. "Camps are hidden all through these woods. They've got hundreds of people. Thousands, by the time the outlying clans show up. The Norms have a pretty good plan, now that they have something the colonel wants."

Michelle glared. "You are not holding babies hostage."

"No, no. They just want to use them to lure some patrols into a trap."

"Dillon, that's even worse! You can't do that!"

"It wasn't my idea. That part's not my job, anyway. Bear asked me to go back to Iron Torr. I'm pretty sure I could get in; the military tried to recruit me, you know. Parker made me a sweet offer, with money and status like I'd never get at the Institute."

I wonder if he accepted. He must have been tempted.

"But the Norms want me to assassinate the colonel, which might screw up my chance at promotion," Dillon said with a wry grin.

"No! How can you even consider that, Dillon? It's a one way trip. Even if you kill him, you'll never get out alive!"

"Without Parker, and minus a few more patrols, the military will leave the clans alone," Dillon pointed out. "They can't keep kidnapping women and using them to make babies."

"Why not?" Michelle snapped. "You're using those same women and babies as bait. What you're doing is just as bad."

Dillon fell silent; and Michelle knew she'd made a point. "It's not our war, Dillon. We need to stay out of it."

"That means we'll have to leave and make it on our own," Dillon said. "It won't be easy. Both sides will hunt us down to keep the other side from recruiting us."

"What do you want to do, then?" Michelle asked. "Choose a side? It's okay if you all want to go back to the Torr, 'cause I still have my prison uniform, you know."

Dillon ignored her sarcasm and turned to Brian and Todd. "What's the best way to keep the girls safe?"

"That's ridiculously old-fashioned," Jeanette interrupted.

"Sorry, no offense," Dillon said. "But you've lived a sheltered life, and I haven't. I've seen things that would give you nightmares. And some of them happened to girls."

Jeanette tossed her head. "We can fight better than any Norm—"

Brian cut her off. "The best way to keep the girls safe is to keep them out of a war. We have to run."

Dillon met Brian's eyes, and the two guys nodded. That ended the argument. The teens slipped back into the village a few at a time to get their belongings. Michelle owned almost nothing, so she retreated to the fire circle and sat there alone. Behind her, Brian and Dillon sat together on the ground, talking in low voices. She watched them surreptitiously, but she couldn't hear what they were saying until Dillon stood up.

"Deal?" he asked.

The two men bumped fists, making Michelle wonder what they'd just agreed to. *Maybe it's a truce,* she thought, but the sorrow in Dillon's expression made her think again. She suddenly felt sure that she knew their secret. *They just agreed that if one dies, the other will take care of me.*

One at a time, Michelle's friends disappeared into the woods. She went last, walking casually at first, then faster, and finally breaking into a run. At the bottom of a slope she took one last look at the village that had become her home. *It's fake,* she told herself, but that didn't clear the tears from her eyes. Smoke from the central campfire rose through the canopy like mist. Under it, something moved. Michelle wiped her face on a sleeve and blinked. Slade peered intently through the leaves. She turned and ran.

Chapter 17: Michelle

Freedom

Michelle dashed through the forest with her friends, her spirits soaring. *We're all together again. We can do this!* With Dillon in the lead, they headed south in a tight pack, every stride taking them closer to home.

The terrain got steeper as the day wore on. By afternoon, the endless run wasn't so much fun anymore. As they gained altitude, large trees gave way to stunted ones, then to scraggly bushes. Above the tree line, only low growing alpine plants dotted the mountainside, giving them no cover. They'd be visible to anyone with binoculars, and if a helicopter flew overhead it would mean certain capture.

The little tribe scrambled over loose rock and leaped from one huge granite boulder to the next. Jeanette began to fall behind.

Brian waited for her. "This isn't a test, Jeanette. Let me help you."

She shook her head, refusing his offered hand. "I'm fine." Blood spread slowly across the leg of her jeans.

"No you're not."

Jeanette dragged herself a few more steps, then hooked a foot on a rock and tripped. Brian caught her before she tumbled down the steep slope. He lifted her into his arms. Tears streaked Jeanette's face. She made faint noises of protest, but she didn't have the strength to make him put her down.

Dillon ran ahead to check out a ledge near the summit. "Let her rest under here."

Michelle crawled under the overhanging rock with her friends, shivering in the cold, thin air. None of them had the right clothes, but hers were by far the worst. Wind blew under the gray skirt, and she'd stepped on its hem countless times as she climbed. Even the thin cotton prison suit would be better, but it was back in Molly's hut. She shoved her hands in the plastic pockets of the colonel's raincoat and turned her back to the wind. People had to huddle to fit in the makeshift shelter, but Michelle didn't mind. She was glad for the warmth. Jeanette needed it more—she looked pale and her skin felt clammy despite the chill.

"We're going to have to take a look at that wound, Jeanette." Michelle rolled up her friend's pant leg and untied the bandage. The wound bled freely, even when she pressed her palm against it. "Lie down. We need to elevate your leg."

Jeanette leaned back against her brother and closed her eyes. Blood dripped from Michelle's hands, staining the frozen earth, but she didn't let it bother her. "The bullet went deeper than they meant it to."

"What do you mean?" Sylvia asked, and then suddenly understood. "Oh! I got shot in the leg too."

"We all did, and no one remembers it. They did it while we were unconscious, to keep us from running off," Michelle said bitterly.

She tore strips from her skirt for a new bandage and applied pressure to the wound. A few minutes later, Michelle met Todd's gaze. "I can't get the bleeding to stop," she mouthed, trying not to upset Jeanette.

"Hold her," Todd whispered to Brian. The two boys switched places. Jeanette's brother took a breath, composing himself. "Try not to touch me while I'm doing this."

"Why not?" Sylvia blurted.

Todd turned on her. "I'm only good with machines, all right? And she's not a machine."

"Geez, sorry."

Todd focused and then passed his hand back and forth across the wound, not quite touching it. In seconds, the bleeding stopped. His sister collapsed against Brian with a sigh of relief. Brian stroked Jeanette's hair and whispered reassuring noises, but he looked scared. They all were. None of them had been so far from home before, with no hope of aid from anyone.

Todd slumped in exhaustion. "I blocked the pain, but I can't really heal it."

Michelle searched the faces of her friends. Todd was completely spent. Sylvia and Brian seemed tired but determined. Only Dillon looked okay. He wasn't even shivering. She wondered all over again what genetic trait he had that the military wanted so badly. Maybe whatever it was gave him that tough constitution.

"Your lips are turning blue," Dillon told Michelle, putting an arm around her for warmth. He turned to the group. "We can't stay up here for long; we need to get off the mountain before dark. But look down there. That's where we're going."

On the other side of the mountain range, ponds gleamed in the sun. The land looked rich, with blue rivers coursing through open meadows. Far away, a herd of elk moved as pinpricks against the vast landscape.

"Looks like good hunting," Michelle managed, trying to sound positive. "We'll just keep working our way south, and eventually we'll get home."

"Next year, you mean." Dillon added. "It's too late in the season to attack that mountain range."

"We don't have to walk all the way home, just close enough to make a call." Todd flicked his wrist, but only got a dull red light from his cell chip.

"Can we just rest for a few minutes?" Jeanette whispered weakly.

"Sure, hon," Sylvia said, squeezing her friend's hand.

They made themselves as comfortable as they could, cuddling like puppies for warmth. Michelle shook with cold, even though Dillon wrapped his arms around her from behind as she curled on her side. Finally Brian backed up against her to lend some body heat, still holding Jeanette in his arms. Dillon didn't seem to mind when Michelle put an arm around Brian and slid her freezing hand under his jacket. "I thought you all should know…Slade saw us go," she whispered.

"I know, I saw him sneaking, the weasel," Brian said. "Don't worry. If he trails us up the mountain, I'll kill him for you."

"You will not," Sylvia snapped, startling them all.

Todd and Brian started to laugh.

"It's not a joke," Sylvia spat.

"Okay, then," Brian said. "Sorry, Michelle, the weasel's under Sylvia's personal protection. I can't touch him now."

"You can't touch him in any case," Dillon said abruptly. "Because I'll rip your head off if you try."

For a tense moment, the group fell silent. Brian propped himself up on an elbow and looked over his shoulder at Dillon, who stared back, eyes dark under furrowed brows.

"It's all right, we'll never see him again anyway," Michelle murmured. No one answered.

Cold wind stirred Michelle's hair, but the slow rise and fall of Brian's chest comforted her. Eventually she fell asleep, tucked securely between the men she loved.

***

A week later, the whole world felt new. The tribe lounged in a sun-warmed meadow, replete from a feast of salmon and blueberries.

Only Dillon bustled around, putting the last few pine boughs over a frame of branches. "Hey, Michelle, it's done. Come on in and see."

She crawled into the dome house through the little round door and stood up inside. The space was roughly circular, with a rock-rimmed fire pit in the middle. A beam of sunshine came through a smoke hole in the roof. The hut felt cozy, with a thick layer of dried leaves and moss cushioning the floor. A deeper pile of moss made their new bed. Michelle sank down onto it, overwhelmed with gratitude.

"What's wrong?" Dillon asked. "You don't like it?"

"No, I love it! It's wonderful. I was just thinking, it feels like a long time since I've had a home, you know?"

"Yeah. It's not the Atherton mansion, but it's all ours."

Michelle wrinkled her nose at the mention of her unhappy childhood home. "I like it better than any mansion at the Institute. Thank you, Dillon.

You're amazing."

Michelle gave her boyfriend a quick kiss and then stopped, glancing shyly through the open door at the people right outside.

"I'll get us a deer hide for a door one of these days." Dillon beckoned her out of sight of the doorway.

She followed, kissed him a couple more times, but then backed off. They'd been careful of Brian's feelings since that day in the chokecherry thicket, and they kept public displays of affection to a minimum. There were plenty of opportunities for privacy in the forest, anyway.

The couple scooted outside to find the others busy building a communal longhouse from bent willows and strips of bark. The roof didn't look all that rainproof to Michelle, but she kept her mouth shut about it. Dillon went off to help the other boys with construction, and Michelle got to work on the leather breeches she was making herself. Sylvia and Jeanette sat down to help with the tedious task. Across the meadow, the boys worked shirtless in the warm sun, raising another section of framing for the shelter.

"He's really changed," Sylvia murmured, glancing at Dillon.

"Really? How?"

"He's putting all that game he kills to good use," Sylvia said. "Haven't you noticed? His shoulders are almost as broad as Brian's now."

Michelle nodded, the trace of a smile on her lips. Dillon had filled out, and he looked a little taller, too. Food was scarce in the slum where he was born, and he'd been lean and wiry. In the forest, on a diet rich in animal protein, he finally put on muscle. That reminded Michelle how young he was. Dillon was only seventeen, but he acted older than Institute guys his age. Boys in the Warren took on adult responsibilities early. At home he would have had a wife and a baby by now.

Michelle watched the guys appreciatively. "I thought you were going to say he's mellowed out. That's the biggest change I've seen. He's so happy here."

Brian came over, carrying something wrapped in a big leaf. He sat down on the ground next to Jeanette and handed the little package over. "I found something I thought you might like."

It held an assortment of berries, which Jeanette loved. "Thanks," she said casually, eating a few and then passing them down to share. Brian waited, obviously hoping for a warmer response, but he didn't get one.

After a moment of silence, Brian stood up. "Um, I should get back over and help those guys," he said. He hesitated and then walked away.

Sylvia shook her head in amazement. "I can't believe you ignore him like that. If a guy that gorgeous liked me, he wouldn't have to ask twice."

"I'm not about to catch him on the rebound," Jeanette said. "So if you want him, feel free."

"I couldn't do that," Sylvia protested, her eyes on Brian.

"You'd be doing me a favor, Sylvia. We know what happens to Rebound Man. Or woman, for that matter."

"What?" Sylvia scooted in closer, until the three girls sat in a triangle.

Jeanette leaned forward and lowered her voice. "It won't matter who he hooks up with after Michelle. The new girl won't last. She'll be all tangled up in his mind with the pain, and sooner or later he'll have to move on. So seriously, go after him if you want to. I bet you won't be sorry. Until I come and take him away, that is." She gave Sylvia a mischievous grin. "That guy's a keeper, and I'm not messing up my chances with him."

Brian took out his frustration on the stakes that secured the new building. He pounded them in with a stone-headed hammer he'd made himself in his first try at tool making. It broke on his last mighty swing, and the stone head flew off, nearly hitting Todd. Dillon laughed, but no one got mad. The guys gave up on construction then and went off hunting together.

***

Days melted from one into the next, and Michelle was happier than she'd ever been. She alternated between foraging for edible plants with the girls and hunting with the boys. They ate well, and she and Dillon had plenty of time for romance in the grassy meadows. She wished those days would never end, but every morning dawned a little colder. One morning Michelle emerged from her hut to find a horrible stench hanging over the camp.

Sylvia muttered from behind the longhouse. In a moment she emerged carrying strings of rotten fish. "Ugh. That experiment was a failure."

"Sylvia, what are you doing?"

"I tried to dry the fish. You know, to preserve it for the winter. I guess it needs to be cut up into smaller pieces, or smoked, or something." Sylvia headed off to dump the rotten fish in the woods.

"I'll go get some more, and we can try it again," Michelle called after her, suddenly worried about the future. Winter would bring deep snows and bitter cold. *We'll be lucky to survive until spring.*

She grabbed the net that Todd made and headed out alone, but Dillon caught up with her before she'd gone very far. He wasn't interested in fishing. She playfully ran away, and he chased her all the way to the stream.

"Help me set the nets." Michelle laughed, slapping his hands away. She tried to untangle the nets on the banks of the crystal clear river, but Dillon kept getting in the way. He put his arms around her and pulled her into the forest while she struggled against him, giggling. Michelle had never really tried her strength against his before, and he pinned her easily.

"Ha, caught you now," Dillon grinned, trapping her against a tree. He kissed her softly, letting his hands slide under her shirt. She ran her fingers slowly across his chest and down the hard-muscled stomach she loved. Michelle played with the top button of Dillon's jeans, deliberately teasing him.

He breathed faster, anticipating. Then a three-note whistle cut through the air.

"That's the alarm," Michelle gasped. Abandoning the fishing net on the riverbank, they ran for camp.

They arrived to find Sylvia and Jeanette dumping water and dirt on the fire, trying to put it out. Choking smoke and dust billowed into the air, making their camp more visible, not less.

Brian dashed into camp with Todd on his heels. "Leave it, let's go!"

"Get what you need, we gotta run!" Todd rushed around, throwing things into a hide bag.

Michelle dove inside the shelter and piled clothes and furs on the deerskin bed. Wrapping everything in an awkward bundle, she crawled back outside and ran to catch up.

"What's going on?" she gasped.

Brian pointed. An army massed like a swarm of ants against the bare granite of the mountain. Behind it, helicopters buzzed into the sky, barely visible against the horizon. "It won't be long 'til they're here."

Everyone fled into the forest, but Todd didn't let them get far. "We need to go to ground. We're way too noticeable on the move."

He led them up a red sandstone ridge not far from camp. Near the top, a rock fall created a small cave. "Uh, sorry," Todd muttered, and in a second Michelle saw why. Twig packrat nests littered the floor.

The rodents scurried away when the teens crawled in, but Sylvia still didn't like it, especially after Todd camouflaged the doorway with brush. "It's dark and creepy in here now," she complained, wrapping her arms around her knees so she touched the floor as little as possible. "I hate rats."

"Oh come on, pack rats are different," Michelle said, trying to ease the tension. "They're cute, they look like big hamsters."

"Shh," Todd cut them off. "People are coming."

"I don't see anyone," Sylvia said, leaning to look out the door. Todd reached out, slapped a hand onto her shoulder and squeezed. The black-haired girl felt what he did, and she shut up fast. Outside the cave mouth, the landscape seemed as empty as ever. Michelle lightly touched Dillon's arm and silently explained. *Todd feels people and animals—he senses the EM fields their nervous systems generate.* Dillon nodded. He knew that already.

Todd tensed, and outside the cave a few Norms came into view. The men slipped quietly between the rocks, gripping rifles. Helicopters thrummed closer, audible but out of sight, and machine gun fire echoed off the mountains. Michelle trembled, but she didn't make a sound. Norms ran for cover as a helicopter swooped over the cave in a strafing run. Bullets ricocheted off rocks and kicked up puffs of dust outside. One young man hid near the cave, wedging his body between some big rocks. Michelle impulsively moved to bring him in.

Jeanette put a hand on her arm, restraining her. "We already agreed, we're not taking sides," she whispered. "They're not after us."

An explosion shook the ground, and Michelle screamed. It didn't matter—no one could hear her over the blast. She ducked, covering her ears with her hands, and ended up with her face against someone's chest. He put his arms around her, and through her panic Michelle dimly realized that it was Brian. When the bombardment ended, she raised her head, and he let her go. Michelle was too frightened to be embarrassed, and no one else seemed to care.

Outside, the Norms bolted away at a run. The teens huddled in the cave for a long time, listening to sounds of battle moving slowly away. At twilight they crept outside.

"I can't believe we were camping close to Norms this whole time," Sylvia said.

"I don't think we were, or I would have known it," Todd answered softly. "They were probably pushed out of their village in the fighting."

"Where should we go?" Jeanette whispered, glancing nervously around. "Do you think it's safe to go back to camp?"

Michelle scanned the landscape for soldiers, but all of them were dead or gone. A few flies already buzzed over the corpses. "I guess so."

Back at camp, they found their shelters destroyed. A crater obliterated Dillon and Michelle's dome, and the longhouse had been reduced to splinters. Smoke hung over the valley like a weird fog.

"They mistook this for a rebel camp. We need to move right away," Dillon said. "Any idea where we should go?"

"Home to Institute Headquarters?" Brian asked sarcastically.

Dillon folded his arms and stared Brian down. "I thought we decided all this a long time ago. Look at those mountains. Crossing them will be hard enough in summer. If we start now, winter will be here by the time we get up high."

People gazed bleakly at the southern horizon, where forbidding white-capped peaks stood jagged against the sky.

Todd nodded. "That'll be a death sentence. We've got to hold on here for the winter, and then head south as soon as we can."

"Right, like we agreed, back on day one," Dillon muttered.

Michelle was barely listening. She just stared at the place her hut had been, feeling bereft. *Dillon built that with his own hands. For me.*

"Come on, let's move," Dillon finally said.

Michelle followed him numbly away. They moved every day or so after that, zigzagging to avoid Norm camps and military patrols. The boys acted unfailingly positive about everything, as though they'd secretly agreed to keep the girls' spirits up. Michelle's nerves were on edge, with or without the forced cheer. Gunfire sounded frequently, and almost every day they saw signs of war. Aircraft droned overhead, and they had to stay alert to avoid patrols from one side or the other.

The boys adopted the conflict as their new spectator sport. The game started with Brian and Dillon keeping score, and pretty soon all three guys were making bets and cheerfully arguing over the outcomes of skirmishes. It worried Michelle, who suspected they got too close to the action when they went off to watch the fighting.

"Norms two, Enhanced zero," Brian shouted after a particularly violent battle.

"Yeah, but the Norms got pounded with heavy artillery on the other side of that ridge," Dillon pointed out. "We all heard it."

"I know, but we only score what we see, that's the rule."

Dillon lost the bet, but he didn't seem to mind handing over his newly made quiver. The animosity between the two guys had all but disappeared, and they acted like friends again.

"What is it with boys?" Sylvia whispered. "Not ten days ago they were at each other's throats."

"Guys get over stuff a lot faster than girls do," Jeanette answered, taking an experienced tone like she was some kind of expert on men.

"If they get along well enough for us to survive the winter, its fine with me," Sylvia said.

Chapter 18: Michelle

Deep Winter

As fall gave way to winter, Michelle got her wish—the war ended. The Norms were snowed in wherever they were, and the military only patrolled by air. The tribe turned its attention to survival. Dillon and the other guys hunted relentlessly, but they burned a lot of calories doing it. Most of what they caught went into their stomachs, just to give them the strength to hunt again the next day.

Every day Michelle tightened the laces on her deerskin pants a little bit more, and tried not to complain. She hunted snowshoe hares with Jeanette and Sylvia, and netted fish from the river until the ice grew too thick to break. The girls pieced together hides into clothing until they all looked like cave people, but the cold went right through even the thickest fur. There in the high mountains, the cold was a palpable force, like nothing Michelle had ever experienced. Every trip outside triggered a countdown. How many more minutes until her feet froze? How long until she gave up entirely and sank into a snowdrift to sleep? After Sylvia did just that and almost died, Jeanette made a new rule. People had to take partners if they needed to go outside, even for short trips to get firewood or snow to melt into drinking water.

Michelle looked up from her sewing when the door opened and a gust of wind brought a flurry of snow inside. The boys came into the longhouse, carrying the carcass of a caribou between them. She jumped up to meet them, tossing aside the rabbit skin she'd been making into a mitten.

"Hey, great job," Michelle exclaimed, but then she got a better look at the frozen carcass. It had been gnawed by animals, and most of the meat was gone.

All three guys looked at her to see what she would do. Their faces were haggard with cold and fatigue. The other girls came over and fell silent, staring in shock at the frozen bones.

"Oh, um, that's okay." Michelle tried to be convincing, but she failed. "Good scavenging."

Sylvia got the hint and jumped on board. "Yeah, thanks, guys! Come get warm by the fire."

There was no post-hunt celebration that night, no dramatic story of the kill. Dinner consisted of a bland, saltless soup made of boiled strips of caribou meat, but at least there was enough to fill their stomachs. Afterwards,

Michelle and Dillon retreated to their bed on the other side of a hide partition. The longhouse had a trench down the middle, so fires could be lit along its length. The fire in their end of the building usually went out since no one sat in there during the day. Michelle brought a burning brand from the main room and re-lit it, stoking it well with wood. Her earthen water bowl had frozen again, so she set it near the fire and got in the hide bed, wondering darkly if she'd freeze to death in her sleep.

Dillon scraped some of the ice from his furs, but he succumbed to exhaustion before he finished and collapsed beside her. The wrinkled hide door didn't provide much privacy, but that wasn't an issue any more. Staying alive took all their energy.

"The snow…is getting really deep," he said softly, like forming words took more effort than he could muster.

"I've been trying to make snowshoes, but the last two pairs I tried broke," Michelle admitted. "I have a new design though, so maybe tomorrow…"

"Look…Michelle?"

Something in his tone made her roll over and look at him in the ruddy light of the fire. "Dillon, are you okay?"

"Yeah, mostly. But the other guys…" He dropped his voice to a whisper. "Don't tell anyone I said this, but…they can't keep up anymore, especially Todd. We wait for him a lot, and…it's getting worse."

"Oh, no," Michelle breathed. She didn't say it, but he knew what she was thinking. This trend could end in one of two ways—springtime or death.

"We've hunted out all the game here. I know it's bad, because we can't move on without shelter, but…" Dillon sighed and fell silent, leaving Michelle to her thoughts.

Packing everything and heading out into the subzero temperatures would be suicidal, but staying there might mean starvation. She pressed against Dillon for warmth and rubbed his leather-clad back with her mitten.

"Tomorrow I'll finish those snowshoes," she promised, but he was already asleep, his face pinched with hunger and exhaustion.

Michelle woke up in the morning with a plan. She slid quietly out of bed and piled her share of the furs on top of Dillon without waking him. After adding more wood to the fire, she pushed aside the hide door and quietly woke the other girls. They whispered together, fearful of alerting the boys. Then Jeanette and Michelle donned their warmest gear while Sylvia paced anxiously around the longhouse.

"Feed them all they'll eat every couple of hours," Michelle murmured to Sylvia.

"I should be coming with you."

"Someone needs to take care of the boys. They're… not doing well. Break the marrow out of those bones and cook that into their soup too."

Michelle leaned in so Jeanette wouldn't hear. "Check on Todd, he's…"

Sylvia nodded. "I know."

Neither of them mentioned it, but they were both worried about Todd. He had a gray cast to his skin, and his eyes seemed too big for his skeletal face. Weeks ago he'd frostbitten the tips of his fingers, and they weren't healing at all. Michelle refused to say it out loud, but she secretly expected him to die within the month.

Sylvia pulled out their last bag of dried berries from a hiding place under her pallet. "I've been saving these, but… it's time. Want to take your share with you?"

"No. Give mine to Todd."

Michelle borrowed Dillon's quiver and bow without asking, feeling like a thief. She and Jeanette hugged Sylvia goodbye and went out into the cold. Moisture inside their noses froze on the first breath, so their nose hairs felt all crunchy. The girls worked together, repairing the snowshoes and strapping them on their feet. A deep ache worked its way into Michelle's fingers, making them clumsy. The girls were both hypothermic before they finished.

"Want to go inside and warm up before we take off?" Jeanette asked, wiggling her toes and jumping up and down in place.

Michelle thought of the fire longingly, but she shook her head. "The guys might try to stop us if we do."

The new snowshoe design worked well, and the girls made good time over the snow. Exercise warmed their bodies, but deep breaths of the frigid air burned their lungs and the icy wind froze any patch of exposed skin. Michelle tied a rabbit fur over her face, breathing into it to warm her nose. Jeanette's face cover was made of white ermine, a gift from Brian.

"I hope you thanked him well for that mask. It's gorgeous," Michelle muttered enviously. Her rabbit skin always shed a little, and she constantly had to spit out hairs.

"Of course I didn't. I'm not stupid."

Michelle didn't argue the point, but Jeanette's stubborn rejection of Brian seemed ridiculous to her. It made no sense to postpone anything, now that they might not have a future.

"Look." Jeanette pointed with a mitten. "Those are their footprints, coming back."

A deep furrow showed where the guys had dragged the caribou carcass through waist high drifts. Floating over the top in show shoes felt easy by comparison.

"They made it a long way," Michelle said. "That means we'll have to go a lot farther to find game."

The great old conifers stood coated in ice, and nothing moved but snow swirling across the ground, pushed by the endless wind. The only colors in that harshly beautiful scene were the forest green of the trees and the white of the snow. The sky remained a dull gray, threatening more snow. By midday the girls had covered twenty miles, but the landscape remained empty except for pinnacles of rock scoured clean of snow by the wind.

"There's no game here." Michelle panted as they hiked up a steep rise. "But the boys bring something back every couple of days. How do they do it?"

"Todd."

"Oh, right. Well if he can do it, you can too."

Jeanette stopped and waved a hand in a slow arc, and then shook her head. "Maybe I'm no good at this. Or else there aren't any animals here. The only things I'm feeling are some kind of rodents, sleeping underground."

That worried Michelle more than ever. Even with Todd's ability to find game, this lifestyle had just about killed them all. *What are we going to do without him?* The girls took a break at the top of a small hill and looked around.

"I'm sorry. I thought for sure if we covered more ground we'd start finding animals," Michelle said.

Jeanette shrugged under her coyote fur mantle. "So did I, or I wouldn't be here."

The river wound through a gulch below, almost hidden under ice and snow. Michelle knew if she followed it, she would eventually come to Iron Torr. Dillon would be welcomed there, but she'd be imprisoned. They were only out there because of her, and her friends could pay for that loyalty with their lives. She stared down at the river, wondering if she should insist on going back. Strange plumes of steam wafted up from the riverbed and condensed into fog in the frigid air.

"Look at all that steam. Could it mean hot springs?"

The girls hurried down the hill to see, but the river flowed as cold as ever, coursing under interlocking plates of ice.

Michelle dropped to a tired walk and looked around. Wisps of steam escaped from small holes in the snow. "That's weird. I thought the steam was coming from the water, but it's not."

"Shh!"

"Why?" Michelle mouthed silently, but her friend didn't answer.

Jeanette ran awkwardly up the hill in her snowshoes. Michelle followed, hoping for a moose or a caribou. She got to the top, and her mouth fell open. "Whoa."

The snow on the other side had been beaten flat by the passing of countless feet, creating a road. The girls crouched on a snow bank above, looking down. At the moment no one passed, but one thing was certain. *People live here.*

Jeanette bounded to the edge and leaped off, landing as well as could be expected. Michelle thought about taking off her snowshoes for the jump, but her companion was already moving down the road. Michelle leaped, landed awkwardly, and hurried to catch up. The road lead to a pair of large upright rocks, and behind them stood a rough-hewn wooden door with a tiny round window near the top. The rest of the building was underground, dug into the side of a mountain. Michelle paused outside, impressed by the design. Dug in as it was, it would be invisible to anyone not coming straight toward the door.

"Come on, Michelle."

"I don't know if that's a good idea. What—"

The door popped open, startling them both. "Get in here! Y' can't hang around outside, you know the rules."

A rough hand on Michelle's coat made up her mind, and she skidded inside, her icy snowshoes clattering on the stone floor. An enormous female Norm slammed the door behind her. Michelle stared at amazement at the cavernous hall. The place looked like an indoor mall hewn of rock, with shops along the walls and passageways branching off in all directions. Lightly dressed people strolled by, talking and laughing together. At the bottom of a staircase, a huge fire circle stood surrounded by stone benches.

"Move it, girl." A fur-clad man clipped Michelle's shoulder on his way out the door. She shuffled out of the way and collapsed onto a bench, struggling to untie the ice-encrusted laces of her snowshoes. Skis and snowshoes cluttered the entryway, and a long wooden rack on the wall held an assortment of weapons, from rifles to spears.

"Y'okay, there?" The fat female Norm bent over the girls in concern.

"Jus' cold." Michelle tried to talk with a Norm accent, but she'd never been very good at it. Keeping her head down, she kept at the laces.

"Get t' the fire, warm yerself. Have some tea."

The snowshoes slipped from her feet, and Michelle obediently headed for the fire. The big woman smacked her in the back of the head with an open hand.

"Y' froze in the head too? Leave yer bow where it belongs."

Michelle glared, but she slid Dillon's beautifully made yew bow off her shoulder and added it to the collection on the wall, hoping no one would walk off with it. That would be hard to explain. Jeanette hung up their snowshoes, warily skirting the unpredictable Norm. They stumbled toward the fire on frozen feet, pausing halfway there to gape in amazement. Blue and orange flames jetted out from beneath a metal sculpture of logs and pine cones.

"It's a gas fireplace," Jeanette breathed. "They know how to use fossil fuels."

"They must have built this place before I enhanced them," Michelle said defensively.

"Of course they did! I'm just glad to be someplace warm, aren't you?"

The girls made their way over to the fire and took over the only unoccupied bench in the ring farthest from the heat. Groups of well-dressed teens mingled there, talking and flirting. As Michelle and Jeanette warmed up, they gradually stripped off their handmade fur cloaks and leggings. Finally Michelle went down to her last layer, the black embroidered vest and deerskin pants. She felt strangely light without her winter clothes.

Nearby, a Norm girl tossed her brunette braids, making a jingling sound with the silver beads at the end of each braid. Each bead held a tiny black feather, gleaming and perfect. The girl giggled with her friends, and Michelle looked up to see them all staring at her. Michelle hadn't seen a mirror in months, but if she looked anything like Jeanette, she was more than a little rough. She self-consciously stroked one of her last ragged feathers, noticing how torn and dirty her fingernails were. The Normal girls looked cute and clean beside her.

The pretty brunette tossed a broken-toothed comb into Michelle's lap. "Ya might try using it sometime," the girl said, and her friends laughed.

Michelle bristled, but Jeanette picked up the comb. "Thank you," she said evenly. The Norms stopped whispering to look Jeanette over. Even half-starved and wearing animal skins, Jeanette still carried herself like royalty. Her thinness only emphasized the perfect bone structure of her face.

Noticing the girl's eyes on her, Jeanette offered a few words of explanation. "We're refugees from the war. We've been surviving on our own out in the forest."

"Why didn't ya just...come inside?" the brunette quipped, but her friends didn't laugh. They just stared at Jeanette in shocked silence.

"Back off, Tina. Why d' ya always hafta be such a bitch?"

Michelle knew that voice. She stood up. "Laird?"

"Michelle!" A dark haired boy pushed through the crowd of girls, but he stopped short when he saw her. "Gods..."

Michelle had to laugh. "I know I must look like hell. We've been on our own since last summer."

The crowd of teens snapped to attention and then started murmuring. "All this time? How'd ya survive?"

Michelle didn't answer them.

"Looks like ya barely did," Laird said, looking her over. "Michelle...yer skin an' bones."

She grinned. "Yep. Got any food?"

"Yeah, o' course, cousin, come on."

Laird took a moment to greet Jeanette, who he hardly knew. Then he gathered up the girls' furs, wrinkling his nose at the wet dog smell, and led them down a stone passageway. Michelle turned her back on the teenagers and walked away without a word.

Hot, dry air blew out of vents at intervals along the floor. As Michelle warmed up, she became increasingly aware that it had been months since her last bath. The cold suppressed smells, but it wasn't cold in there. She shared a horrified look with Jeanette.

"Try not to worry about it," Jeanette whispered. "It's not our fault."

Michelle wasn't so much worried about offending the Norms—at that point she was seriously offending herself. The large passageway branched off into narrow stone hallways. Partway down one of them was Laird's apartment.

"My first place," he said proudly, opening the door with an iron key.

The small oval room had a tiny galley kitchen on the narrow end. Laird's couch apparently doubled as his bed. Off the main room, a nook had been carved into the rock wall.

It took Michelle a moment to realize that the nook was a shower. "Oh, Laird, do you mind if we clean up?"

"Not at all." The look on his face said it all. He'd be grateful, especially since they were all crowded into one small, warm chamber.

There was one small problem—the shower nook stood open to the rest of the room. Laird noticed her discomfort. "I'll get some lunch goin'." He turned his back and went into the narrow slot of a kitchen, leaving Michelle to peel off her doeskin breeches in relative privacy.

After the shower she felt reborn, even if she did smell like a rotten egg from the sulfurous hot springs water that came out of the taps. Michelle sat over the heating vent, letting the hot air dry her freshly washed vest. She'd combed out her ragged braids, and golden brown waves fell to her waist. Life got even better when Laird came in with a big pot of vegetable stew and some bread.

"Thank you! I'm so glad it's not meat," Jeanette said, leaning back and luxuriating in the warmth of the room. "It's all we've had to eat for months."

"Why'd ya run off?" Laird asked. "Ya shoulda stayed with yer clan. We woulda taken care o' ya."

Michelle snorted in derisive laughter. "My clan? We can drop that charade now, Laird. My real clan is a pack of paranoid geniuses built by doctors at a genetic research facility."

"Paranoid geniuses?" Laird repeated.

Michelle felt sorry she shot off her mouth. She ate a little faster in case he got offended and kicked them out. "Enhanced," she explained between bites. "Like the people at Iron Torr—just not military. And they're 2,000 miles away from here."

"Oh, sorry."

"Sorry?" Jeanette interrupted. "You kidnap us, shoot us while we're unconscious, and build this elaborate ruse to turn us against our own people. But that's okay, 'cause you're sorry."

The tension in the room suddenly spiked. Everyone stopped eating. Laird stared hard at Jeanette, biting his lip like he was trying not to blow up at her.

Finally, he took a breath. When he spoke, his voice was soft. "I meant sorry yer all alone here. Starvin' in the cold. I'm amazed any of you survived."

Michelle opened her mouth to tell him that the others hadn't died, but she bit off the comment. She didn't want to give away a possible advantage. Laird's quick eyes turned to her, and he paused to hear what she had to say.

Michelle impulsively blurted out something else and regretted her words almost immediately. "Did you really think you could fool us, Laird?"

Laird's big, rough hands sat awkwardly in his lap. "Once I got t' know ya, I had my doubts. If ya knew what we're goin' through, you'd understand why we tried so hard. The military, they're …" Laird's voice trailed off, and he looked up at Michelle pleadingly.

"I know," she said gently. "They're so much stronger in every way. They're taking your women and killing your men, and if it keeps on like this your clan is going to die out."

Laird flinched at that, and Michelle reached out to take his hand. "It was a good plan, Laird. But no one likes to be used."

He nodded, looking down, but he squeezed her hand.

"This is all very touching," Jeanette said sarcastically, "but it's at least noon already, and we need to be back before dark." She stood up.

Michelle didn't. "I'm not going outside in wet clothes."

Jeanette huffed in annoyance, but she sat back down.

Laird ignored her and focused on Michelle. "Before y' go, um, I'd appreciate if you'd come talk to Wade an' Molly with me."

"Why?"

"They'd probably let ya stay here, fer one thing. How long're ya gonna last outside?"

Michelle sighed. "He has a point," she murmured to Jeanette.

Laird led them down a rough-hewn stone corridor that opened up into a surprisingly airy dining room furnished with heavy wooden tables and chairs. "Wait here for me. I gotta let 'em know you're here… an' see if now's a good time."

Jeanette nodded and leaned back in a high-backed chair, closing her eyes in exhaustion while Michelle scanned the room. Natural light came through frosted glass skylights, and strawberry plants bloomed in containers against the walls. Looking around at the beautiful room, she had to revise her estimate of Norms all over again. They were capable of so much more than she'd believed.

To her surprise, Michelle spotted a familiar set of sturdy shoulders, with a single dark braid hanging down. She jumped up and hurried over to a long crowded table. "Sage! How are you?"

"Michelle!"

The young mother sat at a big table with middle-aged Olivia and some of the other surrogates. They eagerly welcomed Michelle to their group, taking turns hugging her.

"So, no baby for you?" Olivia asked, cradling her blonde daughter.

"Afraid not." Michelle sank into a chair, trying to hide the smile that twitched at the corners of her mouth.

The women looked at her sympathetically, like it must be a tragedy not to be pregnant. *Maybe that's true here, where the clans face extinction. But I'd never get pregnant anyway, without Institute doctors to help.*

Michelle still adored the babies, even through her profound relief that she'd escaped Iron Torr before they implanted her with one of the colonel's embryos. Sage's baby looked more like Mark Parker than ever, but on the happy baby the colonel's ice blue eyes looked cute, not creepy. Michelle exclaimed over all the infants, who had just about doubled in size. Many of them were walking now, or at least crawling. She sat down and held Sage's boy Hunter on her lap. That wasn't exactly restful, since the baby shrieked excitedly and bounced on his little legs while she clung to his middle. His mom obviously needed a break.

Over Hunter's squeals, Michelle peppered the surrogates with questions about where they came from, how they got through the wilderness with the babies, and how life was for them at the Norm stronghold.

"See why I love her?" Sage said to Olivia, leaning over to place an affectionate hand on Michelle's arm. "All she thinks about is other people, even with what she must be goin' through with the news from home."

The surrogates murmured compassionately, and Michelle sat up, eyes wide. "What news from home?"

"Oh Gods, ya didn't know? I'm so sorry." Sage looked horrified.

Michelle practically bit her tongue to keep from snapping at the girl. "What did you hear? Something about the Institute?"

Sage and Olivia quietly handed their babies off to other women and came to sit on either side of her. Olivia reached over to take her hand.

"Honey, you come from Institute headquarters, right? The rich place down south?"

Michelle nodded grimly. The pace at which these Norms broke bad news drove her crazy, but any word from her would just slow them down more.

"Well, I'm sure your family will be all right, and your friends too," Olivia pronounced glacially, while Michelle's tension rose to the breaking point. "But the colonel's planning an invasion. It might have already started, we're not sure."

"How do you know this?"

Olivia glanced over at Sage, but the young brunette didn't answer. Sage gazed bleakly across the room to where her baby played with a group of infants on the floor.

"Sage! Tell me!" Michelle leaned forward and gripped the arms of her chair with white knuckles.

Sage flinched. "They... never paid attention to me...after." The girl's voice was almost too soft to hear.

"What!"

Olivia put a soothing hand on Michelle's arm. "This is hard for her, honey. It woulda happened to you too, if y' hadn't gotten out when y' did."

Michelle suddenly understood and closed her mouth.

Sage dabbed at the tears that welled up in her dark almond-shaped eyes. "The officers, they used to come get us, when they'd been drinkin'," she whispered. "They'd drag us to these party rooms, an' they...they..."

"Never mind, I understand," Michelle said, as kindly as she could. "Slade took you. That was his job."

Sage nodded. "An' when they were done...usin' us, they sometimes drank more, an' talked, an' we couldn't leave 'til they sent guards for us, so..."

"So you heard everything. And they thought you were too stupid to understand."

Sage nodded dumbly.

"When you told me about the doctors putting you to sleep to get you pregnant, that didn't really happen?"

Sage shrugged. "They did that right after I got there. I just didn't want t' talk about the...the other part. Michelle, please don't tell a soul. It's a terrible disgrace." The indigenous girl broke down and cried.

"It's not shameful, Sage, because it isn't your fault. Those rapists ought to be ashamed, not you. But I still won't talk about it, I promise."

Michelle looked across at baby Hunter, who, at only six months, could already pull himself up and stand by hanging onto furniture. That kid couldn't be even half Norm. He had to be Enhanced, and Michelle felt certain he was a clone. The likeness to Colonel Parker was too eerie to be a regular family resemblance. Institute doctors refused to clone anyone, arguing that it halted the evolution of the species. That would all change when the military took over there.

Michelle didn't kid herself that her people had a chance. An attack by their own kind was unthinkable. Headquarters would be completely unprepared, but it wouldn't matter. With all the preparation in the world, they still couldn't resist a full-scale military assault.

When Laird returned, he didn't seem to notice Michelle's pale face and trembling hands. She didn't have a chance to talk to Jeanette, because the Norm immediately took them down a wide corridor decorated with brightly colored textiles on the walls. Laird stopped outside the last chamber and knocked politely on the open door.

The room was luxurious by local standards, with two fireplaces, thick rugs, and rich tapestries on the walls. Wade and Molly sat on opposite ends of a long wooden table, with other adults filling the rest of the seats. Michelle recognized a few of the other people at the table. One of them was the burly dark-bearded man called Bear, the one who'd adopted Dillon. The Norms all looked up in surprise when they saw the girls.

Men stared with undisguised lust, and Michelle wished she'd taken the time to braid her hair. Among the clans, the sight of a woman's loose hair was reserved for her husband. She swore silently. *I could've walked in naked and got less attention.*

Jeanette obviously enjoyed the moment. She tossed her blonde waves and strode confidently into the room, and Michelle hesitantly followed. Laird stood near the wall, not saying a word.

The second Molly laid eyes on Michelle, the heavy-set woman launched herself out of her chair. "Oh, daughter! I feared ya dead!"

Michelle seized the lapels of Molly's jacket with both hands. "I am not your *daughter*. I'm the girl you kidnapped, and poisoned, and shot, and lied to."

The Norm woman strained against Michelle's grip, frozen in place and wheezing from fear.

Wade stood up so fast his chair tipped over. "Michelle!" he bellowed. "What're ya doin'?"

Michelle released Molly and whirled to face him, eyes on fire. "Oh, sorry, *Uncle* Wade. Would you rather we all just kept on lying to each other?"

Wade took an involuntary step backward, glancing at Bear for direction. The big man stood up, and Michelle got ready for a fight. Jeanette got between them fast.

"Nice, Michelle," Jeanette snapped.

"I can't go home because of you now, when they need me more than ever!" Michelle paced the room, ignoring Jeanette's perplexed expression.

The Council sat stiffly, staring at her. They ran things there. As the Norm equivalent of the Conclave, they were accustomed to respect.

Michelle didn't care. "I killed my own kind for you, and if the colonel catches me, I'll be…" A sob choked off her words, but that didn't matter here, in front of Norms.

"Dead?" Laird finished tentatively, and she spun to face him.

"No, worse," she screamed, making him recoil. "They'll get me pregnant, over and over, and they'll steal every one of my babies! I'm sure they already told my mother I died, so she won't send people out looking for me."

Michelle advanced on Molly, shoving Bear aside as easily as she would a child. He staggered back, barely staying on his feet.

"Because of you, I can never go home," Michelle screamed. "I'll never see my real mother again!"

Molly stood her ground, bracing herself against the onslaught. Michelle dissolved into tears and threw herself into an armchair by the fire. No one spoke, and not even Jeanette dared to approach her.

Bear threw himself back down in his chair and stretched his long legs out in front of him. "This ain't worth it. These Enhanced, they're crazy, every last one of 'em. Them babies are gonna grow up t' be jus' like her."

"Babies?" Michelle bounced out of her chair and strode up to Bear, who stood up quickly to face her. "You mean the Enhanced babies from Iron Torr? Do those poor mothers know their kids aren't even related to them, or have you been lying to them too?"

"They know. Now they do."

"Fine," Michelle snapped, turning abruptly away from the big man. "Those kids are better off here anyway."

"So you admit—" Molly started, but Michelle cut her off.

"Don't even speak to me, Molly! You made me love you, and then…you stole my whole life."

"See? That's just crazy talk," Bear put in. "They're all nuts."

"I'm not," Jeanette stated calmly. "Laird, could you please take Michelle out of here?" She turned to Bear. "We need to talk."

Angry and embarrassed, Michelle followed Laird out of the room. They closed the door after her. Two hours later, Jeanette and the Norm Council still hadn't emerged. Michelle dozed fitfully on a padded bench in the hall, but when it got uncomfortable she sat up, listening. Low voices came from the other side of the closed door, but she couldn't make out what they were saying.

She got up and walked toward the door, but Laird got in her way. "Michelle, please don't."

The door opened and Jeanette came out, looking triumphant.

"About time," Michelle snapped. "Sylvia and the boys are probably worried about us. We need to leave now."

"Just listen for a second. It was worth the delay, all right? We've been invited to stay, provided that you don't have any more…outbursts. You do it even one more time, and we're out of here."

"To hell with them. I'm out of here now." Michelle grabbed her furs and ran.

She didn't look back until she reached the front door. The tiny window in the top of the door looked black. It was already dark outside. Michelle swore out loud and grabbed her snowshoes off the wall, letting them clatter to the floor in front of the bench. She sat down and angrily strapped on her fur leggings. It took a moment for her to realize that the fat door attendant had gone away. Michelle lunged for the door, scattering her furs on the floor, and yanked on the heavy iron latch. It had been securely locked, and the key was gone.

Her scream echoed off the high stone walls.

Chapter 19: Michelle

Whiteout

Michelle woke up alone for the first time in six months. She found herself in a small stone chamber, barely big enough to hold the thin pallet she slept on. The last thing she remembered was finding the front door locked. *No, something else happened. Laird gave me tea by the fire while I cried. He must have put something in it to make me sleep. How long have I been here? Overnight, or even longer? Dillon's got to be furious.*

With a panicky feeling, Michelle tried the big wooden door, fully expecting it to be locked. It swung open on oiled hinges. Outside, the stone hallway was empty. Voices came from around the corner. She stepped into the hall and stopped to listen.

"No, she's not unstable, "Jeanette told someone. Michelle instantly knew they were talking about her. "I've never seen her like this, and I've known her my whole life. She's just stressed out. It's been a struggle just to survive, and she feels responsible for us being here."

It's not just a feeling. I am responsible for us being here. I'm the one that sided with the Norms, and then got caught. But who cares, because they're invading the Institute, and—

Someone said something, but the woman's low tones didn't carry as well as Jeanette's higher ones. Michelle still recognized the voice as Molly's.

"It's been a horrible winter," Jeanette said.

"It ain't even half over, darlin'."

Jeanette swore, and the two women laughed together. Michelle felt like walking over there and breaking up their little party, but she pictured Sylvia and the boys huddled around a fire in the drafty longhouse. *Todd won't live much longer. I've got to bring him here, and that means I can't get kicked out myself.*

Michelle composed herself and walked into the dining hall. Light came in low through the windows, and a few Norms were eating breakfast. Molly and Jeanette sat together at a table for two, sipping steaming mugs of tea. They both looked up uneasily as she approached. That, plus the awkwardness of dragging over another chair and sitting down uninvited, was too much. Michelle gave them a self-conscious wave and veered away.

Molly jumped up and pulled over a chair from another table. "Come on, love, sit with us."

'Thanks." Michelle took the offered seat. "So this is your real home," she commented casually. "Nice."

"We do use the villages, in the summer," Molly admitted. "For more than…what you saw. The men like to hunt, and it's good for the kids to get outside." Molly looked different in an elegant dress and soft slippers. She was no peasant's wife. Her hair had been elaborately braided with small white feathers.

"White feathers?" Michelle noticed. "Are you remarried, then?"

Molly averted her eyes uncomfortably, but then looked up and answered honestly. "I was never widowed. Wade's my husband, not my brother."

"Oh, I see. You lied about that to pile on the guilt. I killed Kalie's father. Or was it Jeanette who supposedly killed him? I can't keep track." Michelle laughed musically. "Either way, it worked. I felt really bad about it. So, Wade's really Kalie's dad. Anything else I should know?"

Molly watched her warily. "About the clan? Laird is Wade's son, and mine—our oldest. Strange as it may seem to you, he still considers you family."

Michelle didn't answer. She just kept on looking at Molly with an expression of polite attentiveness.

Encouraged, Molly went on. "Wade an' I, we do too."

Michelle resisted the impulse to roll her eyes. "Thanks, Molly, that's really nice of you," she said in a saccharine voice. Jeanette shot her a tiny nod of approval from across the table.

Molly dropped the topic then, since waiters appeared with trays of food. Steaming platters of eggs, porridge, and toast were placed on their table. It felt like they were back at the Institute again, except that Molly could never pass for Enhanced, no matter how well she dressed. Michelle thought guiltily about Sylvia and the boys, but she still stuffed herself until she couldn't hold another bite.

Michelle sat back and looked at Molly. "We need to be getting back. Dillon's got to be panicking since we've been gone all night."

"Dillon! He's alive?" Molly beamed.

"They all are. I'd like to go get them and bring them here, if that's all right with you."

"Of course they're welcome here! You all are, daught—, I mean, Michelle. But I don't know if it's gonna be possible for you to go out right now, honey."

Michelle ignored that, figuring if the door wasn't unlocked she'd just kick it down. She stood up. "Thanks for the hospitality, Molly."

Michelle headed straight for the front door. Her furs lay scattered around the entryway where she'd left them the night before. She bent down to pick up her bearskin tunic. "Ugh, it's all wet." Snow had melted into puddles on the stone floor. Michelle shook droplets off her furs, accidentally spraying Jeanette with cold, dirty water.

"Hey, watch it!"

"Sorry." But Michelle wasn't really paying attention. Just as she suspected, the door was locked again.

"Whoa, whoa, don't you dare, Michelle." Jeanette hip-checked her, knocking Michelle off balance and ruining the kick she aimed at the door. With a deep boom, Michelle's heel rocked the thick ironclad door against its hinges, but the thick wooden planks didn't even crack. All around the room, heads turned her way. Wade and Molly sprinted for the entryway, with Bear right behind them.

Some girls giggled from over by the fire. "Ooo, you're gotta get it now."

Michelle ignored them. "Jeanette, they can't keep us here when Sylvia and the boys need us." She lined up for another kick, but Jeanette blocked her.

"Wait, you're not locked in, hon," Molly puffed. Running obviously wasn't something she did regularly.

Michelle fixed Molly in a cold stare and pulled on the big iron latch to demonstrate. It didn't move.

"I mean you're not a prisoner, Michelle. The door's only locked 'cause there's a whiteout."

"A what? Oh, a blizzard. It doesn't matter. I can travel in snow."

"This is no ordinary snow," Molly insisted. "You won't be able to see, you'll get lost. People who get caught out in these storms die!"

"Just because you'd get lost doesn't mean I will," Michelle retorted. She started putting on her furs, and Jeanette reluctantly followed suit. "We've got to get back—our friends will be worried about us. Just imagine what Dillon's going through."

Bear swore at the mention of Dillon's name. "He's gonna track you here. What if he shows up an' yer not here?"

"Tell him we'll be back tomorrow. Depending on how fast Todd can travel. He's, um, had a rough winter." Michelle suppressed her paranoia over admitting Todd's weakness. Rules were different among Norms. The weak were nurtured there, not eliminated.

"I still say yer bein' stupid," Wade grumbled, but he unlocked the door for them anyway, sending an icy blast into the cavernous room. "Good luck t' ya."

The girls staggered out into the storm, leaning against the wind. Even in the protected roadway, the wind almost knocked them off their feet. Michelle's eyelashes quickly crusted over with ice, making it hard to see anything. Jeanette's complaining barely carried over the howling of the wind. This time they hiked the half-mile length of the snow packed road, avoiding the steep climb up the icy bank on the side. When they emerged from the sunken road onto untracked powder, the wind picked up to gale force. Michelle extended her arm, and she could barely see her mitten through the thickly falling snow.

"Jeanette, we've got to go back. The Norms were right." She turned to look behind her, but her friend had disappeared in the blinding storm.

"Jeanette!" Michelle screamed, spinning on the spot. She began to run, hooked her snowshoe on a fallen log, and fell into the deep snow. Freezing crystals of ice got up her mittens and down her back as she thrashed to her feet. Her feet and hands ached with cold.

"Jeanette!"

She was alone. Michelle made herself stop and stand still to fight off panic. Running off blind would be stupid. *I'm not that far from the door, I can go back. But not without Jeanette.* She reached out with her mind, sending her silent call as powerfully as she could. She ran headlong into someone's mental shields and accidentally slammed them down. *"Sorry, Todd! Where are you?"*

Michelle felt a wave of disorientation as Todd let her look through his eyes. She saw his view of blowing snow and pine trees, nauseatingly overlaid over her own vision. Trees and rock outcroppings wavered as her brain battled to make sense of two sets of input. *They're outside, looking for us in the storm, but I can't tell where.*

Michelle felt a tug on her mind, and she turned in the direction it pulled her. A minute of walking took her back to the hidden path. Huge snow banks loomed over the road, so the wind dropped off enough for her to look around. No one appeared.

"Todd! Jeanette!" she screamed into the wind, and then she felt a flicker of an answer. "Jeanette? Is that you?"

Another mental tug pulled Michelle down the driveway toward the door. The wind tore at her tunic, beating the heavy leather against her legs. She pushed on, nose and toes numb with cold. Ahead, dark shapes loomed out of the storm. For a split second her mind made them into grizzly bears, but Michelle knew better. Animals had the sense to sleep in their dens in winter. They didn't wander around in storms. She called out, and one of the shapes moved toward her.

Michelle recognized him by the black wolf skin that covered his head and shoulders. "Dillon! Are you all right?"

He said something, but his words were lost on the wind. Their snowshoes clashed together as Dillon pulled her toward the entry by the hand. Michelle made a fast count through blurry eyes, making sure all her friends were there. They were. Jeanette pounded on the door with her fist. Finally someone opened it, and the group tumbled inside. The teenager who let them in gaped in astonishment and sent a boy running for Wade and Molly.

The Institute kids collapsed on the stone bench by the door, slowly extricating themselves from their frozen gear. Jeanette untied her brother's snowshoes, and Michelle helped Dillon pull off his black fur mantle. Patches of frostbite marred his handsome face, but that didn't worry her. The look in his eye did.

"I'm really sorry," Michelle said. "We arrived here late, and they wouldn't let us leave in the dark."

Dillon looked away, and she felt sure he was angry. "It's okay," he finally said, putting a fur-clad arm around her. "This place is amazing. I think you saved us all."

Michelle finally got the chance to ask the question that had been bothering her. "How'd you find us?"

"Todd did it," Sylvia said. "We just followed him."

"We had tracks until the storm started overnight," Todd said modestly, but he still looked proud of himself.

The tribe straggled over to the fire circle, oblivious to the stares of the Normal teens. Todd fiddled with his mittens, trying to get them off, but he gave up and collapsed on a bench. Brian untied the laces that held Todd's mittens on, and when he pulled them off, everyone gasped in horror. Todd's fingers were black with frostbite, and the swollen skin had split in a few places. Michelle winced. *Todd could lose those fingers, and that's my fault.*

Wade and Molly hurried up to the fire circle. "Back already?" Wade growled.

"We found them, just like I said we would," Michelle said.

Wade wasn't impressed. "They musta been right outside then."

"Uh-oh," Molly exclaimed, bending down to take a look at Todd. "Of t' the infirmary with you." She took Todd by the elbow, helping him up, and the girls all stood up to follow.

Wade stopped them. "Ya'll stay here."

"Why?" Jeanette demanded, hands on her hips. "He's my brother."

"'Cause they're gonna strip him nekked an' throw 'im in a warm bath," Wade said.

"Okay then, you'd better do that on your own," Jeanette told Todd. She sat back down amidst giggles from the others.

"Anybody else need medical care?" Molly asked over her shoulder. "If you're injured, come with me now."

Dillon stood up. "Wait a minute. You have warm baths here?"

***

The stone steps felt cold on Michelle's bare feet, but warm steamy air rose up the staircase. The stairs led into the cavern below the Norm stronghold, where hot pools steamed in dark grottos. Flimsy walls with peeling white paint divided the space.

"I knew there had to be hot springs here," Jeanette exclaimed, randomly opening doors to poke her head inside. "Ooh, this one's the best."

The door opened onto a large, dimly lit room with a steaming warm swimming pool. The water looked green under tiny lights that reflected off crystalline formations on the rock walls. The group eagerly went in, and Jeanette tested the water with bare toes. "It's perfect."

"We don't have swimsuits," Sylvia said uncomfortably.

Jeanette laughed, pulling off her shirt. "Like I care."

Michelle moved toward the water, but Dillon tapped her on the elbow and beckoned her back out into the hall. "Look, private rooms."

Other doorways opened into smaller caves, each with primitive hot pools. These rooms had been left in their natural state, except for tiny white lights that glittered from beneath the water. He took her hand and pulled her into one of them.

The steam in the room made it hard to breathe, and Michelle felt claustrophobic in the dark. She liked the other room better. It took a moment to admit to herself that Dillon bothered her more than the room did. He ignored her, focusing on getting out of his clothes. He finally slipped into the water and sat there on a submerged ledge, head back and eyes closed. After a moment, he peered at her through half-closed eyes. "Aren't you coming in?"

"Yeah." She peeled off her doeskin breeches and hung the vest on a hook by the door, feeling insecure. Michelle picked her way over the rocks to the water, conscious of his gaze on her.

"You've lost a lot of weight, but you're not thin…everywhere." He smiled, but she didn't respond, and she wouldn't look at him as she got into the pool and sat down beside him. Delicious warmth flooded her body.

After a long, awkward silence, Michelle finally spoke. "Can't you just talk to me, Dillon? You're mad at me, I know it."

"Did I say that?"

Michelle scratched an itchy, damp curl off one cheek. "You don't need to say it, I can tell."

"Gods…I didn't say one wrong word." Dillon heaved a heavy sigh. "You know how hard it is to be bonded to a telepath?"

Michelle winced at his tone. "I can't help it. It's not like you're stuck with me, you know."

"Yes I am," he insisted, and then he face-palmed, muttering to himself. "Way to go, Freeman. That's the right thing to say."

Michelle giggled despite herself. "Okay, look. I'm sorry we took off without telling you, and I'm sorry I took your bow."

"You should be." Dillon faced her, finally letting his anger show. "Do you have any idea how I felt when I woke up and found you gone?"

"Honestly, yes," she said rebelliously. "But you guys can't do all the heavy work and the hunting too. It's killing you! Look at Todd."

His eyes flashed. "I'm not Todd. I could have gone with you."

"You needed to rest."

"Panicking and hiking through a blizzard all night isn't restful, Michelle."

"You weren't supposed to follow us." Michelle started to sob. "We planned on coming back that first night, but the Norms wouldn't let us out, and Jeanette stopped me from kicking down the door. And I lost it in front of the Norm Council and yelled at Molly and Bear, and he thinks we're all nuts, even the babies…"

Dillon had no idea what she was talking about. "What? Nutty babies?"

She smiled through her tears. "Iron Torr's Enhanced babies are here, with their surrogate moms. Bear says they're all going to grow up to be psychos like me."

Dillon put his arms around her while she cried on his shoulder. "You're not crazy. Whatever you said to them, they had it coming after what they did. It's all okay now. I love you." He subsided into silence, staring away across the dimly lit room while she sobbed.

Michelle wanted to tell him what Sage told her, but it was all too much, and it didn't make any difference anyway. They couldn't do anything about the invasion from here.

When her tears stopped, she sat up to look at him. "What's my age have to do with it?"

"I didn't say anything about—" He stopped. "Oh. I was just thinking how we put you through a lot, and everyone forgets how young you are. You've shouldered more than your share of the responsibility, and it's, um…"

"What?"

He reluctantly continued, looking apprehensive. "Honestly, I think it's normal for you to finally break down once we're safe. You couldn't afford to before."

"Breakdown? Who said I had a breakdown?"

"Jeanette."

"Bitch." Michelle hunched down in the water and crossed her arms. "I hate having no privacy, even inside my own head."

"I hate that too. But let's make the best of it." He gently stroked the tears off her cheek with his thumb, and she turned toward him, running her hands across his muscular shoulders. Michelle hadn't seen Dillon without a shirt in months, and he wasn't as thin as she feared. He'd lost every ounce of fat on his body, but his muscles still remained, standing out in sharp definition. New scars marred his arms and hands, and two big ones crisscrossed the pale skin of his chest. Michelle knew how he got them, and it frightened her.

Dillon and the boys had encircled a wounded bull elk in deep snow. His handmade bow wasn't powerful enough to take down large animals from a distance, so the hunters had to finish wounded prey off with spears. The animal made one last desperate lunge, raking Dillon with its antlers before Brian stopped it with a spear thrust. Dillon could have died that day, but the guys returned triumphant. That night around the fire they told the story over and over, embellishing it more each time. Michelle traced the scars lightly with her finger, thinking about how close she came to losing him.

"You know, I meant what I said," Dillon told her softly, bending down to kiss her throat.

"What?"

"You saved us all, finding this place." He grinned. "It's like a dream!"

Dillon pushed off and floated backward into the middle of the pool, and then reached for Michelle's hands, pulling her after him.

"Wow, the water's deep." She lost her footing and grabbed his shoulders, giggling. Dillon could still stand up, so she wrapped herself around him and half-floated in his arms. He kissed her softly at first, teasing her with the tip of his tongue until her eyes lit with an inner fire. Their minds melded until the boundaries between them disappeared, and she knew exactly how her touch felt on his skin.

Hours later, hunger drove them from their sanctuary. As soon as they opened the door, cold air hit Michelle in the face. She shivered in her sleeveless vest. The stone floor had always been chilly, but now a glossy sheet of ice covered it. Where rising steam condensed and froze, ice coated the walls.

"What the—" Dillon started, and then slipped and had to grab the wall for balance. "Careful, it's slick as hell."

The room with the big green pool was deserted. They hurried up the stairs, clinging to the railing. The door at the top of the stairs stood ajar. Dillon slammed it open, sending the iron latch crashing into the stone wall with a boom. They stood there staring at each other across white clouds of their breath. The entire Norm stronghold was freezing, with not a soul in sight.

Chapter 20: Michelle

In the Womb of the Mother

Michelle sprinted the length of the stone passageway, skidding into a perfectly balanced slide to make the corner. Even in the main tunnels, all the paving stones lay coated in ice.

Behind her, Dillon made a lot of noise as he slid into things and swore. "Wait up! Where is everybody?"

"Probably by the main fire circle, if it's still working."

Michelle dashed into the small apartment Molly assigned them, leaving the door open behind her. She grabbed her pile of furs, smacking each one off the wall in a rain of ice before putting it on. Dillon wiped his icy feet on the gray woolen bedspread before putting on his socks and boots, but Michelle didn't care. That wasn't the Atherton mansion.

"Power's out! Hope they get it going soon or this place is going to be a tomb." Dillon threw on his last layer, the wolf skin mantle, but left the hood hanging down his back. "How'd it get cold so fast?"

She stopped and looked at him, her eyes wide. "Oh, no."

"What?"

"What if it's no accident? The colonel's all about efficiency. What easier way to wipe out the Norms than by cutting off their power?"

"You think he's trying to freeze them to death? Gods! Let's go find the others."

A huge crowd huddled around the main fire circle, which flickered fitfully with faint blue flames. The fat female door attendant policed the area with her typical belligerent attitude, positioning people around the fire. "Babies an' little kids t' the front. You, move back—you've got a coat on. Young fella, don't even think about it." One great flabby arm slammed a teenage boy in the chest, and he staggered backward, almost falling over a family clustered behind him.

Dillon eyed her disdainfully. "What a——"

"Shh, Dillon." Michelle slipped up to the edge of the crowd and waited for an opening. When the woman passed her, she quickly blurted out her question. "What's wrong with the heat?"

"Power's out."

"Obviously," Michelle said shortly. "I meant why."

The woman approached Michelle, who got ready to duck another slap to the head. "I hear yer supposed t' be some kinda genius. Why don'tcha go an' find out?"

"Fine. Where's the furnace?"

A fleshy hand pointed the way down a narrow stone passageway, and Michelle headed down it without another word.

Dillon ran to catch up. "Ever fix a furnace?"

"No, but how hard could it be? Look who built it," she said shortly.

"Sometimes your ego's just out of control, you know that?"

"Go back and sit by the fire with the children if you want to act like that," Michelle snapped, but she shut up when they came around a corner and saw Brian standing there with a dripping armload of pumps and tubing. He'd heard it all, she could tell, and he loved it.

"I'm glad you're here, Michelle, I could use your input on this." Brian didn't smile, but she knew that twinkle in his eye.

"Don't even—" she hissed.

Brian ignored that. "Here's the problem, see?" He pointed to a circular ventilation shaft high in the stone wall, accessed by an old wooden scaffold. "The air pumps run by wind power, and they're freezing the whole complex."

Cold air blew in the round hole and swept down the hall, bringing with it the scent of snow-covered pines. Michelle eyed the rickety scaffold, hoping Brian wouldn't ask her to climb up there. "Doesn't outside air run through the furnace first?"

"Yeah, but the furnace is down. Fuel's gone solid for some reason."

"Solid? Why, from the cold?"

"I thought that too, but warming it doesn't help. Come on, I'll show you."

Norms crowded the furnace room. Todd crouched by the enormous machine, holding his frostbitten hands out of the oily water that seeped onto the floor.

"Can you let 'em in, please?" Todd yelled, and the men stepped back to make room for Brian and Michelle to enter. Dillon followed, but he didn't push to the front.

"They're all clogged with solidified fuel," Brian said, handing the pumps back to Todd. "But why, I don't know."

"Diesel fuel gels in the cold," Todd mused. "But this type of oil shouldn't do that, and you warmed it anyway." He held the clogged pump high, staining one bandaged hand black with oil. "Anybody here ever seen a problem like this? With fuel oil going solid?"

Michelle caught a few guilty looks from the Norms around her, but none of them said a word. She squeezed between the men and squatted down beside Todd. On pretense of examining the gummy fuel dripping from the pump, she brushed her fingers against Todd's arm, and she breathed a sigh of relief at the answer. She turned to tell Dillon there was no sign of an attack, but he'd been pressed back by the Norms who crowded in, trying to help.

A thin gray haired man in an insulated jumpsuit seemed to be in charge, but he deferred to Todd, asking questions in a respectful voice. Clearly these Norms knew all about the Enhanced, and they seemed glad to have a few of their own.

Michelle held the dripping tube up to the faint emergency light. Irregular patches of creamy white stuff floated on the surface of the oil. Suddenly the lights went out. Norms cried out in alarm.

Brian swore. "Sorry." The lights came back on. "Great. Lights and fans are all on the same line. I can't shut off the cold air intake without turning out the lights."

"I can't work in the dark," Todd said shortly.

"Then it's gonna get a lot colder in here."

Michelle breathed into cupped hands to keep her nose from freezing. Inside her boots, she wiggled her rapidly numbing toes. "People are going to start dying," she told the foreman frankly. "We might be able to solve this, but only if you tell us what you know."

"I can't talk about it," the old man muttered. He shivered and tucked his dirty hands in his armpits.

"Please," Michelle said softly. "If someone made a mistake, that's okay. But to fix it, we need to know what went wrong."

The man wouldn't answer. Michelle tossed the oily tube in a bucket and looked at him. He shook his head, scanning the crowd uneasily.

The old foreman bent close enough that she could smell the machine oil on his jumpsuit. "I shouldn't o' let the young feller go. He brought it back, I think."

"Brought what?"

"When they hauled his body out," the old man added, so softly that Michelle wasn't sure she heard him.

Michelle's eyes widened. She barely mouthed the words. "Are you saying someone died?"

The Norm nodded and fell silent. Michelle touched his arm, sending an encouraging vibe. "Why don't we take a walk, so we can talk in private?"

***

Michelle returned from her whispered conference with the old Norm feeling shaken. She strode down the corridor alone, arms folded for warmth, blowing aggravated clouds of steamy breath into the cold air. *I should never have promised to keep his secret. Wade and Molly really need to know about this. But the old man trusted me. He'll get in huge trouble if I tell on him. Maybe we can fix this on our own.*

She quietly gathered the other Enhanced teens and led them into a narrow stone passageway just off the furnace room. The hall grew dim as they moved out of the orange glow of the emergency lights. Ahead, on the left wall, a dark, rectangular gap loomed.

"Careful. This is it," Michelle muttered, raising a hand to halt her group before the ten-foot wide gap.

The hole in the wall opened into a vertical shaft. Everyone clustered nervously, peering down. A cracked wooden platform hung in the center, dangling from worn hemp ropes. Around the edges of the lift, the walls of the shaft disappeared straight down into darkness. Peering into the pit gave Michelle vertigo, but she kept on sneaking peeks anyway, clinging to the stone ledge with a chilly hand. Warm, sulfurous steam rose into her face, but it quickly chilled and condensed in the cold air, making the stone slick.

Brian eyed the rusted pulley system once used to raise and lower the lift. "The foreman sent you here? I'm not convinced this has anything to do with our furnace trouble."

"Me neither," Sylvia agreed. "This thing must have been built generations ago."

"The old guy thinks this has something to do with the furnace going out, but all he'll say is that the place is forbidden to men," Michelle whispered. "Apparently some guy went in, against the rules, and died down there. The foreman's all superstitious, and he won't say anything more. He says I've got to see it, and he'll take me part way."

"Here's an idea," Sylvia suggested. "They could give us a female guide."

"We can't ask for one," Michelle whispered. "He's keeping this secret from Molly, and all the Normal women, I think."

Dillon shook his head. "No way. Somebody died there, and he's only taking you part way? Don't go."

"I have to. This has something to do with why the heat's out. Dillon, there are lots of little kids here, and they can't take this cold for long."

"This makes no sense," Dillon said. "You're not going to fix the furnace by going in a hole."

"Maybe I can. Look." Michelle pointed. Next to the wall of the shaft, a thick pipe led down into the darkness. "I bet that's how they're pulling oil up out of the underground reservoir."

"That's right," the skinny old foreman said, as he limped up to join them. "Didja make up yer mind?"

Michelle swallowed hard. "Yeah. I'm going."

Dillon examined the thick rope that ran over a heavy circular winch. "I don't like it. How old is this thing?"

"Oh, it's a hundred years old, at least," the foreman said. "Maybe more."

"I'm not sure it's safe." Dillon stuck one leg over the edge and pushed on the platform with a boot, testing it.

The white-haired foreman tugged him back by the sleeve. "She ain't heavy, but you are."

With a grunt, the old Norm stepped onto the tiny platform. It swayed but held his weight. Michelle bravely followed him, stepping over the dark gap between the lift and the stone wall. *My body would just fit through there, if I fell.* She forced herself not to look down. Hiding her fear of heights had become a habit, even though it didn't matter among Norms. In the hall, two bearded men gripped hand cranks, ready to turn the gears that would lower their passengers into the catacombs below.

"Remember, not a word," the foreman told them.

The men gave him dismal nods. Then they put their backs into it, and the platform suddenly dropped a few inches. Michelle grabbed for the rusty post in the center, eyes wide. She was nearly eye level with the floor when Brian hopped down to join her. His boots landed with a loud thump on the cracked and rotting wood. Michelle let out a startled shriek. Dillon shouted from above, but the men on the cranks kept working.

"Oh thanks, Brian," Michelle spat. "An extra two hundred pounds is just what we need here."

Brian grinned infuriatingly. "I haven't been that light in years."

The rope hit a frayed spot, making the platform lurch. Michelle clutched the pole and bit back another squeal.

The old Norm gave Brian a dirty look. "Rope breaks, it's you that brought it on us, Goddess knows."

As it descended, the lift slowly tipped to one side, which didn't help. Finally, with a stomach-clenching drop, the other side fell to match. Michelle gasped, and then they were level again. Brian put an arm snugly around her waist. She thought about slapping the uninvited hand off, but couldn't let go to do it. Besides, he did make her feel more secure.

The shaft narrowed as it went down, and an outcropping of rock bruised Michelle's shoulder. "Ouch!"

"Step in, girl." The old Norm pulled her to the center of the lift, uncomfortably close to his body. Fuel-oil and bitter, old sweat filled her nostrils. She turned her face away.

As though he heard the thought, Brian slid a shoulder between Michelle and the Norm, and he held her from behind as the platform dropped into the dark. She didn't know whether to be irritated or grateful, but she didn't break away. There was nowhere to go, anyway. The faint square of light from above faded as they descended. Long minutes later, the platform landed with a thump, surprising her.

"Oh, it's not that deep," Brian said.

"Yeah, it is. Yer not there yet." The Norm switched on a tiny flashlight and shuffled away down a rocky passage. Brian followed. Michelle's skin felt slick with nervous perspiration. She shucked her outer furs, dumped them on the platform, and hurried to catch up.

The path soon turned to rough stairs, hundreds of them, hewn by hand from the bones of the mountain. The rotten-egg smell of the hot springs was stronger there, and it turned Michelle's stomach. The old man moved confidently down the dark stairs while she did her best to keep up. Behind them, Brian walked in almost total darkness. When he stumbled, Michelle reached out and took his hand, keeping her other hand on the wall for support. Handrails were too much to ask for there.

She stepped on a slimy patch of rock and slipped. Brian caught her, and she regained her feet, heart thumping. The place got creepier as they went deeper, and the air began to smell stale. Michelle's respiration and heart rate smoothly increased to compensate, but the Norm wheezed loudly, worrying her. Finally he stopped and stepped aside. It looked like the path ended in a wall, but it didn't. The Norm squatted to shine his light down a waist-high tunnel.

"Gotta stop here…can't breathe." The foreman grabbed Michelle's hand with his calloused one and pressed the flashlight into it. "C'mon back t' the shaft. I'll wait fer ya there."

He pointed a gnarled finger down the tunnel. "End o' the line. You'll know it when ya see it." He laboriously pushed himself up and limped away on arthritic knees, navigating the pitch-black staircase with his hands on the walls.

Michelle hesitated, suddenly very glad Brian was there with her. He squeezed her hand reassuringly and then let it go. The floor of the low tunnel felt slick with the same mold that coated the rocks. Gray fungus reflected eerily in the beam of the flashlight. The air felt warm, stiflingly so. Michelle pulled off another layer of fur. Brian did the same, and they left their clothes piled like a dead animal outside its den. She began to crawl, holding the flashlight in her mouth. It tasted like dirt from the old man's hands. Rocks cut painfully into her knees, but she struggled on with Brian behind her. The passage widened briefly so Brian came up beside her, but then they both stopped at once. It ended in a hole no wider than Michelle's hips.

"He means for us to go in there?" she asked. Dread made her stomach churn.

"He means for you to go in there," Brian countered. "No way am I going to fit."

"Alone?" Michelle turned to Brian, afraid to go on without him.

He squeezed her shoulder briefly. "I'll be right here."

"In the dark!"

"I don't need the light. I won't be moving." Brian said. He hugged her, but he didn't try anything, so she let him. She was grateful for the comfort. "Michelle, if you have any trouble, just yell, and I'll…"

"Get stuck and block the passageway?" She laughed nervously.

"No, I'll go up for Sylvia. She's the smallest."

"Okay, good plan." Michelle wiped her damp forehead and took off her last layer of outdoor clothes, leaving her wearing the vest, leather breeches, and boots. She picked up the tiny flashlight and began to turn away, but Brian caught her with an arm around the waist. He lightly stroked the loose tendrils of hair by her face, his expression torn between love and pain.

"Brian, please don't. That just makes it harder for me."

He dropped the hand off her hair, but stubbornly left his other arm around her waist. His eyes sought hers. "So you do…still…"

"Of course! How could I just forget you? But I can't do that, not to Dillon, and…" She took a breath and told the truth. "And not to myself. It would break my heart."

He cupped her face in both hands, kissed her forehead and released her. "Go on, then. I'll be waiting for you."

Michelle flattened herself on her stomach and wormed through the hole, wondering what he meant. *Waiting here, or waiting…for me and Dillon to break up?* She pushed forward with her toes, moving onward, twenty more feet, then forty. The hole got smaller and tighter, and she couldn't go forward anymore. *Forget it,* she decided, trying to back up. With a grunt, she lifted her hips a little, but the rock pressed down on her and she couldn't move. She was trapped.

Michelle panicked horribly. Oxygen dwindled, and a pounding headache began as she re-breathed the same musty air. Little cries escaped her as she clawed at the rock with her hands. Some of it crumbled, and she realized the tunnel had caved in ahead. With bleeding fingers, she ripped at the debris. More fell from above, sending talc-fine dust into her face. She fought to breathe, but it was impossible. One hand blundered against the corner of a rock. Something soft was stuck there, stuck in… With a surge of terror, Michelle recognized what she held between her fingers. Hair. Human hair, glued to the rock with dried blood. *That man died here. They must have pulled his body out with ropes, dragging it…*

With a cry, Michelle thrashed backward, bumped the ceiling, and brought a huge rock crashing down. She hid her head while the rock slammed into the grit just ahead of her fingertips. When she raised her head and reached forward, her fingers touched the rough surface of the boulder that blocked her in. Michelle threw her head back and screamed.

No answering call came from Brian.

Bracing one hand on the ground, she pushed on the rock with the other, but it wouldn't move. Then she tried pushing in another spot, and it budged, just barely. Using all her strength, she slammed against it with hands and head, heedless of the pain, shoving it aside a little at a time until she dragged her body through the gap, flesh ripping against rough edges of stone. Gasping and coughing, Michelle retrieved the flashlight, which still glowed dimly from under a pile of dirt. She collapsed with her body curled around the light. When she finally sat up, she exclaimed out loud.

The cavern glittered like a jewel. Huge white crystals jutted from the walls and ceiling. Veins of gemstones shimmered in the light. Even uncut, their colors were clear, and lines of green and purple and red lead back into mysterious caverns where the light didn't reach. Michelle sat inside the very body of the planet itself, and to her astonishment, it pulsed with life. She rested against the wall, recovering her strength in the current of fresh air that wafted in from some hidden channel. Raw gems lay scattered among the debris from the cave-in, and Michelle couldn't resist pocketing them. But she wasn't there for treasure.

The pool glowed like a living thing. Experimentally, she switched off her light, and the water fluoresced an eerie green. *Life forms, in the water.* She crawled forward, fascinated. Bubbles rose, and tiny black droplets rose with them, spreading out on the surface. Michelle squatted in the mud at the edge of the pool and prodded the rubbery deposits. Something became clear— something she'd never have known if she hadn't gone into the pit.

There's an oil reservoir under the complex, and some of it has been colonized by bacteria! They break it down to a solid that clogs the engines.

Michelle lingered in the womb of the planet longer than she should have, dreading the claustrophobic passage. Digging with her hands, she cleared the entryway to the collapsed tunnel and saved a few more fistfuls of gems. The air seemed fine there, but it wouldn't be in the tunnel. Taking three deep breaths, she dived back into the darkness, careful not to touch the ceiling and cause another collapse. When she made it back to the wide part of the tunnel, she shined the light around excitedly, eager to tell Brian about the chamber of jewels.

He was gone.

"Brian!" Michelle screamed, scurrying back through the low tunnel faster than she thought possible. The battery of the flashlight slowly died, and the yellow light faded to a single glowing spot that didn't illuminate the passageway. Dashing up the stairs, she slipped and crashed painfully to one knee. Michelle hissed in a breath between clenched teeth, clutching her leg.

"Hey, hey, it's okay!" Brian appeared out of the darkness and grabbed her elbow to help her up. "Sorry, I ran out of air back there and had to retreat."

"Where's, um, what's-his-name?" Michelle knew he could feel her shaking, but she brushed off the impulse to cover it up. Brian wouldn't judge her for that.

"The old man? I sent him up on the platform. He couldn't get enough air down there."

"Oh my God, it was amazing! The tunnel caved in, but there's a chamber full of jewels, and it glows, and the bacteria in the water live on oil, and I'm sure—" He interrupted her with a kiss.

She shoved him away. "Ah! Brian, what are you thinking?"

"Isn't it obvious?" He sounded pleased with himself.

"You know what I mean! Where's the lift?" She pushed past him and peered up the shaft, pointing the useless light even though it didn't help.

"Relax, they're sending it back, after they get the old guy off." He took her hand and drew her out of the faint spot of light. "Please just listen."

"Ouch." She pulled her torn and bleeding hand from his. In the narrow space, heat radiated off Brian's body, tempting Michelle to melt against him. She resisted and leaned on the wall instead.

"Michelle, if there's anything I learned this year, it's not to put off joy, 'cause there may not be another chance."

"I understand, but…you can't…"

"Oh, but I did."

She couldn't see his smirk in the dark, but she heard it in his voice. "Brian, don't you ever take anything seriously? You can't do that, because…honestly, I like it too much, and…you'll make me into the kind of person I don't want to be. If I was your girl, would you want me cheating on you?"

"I wouldn't consider it cheating, as long as you came back and told me all about it. Or even as long as you came back at all."

"You really mean that, don't you?"

"Yeah, I do. Just about all the married couples back home do exactly that, in case you hadn't noticed."

She nodded. "I know. Neil Johnston spends a lot of time with my mother, which is fine with me. He's a good man."

"So am I."

When Brian cupped Michelle's tear-streaked cheek, she leaned her head into his hand for a moment. Then she took his hand in both of hers and kissed his palm.

"Michelle, I love you, but I wouldn't keep you a prisoner. That's not our way—it's a Norm custom. I'm sorry, but it's just wrong. It's primitive and repressive."

"It's not like that for me."

"Then why are you crying?" he asked softly.

Something in his voice made her want to throw her arms around his neck, but she didn't. Then a grinding sound echoed down the shaft from above. The platform was on its way. It hit the ground with a thump, and when they stepped on, Brian put his arms around her again. About halfway up, when light started shining down the shaft, he stepped away, but he didn't stop looking at her until they reached the top.

Michelle had no idea how bad she looked until she saw how the others reacted. Chilly air across her stomach made her clutch the black vest that Molly had embroidered for her. It was covered in dust and torn so badly that it hung off one shoulder. Michelle rubbed a fist across her blackened, tear-streaked face and only managed to add a smear of blood from her hand. The icy air set her shivering.

Sylvia grabbed Michelle's furs off the lift and ran over with them. "What happened down there?"

Michelle didn't know how to explain the horror and the wonder of it all. "Uh, the tunnel caved in."

She actually felt relieved to see Molly, who swept her up in a hug.

"Come with me, I'll getcha cleaned up, darlin'," Molly said, wrapping a fur mantle around Michelle's shoulders. The motherly Norm pointed an angry finger at the foreman. "You're outa your mind, takin' her there."

"She wanted t' go!" the Norm protested.

"That's not fer a *man* t'decide," Molly snapped. "Stella's gonna hear about this."

The old foreman cringed and slunk away.

"Molly, it was worth it," Michelle said. "I figured out how to get the heat going again. I need to talk to Todd."

"He can come to you." Molly twitched her chin at Dillon, who hovered at her elbow, looking pale. "Go get 'im, we'll be back at the hot pools. It's the only place t' get this poor girl washed off."

***

An hour later, Michelle reclined on a massage table while an elderly herbalist treated her wounds. Steam from the hot pools wafted through the warm room.

"It's not a big deal," she told the old woman. "These are minor. They'll all be healed by morning."

"Mornin'? Ha. These'll be weeks in healin'. An' infection's always a risk." The grandmother slathered more salve on the torn and ragged flesh of Michelle's fingers.

"Not for me," Michelle started to explain, but a knock at the door interrupted her. The Norm woman cracked the door.

Michelle heard Todd's voice. "Let him in! Seriously, I need to talk to him." The woman's reluctant expression made Michelle realize there was something special about this chamber. "Oh. Men don't come here, do they?"

The grandmother shook her head. "Never. They're not allowed."

Michelle sat up, wrapping the sheet around her naked body. "It's okay, I can talk to him outside."

"No! Lie down." The woman pressed her back with a surprisingly strong hand. "I know where you've been, an' y' stay here."

The grandmother pulled up the sheet all the way to Michelle's chin before she opened the door. Todd shifted his feet awkwardly in the doorway.

Michelle shrugged apologetically and tried to make it fast. "Todd, you need bleach, or hot soapy water, something to kill germs. Clean the pumps and all the lines. Some organism lives in the caves. It breaks down oil, and I'm sure it contaminated the supply, so make them use different barrels, or whatever..."

Michelle's head fell back, and she realized just how exhausted she was. "Todd..." she held out a salve-slicked hand, and he took it gently in his bandaged one. She began to send him images of her journey to the cavern of jewels.

The old woman slapped Todd's hand away. "That's one of the women's mysteries, and we don't talk about it to men. Even t' you, special boy."

Todd looked dumbfounded and a little offended, but Michelle turned to the Norm in wonder. "You know," she breathed. "How we sometimes communicate by..." Michelle reached out a hand to Todd again, but the Norm warned him off with a sharp gesture. He left without another word.

The grandmother snapped the door closed. "You've been to the womb of the Mother. It's a sacred place. Men cannot go there, nor do we speak to them about it."

Michelle fell silent, staring up at the woman's dark eyes. A wrinkled, blue-veined hand held up a tiny glass vial.

"Young priestesses once made pilgrimages there in coming-of-age rituals. But the last girl to survive that trip did it sixty years ago. The Sisterhood gifted her with this."

The old woman held up a tiny glass vial, and Michelle knew without being told that she was with that same girl, sixty years later.

"Y' offered willing sacrifice, an' you almost gave yer life. The Mother gifted you already. The gifts she gave ya, y' give away, to whoever's most deservin'. This is my gift t' you, and this one ya keep fer yerself." Stella opened the vial. A rough finger lightly traced an intoxicating spot of scented oil on Michelle's forehead, and the old woman whispered, "This'll open yer eyes, child."

Michelle dozed off, surrounded by the exotic scent of the oil. The fragrance carried her into strange dreams of robed priestesses chanting in a crystal cavern. When she awoke it felt like night, although there was no way to tell in the caves. A few candles burned low, filling the room with the warm scent of beeswax. The old woman snored in a chair, gap-toothed mouth open and her gray head tilted uncomfortably against the wall. Michelle tossed off her sheet and stood up. Greasy spots of salve soothed even her tiniest scratch, and bigger injuries had been dressed with clean bandages. Her skin and hair were soft and clean, and someone had even filed her nails smooth. Michelle impulsively spread the old woman's shawl across her sleeping form, and then she reached for her own clothes.

Suddenly the woman spoke. "Don't wear those."

The Norm's quavering voice startled her. Michelle turned. "Sorry, I didn't mean to wake you."

"Don't wear those! You've earned better." The Norm looked even more ancient in her fatigue.

Michelle felt guilty about hogging the one bed while an old lady slept in a chair.

"Don't ya think that. It's my job, an' I'm honored to do it as long as I'm able."

"Whoa," Michelle breathed.

"Creepy, ain't it? Now ya see how people feel." The Norm's voice rose, and one eye reflected madly in the candlelight. "Freak! Abnormal!"

Michelle recoiled, but her feet remained frozen to the floor as though trapped there. She could not speak.

"Oh, you've got darker secrets than seein' into people's heads, I know. Ya carry a heavy burden, child. Gifts of genius… gifts of death." The old woman clung to the arms of her chair and then collapsed back into it, closing her eyes. "They know where you are."

Michelle took in a sharp breath. "Who?"

"He's coming for you, for all you beautiful children. He'll make ya into weapons, into slaves! It's better t' die first, before he turns ya against yer own." Both of the woman's eyes opened.

Michelle inexplicably felt dizzy at the sight. She sank onto the soft rug at the foot of the chair and looked down, letting her long hair hide her face. "I've considered that."

It felt weird to say it out loud. Her darkest secret, her one forbidden thought. She only entertained it when she was certain she was alone, with no well-intentioned telepaths nearby to eavesdrop and fly into a panic.

"But then, I decided—"

"It's better t' kill him first, and if ya die tryin', it all works out the same in the end." The old woman cackled, and Michelle laughed mirthlessly along with her. She didn't even know that woman, but it seemed a relief to not be alone with her thoughts.

Michelle leaned against the chair, letting some of her hair drape across the old woman's knees. "Parker wants Dillon."

"Oh, and a well-baited trap it is! Everything the boy ever wanted, except you. They'll add that in, y'know, if they can. An' if they do they'll change that boy, they'll scar 'im t' the soul. He fights out o' love, now, but that won't last, not at the Torr. It's a dark place. The mountain itself is dark, shunned by the clans long before your kind ever built there."

That wouldn't have made sense to Michelle even a day ago, but after her journey to the cave, she knew what the Norm meant. Underground, the rock itself seemed to breathe, with humming tendrils of energy connecting it to all the life on the surface. *What must it be like under the Torr? Horrifying, no doubt.*

"If I go in after…" Michelle took a breath and made herself say his name, letting him be a real person in her mind. "Mark Parker, and try to kill him, there's a good chance I'll get caught."

"Don't be stupid, girl!"

Michelle flinched at the outburst, and the woman stroked her hair, calming her. "Let 'im come t' you, darlin'. He'll come t' you when he's ready. An' when he does, remember one thing."

Michelle pushed back her curls and looked up. The old woman's lined face took on an ethereal beauty in the candlelight.

"He's hurt others, far worse'n what he's done t' you."

The old woman dressed her in all new clothes, and she wouldn't let Michelle even touch her old ones. Hand-woven undergarments clung to her curves, and over that, a pair of slim indigo pants in the softest wool imaginable. The form fitting long-sleeved shirt was an unusual one, woven from multi-colored yarn that glowed softly in the light.

"Never let 'em braid yer hair again, not while yer here. People need t' know yer not like us, an' y' don't follow our rules."

Michelle objected when the woman flung her old field boots into the waste bin, but they were quickly replaced by better ones, insulated and waterproof.

"Normally ya'd get a dress an' shawl, but this is better. You'll need to be able t' run an' fight."

It gave Michelle a pang to see her doeskin breeches go, since she'd made them herself with help from her friends. But the woman shook out a double handful of uncut gemstones from the pocket first. Gathering them up and cupping them in her hands, the Norm cast the stones across the surface of a small table. They rolled, catching beams of candlelight and throwing off rainbows. The old woman leaned over the table, watching intently as the gems settled into place. Her sharp black eyes suddenly reminded Michelle of a raven's.

"Ya very nearly died," she said, wrapping the gems in a cloth bag and handing them back. "Ya fought hard t' live, and She rewarded ya richly. Remember, all of these, give away. Every last one."

Michelle nodded solemnly.

"These, we're not gonna burn, 'cause each one is a life." The Norm gestured at the pile of Michelle's clothes and furs on the floor. "We'll return 'em t' the Mother, just like we'll do ourselves when we die."

Michelle felt anxious without her outdoor clothes. They meant survival there, and besides, away from the hot springs, the complex would be freezing.

"That blond-haired boy, he fixed the heat, thanks t' you. You'll be gifted with outdoor furs if ya need 'em."

"If?" Michelle repeated, unable to imagine that she wouldn't.

"He'll come t' you, child. He'll come t' you. You're the prize in all this. You and all those beautiful babies, but most of all, you."

Michelle wept when she took her leave of the kind old priestess, and the woman surprised her by catching a few of her tears in a tiny vial. "Powerful magic here, powerful. Sweetwater heals grief, y'know, as much as it can be healed."

Bewildered, Michelle walked back up the stairs, feeling like she'd wandered between the worlds.

Dillon waited for her in their chamber. The place had been transformed. A soft rug cushioned the floor. Colorful cloth hangings brightened the walls, and wrapped packages of bread and cheese sat on the tiny kitchen counter. Even the bed had new covers and piles of soft pillows.

"Each thing is a gift from someone we know," Dillon told her, smiling. "Everything on the bed is from Bear and Elsie."

She giggled. "That's a message. He wants you in there with me, instead of out fighting."

"Yep. The rug and tapestries are from Molly, and the food is from Laird." He sat back on the bed and looked at her. "You look beautiful."

"Better, huh?" She knelt in front of him and put her arms around his neck, but he only kissed her once.

"Michelle, I want to thank you."

She sat back cross-legged on the rug and waited. Finally she had to ask. "For what? Taking a bath?" Michelle giggled.

Dillon looked serious. "For standing by me yesterday, when...it's not your people's tradition."

"What?" Michelle stammered.

"By the Gods, I swear you're not a prisoner. I just can't... I can't do the open relationship thing, I'm sorry."

The blood drained from her face. "How do you know all this?"

"Jeanette got it off Brian, and she transferred the memory to Todd, who gave it to me and Sylvia."

"What is this, a group mind?" Michelle snapped. "I have no privacy at all, even in the bowels of the earth!"

"Try being Sylvia or me—the only non-telepaths in the clan," Dillon said with a wry smile.

"Brian's not a telepath."

"He might as well be. Jeanette spends more time in his head than she does in her own."

They laughed a little, but Dillon still looked perturbed. He leaned against the wall, crossing his arms over his chest. "You know, in the Warren I could have killed him for that."

"Dillon, it was nothing!"

"The way I heard it, you kind of wanted him."

Michelle refused to answer, but the flush on her face gave her away. She felt acutely uncomfortable, mortified, and unfairly angry about it all.

Dillon slid off the bed and sat next to her on the rug. "That's why...I'm really glad you didn't. Otherwise, I'd…"

"Don't say it. Please." She put a finger on his lips, and he turned her hand over and gently kissed her palm.

"Michelle, I'm trying to thank you, not threaten Brian's life."

"Seems like you're kind of doing both."

He pulled her close for a quick kiss. "I guess I am."

Michelle thought of something to change the subject, and she pulled out the bag of precious stones. "Look what I, um, found." She nearly blurted "*was gifted with*," but remembered not to talk about the sacred cavern to the boys.

"What's this?" He turned the bag over in his hands and untied the string that held it closed. Uncut gems spilled into his lap.

"I want to give a few to each of the others, but the rest are for you," Michelle said.

"They're gemstones!" Dillon held up a rough diamond the size of a baby's fist. "You've got a fortune here!"

"No, you do."

Seeing Dillon thrilled was more fun than keeping the gems for herself. He'd never had money in his life, and besides, Michelle had a huge jewelry box at home, if she ever got back there. The Atherton mansion seemed impossibly far away, like something from a particularly vivid dream. The couple sat together on their bed, comparing the gemstones and deciding which ones would be best for each of their friends. The big diamond went to Jeanette, a pair of rubies to Sylvia, and a scattering of smaller emeralds for Todd.

"You don't mind if I give one or two of them to Brian?" Michelle asked.

Dillon shook his head. "No, you should, he deserves something."

"You're not mad at him?"

Dillon didn't answer, but he gently touched her face. She knew he was angry, even though he felt desperately sorry for Brian too. "He's a good guy, really. And in his own way, he's bonded to you, and he can't help it."

"Bonded?" she repeated. "I thought you said that Enhanced can't bond."

"I think he has, in a damaged kind of way. Offering to share you? That's seriously weird. But I get it, because if you…left me for some other guy, I wouldn't stop trying to get you back, even…part time. And even if that new guy was a friend."

"So you won't go off on him if he tries it again?"

"Oh, sure I will. I'll have to kill him." Dillon laughed like it was a joke, but Michelle saw the look in his eye, and it worried her.

A fight between Dillon and Brian would end with one or both of them dead, and she couldn't stand that. She resolved never to let Brian get her alone again. In some twisted way, she was almost glad to have something that took her mind off her real problem--the colonel. *I have to stop him before he launches his attack on the Institute, but how?* That night Michelle lay awake for a long time, picturing Parker's ice blue eyes. *"He'll come t' you, child. He'll come t' you."*

    He knows where I am.

Chapter 21: Michelle

Round Robin

Michelle wouldn't admit it, but thoughts of the colonel influenced her choice of job. At the Norm stronghold, everyone had a workshift, even little kids. Younger ones had small jobs that took only minutes, while teens worked two hours a day. Michelle got slated for a full five hours, the same as any adult.

Molly handed her the order, saying with a sniff, "If yer gonna insist on livin' with a boy, you can work like a grown-up."

"Shouldn't you call him a man, then?" Michelle retorted.

Molly wouldn't answer.

It beat telling Dillon to move out, so Michelle didn't argue even though it wasn't fair. The other Institute teens had two hour shifts, except for Dillon, who got handed another five-hour slip, of course. Michelle deliberately tossed her long loose curls before she walked away, knowing it irritated Molly no end that she'd stopped braiding her hair.

Michelle didn't like any of the open jobs, since they all involved cooking and cleaning, so she invented her own—karate instructor. She pitched the idea to the Council, and it came back with a stamp of approval, on one condition—that Dillon or one of the other guys help her.

"That's sexist," Michelle complained to Sylvia, who wholeheartedly agreed.

"It's ridiculous. They obviously have no idea what you're capable of."

The other girls had no problems. Sylvia loved working in the child care center, which the Norm Council approved of, since teenage girls traditionally learned mothering skills that way. Jeanette designed and sewed clothes, which she enjoyed even if all she had to work with were homespun fabrics and furs. All the boys were grabbed up by the physical plant team, so they helped keep the water flowing and the furnace on. Only Michelle was left shiftless and frustrated.

"Here's what we'll do," Jeanette plotted merrily. "We put up a prize, and you offer to take all comers, round-robin style. Stay in the ring and beat up Norms 'til there aren't any more."

"Do you really think that'll make people want me to be their karate instructor?" Michelle asked. "Or would they all just hate me?"

"Probably both," Jeanette quipped, softening the comment with a grin.

"But at least they'll see that you're qualified."

"I'll do it with you," Sylvia said, shocking Michelle and Jeanette out of their giggles. "You should too, Jeanette. We'll run three rings at a time and get done faster that way."

"Sylvia, um," Michelle began, but couldn't say it. Sylvia wasn't Enhanced, not really. She'd just been recruited because she'd inherited a practically perfect set of genes. *Sylvia can spar, but against male Norms, for hours? Maybe not.*

"Okay," Jeanette blurted, and the deal was done.

Trying to save the situation, Michelle said, "Every fight only goes to the first point, then." That made it more a speed contest, and less a brawl. The girls had nothing to offer for a prize, so they agreed to charge a small entry fee. Norms who won points—if there were any—could divide up the pot.

"Whoo!" Jeanette cheered. "I'll get started making posters, and we'll have it added to morning announcements in the dining room too."

"Shouldn't we ask permission from the Council?" Sylvia asked.

"Of course not." Jeanette looked at her like she was crazy. "They might say no."

***

At breakfast the next day the announcement went out, generating all kinds of excitement among the Norms. "How much is the prize?" men kept asking, until Michelle wearied of saying, "That depends on how many people sign up."

A sign-up sheet hung on the wall, but the girls took to carrying around extras and signing up people who came to ask questions.

"Girls can play too, even kids," Jeanette said, loud enough to be heard from across the dining hall. "We don't have to hit hard, unless you want to."

"What the hell is this?" Bear demanded, getting in Michelle's face. "You startin' fights? On purpose?"

"It's like a game of tag, Bear. First touch wins. Want to sign up for a turn? Pay at the ring."

"No."

"Chicken?" Michelle teased. "I won't hit you that hard. I'm sure Dillon's done worse."

"I'm not scared o' you." Bear grabbed the sheet, and afterward Michelle checked to see if he could really write his name. Some Norms just made their marks. He could, and with decent handwriting too. As Bear walked away, Michelle made a mental note to remind the other girls to watch out for him. *He'll do his best to knock them cold.*

A cluster of men at the other end of the room caught her attention, and she wandered that way. Dillon was in the thick of things, laughing and bantering. He had his own clipboard and a leather bag heavy with coins.

When he took a few coins from a black-bearded Norm and handed the man a slip of paper, Michelle realized with a start that he was playing bookie, taking bets.

"Isn't she a cute little thing?" Dillon said, so all the men turned to look at her. Michelle wanted to make some snappy comeback, but she didn't. Dillon could only be helping, making them see her as weak so they'd be more likely to sign up.

"I'll pay t' play with her," a young ponytailed man said. He pulled out two coins and rubbed them together while the men around him laughed and made suggestive comments. Dillon glared, but that wasn't what stopped the ribald talk.

The old herbalist appeared at the edge of the crowd.

Men made way for her as she came toward Dillon and Michelle. The woman didn't say a word to them, but the men apologized anyway. "Sorry, Stella."

"Won't happen again."

Stella grunted, and the men fell back a few more paces. Michelle hugged the old woman, feeling weird that that she never found out her name until now. Stella gave her a bag, motioning her to open it. Inside was a tank top, multicolored like her long sleeved shirt, only lighter weight and more breathable. A pair of loose, undyed cotton pants went with it.

"Thank you, Stella. I don't know how I would have made it through the day in wool."

Stella just grunted, like Michelle should have expected the gift. Right away Michelle noticed that the old woman's dress matched her own new tank top. They were both made of the same material, fine and glittery. That stood out among the brown and gray homespun fabrics of the Norms. Stella pulled Michelle's head down to her level, like she was going to say something, and then surprised her with a kiss on the forehead. When Stella took the belt off her own dress and held it over her head, the whole room got quiet. Norms stared.

The old Norm wrapped her belt around Michelle's hips and tied it with a knot, while Michelle stood there, perplexed. The belt was really just a scrap of fabric, left over from making the multicolored shirt.

"They know what it means, and they won't be botherin' ya no more." Michelle opened her mouth to ask questions, but Stella turned her back and disappeared into the crowd.

"Come on, place your bets," Michelle called out, seeing that they were about to lose their audience. "You can bet and play too, as long as you bet on yourself," she added, and a couple of men did just that.

"What if I wanna fight, but I bet on you?" a little old man shouted, making the others laugh.

"You can't do that. Otherwise it'd be too easy for you to throw the fight—you know, pretend to lose when you could have won."

"Oh yeah, I could win," the old man yelled, waving his cane. "I was in the war!" The men cheered him, but grandpa placed his bet on her anyway.

***

Back in their chambers, Dillon caught her up in his arms and swung her around, celebrating. "Look at all this money! Win or lose, I get ten percent for holding the bets."

"At least then we could buy some clothes for you," she managed. "You have almost nothing but furs."

Michelle couldn't get excited about the Norms' coins. She paced the room nervously, already overheated in her wool pants and long-sleeved shirt. At least she had something cooler. Michelle tried on the new outfit, imagining that Molly would have had a fit if she'd fought in her bra. The top had an elastic quality, so it clung to her without binding.

"That's hot," Dillon murmured, slipping his hands around her waist, but it was already time to go. On the way out, Michelle suddenly remembered something. She ran back for the fabric belt and tied it around her hips.

"What's that for?" Dillon asked. "That old woman said they'd know what it means."

"That old woman is Stella, the Norm priestess, and I don't even know what it means." Michelle giggled at Dillon's stunned expression.

"Michelle, this—"

"Later. Time to go."

Todd and Brian set up a big stone-walled chamber as a gym, with sparring rings painted on the floor. Butterflies began in Michelle's stomach as soon as she walked in the room, and they only got worse as the crowds began to gather. The girls clustered together in the back, stretching on the floor.

"Anyone regretting this as much as I am?" Michelle muttered.

"Yeah," Sylvia said. "Look at all these people. We have way more than I thought. They must have nothing else to do."

"Oh, come on," Jeanette said. "It'll be fun." But she got up and paced the ring, warming up nervously.

Todd decided to be the master of ceremonies, but without a microphone he had to yell. He stood up on a table to get everyone's attention.

"All right! First off, it's a *game*. No punching hard, okay? And they won't either." The crowd hooted, drowning out what he said next. "I said, you can place your bets any time before you go in the ring." Todd pointed at Dillon, who stood up and waved from his table by the door.

"Fights go to the first point only. Any touch counts as a point, no matter how light. If you win, make sure I get your name before you leave the ring. That's it. Begin!"

On her way to the ring Michelle's stomach quivered with nerves, but when her first opponent waddled in she almost laughed. The bell went off, she popped the chunky little guy in the forehead, and he grinned good-naturedly and left. Michelle fell into a rhythm, sizing up opponents as they approached and deciding how much caution she needed to use. Norms liked to wrestle, which gave her an advantage since she could tag them when they leaned over to shoot in for a grab. They never seemed to figure that one out.

Between rounds, Michelle glanced at the line in front of her ring. It seemed no shorter, even after an hour. She began to worry. She hadn't lost a round yet, but thirst and exhaustion were starting to slow her down. She grabbed a drink of water and got a nasty surprise when she came back to the ring. Bear stood there leering, his big hands already balled into fists. Michelle swore silently, wishing he'd picked one of the other girls. *That's what I get for needling him at breakfast.* Bear pointed across the room, where Dillon was taking bets, head down. Michelle knew what that meant. Bear wanted her to know she was alone now, since no one else would dare to interfere.

Michelle regretted throwing so many fancy jump-spin kicks early in the competition. She'd just been trying to display her skills, but that wore her out. She wiped her forehead tiredly with the end of her belt, wondering how long it had been. Bear's eyes flicked uneasily to the belt, and she caught the gesture. Since it seemed to bug him, she pulled the loose end through her hands a couple more times, and then the bell rang.

Michelle knew he'd be fast, but she had no idea. His speed and power bordered on that of an Enhanced male. That made him faster than her and twice as dangerous. As a result of Michelle's failed attempt to cure the plague, all the survivors received at least one Enhanced gene. It usually wasn't easy to tell which one, but in this case, it was obvious. *Bear got two of them—a double dose of speed and power. I augmented him, and now it's come back to bite me.* She resisted the impulse to tell Bear his famous strength really came from her. It was a short jump from that to figuring out she'd caused all the deaths too.

Bear bent his knees and sprang halfway across the ring, forcing Michelle to dive roll out of his way. She almost went out of bounds, which would have given the match to him, but she regained her feet and skittered away from the green line on the floor. The crowd cheered. His next attack got countered with a kick to the head. He ducked it and rushed in to punch her while she was still on one leg. He threw a powerful right cross, but she knifehand blocked his punching arm, catching him square on the wrist. Bear went pale with pain. He grabbed her by the neck with his good arm and clenched her throat, bringing back horrible memories of her father.

Michelle did the only thing she could to get him off—she grabbed his injured wrist with both hands and twisted. Bear screamed and rolled with it, ending up face down on the floor.

Michelle locked the elbow joint, trapping the big man on the floor.

"Remember, the game's over on the first touch," she called out to the crowd, grinning to diffuse the tension. "If you want more after that, you'll have to sign up for lessons."

The crowd laughed, and suddenly Michelle could feel the mind of each and every one of them. She knew exactly how to play the situation to get what she wanted. It felt weird though, and even the room looked different somehow. Stella stood in the front row, watching everything with her beady raven eyes.

"Bear wants a lesson, doesn't he?" Michelle called out, inducing the audience to agree by applause. "Now, I think he might be a little stronger than me." She paused while men guffawed, yelling, "Ya think?"

"But watch this. With a little encouragement, he does anything I want. Absolutely anything," Michelle said suggestively. Men wolf-whistled and jeered. She flashed her best sexy smile, letting them enjoy the joke.

Deftly rolling over Bear's wrist, she caused him pain in a whole new way, and he rolled with it, ending up on his back. Then Michelle hauled Bear to his feet.

"Front flip, or your arm'll break," she whispered, and she cranked his wrist. Bear flipped and landed hard on his back.

"Great job, Bear! Give him a big hand." The crowd clapped, and Michelle helped Bear to his feet. "Thank you, you were wonderful." She eyed him, hoping she hadn't made an enemy. It was hard to read the expression on his ruddy face. "How's your arm? Todd, can you ask Stella to look at it?"

The big man turned to her, appalled. "Please, no," he muttered. "Not her."

"Okay, no problem. I just thought your wrist…" she whispered. "Todd, never mind, he's fine."

Bear turned away. Michelle went after him, stopping him with a touch. "By the way, thank you for the gifts. The bed is amazing. Dillon and I love it."

"That's the idea," he grunted, but his habitually cross face broke into a smile when she stood on her tiptoes and kissed him on the cheek. He hugged her back while people clapped.

"So, do you think I'm qualified to teach karate or not?" Michelle asked.

Bear nodded, rubbing his wrist with a rueful grin.

Michelle dispatched the rest of her line without anyone getting a touch on her. She high-fived triumphantly with Todd, and then they watched Sylvia and Jeanette spar the last few people in their lines. Sylvia's line ended with a string of kids from the day care center, and she danced around with each one for a couple of minutes before touching them lightly on the nose. Kalie went last. Mollie and the other parents cheered, and Sylvia hugged the little girl as she left the ring, praising her richly.

Jeanette only had one more challenger, a big one.

Michelle took a sharp breath. "Brian! He's not supposed to participate. It's just for Norms."

Tension crackled in the air as Jeanette and Brian argued under their breath. Norms heading for the door came back to watch. Brian wouldn't back down. He circled the ring like a lion, light glinting off his long blond hair. Michelle shot a questioning look at Dillon, who nodded and raised six fingers. Brian had bet on himself, at six to one odds. In his favor, of course.

"Dillon should have told him no!" Michelle hissed to Todd. "Why'd he take the bet?"

Todd shrugged, bowed them in, and started the match. Jeanette ran for her life.

She stayed in bounds but danced and weaved, trying to stay out of reach. Anyone could see she was hopelessly overmatched. Brian toyed with her, faking punches and kicks just to see her flinch. Then he covered the width of the ring in one tremendous spring and backfisted her hard across the face. The impact could be heard across the room. Norms gasped. Jeanette's face turned white except for the flushed red spot where he hit her. Tomorrow it would be a huge black bruise, but she put her feet together, bowed to him, and then politely left the ring. In seconds she was lost in the crowd.

Todd and Michelle stared at one another for a moment, aghast. Then Michelle remembered where they were. "You're still on," she muttered.

Todd leaped onto the table, thanked everyone for coming and reminded winners how to collect their bets. The girls moved slowly toward the door, accepting congratulations on the way. Michelle totally forgot to ask Sylvia how she'd done. Dillon stood in the center of a clamoring crowd, juggling betting slips and money. Michelle caught his eye, waved goodbye, and escaped into the cool air of the hallway. Jeanette was nowhere in sight.

After a shower, Michelle climbed into their new bed and fell asleep. Dillon came in quietly, but she woke up at the sound of the door opening.

"Heya, love," he whispered. "How're you feeling? You were awesome."

She put her arms around his neck, already feeling her muscles twinge from just that small motion. "Sore already. Tomorrow's going to be worse."

He gave her a kiss and then stretched out beside her on the bed. "Michelle, what the hell happened with Jeanette and Brian?"

"I have a pretty good idea."

Dillon rolled over on his side, propping up his head with one hand. From the look on his face, he already knew, but he wanted to hear her say it.

"He's punishing her for gossiping. He trusted her with that memory, and she spread it around to everyone."

Dillon looked grim, and she put a gentle hand on his chest. "Let it go, please?" she begged. "I know you don't like him hurting girls. "

"That's an understatement."

"But if you get in his face about it, it'll never end."

"Okay, Michelle."

"Besides, I hate to say it," Michelle went on. "But she deserved it."

"I said okay!" Dillon snapped.

Michelle shut up and watched him anxiously. In a few minutes she sat up in bed. "I'm going to go check on Jeanette. Want to come with me?" She added that last part as a peace offering, not really expecting Dillon to come along.

He got up right away. "Absolutely."

As they slipped down the hall to Jeanette's room, Michelle wondered how Dillon got so attached to Jeanette. But he obviously was.

Jeanette's room stood open and empty, which worried Michelle. "Maybe she's in the infirmary."

"I seriously doubt she'd go there unless someone made her. She's got too much pride for that," Dillon sighed. "Want to check anyway?"

They cut through the dimly lit dining hall on their way to the infirmary tunnel, but they didn't have to go any farther. Jeanette and Brian slept together on a double chaise lounge, her head on his shoulder. The bruise on her face stood out clearly from across the room, but their hands were entwined like they'd been linked when they fell asleep. Michelle found the scene charming, but Dillon didn't. She had to pull him away by the hand, and she kept hold of him all the way to their room.

"How can you just accept that? How can she?" he argued, once they closed their door. "I thought you'd be opposed to men beating up pretty girls."

Michelle shot him an irritated look for the pretty girl thing, but he didn't seem to notice.

"She went into the ring, it was fair, and besides, I have bigger problems," Michelle said tiredly, groaning in pain as she sat down on the bed.

"Bigger problems? What, like Brian? Are you jealous?" Dillon demanded, following her.

"No." She stretched out without another word.

"Michelle, don't shut me out!"

"Trust me, you'd rather be shut out of this one."

Dillon looked hurt, and for a moment she thought he was going to leave, but he just took off his shirt and got into bed. He stared at the dark ceiling for a moment, and then reached over and took her hand. At first Michelle didn't notice, but a slight tingle began. She realized with a shock that Dillon was initiating a link. *He's not supposed to be able to do that, ever. He doesn't have the gene!*

Instead of helping, she waited, letting him show her what he could do. In a moment, the link formed, weak and tentative, but only because she wasn't adding anything to it. Michelle reached out for him, drawing him softly into her mind. Dillon closed his eyes and shuddered a little as she lit up the pleasure centers in his brain.

"So Jeannette taught you," she finally whispered. "You have her style, the way she initiates...it's really beautiful. I'm blown away, completely impressed. What an amazing surprise." She moved to kiss him, but he sat up.

"Michelle, who's attacking the Institute?"

Chapter 22: Michelle

Leveling the Field

Dillon called an after-breakfast meeting in their quarters to discuss Iron Torr's attack on the Institute. Brian arrived with Jeanette and a bad attitude. Dillon eyed the pair as they came in the room, but he didn't say anything.

Brian took a preemptive strike. "Hey, we worked it all out, and it's none of your business anyway, Freeman."

Dillon looked Brian in the eye. "That's not what we're meeting about, but since you brought it up, hit her again and I'll slit your throat."

"Where do you get off getting all possessive over Jeanette? Thinking about adding her to your little harem?"

"It's not like that, you moron," Dillon spat. "Look what you did to her face!"

Jeanette's left eye was swollen half shut, and a huge black and blue bruise covered the side of her face. When she spoke, her voice sounded uncharacteristically small. "I don't know about your martial arts training, Dillon, but at the Institute girls go toe to toe with men, and we sometimes get hurt. We prefer that to being sheltered, honestly."

"He could have won the match without wrecking your face," Dillon insisted. Around the room, people chimed in to agree.

"That reminds me, Dillon," Brian interrupted. "I did win, and you owe me a lot of money."

"Stop it, both of you," Sylvia snapped. "Don't you guys ever think of anything besides yourselves?"

The outburst shocked them all, mainly because it came from her. Sylvia was always the first to agree to a new idea, the first to give in during an argument. Now she stood between the boys, eyes blazing. Dillon nodded, letting her make her point, and Sylvia backed off.

In the moment of silence that followed, he dropped the bomb. "I called this meeting to tell you that Iron Torr is invading the Institute."

A collective gasp followed. Michelle sat on her bed and let the talk swirl around her, rousing herself only to argue against the idea of bringing Sage in to re-tell her story. The situation seemed hopeless. The colonel's logical move would be to execute the Conclave immediately after invading and replace it with his own officers.

Michelle pictured him lining up the Conclave to face the firing squad.

Her pregnant mother Victoria would be the first to die, along with her unborn baby girl. *When the troops arrive, Dillon's little sisters will melt into the Warren and disappear. If they get caught, they'll bide their time until they can scale the wall. Seth would have done that too if he hadn't been assigned to security. He'll be on the front line now with those tattooed freaks, the Toklats.*

Todd's warm shoulder pressed against Michelle's. She turned into it to hide the tear that streaked her cheek. He tried to send waves of comfort, but they faltered. Both of his parents were on the Conclave. At home, that put him in an enviable position, protected against the doctors' purges of weak offspring. But in an invasion, rank worked against the Morleys too.

Raised voices snapped her out of her thoughts. Dillon and Brian were at it again. Michelle jumped off the bed to break it up. "All right, that's enough," she said sharply, as the two guys glared at each other over her head. "We can't be at each other's throats when we're about to lose our home."

There was a momentary pause, and then Brian started to argue. Michelle cut him off. "Seriously, Brian, shut the hell up."

Brian flinched and put a hand to his head. "God, Michelle!"

Michelle ignored him. "Jeanette!"

The blonde recoiled like she'd been slapped. "What?"

"He apologized, right?"

"Yes," Jeanette said softly from her spot on the floor.

"Good, 'cause what he did wasn't okay. But it's over," Michelle said. "Okay, Dillon?"

"Fine, but you're all totally screwed up, if you ask me," Dillon said.

Michelle glared. "Do I need to melt your brain? It's over, I said!"

Dillon put his hands out in a capitulating gesture and shut up.

Michelle whirled on Brian again. "I totally understand why you did it, but if you hit her again, in the ring or out, I will personally help Dillon kill you."

Brian's eyes widened as he figured out that she wasn't kidding, and he nodded. "I'm sorry. I told her I am, and it was just because she told everybody—"

"We know," Michelle interrupted. "Now we need to figure out how to take down Iron Torr."

The room got very quiet, and Michelle added, "By the way, Brian, you're not getting paid. That's our war chest now."

The meeting ended with nothing decided. People trickled out. Brian helped Jeanette up off the floor and walked her to her apartment a few doors down the hall. "I'll be back to check on you after my shift, all right?" Brian said, his golden blond head bent attentively over her platinum one. Dillon rolled his eyes in disgust.

"Looks like Molly gave Jeanette the day off," Michelle said to Dillon, but he only grunted in a pissed-off way, grabbed his jacket, and left.

Michelle dreaded her workshift. *What a waste of time, teaching karate to*

Norms instead of planning a strike on Iron Torr. I guess I'd better get over to the gym, in case anyone actually shows up. It counts as a workshift, anyway, so Molly can't bitch.

When Michelle opened the door, she almost backed out of the room. The place was packed. Excited Norms milled everywhere, talking and laughing. Michelle tried bringing class to order by clapping her hands the way Sensei did back home, but the Norms just applauded her right back and kept on chatting. They didn't get it.

Finally Michelle jumped up on the table. "Thank you all for coming! I didn't expect so many people."

They all stared, like they were hoping for something better.

"Okay, um, line up and I'll show you some basics."

Karate class was a disaster. Over a hundred people were there, and everyone did everything wrong. People in the back couldn't hear over the chatter, and a scuffle broke out in line as some boys started play sparring. Michelle raced around trying to maintain order and teach too, and finally she gave up. She grabbed a teenager and sent him off with a message for her friends—help!

No one showed up.

When the class finally ended, Michelle sagged against the wall, feeling like she'd run twenty miles. Through the departing crowd, she glimpsed Sylvia sitting on the sidelines, arms folded, like she'd been there a long time. *She's here! Why didn't she step up and help, then?*

By the time Michelle made it through the press of happy, sweaty Norms, her friend's long black braid was disappearing around the corner.

Michelle ran to catch up. "Sylvia! Thanks for coming. Um, want to walk back with me?"

"No, Michelle, I really don't."

Michelle felt a sudden, palpable ache in her chest. She only stared at her best friend.

Sylvia sighed heavily. "I just came over to talk to you, and after this, I don't want anything to do with you. And I don't think Jeanette does, either."

Michelle couldn't talk over the lump in her throat. Tears welled up in her eyes.

"Michelle, I know you've been under a lot of stress, but we all have. The way you snap at people literally hurts. So threatening to melt our brains isn't funny. We know you could do it if you wanted to."

"That's ridiculous," Michelle said, but she knew it wasn't, not really.

"Tell that to your father," Sylvia said sarcastically. "Oh, that's right, you can't. He doesn't understand much of anything anymore, after what you did to him."

Michelle walked back alone, head down, remembering the brilliant, charismatic, abusive father Grant Atherton had been. *I wanted payback, and I got it. Now he's got the mind of a preschooler. Sylvia's right. I'm dangerous. I lack self-control.*

I don't deserve this power.

The stone corridors were deserted except for a slender, dark-haired boy ahead of her. Hoping to walk with a friendly student, she lengthened her stride, but he glanced over his shoulder and sped up. Michelle winced. The boy seemed strangely familiar, but she hardly glimpsed him before he disappeared around a corner. Something about him intrigued her. Feeling absolutely insane, she left the route toward her apartment and followed him.

The boy led her into a part of the complex she'd never been in. Soft hand-woven carpets covered the floor, and surprisingly good art adorned the walls. A few peeks through open doorways revealed the beautifully furnished apartments of high ranking Norms. Michelle tried not to feel like a recruit at the Institute, relegated to her tiny stone cell. *I should be grateful just to be here at all.* The hall came to a weird intersection that opened in five different directions. She stopped there. A rustle down one of the corridors alerted her, and Michelle broke into a run, tearing down hallways and surprising a few well-dressed Norms coming out for lunch.

The dark-haired boy ran too, forcing Michelle to sprint hard to keep him in sight. That was all she needed to be sure. "Slade!"

Slade bounced a hand off the wall and disappeared around a corner. Gasping for air, Michelle rounded the corner after him. A pair of large double doors stood there, closed tight. She slammed the doors open and recoiled, mortified. Wade and Molly stared disapprovingly from their places at opposite ends of a long wooden table. Slade sat between them, and Bear glared from his chair next to Dillon. Jeanette and Brian just looked pained. Michelle had interrupted a formal meeting of the Norm Council.

"Sorry," she gasped, backing out of the boardroom.

Michelle would have fled in humiliation, but a beautiful black-haired woman turned and froze her in place. The two females locked eyes.

"Hello, Brooke. What a surprise," Michelle said evenly. She didn't speak to Slade, who looked fit and well-fed, if wary. His winter hadn't been at all like hers.

"Since ya crashed the party, ya might as well sit," Wade said, in a tone that said he was giving her something she didn't deserve.

Michelle almost refused, but curiosity trapped her. She took an empty seat next to Brooke, taking the opportunity to look the woman over. Brooke held herself differently. Her old submissive posture had disappeared, replaced by one of regal elegance. *Is that an act, or is she free of the colonel now?*

"How're things at Iron Torr, Brooke?" Michelle asked in a conversational tone, but Brooke barely spared her a sideways glance and didn't answer. Almost as soon as Michelle sat down, Brooke stood up, ending the meeting. Michelle was offended, so she didn't say another word.

Brooke glided over to Wade in her high-heeled, black leather boots and took his hand. Wade's breath caught at her touch. He stared at the gorgeous woman with his mouth open. His wife narrowed her eyes at Brooke from across the table, but only Michelle noticed.

"Do consider my offer," Brooke purred. "It'll be good for both of us." She left that hanging like a promise as she strutted out of the room, with Slade in her wake. Bear practically trampled Wade trying to walk her out.

Michelle sat frozen in her chair. Molly and a cluster of Norm councilmen swept up Dillon and Brian, and then only Jeanette lingered in the hall outside. Michelle didn't move, and finally Jeanette came back in.

Michelle counted her breaths in the way Seth taught her, determined not to keep snapping at people. *I know why I wasn't invited to the meeting—no one can stand me.*

"What does she want?" Michelle deliberately kept her voice calm. *If I want to have any influence at all, the tantrums have to stop.*

"Brooke wants the Norms to invade Iron Torr before the colonel hits the Institute. Most of her relatives are back at Headquarters."

Michelle opened her mouth to scoff at their chances, but she bit back that comment and substituted another. "Is she helping the Norms with strategy?" *Or just sending a bunch of men to their deaths on a huge testosterone rush?*

Jeanette slumped tiredly into a chair, touching her black eye lightly with her fingertips. "I'm sure she would if the Council agreed, but they haven't yet."

"Wade and Bear are for it, I presume?"

Jeanette shook her head. "They're not. Molly's the biggest supporter of the idea."

"No way!"

"Molly's afraid for the children," Jeanette said softly, turning in her chair to meet Michelle's eyes. "She thinks it's only a matter of time before this place gets overrun."

"She's probably right. So she figures an offensive is the best move. Still, the Norms don't stand much of a chance."

"I hate to tell you this, Michelle, but they're putting up a better fight than our families will," Jeanette said.

Michelle didn't answer, but she knew Jeanette was right. *Norms can hide in the forest, but Institute mansions make easy targets for artillery.*

***

Michelle left the Council chamber, wandered the halls alone, and ended up in the giant, dome-roofed common room by the entry. Lunch was being served back in the dining room, so the benches by the gas fire pit stood empty. Even the bad-tempered gatekeeper had gone off to eat. Michelle opened the heavy door to look outside. Snow blew over her shoes, but droplets of water fell from sundrenched icicles. In a month or so, the colonel and his troops would be on the move again. She slammed the door and barred it, like that could keep an army out.

Tears of frustration rose to her eyes. *I'm trapped, but the colonel's not. His helicopters could make it to Institute headquarters in a matter of hours.* She sat by the fire alone. None of her friends came looking for her, not even Dillon. Michelle stared into the flames, remembering the day the heat went out. *If I could do that to Iron Torr, Parker would be as trapped as I am.*

She slowly made her way down the stone stairs toward Stella's quarters. The door opened before she even raised a hand to knock. The old woman wouldn't listen to a word until Michelle ate a piece of brown bread and dutifully sipped at a steaming cup of bitter tea.

Finally Stella sat down in a threadbare chair opposite her. "Tell me, child. What burdens ya?"

"Same problem," Michelle whispered. Her throat felt tight, and it hurt to talk.

Stalla barked out a laugh. "It ain't the same, seein' as how ya changed yer mind. I told ya he'd come, but you ain't gonna wait fer him, are ya?"

Michelle never got used to Stella reading her mind like that. It would be a terrifying trait in an enemy.

"Of course he's afraid o' you, child," Stella answered, as though she'd spoken aloud. "He don't know why he is, but his instincts work jus' fine."

"You think Colonel Parker senses I can hear people's thoughts, and that scares him?"

Stella shook her head solemnly. "No, but think about him. He's a big man, always workin' on makin' himself bigger."

Michelle laughed. "You think he's insecure?"

"I reckon he is. And he's got a hunch that you'll spot his weakness."

"How do you really know all this, Stella?" Michelle blurted. "You never even met him."

"Am I wrong?" the priestess retorted. "You have spotted it, haven't you?"

Michelle nodded, pressing her hands together to keep them from trembling. "But I didn't lift it out of his head. I first thought of it in the cave. Stella, do you remember that glowing stuff, in the underground pool?"

The old woman nodded, dark eyes alight.

"It's alive. It breaks down oil and gasoline, so the fuel won't burn. If the colonel's fuel depot got infected…that would shut him down. At least until they figure it out."

Stella said nothing. The old woman's shiny, birdlike eyes bored right through Michelle, reminding her why Bear feared his priestess. Michelle met those eyes without flinching. The Norm could read her to the core, so evasion was pointless. Stella raised an eyebrow, asking a silent question.

"I could probably get into Iron Torr," Michelle answered over the lump in her throat. "But…I don't think I'll get out alive."

"Likely not," the old woman said, startling Michelle with her bluntness. "Levelin' the field, that's worth yer life? Why? It won't end the war."

Michelle struggled to explain. "All this started when I enhanced the Norms, trying to cure the plague. They never would have rebelled before I changed them."

"So everything that goes wrong in the world is your fault now," Stella huffed.

"Not everything. But this much is," Michelle said earnestly. "This is the only way I know to make a difference."

Michelle thought of the millions of Norms who died of Doctor Salomon's plague. Billions more died because of her own egotistical certainty that she could cure them. *Like I could take five minutes and cure a disease designed by a hundred-and-fifty year-old genius. The augmented survivors are my fault too. These new, smarter Norms aren't satisfied with lives of servitude, and they started a war over it. This is the only way to atone for what I've—*

"Bah!" Stella suddenly shouted, right in her face. Michelle rocked back, clutching her head in pain. Telepaths could listen to people's thoughts and subtly add new ones. But cutting a thought off in midstream was something Michelle had never seen done. It felt like being slapped in the head, on the inside.

"This ain't new," Stella grunted. "You did it to yer own friends, this very mornin'. Taste o' yer own medicine, an' not very pleasant, is it?"

Michelle gasped. Tears rolled down her cheeks. Her head pounded, and her stomach roiled with gradually subsiding nausea. "I did this? I didn't know...no wonder they're so mad. I'm a monster."

"No sense in beatin' yerself up, girl. Goddess knows, there's enough people eager to do it for ya." Stella chuckled. "If ya could do that from a distance, then you'd really have somethin'. Every time Parker has a thought— *bah!*" The old Norm cackled harder. "He'd piss himself!"

Michelle laughed weakly even though it made her aching head pound even harder. Stella stood and opened a cabinet, where stacks of fur-wrapped bundles lay. One at a time, the old woman tossed them to the floor. Michelle untied the cords and found thick boots and a handmade set of outdoor furs, all expertly cut and sewn in exactly her size.

"Stella, you knew."

Tears glistened in the Norm's eyes. "I wouldn't let ya go, child, but I don't see another way. You're the only chance we got."

Chapter 23: Michelle

Willing Sacrifice

Stella crouched in the pine-scented forest. She scraped aside slushy snow with her bare hands and sculpted freezing mud into little mountains and valleys. Beneath her hands, a model took form, showing a steep ridge overlooking a river. Snow soaked the old priestess's skirts, and her wrinkled hands were red with cold. Michelle squatted guiltily beside her, dry and comfortable in new furs.

Stella jammed a black rock into the mud to represent Iron Torr. "Ferget it! I'm goin' back t' sit by the fire. Yer the one goin' into the dark."

Michelle turned her attention to the map and mentally photographed it. She closed her eyes for a second and saw every detail in her mind's eye.

"Watch now," Stella said, poking at the model with a twig. "This is the entrance, here, where the river goes under the mountain. Beware the path along the cliff; it's slick from spray. The Torr is anchored here, in the bedrock under the cave floor. When they were buildin' it, they used local labor. Men needed t' go up an' down, so there had t' be ladders. Unless they blocked up the holes, ya might be able t' get in from underneath, like a rat."

"There had to be ladders?" Michelle repeated. "So you don't know for sure."

"I don't. My granddaddy did."

Michelle gave her a dubious look, and Stella smiled mirthlessly. "Want a sure thing? Stay home."

"Too late for that."

"Listen, child. Drownin', falls, gettin' lost—all these things can happen in there. But those aren't yer real problems."

"Right. The colonel is," Michelle said, nodding. "And his men."

"No! Before ya ever get to him, or his fuel supply, it'll find ya. It might not interfere," the old woman muttered darkly, almost to herself. "But I don't know it well. I only met it once and heard the stories."

"It? What?" Michelle had no idea what the Norm meant, but the old woman's weird talk was starting to make her palms sweat. She pulled off her mittens and rubbed her hands on her pants, half afraid to ask the question. "What stories, Stella?"

The old woman snatched up Michelle's warm hand in her freezing, muddy one and squeezed it so hard that it hurt. "Stories are medicine!

Sometimes you need 'em more than you need food."

Though her eyes were open, Michelle's world went dark. She took a ragged gasp and tried to pull away, but her body didn't respond.

The darkness around her resolved itself into shadows, and she found herself in a damp cavern, cool mud squishing under her bare feet. The cave smelled faintly of sulfur, mold, and rodent droppings, but a cool mist rose, making this the perfect place to rest on a hot day. A blonde girl in a tattered homespun tunic walked at her elbow. The blonde girl looked about ten, but she stood only an inch or two shorter. The two children exchanged a secret smile, and Michelle knew they weren't supposed to be there.

Rivulets of moisture ran down the walls, and the cave's humidity made her hair cling damply to the nape of her neck. Somewhere in the darkness, the river plunged into a pit, where it traveled a short way underground before emerging on the other side on the mountain. Michelle tried to turn her head but couldn't. She was a passenger, gazing through another girl's eyes, with no control. That frightened her. She willed herself to stop, but her host's little feet carried her deeper into the shadows. The mud-caked floor turned to slippery rock and began to slope down. This close to the pit, vibrations of agitated water thrummed through the cave floor.

"C'mon, Stella," the blonde child whispered, and she took a few more tentative steps. Michelle's panic grew. One slip and they'd plunge into the roiling water.

Faint light from the cave mouth filtered through a cloud of vapor rising from the pit. In unspoken agreement, the two girls picked the darkest spot to make their nest. The blonde child sat down first, and Stella followed. A feeling of profound peace enveloped them as they lounged on the cool, damp earth. An ancient presence slid from the pit and lay there, just out of sight.

Michelle's host sat up and looked around, but nothing moved. Still, she had no doubt. Something was there. Instinctively, Stella reached out with her mind while Michelle watched, paralyzed. The thing billowed toward them like mist, seen and unseen. It exuded evil. From her hiding place behind Stella's eyes, Michelle felt it watching her across time.

The little girls scrambled to their feet, making breathy sounds of panic. Michelle's lips parted on their own, and another girl's voice came out. A child's voice, quavering with fear. "Something's watchin' us, Darla."

"Let's get out o' here," the blonde child said abruptly.

The girls whirled and ran. Forgetting their friendship, they raced toward the mouth of the cave. In her panic, Stella cut off the smaller girl. Darla slipped and grabbed at a stalactite, which came loose and crashed to the cave floor. She cried out, but recovered and kept running. The mist flew behind them. Tendrils spread out to the sides, trying to wrap around them and cut them off from the only way out. The girls sprinted desperately as the gap closed, and with only inches to spare, they burst into sunlight. The thing watched them from the darkness, though it had no eyes.

Michelle gasped as her consciousness returned to her own body. Sunshine glared off snow, sending stabbing pains into her dilated eyes. She blinked her tears away, dimly wondering how she'd gotten forty paces farther into the woods.

Stella clutched Michelle's fur-clad arms with wet fingers. "It once chased a man deeper in. He got trapped in there, or lost. No one went in after him. His screams echoed out o' the cave for days."

Michelle trembled. "What is that thing? What does it want?"

"All we know is that it feeds on fear."

"I'm afraid of something every day of my life," Michelle confessed, eyes wide.

"Then it'll feed on you."

***

Even in wet shoes, Stella insisted on accompanying her as far as the river. Michelle bargained the whole way. "Are you sure that's the only way into the fortress? Maybe I could reach the fuel depot without going through the caves at all."

"Go bang on the front door then," Stella grunted.

Great slabs of ice broke up on the river's surface, and they churned against one another, making deep grinding sounds she felt in her bones. Michelle suddenly found a million things she wanted to say. "Don't let Dillon go after me. Seriously, lock him up if you have to. He'll try to follow me, and he'll get himself killed. Tell him I'm deep in meditation, or off doing priestess stuff with you, and I can't be disturbed."

Stella let out a pained laugh. "You *are* doin' priestess stuff, girl. What d'ya think a priestess does? She serves her people in willing sacrifice."

Michelle choked up, and a single tear rolled down her cheek. The wind chilled it until it felt like ice.

Stella hung a little round jar of contaminated fuel oil on a cord around Michelle's neck, tucked it in for warmth, and chanted a blessing in some forgotten language while making strange and graceful gestures around her head. Then she silently handed over a leather backpack brimming with food and extra furs.

Michelle strapped it on with hands that suddenly felt weak and clumsy. She embraced the old woman. "Goodbye. Thank you for everything, Stella."

Before she could change her mind, Michelle bounded for the riverbank and leaped from one boulder to the next, racing the swirling ice. When she paused to look back, the priestess was gone. Michelle checked to be sure she was alone, and then leaned on a tree and sobbed, icy bark rough against the soft skin of her face. When the relentless cold crept through her furs, she set off through the snow.

Travel over icy riverside rock was hazardous, but there she left fewer footprints to alert the colonel's scouts. *Or more likely,* she reflected guiltily, *fewer tracks for Dillon to follow me by.* She hiked until the sun set and then pressed on through deepening twilight, delaying the moment when she had to set up camp alone. Eventually full dark came on and walking became all but impossible. Stella had packed dry tinder and a flint-and-steel for her, but a fire was out of the question. It would stand out as a beacon to Parker's sharp-eyed Enhanced soldiers.

Michelle crawled under a pine tree and tucked boughs in to make a rough shelter, feeling lonelier than she ever had in her life. She shivered into her furs and dozed, but whenever the wind shifted it dusted powdered snow onto her face, waking her.

At the first light of dawn she broke down her shelter and tried to sweep footprints away, but she soon gave up and set off along the river. *Dillon's not stupid. If he finds that trampled snow he'll know it was my camp, with or without footprints. He'll never understand, but there's no reason to give all our lives when one will do. Besides, it's my responsibility.*

Bah! Michelle told herself, trying to stop the dark thoughts, and giggled aloud, feeling crazy. Her laughter died when she rounded a bend in the river and spotted the Torr for the first time. It stood out as a tiny black dot on a faraway mountain. She watched it on and off as the day crawled by, but it never seemed to grow any larger. Finally, driven by worry that the colonel could mount his offensive at any moment, she began to run.

Running over ice-slicked rocks took her mind off her problems. Michelle's life fell into a pattern of running all day and then trying, but failing, to sleep at night. Her pace flagged toward the end of the fourth day, when the food ran out. Scraping the bottom of the bag yielded a few more fragments of jerky, but it didn't matter. The Torr stood only a few hours away. In a fit of paranoia, she left the riverbank and entered the shelter of the trees.

***

From the edge of the forest, Michelle craned her neck and looked up. The black tower loomed over her like a monster. Its long shadow cast a strip of forest into twilight. Iron Torr seemed deserted from the outside, like it usually did, but she sensed the lives inside. Anxiety and stress radiated from the walls, with occasional flares of anger. *They're going to be a whole lot madder when the power goes out.*

Near the top of the tower, someone switched on a light. Michelle ducked back under the pines and burrowed into a snowdrift, hoping it would hide her from watching eyes. As she waited for darkness to fall, nervous sweat chilled on her body, and she clenched her teeth to stop them from chattering. Eventually a deep sleepiness overcame her, and her freezing feet went comfortably numb. Thoughts became sluggish, but she dimly realized what that meant. *If I stay here much longer, I'll fall asleep and die.*

A little herd of does and yearling fawns came through the trees toward the river, their nostrils flaring when they caught human scent. They hesitated, but thirst won out. Large ears flicking, the deer picked their way down the steep side of the canyon. *There's the path down the cliff.* Making the approach in twilight was risky, stupid even, but the thought of entering that cave in the dark was terrifying. *It won't matter, it's dark inside anyway*, Michelle told herself, but that didn't help. She wiggled out of the snowdrift and hurried toward the path, keeping low. Spray from the river a hundred feet below froze a glaze of ice onto the cliff, constantly wetted by more churning whitewater. Three steps down the trail, Michelle glanced out at the deer, and her numb, frozen feet shot from under her.

She landed hard on her back and went into a sickening slide off the edge of the escarpment. Sharp rocks tore her furs and gouged her flesh as she tumbled down the steep slope. Michelle clutched at an outcropping of stone, but it came loose and crashed into the freezing river beside her. The shock of the cold water took her breath away. Icy fire licked her wounds. She scrambled toward shore as the powerful current sucked at her legs. Even in knee-deep water, the river could take her.

Sodden furs weighed her down, and it took all Michelle's strength to pull herself onto the shore. She collapsed on a flat rock, whimpering in pain. A fawn swept past in the water, bleating piteously. Its mother followed anxiously along the shore. Despite all the deer she'd killed, Michelle gasped in horror when the youngster disappeared into the mouth of the cavern. In time, its body would reappear on the other side of the mountain, where it would feed the scavengers.

Soaking wet and bleeding, Michelle dragged herself along the riverbank. Despite the protective furs, her knees and elbows burned. Blood ran freely from a cut on her lip, and her side ached so badly that she could hardly breathe. She limped into the cave, instinctively aware that something evil was inside. And it smelled her blood.

Chapter 24: Michelle

Into the Dark

Twilight didn't reach far into the cave, but thanks to Institute doctors, Michelle saw in the dark like a cat. A feeling of déjà-vu overwhelmed her as she limped into the cavern's mouth. It looked just like she—*no, like Stella*—remembered it, except for one thing that made her heart sink. Big boot prints tracked through the mud. Lots of them, and they all lead into the cave. Michelle's own prints looked delicate beside them. *Soldiers. Enhanced ones, I'm sure. Norms aren't that big.*

The cave looked deserted, so Michelle limped into the darkness, following the prints. When she stepped partway off a flat rock, pain lanced through her hip. A soft cry of pain escaped her. Her left leg burned like fire. She crawled into a shadow and collapsed on a boulder, trying to quiet her ragged breathing. The only sounds were the soft dripping of water and, farther away, somewhere off to her right, the roar of the river plummeting into the earth. She felt lightheaded, and the smell of wet guano turned her stomach.

Pushing with her arms, Michelle sat up, but it took all her will to force herself onto her feet. *Face it. This is a one-way trip. I'd better go now, so I can do this...before I can't walk anymore.* She struggled deeper into the cave. Ahead, the path narrowed to a ledge that tracked around the left side of the watery pit. The black stone was slick with spray, but not frozen. Inside the cavern, it seemed oddly warm, but maybe that was just the blood pooling in her boot. She crept along. The path abruptly disappeared into shadow. Reaching forward with her one good foot, Michelle felt only air. She clung to the wall, trembling. Fumbling in the dark, she discovered that the ledge sloped down in a mound of loose rock. She bent her knees and slid about ten feet down to a flat place where a pool of still water lay among timeworn stones. Behind the great stones, the river roared into an abyss. Scrabbling sounds reached her, and a breathy panting. Something moved in the black pool. Terror prickled the skin up her back.

The panting continued, rapid and shallow. Sounds came from the water's edge, like something was trying to climb out and come after her. Cold dread washed over Michelle. She wanted desperately to run for the mouth of the cave and forget that insane plan. A shadow moved on the side of the pool.

Oh, it's only the fawn! Grunting in pain, Michelle crawled toward it. The fawn's slender forelegs were thrown up on the rock in such a strange angle that at first they looked broken, but the side of the pool was too steep to allow it to crawl out. Its body hung below, invisible in the dark water. Reaching out a slow hand, Michelle cupped the little muzzle. The fawn lay still, eyes huge in the dark. The baby didn't have the strength to flee. Its fur felt coarse and prickly, and warm blood ran over her hand.

"Nothing should have to die like this." Michelle grasped the front legs and pulled while the little deer struggled. One sharp cloven hoof caught her in the arm, and she accidentally let go. The fawn thrashed and disappeared underwater. Michelle moaned aloud to see it go.

In a moment the swirling water brought the deer around again, lower in the water and bubbling through half-submerged nostrils. Michelle put a boot into the water and then waded in waist deep. Cold water flooding across her stomach made her suck in a breath with a hiss. She caught the fawn in her arms. It hung there, exhausted. For a moment she didn't move. Icy water numbed her pain, and she wanted to relax, float, and forget everything. Then a hoof caught her in the knee, so she wrapped her arms around the baby and tried to lift it. Its slender forelegs hooked the rocky edge with surprising strength, and when Michelle boosted the haunches, it scrambled from the pool. She crawled out after it and sat there talking to herself.

Idiot. After all the deer you've killed. Don't trade one for everything back home. Get moving.

She regained her feet with an effort and then herded the fawn up the pile of loose rock. The animal sniffed the air and moved toward freedom on shaky legs, but partway up, it stopped. In an avalanche of gravel, the fawn bounded back down. It stood there trembling. With a chill, Michelle saw why. A formless mist hung in the air above the ledge. Terrified tremors shook her, but she stood her ground. There was nowhere to run. Her breathing came faster, and Michelle broke into a sweat like she always did before a panic attack.

"Damn you, Doctor Salomon," Michelle gasped aloud. *It's his fault I have this panic disorder, his mistake, and now it could mean I'll die for nothing in this cursed place, without accomplishing my mission.*

The mist crept closer, and Michelle's heart raced so hard that her chest ached. Hot blood coursed through her freezing hands and feet. She moved a few steps toward the thing on trembling knees.

"What do you want?" she suddenly shrieked, forgetting all about the soldiers who might hear her.

The entity made no answer. It watched her malevolently, and then slid a few inches closer. Michelle's pounding heart accelerated the blood loss. A wave of dizziness made her stagger.

"What are you gonna do?" Michelle shouted, but her voice sounded small, swallowed by the roar of the pit. She swung a boot through a puddle, splashing water at the place where the thing hung invisibly in the dark. It didn't react. Terror fueled her anger, and Michelle lost control.

"What are you gonna do, kill me?" She bent and hurled a handful of stones, but they ricocheted off the rocks and came back to pelt her. She advanced on the entity, waving her arms insanely. "Beat me, like my father did? Rape me, like Salomon? You can't hurt me. You don't even have a body," she shrieked, flinging another rock.

The stone bounced off the wall and accidentally hit the fawn, so the little deer bounded in terrified circles. "Oooh, sorry, sorry," Michelle murmured, changing her tone to a soft one. She reached out an arm to steady the creature, but it shrank from her. "Let's get you out of here."

She put a hand behind the fawn's hindquarters, prodding it toward the ledge, but the mist blocked the way. "Move over," she snarled, and she was surprised and gratified when the evil thing swirled silently off the ledge to hover over the black pool. When she stepped forward to shove the fawn up the hill, the entity swept up behind her in a rapid arc. She screamed. The fawn bounded up the slope and disappeared, but by then the thing had its ice-cold claws in Michelle's back. It clung to the nape of her neck, touching her…invading her.

"Get off!" Michelle whirled as though to strike the formless thing. A bright light blinded her. The mist let go and slid into the shadows.

Behind the light stood a man, visible as only an outline. The flashlight shook, making shadows waver nauseatingly. "Well, if it isn't Michelle Atherton, crawling around my cellar like a thief."

He sounded oddly constricted, and she almost didn't recognize his voice. *Oh, no. It's Colonel Parker.* It took a moment for Michelle to register his tone as fear. Rigidly suppressed fear, bordering on terror. Men's voices echoed in from behind the colonel.

"Who are you talking to?" Parker demanded, casting his light around the stone chamber. The beam reflected off the pool and glinted weirdly off his pale eyes, making him look otherworldly.

"A demon," Michelle said, a manic little smile quirking the corners of her mouth. The cold from her legs gradually spread up her body, and in the back of her mind the automatic countdown began, ticking off the minutes until she'd lost too much blood and no help in the world could save her.

Parker made a guttural sound of disdain. "That's the best story you can come up with?"

"Okay, fine." Michelle walked toward him, taking careful steps to conceal her weakness. "I didn't come here alone, obviously. I'm not the only person you ever hurt, am I? They're here too, hiding."

Behind her, the mist changed course to creep toward the colonel. Michelle knew then that some part of him believed her. He was afraid. She stepped aside, clearing the path between Parker and the entity. "They're going to hunt you down, Mark."

Parker glared at her for daring to call him by his first name. The mist picked that moment to attack. It swept forward. The colonel gave a great strangled cry and stumbled for the passageway, for the chamber where light and people and machines kept the darkness away. It caught him like a spider with a fly, and he went to his knees, gurgling.

Michelle stared, horrified. *Not even Parker deserves this.* She took a hesitant step forward, and then made a decision. "Back off," she cried, waving her hands.

The creature spasmed weirdly as though she'd slapped it. Concentrating, she limped forward and exerted the force through her hands again. Pain stabbed up her leg and hip with every step. The mist gave way reluctantly, leaving a few hungry tendrils behind as it retreated. With a breath of fetid wind, the thing retreated to hang over the pond again. When Parker scrambled to his feet, Michelle let out a relieved sigh. Then he grabbed her by the throat.

"Here, in here," Parker bellowed. Feet pounded, and soldiers with flashlights raced in. "Take her. Search this place for more spies!"

Strong arms dragged Michelle down an endless stone passageway. Eventually it opened into an immense, well-lit chamber. Helicopters and jeeps stood in orderly rows while jump-suited men readied them for a mission. The soldiers threw Michelle roughly on the floor, and she saw the huge white fuel tanker, five hundred feet away, on the other side of the chamber. *If I was alone, could I walk that far?*

"Sir, she's hurt," a man said.

"Like I care," Parker said. A few of his men chuckled.

A young man bent over Michelle, but his face kept slipping out of focus. He picked up her wrist and felt the pulse. "She's in bad shape, sir. If we don't stop the bleeding she won't make it."

Michelle tried to say something, but her mouth didn't want to form words. The pain kept her in her body, and she concentrated on it to stay focused. *I was so close.* The fuel tanker looked like a blurry white blob, impossibly far away. Men's voices spoke around her. One of them stood out.

"That's the Founder's spawn. I suppose she might be useful as a hostage," Parker said, pinching her chin to turn her face toward him.

Michelle cringed as Parker bent close to her and leered. "You've caused a lot of trouble."

"Do you want to keep her, sir?" asked the young medic who had taken her pulse. "I hear she carries some rare genes. Exceptional ones."

"Might as well," the colonel grunted.

The medic pulled out a pair of bulky shears and quickly clipped off her torn leather jacket. Michelle gasped in pain as he pulled a strip of fur out of a clotted wound over her ribcage.

"I don't know if her genes are exceptional, but her tits sure are," some soldier said, making his friends laugh.

Michelle reached out a weak hand for her clothes, but the medic pushed her arm aside and started cutting off her blood-soaked leggings.

"Keep her alive," Parker ordered, moving away. "I have questions for her."

Michelle woke with a start when someone pricked her finger and scraped a vial across the bloody fingertip. She didn't remember passing out. She lay on a gurney, wrapped in blankets. They'd rolled her to the other side of the chamber, just under the roof. A med-evac helicopter waited nearby.

"What's this?" the medic asked. He tugged on the vial of oil around her neck, and Michelle reached up a hand to cover it.

"It's one of those totems," another man answered. "Stupid Norm superstitions."

The medic held up a syringe, squirting a droplet of amber liquid from its tip, and Michelle waved it off. "No…no painkillers."

"What? Why not?"

"It's…against my religion." Her head fell back, and she laughed weakly at her own joke.

"Suit yourself." The medic quickly threaded a needle and began stitching up a gash in her leg. Every pinprick burned, but Michelle focused past him. The giant fuel tanker squatted nearby. It took up practically the entire length of the hanger. Footsteps approached, and a blue-eyed officer came into view. More men gathered behind Michelle's head, where she couldn't see them.

"She is gorgeous," said the officer, yanking up the blanket to look. Cold air flooded in. With an outraged sound, Michelle snatched the blanket back. Another man ran strong fingers through her tangled curls, hurting her. She made a soft cry of pain, and the fingers gripped harder. She recognized the laugh before his face came into view. *Parker.* Ignoring the medic, the colonel shoved a hand under the blanket. She tried to fend him off, but he pinned both her wrists in one big hand and ran the other one over her breasts and then down her stomach, rubbing painfully over the open wounds there.

Michelle thrashed on the stretcher, but the colonel held her down. "Don't touch me, or I'll feed you to that…thing," she hissed.

Parker let go and slapped her hard across the face. Blood ran from Michelle's nose onto the crisp white pillowcase, but she saw his expression, and he looked pale. *He knows I can beat it, and he can't.*

"Sir," the medic said in a patient tone, the closest he could come to a reprimand of his commanding officer. The young man held up his suturing needle and waited. "Should I finish later?"

"No. Finish now. I want her alive. And do a good job, I don't want her scarred."

"There won't be scars, sir. Scans indicate that rapid-healing mutation. She'll be as good as new by day after tomorrow, at the latest."

"Good." Parker leaned over Michelle and played with a few of her curls. "Brooke's been a giant pain in the ass lately," he whispered. "Maybe it's time for a replacement."

Michelle snapped her head around and tried to bite his hand, but Parker only laughed. "I can't wait to see the look on the old man's face when he sees me with his precious great-granddaughter. On a leash."

Parker walked away, and a few moments later the unmistakable tap of a woman's high heels approached. A black haired woman in a fur coat stood over her.

"Brooke! You've got to help me," Michelle begged, and then she got a better look at the colonel's wife. Brooke's perfect features were rigid with fury.

The beautiful woman kept her voice low, almost playful, but her dark eyes flashed. "You sure know how to work it, don't you, little girl? Just enough fight to keep him interested. Whoever trained you did one hell of a job."

Michelle flushed scarlet and took a breath to answer, but Brooke didn't wait to hear it. She turned on her heel and stalked off, leaving Michelle alone with the young medic. The suturing took forever. It hurt more than she expected, and she wished she'd taken the painkiller. The dark-haired medic looked like he could have been the compassionate type, under other circumstances. He gently turned her onto her side to clean a gash on her hipbone, working around the IV that trickled synthetic blood replacer into her arm.

He talked to her as though she was a normal patient and not a prisoner at all. "That cut on your leg opened an artery. You lost a lot of blood. What happened?"

"I fell down the ravine into the river," Michelle whispered, leaving out the weird parts.

The medic slid a hand under her head, and she tensed, but he only held a cup to her lips. "Drink. Just a little, or it might make you throw up. Okay, I'm done here. Take care."

When he left, Michelle felt sorry to see him go. She lay on her back, watching the blood replacer drip from its bag overhead. No one paid any attention to her. It hurt to lift her head, but if she strained her neck she could see the white cylindrical fuel tank. A worker took the nozzle and pulled its long hose over to a nearby helicopter, but Michelle focused on the tank. Rungs on its side lead up to a port at the top. She began picking at the tape that held her IV needle in place. Workers busied themselves around the hanger, and no one was near. Parker and a few of his officers clustered on the far side of the hanger, talking. *This is my chance.* Michelle took a deep breath and yanked the needle out sideways. Pain flashed. Blood, real and synthetic, poured out of the torn vein.

Michelle rolled off the gurney and almost fell. Cold wind whipped around her naked body as she limped rapidly to the tanker and began climbing.

Halfway up, a mechanic spotted her. "Hey! What are you doing?"

The jump-suited man ran toward her, and Michelle scrambled up faster. The port on top was made for Enhanced men's strong hands, and she struggled with it, breaking a nail to the quick. Soldiers spotted a naked girl on the fuel tank. With catcalls and whistles, they swarmed toward her. The circular lid gave way with a sigh, sending fumes into her face. Michelle ripped the cord from around her neck just as the mechanic grabbed her ankle with grease-blackened hands. She kicked him in the face, but a couple of soldiers jerked her off the ladder. She fell hard on her back, still clutching the vial of contaminated oil in one fist. Michelle elbowed the nearest man in the ribs, trying to create an opening, but he leaned on her and she couldn't move him.

"Bah!" Michelle howled, letting all her fear and rage loose in a mental blast.

Soldiers recoiled, clutching their heads. Aiming fast, Michelle tossed the vial. It rotated, catching the light, and then she saw her mistake. *The cork's still in.* She fell back, shrieking, her head exploding in the men's reflected pain. *I failed.*

The glass vial shattered against the lip of the open fuel port.

"What're you doing?" the mechanic bellowed.

"That's my amulet. It's cursed, and now you are too," Michelle spat triumphantly.

Parker and his officers arrived in time to hear that. "You really bought into that pagan mumbo-jumbo," he laughed.

Someone jammed a needle into her arm, and she passed out.

***

The thrumming of the helicopter Michelle rode in woke her. A bag of synthetic blood swayed from an IV stand above her head.

The familiar face of the medic looked down. "You tore out some stitches, but I fixed them while you were sedated."

"Where are we going?" Michelle's throat felt dry, and talking hurt.

The medic offered her a sip of water. "Off to knock down those insurgents. You'll feel safer when that threat's gone. And then you get to go home. Home to Iron Torr."

"No." But her shout died and came out as a whisper.

A sunbeam lanced through the window, and it took Michelle a moment to realize that it must be the next morning. They'd kept her sedated all night while final preparations were made for the assault. For a sick moment of fear, she pictured contaminated fuel clogging the helicopter's engine, sending her down to crash in a ball of fire. *I'd rather die than let them land and kill everyone,* she told herself, but she still listened to the engine anxiously. It hummed smoothly along.

Michelle moved a little, and restraints dug into her bruised flesh. Yellow nylon straps held her down. She grunted in pain, loud enough to make soldiers' heads turn. The helicopter was packed with uniformed men. A flash of tension across the medic's face alerted her. The young man shot her an apologetic look and moved away.

Parker took his seat. "How's my pet?"

Michelle stifled a nasty answer and tried to smile a little. "Better. Hard to breathe."

Surprisingly, Parker reached under the gurney and loosened the strap across her chest. Michelle took a deep breath, stretched her neck, and glimpsed a familiar sleeve with a black number 24 on it. *I'm back in my prison uniform. He's making a point.*

When Michelle looked up at his face, Parker petted her head like she was a dog. She suppressed the urge to try and bite him again. "What are you going to do with me?"

Parker didn't bother to answer. He just let out a breathy laugh and moved away. Michelle closed her eyes, but tears leaked out the corners and ran down her temples to dampen her hair. Her eyes flew open when a man's finger wiped them away. Parker was back. He put his finger into his mouth, tasting her tears. Disturbed, Michelle turned her face away.

"Now, don't cry," he said, loud enough that all the Enhanced heard him. A few men chuckled at her humiliation. "You behave yourself, and we'll get along just fine."

Michelle flushed, but she held herself still. *I am going to kill you,* she vowed, and then quashed the thought for fear he'd heard it through his hand on her shoulder. He hadn't.

"Why'd you bring me along?" she whispered.

"Why not?" Parker gave her a fake, white toothed smile. "We're going to be spending a lot of time together."

Michelle couldn't help shooting him an irritated look for that.

"Oh, all right," Parker said. "It's just more efficient this way. Saves me a trip. I won't need you at the insurgent base, but I will at Headquarters."

"For what?"

Parker looked away, speaking to someone out of sight. "What do you think? When we let the Founder see her, should we drag her out naked?"

"If you say so, sir." The other man laughed in a mean way.

Fool. He's trying to use me against the Founder. Parker ought to know by now that G.G. doesn't care about me.

Michelle closed her eyes tight. Too soon, the helicopter descended, preparing for a landing.

"Colonel, please!" Michelle twisted under her restraints, trying to look over her shoulder. "There are children in there, noncombatants. Please don't do this."

"Children?" The colonel repeated sarcastically. "Well, we'd better clean the place out before they breed any more of them."

"Some of them are yours! Your clone—" Michelle stopped herself, suddenly afraid she'd endangered the surrogate mothers more by reminding him of them.

"How'd you know I have a clone?" Parker shook his head in disbelief. "Anyway, it's not our top priority. I'll pick it up if I can. Maybe I should, just to piss off Brooke." He shared a chuckle with his men.

"Excuse me, sir," an officer said. "Our operative reported the clone inside the underground complex. Do you want us to locate the child before deploying heavy artillery?"

The colonel snorted. "Finding it could take hours. If it dies, the doctors can always make me another one."

"It?" Michelle gasped. "He's a baby boy!"

But the colonel had already turned away. "Prepare the explosives, men."

Chapter 25: Dillon

Not Coming Back

Dillon knocked on Stella's door. "Stella, it's Dillon. Again."

Stella didn't answer. Dillon leaned on the stone wall opposite the door, arms folded. The old woman's woodstove squeaked loudly when she opened it, and her kettle whistled for a moment before she pulled it off the heat. Dillon knocked on the door again and settled back to wait. Long minutes passed while he bumped the heel of his boot softly against the rock. His self-control began to unravel.

Suddenly he pushed off the wall, took a big step forward, and pounded on the door so hard his fist hurt. "I know you're in there, Stella! I need to talk to you—"

The door opened a crack. One of the crone's shiny eyes stared through the slit.

"About Michelle, I know," Stella interrupted. "Like I told ya yesterday, an' the day before that. She's deep in meditation, an' I'll send 'er out when she's done." Stella tried to close the door in Dillon's face.

He shoved his fingers in the gap and stopped her. "Bull. Nobody meditates for four days straight."

The old woman put one bony shoulder on the door and pushed, but Dillon held it against her with one hand. Slowly, against her resistance, he pressed the door open. A wave of muggy, sulfur-tinged air rolled out into the hall. Dillon stepped into a low-ceilinged chamber, barely big enough for a massage table, a few chairs, and the oversized stove. Michelle was nowhere in sight.

The priestess hissed as he crossed the threshold. "Men're not allowed in here. As y' well know."

Dillon met the old woman's glare with one of his own. "Sorry. I guess somebody'll have to wash the floor now."

Heat pounded off the wood stove, making the small stone chamber into an oven. Moisture from the nearby hot springs beaded on the walls. Dillon felt like he was drowning.

A closed door stood at the far end of the room. *She must be in there.* Dillon pushed past Stella, opened it, and swore. It was only a closet, crammed with jars full of herbs. He whirled. "You lied to me! Where is she?"

The old Norm's hands trembled. "Off doin'…priestess stuff."

Dillon towered over her, fists clenched. "Where?"

"Go ahead an' punch me if yer gonna," the priestess said, her jaw thrust forward obstinately. "'Cause I ain't tellin'."

"I've never hit a woman in my life." Dillon flung himself into a moth-eaten chair. Stella didn't look happy about it, so he decided to stay.

"Yeah? Well, there's a first time fer everything." Stella stepped over his long legs, heading for the door. Dillon reached out a hand and slammed it before she got there. The room suddenly got a thousand times hotter.

Stella fixed the tall boy in her beetle-black stare and hobbled over to a huge basket of wood next to the stove. She tucked a few chunks under her arm and reached for the door of the stove. Dillon put one big boot against it and held it closed. He shook his head grimly.

Sighing in defeat, Stella dropped the wood and lowered herself into the one remaining chair. The pair stared at each other in silence as minutes ticked past. Thirst burned Dillon's throat, and chewing at his tongue didn't help. Stella sipped at her tea, but she didn't offer him any.

Dillon spoke first. "Something happened to Michelle, didn't it?"

Stella looked down. "She said…I'm not supposed t' tell."

Dillon wanted to bellow, but he bit his lip and tried another tactic instead. He leaned forward, pleading with his eyes. "Stella, please don't do this to me. I love her."

"I promised," Stella muttered, shaking her gray head. "But it don't matter now."

"Tell me the truth. Is Michelle…alive?"

Tears tracked the woman's wrinkled face. When she spoke, her voice was low. "The stones say she is. But I can't see her anymore."

"Where'd she go?" Dillon asked, using all his willpower to keep his voice low and even. He failed.

"I promised 'er I wouldn't tell you. She's afraid you'll go after her an' get killed. But it's too late now, too late fer ya to follow her. What's done is done."

Dillon abruptly pushed off his chair and stood over the priestess. "Stella, tell me," he bellowed.

The gray-haired woman didn't cringe. Instead, she sat bolt upright, one bony finger pointed right between his eyes. Stella pursed her lips and forced a burst of air out. A hot bolt of pain blasted through Dillon's head. With a cry, he fell backward onto the floor and curled up there, fighting not to vomit. Ten minutes later, he raised his head, ashamed of himself for badgering an old lady and losing. He wanted to leave, but his shaky legs couldn't carry him.

When Stella finally spoke, she wouldn't look at Dillon, but only stared at the flickering flames in the stove. "I know yer sorry. Ya don't have to say it."

A guilty flush spread across Dillon's face. "I am."

Stella nodded. "That ain't important now. Michelle is. I told her he'd come for her, but she wouldn't wait."

Dillon's breath caught in his throat. "He? Who?"

Stella bent to wipe her eyes on an indigo shawl, so her voice came out muffled. "Parker."

Dillon dragged his aching body to a sitting position and slumped against the wall, his head in a hand. *If Michelle's gone after Uncle Mark, she's going to lose. She has no idea who she's dealing with.*

"She's gone t' the Torr, all alone," Stella whispered. "To plunge 'em into the dark."

The old priestess took a squat earthen vial off a shelf and dropped it into Dillon's hand. When he pulled the cork out, it left a black smear of thickened oil across his palm. Comprehension dawned. *Michelle's trying to sabotage their fuel, but it won't make any difference. We dealt with that problem in a matter of hours, and the military will too.*

The old woman began to keen softly, rocking in her chair. "Michelle… ain't comin' back," Stella said between sobs. "She knew it …when she left."

From the floor, Dillon reached out and took the crone's spotty, blue-veined hand. They grieved together in silence while the fire slowly burned to ashes. Eventually, Dillon came to a decision.

Stella seemed to feel it. "I know, you gotta go after her, 'cause that's what men do. Even if it's stupid. And it is stupid, y' know."

Dillon nodded weakly, grateful to the priestess for not trying to stop him. He got to his feet, leaned down, and gently embraced the old woman. Then he walked up the misty stairwell alone.

By the time Dillon entered the main tunnel, he was moving fast. Shoulders set and eyes rigidly forward, he ignored the Norms that scattered out of his path. In his wake, people whispered and stared.

What am I gonna do? I'm not even sure how to get to Iron Torr from here. Who knows the way?

Dillon lurched sideways, grabbed a nearby Norm by the collar, and lifted the unfortunate man to his toes. "Bear! Where the hell is Bear?"

The Norm clawed at Dillon's hands. "I dunno. Let go o' me!" The man pulled free and disappeared down the tunnel, cursing.

Dillon let him go. No one answered his knock at Bear's apartment, and the Norm Council chamber was deserted. He slammed the big wooden door, rounded the corner and came face to face with Slade.

After an uncomfortable silence, Slade spoke. "Hey, um, haven't seen you in a while."

Dillon shrugged. "I thought you were back at the Torr."

"I was, but, you know, orders." Slade ran an uneasy hand over his dark hair.

Dillon quirked a lip. "Orders, eh? Whose?"

"This time? My mother's," Slade admitted. "Dad would have a fit if he knew I was here."

"I don't know how you choose who to mind," Dillon said with a wry grin. "They never agree."

"I mostly obey whoever's there at the moment," Slade said. "Otherwise I pick the option that's least likely to get me killed." He glanced around and lowered his voice. "Um, speaking of which, you should come with me."

Dillon wasn't processing very well. He shook his head. "Come with you? I can't. I've got problems. Michelle's missing."

"I know," Slade mouthed, giving him a significant look. "So come with me."

Dillon froze, all his attention on his cousin. "You know where she is?"

"Not exactly," Slade muttered. He grabbed Dillon's arm and started him moving down the hall. "Come on, we can't talk here. Get your outdoor gear."

The pair fell into step, moving rapidly through the maze. "This part of your orders?" Dillon asked.

Slade shook his head and muttered something that Dillon didn't quite catch. It sounded like, "Get me shot."

Heavy footfalls approached from a side passage, and Bear burst into view. "Freeman! I hear yer lookin' fer me."

"Um, yeah." Dillon didn't know what to say. He'd wanted Bear to tell him the way to Iron Torr, but now that Slade was here, that didn't matter anymore. Slade knew.

Bear stared him down. "Folks say yer goin' off on people again. I thought we was done with all that."

Dillon sighed. "Sorry. Um, you might have heard, Michelle's missing. Four days now."

The big man looked grim. "Alright, Freeman. Get a grip. I'm gonna tell ya somethin' nobody else will."

Dillon's stomach clenched while he waited for the hammer to fall. *They found her body.*

Bear folded his arms across his chest. "Some women just ain't worth it. Sure, she's pretty an' all. But that one's been nothin' but trouble since y' took up with 'er."

Dillon didn't answer. He just concentrated on getting his heart going again.

"Look, son." Bear put one big hand on Dillon's shoulder. "If yer gonna start a family with a woman, she's gotta be reliable. That one?" Bear shook his shaggy head. "She's prob'ly run off with some guy."

If I tell him she's gone back to the Torr, he'll figure she switched sides, or he'll think she's been spying. Dillon glanced uneasily at Slade, who looked like he was trying to blend into the wall.

"Slade," Bear said abruptly.

Slade flinched, and for a second, his slanted eyes narrowed to slits.

"Remember. Afternoon meetin' with the Council. We got a lot o' questions for ya."

Slade nodded, looking sick. Bear didn't seem to notice. The big Norm patted Dillon on the back and turned away. Before Bear rounded the corner, he paused and looked back over his shoulder. "Just wonderin'...y' seen Brian lately?"

Dillon swore. "She's not with Brian!"

"Alright, alright. If you say so." Bear lifted his hands in a capitulating gesture and turned away.

With Slade scampering beside him, Dillon strode to the furnace room and straight-armed the door open. Brian was there next to Todd and the old foreman, elbow deep in a partially disassembled pump.

Brian looked up, startled, and met Dillon's eyes. "What?"

"Nothing," Dillon grunted. "Sorry."

"Yer late t' work, Freeman," the foreman said shortly. "Give us a hand here."

Dillon didn't answer. He snapped the door shut in their faces and took off for the apartment he shared with Michelle.

Slade ran a few steps to catch up. "I could have told you that."

"What? That Michelle's not with Brian?" Dillon hurried through the dining hall and turned sharply down the tunnel toward his quarters. "How would you know?"

"Because..." Slade's voice trailed off.

Dillon stopped walking and stared.

Slade inched away, ready to dodge a punch. "Because...she's with my father."

"Figures." Dillon folded his arms and fixed his cousin with a hard stare. "So, where do you stand in all this?"

Slade sighed and then resolutely squared his shoulders. "Whatever I do is wrong by somebody's accounting. At this point, I might as well do what I want. Either way I'm screwed."

Dillon nodded, daring to feel hope.

Slade pushed him toward the door of his apartment. "Get your gear. Looks like I'm gonna miss that Council meeting."

***

Dillon hiked along a trail that snaked up a steep ridge, legs and lungs burning. Sunshine glinted painfully off the snow, making his eyes water. Hardly anyone could push him to his limits, but Slade was doing one hell of a job of it. At least it took his mind off Michelle. His borrowed snowshoes were the only reason he hadn't fallen even farther behind. Light and sleek, those came straight out of some storeroom at Iron Torr—no doubt one that Slade had stolen a key for.

"How come you didn't bring a snow machine?" Dillon gasped.

Slade spoke between rapid breaths. "Sure, that'd be smart. Make a lot of noise. Probably get shot right off my sled."

Slade topped a false summit at the base of a larger ridge and waited there while Dillon slogged up to meet him. "I'm not very popular here, in case you hadn't noticed."

Dillon winced. "Um, yeah. I noticed. Sorry."

"Goes with the territory," Slade said airily, like it didn't matter, but Dillon knew better. Slade's whole life revolved around his friends.

Whatever he does, someone's going to hate him. He's Uncle Mark's pawn, when Brooke doesn't yank him in another direction, and now the Norms are using him too. I'm glad I'm not Slade, even if he will command his own army someday.

Dillon poured a handful of snow into his mouth and let it melt on his tongue. "Wish I'd remembered to bring water."

"We're almost there anyway."

The Torr was visible as a tiny black line against the sky. Dillon laughed. "Sure, almost. Hope you've got three or four days worth of food in that pack."

Slade sat down on a nearby boulder, unstrapped his snowshoes, and began tying them to the outside of his pack. "We climb from here."

"Climb?" Dillon raised an eyebrow. "What, we're not going to the Torr?"

Slade shook his head. "That's…not a good place to be right now."

Dillon hid a smile. *The attack worked! Uncle Mark's got to be livid.* Dillon's smile faded, and a worried line appeared between his eyes. *He's furious, and he's got Michelle.*

Slade started up the icy ridge.

Dillon stared back at the dark tower, feeling torn. "Slade! Where the hell are you going? We need to get back to the Torr and find Michelle."

"She's not there anymore," Slade said over his shoulder. "Just remember, you didn't hear it from me."

Dillon swore like a Norm. He took off his snowshoes and followed, pulling himself up the slippery slope one gnarled tree trunk at a time. At the top, Slade jumped off the edge and let a drift of deep snow carry him down the other side. He emerged, shaking off the powdery white snow.

Dillon stared down at him from above. "That was stupid. You'll be all wet when the snow melts, and it's almost sundown."

"That won't matter," Slade grinned. "Not where we're going."

"What, we're not camping?"

Slade didn't answer, so Dillon slid down the hill after him, getting snow down his own back in the process. He stood up, still gripping snowshoes in his mittens, and shook like a wet dog. Ahead lay a crevice in the rock. Slade motioned him inside and then followed. Dillon gazed around in wonder. The place wasn't exactly a cave, since the whole thing was above ground, but a ledge extended overhead and sheer rock walls rose on all sides. A campsite waited there, complete with sleeping bags and battery powered electric lamps.

Dillon dumped his gear and pushed back his hood. "You left the lights on. And it's warm in here. Are you running heaters too?"

"We don't need 'em," Slade said, unzipping his jacket. "Hot springs run close to the surface here. Feel this." He put a hand on a shelf of rock.

Dillon pulled off a mitten and followed suit. The warm stone steamed a little under his damp palm. "Nice."

Slade spread out his jacket to dry on the rock. "Sometimes we base camp here, when we're out on maneuvers. As far as I can tell, the Norms don't know this place exists."

When Slade pulled his boots off and walked across the cave in stocking feet, Dillon followed suit. A lamp glowed gold in the dim light, encircled by thin foam pads, like Norms around a campfire. The boys sank down there and made themselves comfortable.

"We can't have a fire here on account of the smoke, but we'll be comfortable for the duration," Slade said.

"Duration of what?" Dillon shifted impatiently. "What are we sitting around for? Look, Slade, we've got to get moving. Your dad's .got to be furious, and I'm afraid he'll take it out on Michelle."

"Oh, I'm sure he will," Slade said with a shudder. "If he hasn't already."

Dillon narrowed his eyes.

Slade licked his lips uneasily. "So, I gather you heard all about your girlfriend's solo attack on the biggest garrison in the hemisphere?"

Dillon gave him a brief nod. "I found out after it happened. I didn't know she was going to do it, I swear, or I would have stopped her. It was stupid."

"It was damned effective, Dillon. Lights are out, and we're freezing our asses off over there. Everyone's paranoid as hell, waiting for an attack that never comes. I've never seen my father so mad."

Dillon tried not to look surprised. *They haven't figured it out yet?*

Slade sat up and wrapped his arms around his knees. "Sorry, but there's nothing you can do to help Michelle now. She got herself into this."

Dillon couldn't help noticing that his cousin said "you" instead of "we." *He's not going to help me. That's what Michelle gets for trying to kick him in the groin every chance she gets.*

"We'll just lie low 'til it's over," Slade concluded.

"Until what's over?" Dillon repeated apprehensively. "What's he going to do to her?"

"Not to her." Slade looked at his watch and spoke to the room at large, without looking at Dillon. "Should be starting any time now."

Dillon looked at him sharply.

Slade didn't elaborate, so Dillon got up and went to the mouth of the cave to look outside. A slender figure stepped from the shadows, holding an assault rifle in practiced hands. Dillon froze. The woman turned slightly, so she wasn't silhouetted quite so sharply against the light.

"Marcia? Is that you?"

"That's right, lover," Marcia said, leveling the gun at Dillon's chest. "Now go sit down. A lot of people are going to die today, and you're not one of them."

"I'm not?" Tingles of relief passed through Dillon's legs, leaving them weak.

Marcia shook her head, but the gun didn't waver. "Not unless you do something stupid. I've got orders, but they're real easy ones. All I have to do is keep you here, nice and safe."

Dillon carefully kept his hands away from his sides. His mind raced. *An attack! I need to get back to the compound and warn them.* He edged toward the door.

"Don't try it, Dillon," Marcia said, moving to intercept. "I don't want to shoot you, but I'll put a round through your foot if you try and run. Nothing personal, but your aunt will have my head if I mess this up. It's me or you, and I like me better."

Dillon made a decision. "Okay, I'll just…go sit down."

"Good call, lover." The barrel of Marcia's rifle tracked him all the way back to the circle of light around the lamp. "The girls all want you around for the next party. I think you set some kind of record."

Chapter 26: Michelle

Reluctant Sacrifice

Michelle squirmed against her bonds, trying to look out the windows of the moving helicopter. She only saw sky. Then treetops appeared, and all around her, helmeted men readied their weapons. Before the aircraft touched down, soldiers opened the door and leaped out. The friendly medic went with them, wearing a helmet and an armored jacket bearing a reflective red medical insignia. He carried a sidearm and a first-aid bag. Michelle watched him go with a pang.

Out the open door lay the snow-packed road into the Norm base, with the familiar wooden door at the end. Two soldiers stayed outside to guard the aircraft. *They already knew where the base was. Parker just let the Norms live until it was convenient to kill them.*

The blades stopped whirring, and Michelle lay there alone. Cold wind whipped through the open helicopter door, ruffling her hair. A short, sharp explosion came from the door of the Norm complex, and then muffled gunfire echoed from inside. Michelle screamed until her throat hurt, strained against her bonds with all her strength, and even tried rocking the stretcher to knock it over, but it was secured to the wall.

Planes approached, low and fast. The DNA double helix logo stood out on their wings, black paint stark against the gleaming white background. *Institute headquarters!* Michelle groaned. *What are they doing here? Helping to wipe out the Norms?*

Then the strafing began. The pair of soldiers outside leaped for the helicopter but died in a spray of blood before they reached the door. The attackers turned and came back for another pass. *Headquarters is attacking Parker's army!*

Michelle screamed and fought, but could not move. A missile roared down and exploded, sending up a fireball.

Colonel Parker pounded back into the helicopter, followed by a small group of men. "Go, go!" Parker bellowed at the pilot. He took the copilot seat and grabbed the radio. "All forces, abandon the mission against the rebel base. We are under attack by Headquarters, repeat under attack by Headquarters."

The pilot tried to fire up the engine. It choked, caught for a few seconds, and died.

"What's wrong?" Parker cried, scanning the sky for more attacking aircraft.

The pilot fought to start the engine. "I don't know, sir!"

Michelle knew. *It took time for the contaminated fuel to gel, but now we're all trapped.*

Overhead, two shining white airplanes swooped in, and a grounded helicopter went up in an earth-shaking explosion. The shock wave rocked the colonel's aircraft. Debris rained down, cracking the windscreen. In the moment of shocked stillness afterward, the men leaped up and bolted for the door.

"Wait," Michelle shrieked. "Untie me!"

No one even spared her a glance. Parker and his officers ran for another helicopter, but it too choked on the thickened fuel and died. In a minute they came out and sprinted for the woods. Michelle writhed, choking on the acrid smoke. Outside, gunfire rattled and men ran past. None of them heeded her calls for help. Another missile jetted through the sky, and the helicopter beside hers went up in a blaze of gold. Michelle couldn't hear herself scream over the sound it made.

Burning debris flew in all directions, under her helicopter, and through the open door. The aircraft began to burn. Heat blistered her face, and the smell of burning plastic made her ill. Michelle threw all her strength against her bonds, twisting and fighting.

A dark figure appeared in the doorway, silhouetted against the flames. "Michelle! By the Gods!"

"Laird!"

Her cousin raced in and fumbled frantically with the straps.

"Underneath! The catch is under the stretcher," Michelle cried.

Smoke filled the helicopter, turning daylight to darkness. Flames spread rapidly. Laird swore, coughing on the smoke. He ripped the stretcher free from the wall and gave it a powerful shove toward the door. It careened outside on its wheels and fell over sideways, dumping Michelle onto the melting snow. Laird made it to the doorway, and then the entire helicopter exploded.

He died instantly, engulfed by fire.

Shrapnel rained down as flaming pines darkened the sky with smoke. Michelle hid her face in the slush and sobbed, still strapped to the overturned stretcher. The world got strangely quiet, and in time a smoke-blackened face bent over her. The man's lips moved, but no sound seemed to come out. Michelle's ears rang, and her heart sent sharp pains into her head with each beat. Dropping to his knees, the man released the straps, letting her battered body roll into the mud. She couldn't tell if he was Normal or Enhanced. It didn't matter. The man left as quickly as he arrived.

Michelle lurched to the doorway of the Norm stronghold. It yawned open, the floor black with charred splinters of wood. Inside, a great gout of fire spouted from the gas fire pit. Norms ran everywhere, pursued by Enhanced with automatic weapons. Parker's soldiers obviously hadn't heard the order to withdraw. Michelle drifted through the nightmare in a haze of shock. Brooke Parker sprinted past, in uniform and attended by a grim-faced platoon of female soldiers. The women chased a cluster of Normal boys around a corner, and moments later, gunfire and shrieks echoed down the stone corridor.

Michelle's mind snapped into gear, and her breath began to heave in panicked gasps. One thought broke clear. *I need a weapon.* A rack of bows and arrows hung on the wall by the door, but Enhanced soldiers had already taken up positions there. One of them pulled an electronic pad from his pocket, checked it, and looked at her again. *He knows who I am.* When Michelle met his eyes, he pointed at her. Panic rose, making her throat tighten with pain. She turned and ran. The soldier dashed after her. A Norm's arrow zipped past her shoulder. Michelle whipped her head around in time to see the soldier clutch at a feathered shaft protruding from his armored chest. He slapped the arrow in half without slowing down.

Some Norms had barricaded themselves inside the shops that surrounded the common area, and they rained projectiles on the invaders from behind piles of overturned furniture. Arrows and thrown knives littered the floor.

"Take head shots," Michelle shrieked as she darted past. "They've got body armor!"

The next arrow nicked the soldier's forearm, sending a spray of blood into the air. He ignored it and grabbed for Michelle, but she slipped away and dashed barefoot down the hall. On her left, a wide wooden door stood open. She shot through, slammed the door, and threw the great iron bolt.

Suddenly the world went still. Michelle stood trembling at the top of the stone staircase that led to the hot pools. Sulfurous steam wafted up through the air. Sobbing, she half-fell down the stairs. Stella met her near the bottom, clutching a pair of handmade hunting spears. The old Norm got a bony shoulder under Michelle and helped her the rest of the way down. "Child, are y' hurt?"

Michelle shook her head. The woman's voice barely penetrated her ringing ears. Her exhausted body slid down the wall until she slumped on the stone floor. "Laird." Michelle's voice came out as a hoarse croak. "Laird's dead."

"Oh, darlin', not yer cousin! I'm so sorry." Stella squeezed her shoulder briefly, and then she began to hobble up the staircase.

Michelle hauled herself back to her feet. "Stella! Where are you going?"

The old woman held up the spears, her jowls set in a stubborn line. "I'll mourn the dead later. Right now, there's work t' be done."

Michelle limped up to join her. "Do you... want to let me do that?"

Stella reluctantly handed over the spears. Michelle took both shafts in one fist. Stella followed her to the top of the staircase, where rising steam choked the air. The old priestess touched Michelle's forehead with a finger, mouthing a silent prayer. Then Michelle whipped the door open, slammed it in Stella's face, and ran. Pain and fear disappeared in an enormous adrenaline rush. Angry shouts came from the dining hall. Michelle followed the sound. She peered around a corner.

Soldiers in helmets and body armor gathered outside the dining hall, where a great pile of wooden tables filled the doorway. Most of the men had their backs to her as they worked to clear the barricade. Enhanced males lifted heavy tables and tossed them aside while other soldiers stood behind them with shouldered rifles. Beyond the barrier, children wailed. The sound clenched Michelle's stomach into a knot. *Children! How could they?* Michelle desperately looked around for help, but the only defenders were either badly wounded or already dead. *Parker meant it when he talked about wiping out Normal kids. Does he know they're illegally augmented, or is it his idea of a permanent solution for the rebellion?*

Her breath rose in panicked gasps, and she fought for control. *I'm all alone. I have to do something.* To calm herself, she began to count backward from a hundred, the way Seth had taught her, but it didn't work and she was running out of time. Michelle narrowed her eyes. *To hell with it.* She readied a spear in her right hand. *I wish I was better at this. I could never even hit a deer.* Aiming carefully, she drew back her right arm and threw.

The spear missed the soldier she was aiming at, but hit the man beside him, impaling him in the nape of the neck. The man died instantly, slumped face-down across the barricade. Parker's Enhanced opened fire when they saw her, but Michelle had already ducked around a corner. Bullets ricocheted off the great stone blocks that held up the cavernous ceiling.

"Hold your fire!"

"She's Enhanced," a man shouted. "Take her alive!"

A group of them took off after her. Michelle launched her second spear and then ran. The rushed throw only took the leader through a bicep. All Enhanced were well schooled at overcoming pain, and Parker's men most of all. The officer went to his knees and began the grisly job of pulling it out. One man stayed to help him. Three more sprinted after Michelle, and she had no hope.

She tried anyway, wheezing with pain, and rounded a corner to face a horde of Norms pounding toward her in numbers great enough to fill the passageway. Michelle recoiled as the oncoming rush split to go around her. They converged on the other side, screaming a war cry. The sound was horribly familiar, but her shell-shocked brain didn't put it together until she saw the spiky blue tattoo around a man's left eye. Another tattooed man raised a hand to call a halt, and his gang took positions at the corner. On his command they opened fire on the soldiers from Iron Torr.

"Toklats! How the hell?" Michelle said aloud to no one. No way could the gang from the Warren be here, two thousand miles from the slum outside Institute walls, but their blue facial tattoos were unmistakable.

More Enhanced appeared, this time in navy blue jackets bearing the double helix logo of Institute Headquarters. Ignoring her, they swarmed through the halls while explosions rocked the complex. Michelle wove frantically among them, searching for her friends.

A familiar voice came from a tunnel that branched off to the left. "Children, stay together. Keep moving."

"Sylvia?" Michelle swerved that way, toward the furnace room. In the narrow side passageway, she was finally clear of the press of bodies.

Soft whimpers came from high above her head. Michelle looked up and gasped. Three stories up, Sylvia herded her daycare class across a rickety wooden catwalk. Frightened children edged toward their hiding place, a ventilation shaft high on the wall. Sage led the group, carrying Parker's clone-baby Hunter on one hip. Frayed ropes served as guard rails, but most of the children were hardly more than toddlers. Their little bodies could easily slip under the ropes and fall. With a baby under one arm and little Kalie clutching her other hand, Sylvia couldn't even grab the rope for balance. The entire scaffold wobbled under her feet.

A narrow handmade ladder rose up the right side of the structure. From there, a long, flexible wooden bridge led across to the ventilation shaft. Michelle ran toward the ladder, anxious to help but afraid to add her weight to the creaking structure. It must have been built generations ago.

Sylvia's bright eyes swept the floor below. "Michelle, look out behind you!"

Brooke Parker strode around the corner, speckled with blood and attended now by only one soldier, a sturdy round-faced woman of about eighteen. The pair brushed disdainfully past Michelle, who stood there empty handed.

Brooke's gaze flicked from the children to the soldier beside her. "Kill them all. Retrieve the bodies."

The girl soldier stared for a second too long, and Brooke snapped, "For testing. To confirm that we eliminated the clone."

"Yes, ma'am," the girl choked out, but she stood rooted to the spot. Her freckled face had gone stark white.

"Sylvia," Michelle screamed. "They're after the kids!"

"Run!" Sylvia shrieked.

Children's high-pitched screams echoed down the passageway. Little feet pounded across the swaying catwalk. The rusted old bolts creaked, and a few splintered free, threatening to send the whole structure crashing down. The girl soldier reluctantly raised her rifle.

"No," Michelle bellowed, charging forward.

The young soldier swung her rifle around, targeting her at point-blank range. For a split second, Michelle stared down the barrel. Her heart clenched like it would stop.

Brooke Parker slapped the rifle down. "Stop!"

"Ma'am?"

"She's the one," Brooke hissed. "We can't kill her."

Michelle had no such compunction. She sidestepped, dodged the soldier's rifle barrel, and struck hard for Brooke's throat. The blow glanced off the woman's cheek instead. The young soldier pivoted her rifle and clubbed Michelle hard in the jaw. Pain exploded through Michelle's head as she fell. The stone floor felt gritty against her teeth. Before she could move, the soldier pinned her and got one arm around her neck in a choke. The muscular girl leaned into the hold, her breath hot in Michelle's hair.

Michelle struggled. Her vision went red, and then began to fade.

"Stop it, Jensen!" Brooke grabbed the soldier by the collar. "Let her go, now. That's one rule even I won't break."

Jensen let Michelle go and stood over her. Michelle lay still, gasping for breath as her strength trickled back. She kept her eyes narrowed to slits.

"I know what you're feeling. You can control this, Britta. Take some deep breaths," Brooke told the soldier.

After a moment, Brooke said, "That's better. Remember her? She's the one they mentioned in the briefing."

"She's the one?" Britta Jensen repeated. "The girl that the doctors want?"

"Right. Either way this plays out, we'll need her," Brooke said. Her voice sounded far away. The soldier asked a question that Michelle didn't catch, and Brooke answered. "The clone...that's a piece we can take off the board. It's prohibited under Institute rules, in any case."

"Yes, ma'am."

"Things are in flux." Brooke said. "Stay close to me. I'll help you land on the winning side." Her voice faded as they walked away.

The deafening sound of gunfire erupted in the narrow stone tunnel. Brooke swore when bullets ricocheted off the walls. "Stop it, you idiot. You'll kill us both. We'll have to catch up and use our knives."

Michelle struggled to her feet, hurting in a thousand places. The two women were already high above on the catwalk. They walked single file, with Jensen leading and Brooke a few paces behind. Kalie's little brown ponytail disappeared into the tunnel ahead of them. Michelle ran for the ladder. Rusted bolts worked their way loose as she climbed, so the rungs wobbled more as she went higher. She gulped and kept going.

Michelle stepped onto the wooden scaffold. It was barely wide enough for her to put both feet together. She forced herself not to look down. "Hey, bitches!"

Jensen turned with a feral grin and ran a few paces back, balancing lightly on the narrow boards. Brooke was in her way. The soldier tried to squeeze around her commanding officer, who clutched the rope handrail.

"Stop it, Jensen," Brooke hissed. "Control. Like we practiced. Breathe."

Jensen leaned and peered around Brooke, first on one side and then the other, a predator crazed with the proximity of its prey. The bridge swayed nauseatingly with her motions.

Something clicked in Michelle's mind then, something she'd never realized before. *Doctors at Iron Torr breed for aggression. It backfires during battle, though. That soldier can't follow orders.*

"Having discipline problems, Brooke?" Michelle taunted. "I guess that last enhancement was a mistake. You'll have to cull every last one of them. Hear that, girl? They're gonna cull you when it's over."

"Shut your mouth, Michelle," Brooke spat.

Jensen's blue eyes turned to her commanding officer. Michelle recognized the expression. *Target acquisition.*

"She's lying," Brooke said evenly. "Trust me."

Jensen took a breath and seemed to get a grip on herself. Her wild eyes flicked back to Michelle and locked there.

Brooke slung her rifle over one shoulder, gripped the girl's uniform jacket, and shoved her backward. One hand still clutched the rope. "Not her. The clone. Get the clone."

"Come on," Michelle shouted. "Fight me, not a little baby!"

The soldier tried to bull past Brooke. Brooke cried out, let go of Jensen's uniform, and grabbed for the handrail instead. "Britta, please."

The woman's white-knuckled grip looked painfully familiar to Michelle. *Oh my God. She's afraid of heights, just like me.*

In a moment of complete insanity, Michelle shook the scaffold as hard as she could. Brook shrieked and fell to her knees. Ancient wood cracked, and a couple of support struts came loose and clattered to the floor. The whole catwalk lurched.

"Stop it," Brooke screamed. She let go of the swinging boards long enough to slap ridiculously at Jensen's knees. "Go! Kill the clone."

"But, ma'am, it's only a baby —"

"Kill it, before my son is disinherited entirely. Do you think he can compete with that? No one can."

Jensen turned her back and in a moment she disappeared into the narrow ventilation shaft.

Brooke shouted after her. "Jensen!"

The girl stuck her head back out. "Ma'am?"

"Don't fire your gun in a tunnel this time, you dolt. Use your blade."

Britta Jensen flashed her commanding officer an irritated look, quickly masked, and disappeared. Michelle launched herself across the narrow catwalk. Boards cracked under her bare feet. Brooke's leg flashed out, unbelievably fast, and Michelle barely dodged the kick. She grabbed the woman's arm, trying to throw her off the bridge, but Parker had married Brooke for a reason. She was the best of her generation.

With unbelievable strength, the black-haired woman broke Michelle's grip and shoved her back. Michelle's feet skidded on the old boards. Brooke tried to shoulder her rifle, but Michelle danced forward, open handed, and karate-chopped the woman's arm. The gun clattered to the rock floor below. An agonized scream came from inside the ventilation shaft. Brooke howled and scrabbled forward, dragging Michelle, who refused to let go. Brooke pulled her into the dark.

With a quick twist of her body, Parker's wife smashed Michelle against the wall and tore free. Pain lanced through Michelle's head. She sank to hands and knees, fighting dizziness. By the time she regained her feet, Brooke had disappeared. Michelle froze, listening hard. Sniffles and scuffling sounds came from children hidden in small air vents that branched off the main line. Fear crawled up Michelle's back. *Brooke could be lying in wait inside any of those passages.*

Cool air flowed down the shaft, carrying the nauseating smell of burning oil. Michelle took a few tentative steps farther into the tunnel, and her foot nudged something soft. Britta Jensen lay crumpled in the shadows, blood soaking the tendrils of blonde hair that escaped her helmet. At first Michelle thought she was dead, but then the girl moved feebly.

Behind Jensen, something pale caught the faint light. Sage's dark skin and hair melted into the shadows, but the knife in her small hand stood out clearly. It was a curved arc of white bone like those carved by the northern indigenous tribes, a twin to the one buried in the soft hollow between Britta's neck and shoulder. The girl soldier's wheezing breath filled the narrow tunnel. Michelle stared, horrified. Somewhere in the dark, Sylvia began to sob.

"Brooke, I know you can hear me," Michelle said. Her voice echoed back at her. "We don't have to make this any worse than it already is. Tell Jensen to let me help her. She doesn't have to die."

"Michelle, no!" Sylvia's voice broke. "She's a baby killer."

"How many men have I killed, Sylvia? It has to stop somewhere."

The sole of a boot whispered against rock. Michelle snapped her head around to find Brooke standing behind her. A tingle of fear shot through her body. Sylvia and Sage immediately moved in to back her up.

"Three against one. Or two and a half, anyway," Brooke snorted, glancing dismissively at Sage and her white knife. "Still, not exactly favorable odds." She sighed and made a tired gesture of capitulation with one hand. "Jensen. This bleeding-heart idiot wants to save your life. Submit."

With that, Brooke moved down the tunnel and sat down with her back against a wall. Michelle let out a shuddering breath. She crawled up to Jensen and realized Brooke's order had been unnecessary. This girl couldn't fight if she wanted to. Michelle reached down and gently pulled off Jensen's helmet. Without it, the blonde-haired girl looked younger and more vulnerable. The sight touched Michelle's heart. Jensen's face could have been pretty, without blood and dirt all over it.

You're trapped here, just like me, damaged by some doctor's mistake. I get scared and you get mad, but we're both broken in the same way.

Jensen's hoarse whisper startled her. "She's right, you know. I am a baby killer."

"But you didn't kill them, did you?" Michelle asked softly. "Even though you were ordered to. That's worth something."

Michelle tugged hard at a hole on the shoulder of her prison uniform. A black- embroidered number twenty-four ripped off, along with most of the sleeve. She pressed the folded cloth to Britta's wound, but left the knife in, afraid the girl would bleed even more if she pulled it out.

"You don't understand." Britta spoke slowly, as if moving her lips took a special effort. "You don't know why those *Norms*," she spat the word, "raise our babies."

"Efficiency," Michelle murmured as soothingly as she could. The girl was losing a lot of blood. Working around the knife, Michelle pressed both hands against the wound.

"I've had two," Britta whispered. "But I got mad when they cried, and, and…"

With a shock, Michelle put it together. Dropping the cloth, she sat back on her heels and stared down at the soldier's ashen face. "Oh. They bred for aggression, and you turned it against your own—"

Britta suddenly raised her voice and cut Michelle off. "I *swore* I'd never do it again! But they never gave me another chance."

"How many…" Michelle battled to keep her voice even. "How many of you have this, um, new enhancement?"

"Just about everyone under thirty. Except for Slade and a few others." Britta croaked out a weak laugh. "They're soft."

A cold detachment came over Michelle, and, against her will, a part of her began to wonder how to selectively eliminate a generation. She shook her head to banish the thought and leaned forward again, pressing on the bandage to staunch the bleeding.

Sage stalked out of the side tunnel, still holding her knife. Little Hunter toddled after her. "Michelle, don't talk with her. You'll have nightmares."

Michelle nodded as calmly as she could. "I probably will, but the Conclave needs to know the truth. They'll put a stop to this."

"Your Council. Yes." Sage took a step toward Britta and slowly squatted down, holding the knife over the woman's prone form. "This is a great crime, making mothers into killers. But we can't heal her heart. It would be kinder to let her die."

"To kill her ourselves, you mean," Michelle said frankly, eying the bone knife. Her hands continued to press gently on the wound, while Britta writhed beneath them, hissing in pain. "Maybe you're right, Sage, but I just can't."

"I can," Sage said. She rotated the bone knife in one hand, so it arced down over the girl's throat. "It would be a kindness."

Hunter stood beside his mother's knife arm, his eyes fixated on the circular spot of blue sky where outside air entered the compound. He began to walk that way, weaving unsteadily on his tiny feet. Sage noticed immediately and stood up. "Hunter, no!"

Brooke moved faster than Michelle thought possible. She sprang to her feet, snatched up the toddler under one arm, and leaped out the open window.

Sage screamed. "Hunter!"

Michelle swore. She dashed to the circular opening in the stone wall with Sage on her heels. Forty feet below, Brooke had already regained her feet. Snow coated her green uniform. Under her arm, the red-faced baby wailed and kicked vigorously.

"He's not hurt, Sage," Michelle began. Sage's sobs almost drowned her out. Michelle grabbed the young mother's shoulders and looked her in the eye. "I'll get him, okay? I'll get him! Stay here. Help Sylvia."

Michelle shoved Sage away from the round window and stood there alone, gripping the sides of the hole with both hands. Michelle's knees shook a little, and she felt a grudging respect for Brooke, who'd jumped despite her fear of heights. Cold, smoky air hit her in the face, laced with the sickening smell of burning hair. From her vantage point, it was clear that Norm fortress was more than a network of tunnels. A huge, half buried stone building enclosed the complex. From the front, nothing showed but the wooden door set into the mountain. Around back stood a high stone retaining wall, well hidden by a tall outcropping of red rock dotted with stunted trees.

Brooke's forest-green uniform disappeared into a grove of snowy pines at the base of the ridge, while Hunter's wails continued to broadcast her position. A man's voice carried faintly on the wind. Michelle leaned out the window. A green-clad figure stood alone in a grove of wind-twisted pines. *Parker! Brooke knew he was out there—that's why she jumped.*

Parker's voice came from around the corner, in back of the giant building. Michelle couldn't make out his words. Driven by curiosity, she eased out the window onto the narrow stone ledge that ran along the outer wall. Belly pressed close to the giant stone blocks, Michelle shuffled sideways, heels hanging off the narrow shelf.

An accidental glance at the snow-covered slope below triggered a wave of vertigo. The stiff breeze didn't help. She spread her fingers over the rough-hewn rock and hung on until the dizziness passed. Michelle gritted her teeth and pressed on, stopping just short of the corner. Clinging to a squared-off slab with both hands, she leaned out to peek.

Brooke and her husband stood together, knee deep in snow. Brooke still held Hunter, who had stopped struggling and now looked around with bright-eyed interest.

"Think of it as a peace offering," Brooke said. She held out the toddler.

Parker didn't take the child. "Your timing couldn't possibly be worse. Like I need a squalling baby in the middle of a campaign."

"No problem. It's not my clone, I don't care," Brooke said lightly. A faint smile touched her lips. She set Hunter down at her feet.

The baby fell forward in the deep snow, floundered, and began to cry. The sound made Michelle want to rush over and pick him up, but she held still, her stomach pressed flat against the wall. In a moment the crying stopped, so she risked another glance around the corner. Colonel Parker now held the baby. To Michelle's surprise, he was using his sleeve to wipe snow off Hunter's face.

That's his child, Michelle told herself, but it still felt like a kidnapping to her. A cold wind cascaded off the glacier, hissing granules of crusty snow against the wall, and she missed part of what Parker said next.

"...hell of a mess. I wish I knew how Headquarters got wind of this. We're going to have to go with the Trojan horse."

Trojan horse? Michelle cocked her head, unsure if she'd heard him right.

"Don't worry, I already have everything in place," Brooke said confidently. "But now I won't see you for months," she added in a more intimate tone. "I'll miss you." She leaned in and gave her husband a passionate kiss on the mouth.

Afterward, Parker walked into the woods, still carrying the baby, while Brooke started back around the building. Michelle sidestepped as fast as she could, but Brooke's strides were long, and in moments she caught up. Michelle froze, praying the woman wouldn't look up. She did.

Brook gave a shout, and a patrol of Enhanced sprinted around the fortress. Over Brooke's shrieked protests, they opened fire. Michelle dove into the hole. A searing pain slashed across the back of her calf. She struggled down the tunnel, fleeing the light, and crashed into Sylvia.

"Michelle, you're hit!"

Michelle began to answer as a new wave of explosions rocked the compound. Children screamed. The girls clutched each other and tumbled to the floor. An eternity later, the blasts finally stopped. In the dim light from the open window, Michelle checked her leg. It had only been lightly creased by the bullet. The slash arced painfully up her hamstring, but it wasn't deep. Sylvia tore off Michelle's remaining sleeve and used it to bind the wound, and then went around pulling toddlers from their hiding places.

Sad-faced kids collapsed on the floor like a pile of puppies. The toddlers quickly fell into an exhausted slumber, while Sage sat alone, weeping quietly. Sylva brought back the last baby, added him to the nest, and sank down beside Michelle.

Michelle sat in silence for a few minutes before she spoke. "Sylvia, I just want to say, I'm really sorry we're not friends anymore. I understand, after that, uh, brain-melting incident."

Sylvia's grin looked white against her dark face. "Just melt Parker's brain for me, and his wife's too, and we'll be even."

"Really? You're not mad at me anymore?"

"No. I've got bigger problems, Michelle. We both do." Sylvia reached out and briefly squeezed Michelle's hand.

Grateful tears coursed down Michelle's face. Eventually she dozed, holding Mollie's five-year-old daughter in her arms. The sun set outside, and the tunnel was cast into abject blackness. When Jensen dragged herself from the tunnel and climbed down the creaking scaffold, Michelle didn't try to stop her.

Chapter 27: Dillon

Disposable Children

Dillon sat on the floor of the rock shelter in the forest, acutely conscious of the gun trained on his back. A horrible itching began between his shoulder blades, right where Marcia was aiming, but he didn't dare scratch it.

Slade provided no sympathy. "I'm warning you, Dillon. Marcia's not the only one with orders. Try to walk out of here, and I'll blow off your kneecap."

Dillon's eyes widened. "Why?"

"So you don't run back there like an idiot and get yourself killed over a worthless bunch of Norms. The doctors say you carry some rare genes, and that makes you valuable."

"Oh, thanks, bro," Dillon said sarcastically, eyeing the holstered pistol on his cousin's belt. "I'm really feelin' the love now."

"That's the army's motivation. Mine's different."

"What, you have your own agenda?" Dillon asked. "Why am I not surprised?"

"Agenda? You're *family*, Dillon, so I pulled you out of a certain-death situation. On my mother's orders, I admit, but I would have come back for you anyway. Call it an agenda if you want, but I cut it really close back there. We stuck around way too long. Trust me, you don't want to be there when the shelling starts."

"Shelling?" The first explosion struck. Dillon reflexively rolled out of the light, heart pounding, and then belatedly registered that the blast had come from the other side of the ridge. His guts twisted. *The Norm stronghold! All my friends are there, except Michelle, thank Gods.*

"Hold still, Dillon," Marcia snapped. She turned her head toward the sound of faraway gunfire, gripping her rifle hard enough to make tiny muscles stand out along her forearms.

"Easy, Marcia," Slade said, eyes wide. "Keep your finger off the trigger, please."

"Don't tell me how to do my job, Lieutenant," Marcia said shortly. "I'm completely clear on my orders."

Behind her, a man's shadow crossed the open doorway of the rock shelter. Marcia whirled and squeezed off a few shots. In the enclosed space, the report of the rifle was deafening. Everyone cried out.

"What the hell are you doing?" Slade bellowed.

Marcia turned toward Slade, and in that instant the attacker burst through the doorway. Executing a tight forward roll, Brian slammed into her legs, sending the gun flying. Marcia fell with a grunt and cracked her head hard on the ground.

By the time she sat up, Slade had her rifle cradled in the crook of his elbow. "Settle down, Marcia, we know him!"

Dillon bent over the intruder. "Brian! Are you okay?"

"Watch her, Dillon," Brian moaned.

Dillon shot a frantic look over his shoulder. Marcia lay in the dirt, looking pissed. One hand clutched the back of her head.

Dillon went back to pressing on the gunshot wound in Brian's thickly muscled thigh. Fresh blood stained his palms. "Slade, Slade! What do we do?"

"Calm down, it doesn't look fatal." Slade slung Marcia's rifle over his back and hurried across the shelter to retrieve a medkit. On Dillon's nod, he injected Brian with a painkiller and then went to work on the wound.

"It could have been a lot worse," Slade murmured, methodically cutting away Brian's jeans with stainless steel shears. "See, it went in here," he pointed, "and there's the exit wound. It missed the bone. I just need to stop the bleeding."

Soon Slade had his patient bandaged, wrapped in a blanket, and lying on one of the mats. Brian drifted, so doped up that he barely twitched when the hollow boom of heavy artillery reverberated across the mountain.

"Brian," Dillon whispered. "What are you doing here?"

Brian's voice sounded far away. "I followed you, since you were going off with that weasel. I figured he was up to no good."

"Hey, I'm not the one who shot you. Don't make me sorry I patched you up," Slade snapped.

Dillon kept a wary eye on Marcia, who sat trembling on the ground a short distance away.

Slade turned to look at her too. "What were you thinking, Marcia?"

"I didn't know he was Enhanced," Marcia said defensively. "He snuck up on us. It wasn't my fault."

"Quit whining," Dillon growled. "You're not the one who's hurt."

"I will be! You have no idea what's going to happen to us if we fail," Marcia cried, her voice getting louder and more hysterical with every word. "We'll all be erased, erased, just like—"

"Marcia!" Slade's voice cut across her words. "Don't."

"Why not, Slade? You don't want the perfect Headquarters kids to know how disposable we are?"

"Disposable?" Dillon repeated. "Tell me."

"Marcia," Slade spat, but Dillon made an abrupt slashing gesture right in his face. Slade shut up.

Marcia sat quietly for a minute. When she finally spoke, she sounded much younger. "I first learned about them when I was nine years old."

Dillon leaned forward intently, raising his eyebrows in an unspoken question.

Marcia swallowed hard and continued. "My mother tells me I'm the oldest, but she's a liar. I know, because I found my sisters' names carved into a tree behind the Torr, along with dates. Dates from before I was born. That was back before the insurgency, when we could still play in the woods. I had three older sisters, and at least two brothers, I think. They all disappeared."

"What, like they died? Some disease, or an accident?" Dillon asked.

"No, Dillon," Slade said softly. "You don't get it. She means they *all* disappeared. An entire generation. I wasn't the only kid my mother ever had, either. I'm just the only one she'll admit to."

"Same with all the families," Marcia added. "We think all the parents murdered all the children."

The matter-of-fact way she said it made Dillon feel ill. "But...why?"

Marcia sat straight, jaw clenched. Her words came out clipped. "Dillon, when people have lifespans of hundreds of years, children become disposable. Our parents have plenty of time to experiment and try new enhancements. If the offspring don't pan out, they just wipe us out and start over."

Brian writhed on the mat, and Dillon knew he'd heard every word. He put a hand on his friend's shoulder and squeezed. A minute passed before he could speak. "Slade, how'd you find out about this? From Marcia?"

"No," Slade answered through tight lips. "A few of us came to it independently, but we didn't dare talk about it. I found out the winter I was seven, when my dad decided to take me skiing. My old ski boots were too small, and I thought I'd impress him if I handled it all by myself. So I took a key to the storeroom and went down there alone to try on boots...and that's when I found it."

For the first time, Brian spoke from his pallet. "What?"

Slade pushed his hair back with both hands and closed his eyes. "A name, in kid's writing, on the lining of a boot. You probably wouldn't see it unless you pushed back the tongue to put the boot on. It said Joey Parker. I didn't see how some stranger had my last name, so I looked for more. I found his name again, on a boot that might fit a sixth grader. Now he's Joe Parker. The last one's on an adult-size boot. It's burned into my brain, so I see it in my nightmares, y' know? Joseph Lawrence *Parker*," Slade spat, enunciating each name. "They named him after my *father*."

"I thought your dad's name was Mark."

"Mark Lawrence." Slade hunched on his pad, staring across the shelter at his shadow on the wall. "I found out later that my brother made it to seventeen. That's how old I am now."

"Me, too." Marcia's lower lip trembled. "A few of us are older than that now, but we're not sure if that means they're safe."

Brian winced as he pushed himself to a sitting position against the wall. "At Headquarters, they cull offspring every year, starting with newborns. Every year you survive improves your odds of going the distance. If we make it to eighteen, we're home free."

"But not the whole generation," Marcia cut in anxiously. Tears spilled from her eyes. "Not everyone, right?"

Brian answered her gently, as though she hadn't just shot him. "That's right. At Headquarters, they never cull the whole generation."

"I can't believe it," Dillon said bitterly. "They're your *parents*, and they don't love you at all."

"That's the weird thing," Slade said, his voice husky. "I think they do love us. It really tore them up to cull Joseph, but they did it anyway. For the good of the bloodline."

Dillon made an angry retching sound deep in his throat. "That's sickening, Slade! What makes you think they care at all?"

"Because, when I hauled the ski boots upstairs and asked my parents about Joe, my mom got hysterical, screaming and crying. Late that same night, she tried to kill herself." Slade wrapped his arms around himself, staring blankly into space. "It was snowing, and she ran up the stairs to the top of the tower. The whole platform was a sheet of ice. My father stopped her from throwing herself off. They struggled, and he nearly went over the edge along with her. Neither one noticed me, but...I followed them up there. I saw the whole thing."

No one had an answer to that. The boys sat together in silence, listening to faraway gunfire and the soft sounds of Marcia's sobbing.

The crackle of a handheld radio startled Dillon to alertness. Marcia pressed a hand over her mouth to stifle her sobs.

Slade snatched up the radio and pressed a red button. "Slade here."

Dillon didn't catch all the words over the static, but the voice was recognizable. *Parker!*

"Yes, sir," Slade said evenly. "Dillon's here. He's fine. Everything went perfectly." He paused for a moment to listen. "Thank you, sir. Slade out." With an oath, Slade tossed the radio aside. "He'll be here in less than ten minutes!"

Marcia madly scrubbed her tear-streaked face with a sleeve. When she knelt down to dim the light, it made her red, puffy eyes a lot harder to see. Dillon couldn't help admiring her attention to detail.

"What should I tell him, Slade?" Dillon asked in an urgent whisper.

Slade handed Marcia back her rifle and sat down beside the other boys. "It's up to you, but if you tell him you defected because of the way he treats the Norms, he won't take it well."

Dillon instantly caught the implication. "You're saying I'm disposable too."

"Damn right you are. Think fast and make yourself useful, 'cause…" Slade's voice trailed off. "Because you're like a brother to me, okay? The only one I've got. So don't be a moron."

Too soon, the radio came to life again, with Parker announcing his arrival. Slade and Marcia stood up respectfully, leaving Brian and Dillon sitting against the wall.

A shadow blocked the sliver of late afternoon sunlight that entered the shelter, and then Colonel Parker was there, larger than life and crackling with energy. Dillon found himself scrambling to his feet too, in some instinctive puppy response to the presence of the alpha male. When Parker's pale eyes fell on him, Dillon froze.

"Dillon!" In a few long strides, the big blond colonel covered the distance between them.

Marcia stood ready with her rifle, and Dillon knew he was trapped. *I'll never make it to the door alive, and anyway, I can't leave Brian.* With an effort, he stood his ground and pulled his gaze level. "Uncle Mark."

Parker swept him into a one armed hug. Dillon let out his breath, and the tense muscles across his back went loose. Something small wiggled between them, and a baby's tiny face looked out at him from the crook of his uncle's arm. Dillon recognized the child with a start. *That's Hunter! Sage must be out of her mind.*

"Thank God I found you, Dillon." Parker gave him a white-toothed grin. "Actually, it looks more like I should thank Slade. Well done, son."

The colonel hugged Slade, who looked relieved nearly to the point of tears. "Dad, I thought you might want the Halstead boy, so I brought him too." Slade swept his gaze around the chamber. No one called him a liar.

"Halstead." Parker acknowledged Brian with a nod. "Brian, right? You scored high. We can find a use for you." He paused, as though expecting thanks, but Brian said nothing.

Dillon was just opening his mouth to ask about the baby when his uncle marched over to Marcia and abruptly dumped the kid on her.

"Sir? Sir!" Marcia desperately juggled the toddler and her assault rifle, unable to get a secure grip on both of them at once. "I have no idea what I'm doing here."

"You're a female, figure it out," Parker said, turning away.

Slade smirked at her over his father's shoulder, and Marcia shot him an evil glare back. "Lieutenant, I'm going to need you to take over security," she said, handing Slade the rifle. "I have…other duties." She cradled the baby awkwardly, looking livid.

Parker had already lost interest in her. "Dillon, I owe you an apology," he said.

"To me?" Dillon was stunned. *I bet Parker's never apologized to anyone in his life.* A fast glance at Slade's astonished face confirmed that.

"Brooke said I should never have taken you into combat so soon after activating your enhancements. She was right."

Dillon stood rooted to the spot, unsure of what to say. "Well, I did ask you to take me along, sir."

Parker made a dismissive gesture. "You're too young to have good judgment. I should have listened to the doctors. Dillon, did you, uh, ever see things moving, that shouldn't have?"

"You mean hallucinations? Oh, yeah. That's why I, um...got lost. But I'm all better now," Dillon hastened to add. *I'm not buying his concerned father act. If Parker thinks I'm nuts, he'll put a bullet between my eyes.*

Parker glanced at his watch. "Look, I don't have time to talk now, but sit tight, and we'll get you home when the campaign's over. It's winding down now."

Dillon swallowed a wave of burning acid that rose in his throat. *That means most of the Norms are already dead. Where are Bear and Elsie and our friends?*

Parker didn't seem to notice Dillon's nauseated expression. He was busy watching his clone baby struggling in Marcia's arms. "I've got to go back and take command of the operation again. But remember, boys, family always comes first. The most important thing was to rescue your little brother there."

"Brother? He's your clone, right? So isn't he technically my uncle?" Dillon blurted, and immediately regretted it.

Parker's ice-cold eyes flicked over Dillon. The colonel didn't answer. Dillon's stomach muscles tightened with nervous tension. He stood there, silent and bewildered, as Parker turned his back and left the shelter without another word.

The teens breathed sighs of relief. Dillon and Slade waited in silence at the entrance, watching Parker hike up the snowy hillside to rejoin his men.

"Congratulations," Slade whispered, as though his father might somehow hear. "You just ran afoul of another one of his unwritten rules."

"What, we're not supposed to call Hunter a clone?"

"Apparently not."

"Nice of him to tell us."

"Welcome to the family," Slade said, rolling his eyes. "This is how I find out half the things I know."

Marcia bent down and let Hunter slide from her arms. The little boy crawled a few paces and then pulled himself up, using Dillon's pants leg for balance. Then he set off on tiny feet to explore the shelter. Marcia dutifully followed the toddler in circles, making sure he didn't get hurt. Slade laid the rifle carefully on a high ledge of rock, out of the baby's reach, before he returned to his spot by the door.

"So, here's a question for you guys," Brian said, from his spot by the wall. "Why does Parker get to be the boss?"

The other boys started to laugh, but Brian waved it off. "Seriously. Think about it."

Dillon shrugged. "Parker's top dog because he's the biggest badass. He's stronger, smarter, and meaner than the rest of us." He peered out the door at his uncle's retreating form. The colonel plowed through thigh-deep snow, climbing the steep ridge without slowing.

"My point exactly." Brian grinned at their perplexed expressions. "Gentlemen, consider this." He glanced across the room at Marcia and lowered his voice. "Stronger, smarter, meaner—those are all genetic traits. Parker essentially inherited his position, even though he's a psychopath."

"Bravo," Marcia interrupted from forty feet away. The boys flinched. "Yes, Brian, I can still hear you, even if you whisper."

"Sorry. I didn't know how loyal you were to the colonel."

"I'm loyal to my *friends*, Brian," Marcia said, walking toward him. "I'm loyal to *Iron Torr*. Not to whoever happens to run the place. Especially if that man kills children. I just can't get past that."

"Good. I can't either," Brian said shortly. "But my point is that Hunter's got the same genetics as Colonel Parker. So he'll probably rule us all someday."

Marcia stood over Brian with the toddler in her arms. "I believe you're right. In fact, I'm certain of it."

Slade looked at Marcia dubiously. "Oh, please."

"Tell, me, Slade. Have you ever beaten your father at anything?" Marcia snapped. "Even once?"

"Not yet," Slade said. "I will someday, when I'm a little older."

"Don't delude yourself. You'll never win. Your father bred you to be weaker than he is, and dumber, too." Marcia moved to the entry of the shelter and glanced out. Parker was still visible, striding away through the trees.

"You're saying he's held us back, on purpose, since we were…embryos?" Slade breathed.

"Obviously," Marcia snorted. "No one ever beats him at anything, and I bet he designed us that way. So if we plot against him, he can squash us."

"It makes sense," Slade mused. "His ego won't let anyone best him, even his own son. This clone is the only one who'll ever be able to match wits with him."

Marcia nodded gravely. "You know, if we can prove that the colonel blocked the evolution of the species—"

"That would be a clear violation of Institute law," Slade finished triumphantly. "There's our loophole, by the way."

"Loophole?" Brian repeated.

"Sure. We'll need that for the Conclave investigation that'll take place after we…" Slade glanced outside, dropped his voice to a whisper, and continued. "After we overthrow my father. It'll legitimize the new government."

"You're crazy," Marcia hissed, her breath steaming in the cold air. "We're going to stage a coup, *ourselves*? Not just report him to Headquarters?"

"Headquarters can't stop him. They don't have the firepower." Slade voice took on the clipped tone of his father. "We have to do this. For my brother. For his whole generation."

Marcia stood very still. It took her a long time to answer. "Okay, then. I'm with you. Even if we get crushed. And we probably will."

Slade swallowed hard. "Yeah."

"But if we succeed? We'll *rule.*" Marcia flashed a shaky grin, but her smile quickly faded. "It won't be easy. The colonel won't step down without a fight, and we can't match his strategy."

"Maybe Hunter can help us, in a couple of decades," Slade said. "If I'm lucky, he might even take my father's place. You know I never wanted the job."

Marcia nodded. Dillon and Brian shared an astonished look, but neither one said a word.

"But we've gotta make sure he's raised right," Slade went on. "Without the kind of abuse my father got. That's what made my dad...how he is." He reached out and lifted the toddler's tiny hand. "Hey, little guy. You're not going to grow up to be a mean man, are you? Not if we raise you right."

"Don't look at me." Marcia shook her head, shifting the baby clumsily. "I'm not the maternal type."

"His surrogate mother is," Dillon interrupted. "She loves him. Give him to me, I'll take him back to her."

Marcia fell silent, considering. "Slade, I say we give them the clone, on one condition. You and I get to be his loving aunt and uncle, which means we have to visit him a lot." She looked hard at Dillon. "Be aware, we'll take him back when we're ready, so you better keep us up on where he is."

Dillon gaped. "Am I supposed to tell his mother that?"

"Of course not," Slade said sharply. "That's your responsibility. If they move him and you fail to check in, we'll track the boy down and take him, no matter how old he is."

Dillon rolled his eyes. "What, and raise him in the dorm?"

Marcia let out a tense laugh. "No. A foster family, our choice this time."

"Fine."

Marcia looked coolly down at Brian. "You all right with that?"

"That depends." Brian folded his arms and stared right back. "What's going to change back home?"

"Say we win. We'll support Headquarters, and defend you if necessary." Marcia offered. "But the culling's got to stop."

"Except at the molecular level," Slade put in. "We can still pick the best genotypes, right?"

"Sure, genetic engineering is fine at the cellular level, but no more murdering children," Marcia said. She turned to Brian. "And you'd better make sure that's the case back at Headquarters too. Do what you have to do."

Brian seemed to consider the idea. "Well, I'll probably be on the Conclave someday."

"Sooner, if a few selected people had terrible accidents," Marcia said pointedly.

Brian winced. "Marcia! These are our parents you're talking about. But I agree with you about the culling. It's got to stop."

Slade raised an imaginary glass. "Here's to long lives, and long-term plans."

"I'll drink to that." Tears glistened in Marcia's eyes. "Just think about it, Slade," she whispered. "We could actually love our children. All of them. Even the imperfect ones." For the first time, Marcia held the baby softly, like a mother would.

A chilly breeze blew into the rock shelter, swirling snow around them. Hunter snuggled against Marcia while her tears ran into his white-blond hair. She reluctantly handed the child off to Dillon. "Take him. Give him back to the Norm who bore him, if you think she's a good choice."

"Her name is Sage. She's indigenous. I don't know what tribe. And yeah, she's a perfect choice. If she's still alive, after all the fighting." Dillon paused to listen for sounds of gunfire. There were none. His heart sank. "Sounds like the insurgency's over."

Slade only shrugged. "Good. The Norm problem's settled for now. We've got maybe twenty years to plan, and we'll need every minute of it. By then, Hunter will be old enough to help."

Marcia paced the shelter, becoming more aggravated as the minutes ticked past.

The toe of one boot ground hard on the gravel as she turned on Slade. "This is the lamest plan I ever heard. We're going to give up our little genius here?" She waved a wild hand at the kid in Dillon's arms. "Hunter's going to be loyal to the Norms, not us. Besides, we might not have twenty years. In that time we could all be culled. It could happen again. We could all die!"

Slade wouldn't even look at her. He leaned calmly on the slanted rock wall, watching his father scramble to the top of the ridge. "You got a better plan, Marcia? Fine. Cough it up."

"Cut the head off the snake, that's what we ought to do," Marcia shrieked. She snatched the gun off the ledge, sweeping the room with the muzzle of the rifle.

Slade ducked. Dillon spun away, protecting the clone baby with his body. A burst of gunfire stabbed his ears. Hunter shrieked and thrashed against his chest. Outside, almost a mile away, a bullet tore through Colonel

Parker's left cheek, streaked through his open mouth, and exploded out the other side of his face. Dillon's recently enhanced vision made a leap, suddenly magnifying the scene. He fought to shut it off, to look away, but the nightmare scene held him. Mark Parker stayed down for long minutes, hidden by deep snow. When he clawed free and struggled to his knees, the right side of his face was virtually gone. Parker's jaw churned, teeth showing between bloody shreds of flesh. His monstrous head turned. One pale blue, bloodshot eye looked down upon their shelter.

Marcia's face went white.

"He's still alive," Dillon howled. "He knows it was us, so finish it! Get 'im, go!"

The Enhanced girl burst into the freezing forest with no coat on, no gloves, only the rifle in her hands. In four long strides, she reached the shelter of the trees. Clutching the baby, Dillon reeled back against the wall, his lip twisted in horror. Half of him wanted to run to his uncle's defense, while another half cheered on the man's killer. The image of his uncle's ravaged face, part skin, part skull, filled his mind.

Slade slid to the floor and sobbed, head in his hands. He made no move to help his wounded father. The sun sank toward the west. Occasional bursts of gunfire came from outside, startling the boys. The fighting sounded farther away each time.

Brian struggled to his feet, causing a fresh bloom of blood to spread across his bandage. "Come on. We've gotta move, before Parker's men get here. You coming, Slade?"

Slade sat a little straighter and pushed a strand of black hair from his eyes. "I need to stay here, so it looks like I'm following orders. That's my only chance for power, now that my father's…gone." He swiped away a tear and then set his jaw in a hard line. "There's going to be an investigation. If I handle it right, my mother will take command until I'm old enough. Then I guess it's my army, like it or not." His narrow shoulders slumped, and he turned away, staring silently into the twilight.

"Brian, you're in no shape to travel," Dillon said. "And Slade's right. Running only makes us look guilty. We should stay here and get our story straight, in case soldiers show up. What are we gonna say?"

Slade didn't answer right away. He got to his feet, shivering, and moved deeper into the shelter. Dillon had just about given up when his cousin finally spoke. "We're not blaming Marcia. We'll say we spotted some Norms in the woods. Marcia was concerned about the colonel's safety, so she went after them. We don't know what happened after that. Remember, we don't know my father was shot until they tell us."

"Good enough," Brian said. "Only weren't you both supposed to stay here?"

"Yeah. We'll have to admit she disobeyed orders, but only to defend her commanding officer. If I spin it right, she'll get a medal. If she's still alive." Slade slumped to the floor and covered his face with his hands.

The day wore into evening. Slade refused to eat, but Dillon and Brian devoured a couple of military ration packs each. The only person who seemed to really enjoy his dinner was Hunter. With only a few teeth, the toddler gnawed through a surprising portion of reconstituted beef stroganoff, and he totally destroyed Slade's canteen with sloppy backwash. Afterward, tucked snugly into a military-issue sleeping bag, Hunter fell into a peaceful sleep.

Dillon had a restless night, disturbed by dreams of Parker, half his face gone, staring them down with his one good eye. *He looked right at me. He knows what we did! Parker might be dead, but what if he's not? He'll hunt us down.*

Sunrise seemed to take forever to arrive. In the morning, Slade handed out another round of unappetizing ready-to-eat meals, this time a greasy stew. There was no sign of Marcia or Parker's soldiers. Overnight, the sounds of fighting at the Norm compound had ceased. Dillon dreaded going back, but he had to know.

Is anyone still alive?

Dillon helped Brian into a borrowed pair of snowshoes, then strapped on his own. He knelt to wrap Hunter in his black wolf skin mantle. "Come on, buddy. It's cold outside." He picked up the bundled baby and turned to his cousin. "Take care, Slade. Don't forget, I'll always be your brother. No matter what."

"I'll always be yours, too, Dillon. Be careful out there." The two guys shared a brief hug.

Brian nodded to Slade as he shuffled past, politely ignoring the tears that streaked the other boy's face. They left Slade standing there, alone with his grief.

Cold, smoky air hit Dillon in the face. The rising sun glowed sullen red through a haze of smoke. He tucked the baby under one arm, put a shoulder under Brian's, and began hauling both of them through the snow. In their wake, the boys left a wide, trampled trail, speckled with occasional drops of blood.

Chapter 28: Michelle

Time's Up

Michelle woke shivering at dawn, stiff and sore, and settled little Kalie against the warmth of Sage's side. The surrogate mother had finally fallen asleep. Puffy shadows under the woman's eyes remained as relics of her tears.

Michelle woke Sylvia as quietly as she could. "Sounds like the fighting's over. I'm going to go take a look around. Do you want to come along?"

Sylvia nodded, and the girls tiptoed out to the scaffold together. Below, the corridor was deserted. The air smelled like gunpowder and smoke. The old wooden scaffold was in worse shape than Michelle remembered. When Sylvia put a foot on it, the whole bridge sagged.

"Lucky I'm light." Sylvia clung to the rim of the ventilation shaft with both hands and slowly eased her weight down onto the narrow boards. "Eeek, I hope it holds! You practically ripped it out of the wall, Michelle."

Michelle leaned out of the shaft to steady the scaffold. Several large bolts hung from splintered beams, torn free and leaning at odd angles. "I can't believe I did that. Sorry."

"Don't be sorry. If you hadn't, I'd be dead, along with all my daycare kids."

After Sylvia was safely across, Michelle started over the narrow bridge, knees shaking the whole way. At the bottom of the ladder she wiped her sweaty hands on her pants and looked around. Faint noises from the main hall made her twitch. "Who won, Headquarters or Iron Torr?"

Sylvia straightened her shoulders. "Let's go find out."

In the main hall, the gas fireplace was back under control. Around the blue and orange flames, a group of Parker's green-uniformed soldiers sat on benches under the watchful eyes of their Institute captors. The girls skirted the group.

"Most of the soldiers from Iron Torr are gone," Sylvia whispered. "See? Blue uniforms everywhere. Headquarters is in control."

Michelle breathed a sigh of relief. "Where'd Parker's soldiers go? They can't all be dead. I don't see that many bodies."

"They probably retreated. I wonder how Headquarters found out we needed them?"

"Good question. I doubt the Norms contacted them."

Michelle scanned the hall. The Institute's well-oiled machine was already at work, bringing order to chaos. Blue-uniformed Toklats and teams of Normal teenagers hauled the injured to an Institute surgical tent outside.

"We need to find Jeanette and the boys. Hope they're not hurt. And I need to talk to Stella." Michelle turned to find the old woman already hobbling toward her through the crowd, a lumpy bundle in her arms.

Stella shoved the bundle at Michelle. "Go wash. Meet me outside. You're needed to officiate at the funerals."

"Oh, God."

"Why only one? Might as well invoke 'em all," Stella snorted. "Goddess knows you'll want the help."

"Michelle, I'll try and find Jeanette and the others," Sylvia said. "They'll help me get Sage and the kids out of the ventilation shaft. You're needed here."

"Thanks." When Michelle looked back at Stella, only a second later, the priestess had vanished.

Michelle headed for her tiny apartment with the wool-wrapped bundle in her hands. Dillon wasn't there, and neither were his furs or boots. *He's outside, probably fighting.* She wrapped her arms across her stomach and squeezed until the urge to scream passed. Numbly, Michelle stripped and stepped into the little shower nook. Steaming sulfurous fumes rose around her. The hot-springs water stung every cut and scrape, but it washed away the stench of fear. Old blood swirled around her feet before it disappeared down the drain.

Michelle twisted her wet hair into a single long braid and tied it off with a red string that had held the bundle closed. *I'm supposed to go out there and be their priestess? Getting shot at is less nerve-wracking.* She unfolded the soft wool to find a long-sleeved dress and a pair of knee-high leather boots. The dress was made entirely of Stella's familiar shiny cloth. *Priestess cloth. I guess I rate more than just a belt and shirt this time.* Michelle pulled the dress over her head. It fell to mid-calf, and the woolen wrapping turned out to be an indigo shawl exactly like Stella's.

Outside, the air held a hint of spring. Countless feet had churned the slush into mud. Michelle paused for a moment at the burned-out hulk of the helicopter where Laird died. There was nothing left of him at all. With an effort, she walked on by, clutching the shawl around her, and took her place beside the Norm priestess. A long line of exhausted Norms stretched around the building. Stella worked her way along it, chanting in the ancient language that only she seemed to know. Families waited, many with wrapped corpses at their feet. The old priestess slowly moved down the line, giving comfort and blessings to them all. Michelle followed Stella, copying her motions as well as she could.

Somewhere behind the complex, an explosion tore through the air. Michelle screamed, along with half the Norms around her.

"That's just yer people, makin' us a mass grave." Stella spoke gently, so

Michelle didn't feel ashamed. "It's a gift. So we don't have to dig. The ground's still frozen."

Michelle nodded shakily, and Stella began her chant again. The ritual was choreographed, almost like a dance, words intertwined with gestures of blessing, timed to the touch of aromatic oil on a mourner's bent head. Michelle soon realized that the words repeated. Though she didn't understand them, she learned the sounds and began to chant along. When Stella pressed a vial of oil into her hand, she understood, and took her place at the head of her own line of grieving Norms.

In time, the chanting put her into a kind of trance. Faces appeared and disappeared. Some she knew, and others were strangers. Michelle gave each of them some of her energy, healing their trauma as well as she could. She tried to emulate Stella and not change the rhythm, whether the person was a friend or a stranger. Bear passed under her hands, looking half dead, and she poured a double dose of strength into him. But when Molly and Wade appeared in her line, pale-faced and haggard, Michelle's chant faltered and then died.

"We lost Laird," Molly told her softly. "There's no body. Witnesses say he died in an explosion."

"That's true. He died saving me." Michelle admitted. "I was tied up inside Parker's helicopter." She swallowed hard and told the whole truth. "Which wouldn't have been sitting there, except that I sabotaged their fuel, so they couldn't take off. Laird got me out just before I burned." Michelle watched their faces, expecting angry recriminations.

Molly enclosed her in a hug. "You're why we won the battle, then," she whispered. "Bless you."

"And Michelle?" Wade said gruffly. "I don't want ya t' hear it from no one else. Um...Kalie's missing."

Molly's sobs cut off Michelle's answer. The stocky woman put her arms around Michelle and hugged her tight. "You're my only child now."

She really means that. Tears sprang up in Michelle's eyes. "No, no, Kalie's fine! Sylvia and I hid her, along with a bunch of other little kids. Sage is with them."

Wade and Mollie sagged in relief. "Where?"

"In the ventilation shaft opposite the furnace room. Only be careful when you go to get them out, the bridge is close to collapse."

"We will! Oh, thank you, daughter!"

"Wait." Michelle performed the ancient Norm chant for them, and after she placed a spot of oil on each of their heads, they all stood for a moment in silence. Then she said, "I'm so sorry about Laird. It was all my fault."

"Don't ever say that," Wade said. "You're our girl. You're family. Laird died t' show you that."

Michelle gazed at him without saying anything, grateful tears streaming from her eyes.

"Michelle?" Wade choked up and couldn't speak for a moment. "I just wanted to say…we honor yer sacrifice too."

"Mine? What do you mean?" A wave of cold dread washed through her.

Wade took Michelle hands, so the vial of oil lay pressed between their palms. "Dillon. Nobody found a body, but we ain't seen 'im. Not since yesterday."

Michelle set her jaw stubbornly. "He'll be back."

"Sure he will," Wade said. He hugged her as gently as a loving father could, and then led his wife away.

Aware of all the eyes on her, Michelle wiped her face on her shawl and moved on down the line, comforting herself in the chant. Deep in her trance, she didn't notice that she'd reached the end of the line until she came upon the last person, a tall man with his head deeply bowed under a hooded cloak. She dug deep for her last vestige of strength, trying to give him the same healing she'd given all the others. The tingling in her hands told her she had just enough left, and she began the litany, eyes closed in concentration. As she made the graceful gestures of blessing, she let her strength trickle into him. Her knees started to shake a little, but this man was the last one, so she kept on going, too upset to care if she ended up face down in the mud or not. Michelle opened her eyes to touch his head with oil.

Great-grandfather!

Her hand froze in midair, and then, deliberately, Michelle pushed back his hood and anointed his silver head. She swallowed the questions that rose to her lips and finished the chant, letting the last of her strength flow into him.

Just as her knees buckled, the old man lifted her lightly into his arms. Power coursed through his hands and thrummed through her body, more than she ever imagined possible. She breathed it in like air, and it filled her with light. Questions filled her mind, but her lips could no longer form words.

This …magic? It's an old Norm power. Enhanced never do it, except for me. And him?

Great-grandfather said something in the old language, and she didn't understand. Stella did. The Norm priestess suddenly stood beside him, though Michelle hadn't seen her approach. The elders talked quietly together, their melodious words flowing around her.

***

Michelle awoke on a makeshift surgical table in the Institute's medical tent, portable electric lights glaring into her eyes. Jeanette hovered over her, wearing Institute-issue scrubs. Doctor Williams snapped his used latex gloves into a waste barrel and joined her at Michelle's side.

"Doctor, I've checked her for injuries, but they're all a day or two old, and mostly healed already," Jeannette said in a rare respectful tone. "Could she be bleeding internally?"

"Try the simplest explanations first," Doctor Williams said. He bent over Michelle, light gleaming off his broad forehead, and began gently prodding her abdomen. "When was the last time you ate?"

"Um, I don't remember. Three or four days ago."

"Your body is a machine, Miss Atherton. It won't operate without fuel, no matter how elegantly enhanced you may be."

"Oh, I'm way more than a machine," Michelle murmured, remembering the tingling power that had filled her soul with light, but Doctor Williams had already moved on to his next patient.

***

Hours later, Michelle sat on a damp log outside the medical tent, chewing on a hunk of bread and watching people come and go. Norm families finished their private graveside rituals and trudged past her into the warmth of the great hall. The last rays of sun lit the trampled pathway to the Norm stronghold. At the end of the road, a group of men rebuilt the wrecked door. Their hammering shattered the stillness of the forest.

Michelle shivered under her shawl, but she refused to go inside. The sun sank below the crowns of the pines, leaving the medical tent speckled in shadow. Institute helicopters buzzed in and out like bees, evacuating the most serious injuries. Blue-uniformed Enhanced and their Toklat security guards began to assemble out front with their equipment. Occasional groups of insurgents limped out of the woods, and Michelle jumped up to question them. None of them had seen Dillon for a day or two. No one knew where he was. Her apprehension grew.

Jeanette finally came out of the medical tent and sat down beside her.

"Dillon's missing," Michelle said in a low voice.

"So's Brian," Jeanette said. At the surprised look on Michelle's face, she added, "In case you hadn't noticed."

"I'm sorry, I…"

Jeanette faced her without smiling. "You should be. Go ahead and melt our brains, Michelle. Have a total breakdown, you twit. And then you go off without telling anyone and attack Iron Torr all by yourself. Way to say you're sorry."

Michelle stared. "I…really am."

Jeanette gave her a little smile. "I know. It's okay. I've got to find Todd, and then we're going out to look for Brian and Dillon."

"Good, I'm going with you." Michelle stood up, resolutely ignoring her aching leg. "I'm afraid Parker's soldiers captured him and took him back to the Torr."

"Without vehicles? They're not going to drag him all the way back there on foot."

Maybe Parker's soldiers shot him. "I need to find him, Jeanette. He could be lying injured somewhere."

"You're not going out dressed like that," Jeanette said shortly. "Nights are still bitter around here."

Michelle always hated it when Jeanette treated her like a child, but just this once, she didn't argue. "Fine. I'll go change, meet you here in a few."

Movement on the edge of the woods caught her eye. "Look! That's them!"

Michelle dropped her bread and ran for the trees. Dillon and Brian struggled toward her, arms around one another, their snowshoes dragging through wet snow. Brian was limping badly, and blood soaked a bandage on his thigh. Dillon had Brian's arm slung over his shoulder, and he half-carried his friend toward the compound. Dillon carried something tucked under his other arm, something he'd carefully wrapped in his black wolf-skin mantle. Then it wiggled, and a smile broke across Michelle's face.

"Here, take him." Dillon grinned proudly, like he always did after a good hunt.

"Is that Sage's baby?"

"The clone, yeah. Careful, he's sleeping."

Michelle gently took the bundled baby in her arms without waking him. Hunter's cheeks glowed with warmth, and his pink rosebud lips moved rhythmically, as though he dreamed of nursing. Dillon wrapped an arm around her, but he couldn't let go of Brian. For one glorious moment, Michelle found herself held by both of them at once, with no jealousy or competition between them at all.

Michelle shifted the baby onto her shoulder and gazed up at their faces. She hugged them both, leaning against Dillon's chest and reveling in the sensation of Brian's hair tangled between her fingers. No one said a word until Jeanette came over to help Brian out of the forest. She led him toward the med tent, but he stopped short and collapsed on a fallen log, head bowed. Jeanette sat down beside Brian and took his arm, but he refused to look up. Without speaking, she knelt at his feet, untying the laces of his snowshoes.

"Somebody get Sage," Michelle called to the workmen by the door. "Sylvia knows where she is. Tell her Hunter's back!"

"Yes, ma'am," one of them said. The man immediately dropped his hammer and ran.

Dillon tucked Michelle softly under his arm. Joy surged through her to see him so vibrant and alive, and completely unhurt. His body felt warm and strong, and when he smiled down at her with those white teeth and blue eyes, he looked unbelievably handsome. Heat shot though her, and suddenly she wanted nothing more than to drag him straight back to their apartment. *Even if I can't bring Brian too,* she thought, and then flushed, worried that Dillon had heard her.

"Oh, Dillon, I thought you were —"

Dillon interrupted her with a soft kiss on the mouth. "I know. So did I, for a while there. I'll tell you all about it later. Right now, let's get this baby back to his mom."

A commotion at the door heralded Sage's arrival. She burst outside, followed by a crowd of young mothers with infants.

"You should be the one to deliver him." Michelle carefully maneuvered the sleepy baby back into his arms. "Go on, you're the hero who brought him back. Let her thank you."

Dillon moved off to be engulfed by a crowd of beaming young women, who showered him and the baby with hugs and kisses.

Brian looked Michelle up and down from his spot on the log. "You've got a new look. It's, uh, more than fashion, I take it?"

"Yeah. It's from Stella, the priestess." Michelle came over and sat beside him. Jeanette had disappeared, probably back to the medical tent.

"It suits you," Brian said. "People sure treat you differently now. Those guys by the door jumped to serve you."

"It's not like that." Michelle looked down. "I ...I really serve them."

"Not anymore. The Conclave's here to take us home." Brian nodded at the landing zone, where a sleek white helicopter had just touched down.

When the helicopter door opened, two well-armed bodyguards emerged first, followed by Michelle's hugely pregnant mother, Victoria. The rest of the Conclave followed by rank. Michelle's great-grandfather, founder of the Institute, came out to meet them. Their whole group immediately got swept up by Enhanced soldiers and members of the Norm Council.

"They haven't seen us yet," Michelle whispered. She pressed against the warmth of Brian's shoulder, wishing she could hide behind him. "I mean, I love her and all. And I really did miss her. But I'm not ready for all this to end so suddenly."

"Don't worry," Brian said, putting a leather-clad arm around her. "We won't have to leave right away. You'll still have time to say goodbye to everyone."

Michelle nodded weakly, but then tears started rolling down her face and didn't stop. She cried for all the dead and injured Norms, but most of all she cried for Laird, who had died for her.

Through her tears, Michelle gazed at the happy crowd of Norms around Dillon, who was making the rounds with Hunter and Sage. "Brian, I'm not sure I want to go back."

Brian squeezed her shoulder. "I feel the same way. But we've got to grow up sometime. They'll be—" He abruptly stopped.

"What?"

"Sorry. Bad time to bring this up. Never mind."

"Brian, what?" Michelle twisted on the log to face him.

Brian paused reluctantly before he spoke. "Our disappearance put them almost a year behind schedule, so they'll be pairing us up immediately." He took one of Michelle's chilly hands in his warm one. "You're too important to stay here. You know that. You have a duty to the community."

Her eyes went to the Norms.

"No, *our* community, Michelle. The Institute, where everyone's hopes hang on you."

"On me, having babies, like some farmer's prize heifer."

"On you, having babies with a man who loves you." Brian touched a few tendrils of hair that blew free from Michelle's braid, but she only stared down at the bloody bandage on his thigh. "Someone approved by the Conclave, who'll give you the life you deserve. Someone you can take to parties without people whispering about you behind your back."

Michelle frowned at him for that, but Brian stared back unflinchingly. "Michelle, I'm only telling you the truth. The Conclave will never pair you with Dillon. They were willing to give you some time to grow up, but they never meant to leave you with him long term."

Brian stood up, wincing with pain, so Michelle jumped up to slide a shoulder under his. He leaned down to whisper in her ear. "Time's up. And before you declare war on the Conclave, please remember one thing. Because Dillon's my friend. The best I ever had, and I love him like a brother."

"What?"

"Remember how his father died."

Michelle's stomach clenched. "What do you mean?" she gasped. "I thought Salomon ordered him shot."

Brian's gaze locked on the Founder's silver head. "That's what *he* wants you to think."

When Brian turned back to Michelle, his eyes softened. "I know Dillon would be hurt...hell, more than hurt. Devastated, if you left him. But I don't want to find him with a bullet in his head either, and things are going that direction. Unless the Conclave sees it's over between you two. Then they'll have no reason to eliminate him."

"Are you sure? There's got to be some other way."

"All I know for sure is, either way, I lose." Brian sighed. "I lose a brother, or I lose the girl I love. Either way."

Jeanette came out of the med tent, carrying a suturing kit. Michelle had forgotten all about her. Jeanette bowed her head for a moment, and Michelle realized that her impeccably controlled friend was trying not to cry. *Jeanette heard that. All of it? Probably.* Brian's arm suddenly felt way too heavy on her shoulder.

When Jeanette finally spoke, her voice sounded tender, but not hopeful.

"Brian? Are you ever going to let me bind up that wound?"

Brian spoke so softly that Michelle barely heard him. "I'm…not sure anyone can." On heavy feet, he trudged toward the med tent, leaning hard on Michelle the whole way.

At the door, Michelle handed him over to Jeanette. "Take care of him."

Jeanette looked pale, and her blue eyes gleamed with unshed tears. "I'll do my best. I always have."

Michelle nodded and turned away. She hadn't taken two steps when men began shouting from the edge of the woods. A pack of blue-uniformed Toklats dragged a prisoner out of the forest by a rope. The man's hands were bound, and mud coated his body. As the tattooed Norms passed Michelle, their dark-haired prisoner struggled to regain his feet, but tripped and fell on his face again. The reflective medical insignia on his jacket flashed red through the grime.

"Stop!" Michelle cried. "I know this man. He's the medic who treated me. Let him go."

The black-bearded Toklat with the rope looked at Michelle sideways, but didn't answer. He kept walking. The white of his left eye stood out garishly against the spiky indigo tattoo that surrounded it. It gave her the creeps, but she grabbed the man's arm anyway. "Stop it, I said!"

The Toklat tried to shake her off, but failed, and their group came to a ragged halt. When the young medic struggled to his feet, another Toklat kicked him in the stomach. The prisoner sank back down in the slush with a groan.

"Leave him alone," Michelle shouted.

Fifty Norms converged on her protectively, all yelling at once. "Dincha hear her? She said t' let 'im go!"

"Do what the priestess says, or yer goin' in the hole with the corpses, dead or alive."

The bearded Toklat dropped the rope and backed off, looking to his boss for instructions. "Uh, Seth?"

Michelle's brother came through the crowd, grinning broadly. "Hey, little sister!" He gave her a quick hug. "Since when do you have this much clout?"

Michelle returned the hug and then stepped back, looking serious. "Call off your dogs, Seth. That's a good man there, and he doesn't deserve this."

"If you say so." Seth waved the Toklats off the young medic. "Go on, guys. Take a break."

The tattooed men looked around apprehensively at the hostile Norms and grunted a few apologies as they left.

Michelle untied the medic's hands and helped him to his feet. "Are you okay?"

"I think so," the man gasped. "Only bruises."

Michelle turned to the nearest Norm, a kind-looking middle aged man.

"Please take this man to the pools and get him washed off, and then get him dry clothes and bring him back out to the med tent. I want the doctors to have a look at him."

"Yes, Priestess." The Norm quickly obeyed.

Michelle caught her brother's raised eyebrow, but there was way too much to explain. "We'll talk later, Seth. So much happened. I missed you."

Their mother hurried across the slushy ground, moving fast for her bulk. "Michelle!" Victoria drew her daughter into a hug, with her giant pregnant stomach between them. "I'm so glad to see you! We were worried sick. Search parties have been in the field since last summer, but with the hostilities, they didn't make any headway."

"Mom, you shouldn't even be here in your condition. You look like you could deliver any second."

"Then I'll do it here," Victoria said. "Why not? Normal women do it all the time."

"Why not?" Michelle repeated. "What did the doctors say about that?"

"To stay home, of course, but I didn't listen to them," Victoria said airily. "You're my daughter, and I love you. If that means giving birth here, I'm sure I'll be just fine, and so will your sister."

Michelle rolled her eyes. "Mom, really!"

Victoria took Michelle's elbow and walked her out of the press of people. "I think you showed real leadership there. Displaying mercy to an enemy, and *right* in front of everyone. Well played."

"It wasn't a game, Mother. That man is a medic—"

"Excellent, you salvaged someone with real value to the community. See, I knew you'd do well! And, along that same line, come with me. I think you'll appreciate this."

Victoria swept into the Norm complex like she owned the place. Iron Torr soldiers still clustered by the fire, guarded by Enhanced from Headquarters. Without guns and helmets, Parker's soldiers looked younger and much less frightening.

"Victoria, darling," Brooke gushed. She came over and kissed Michelle's mom on both cheeks.

Michelle gagged on the inside. *Oh, please.*

"I see you've found your daughter," Brooke said. "We've been through so much together." She took Victoria's arm and lowered her voice. "We became very close, but she's a bit ticked off with me at the moment. Normal teenage rebellion, I'm sure, exacerbated by stress. She'll get over it."

"Of course she will," Victoria said, giving Michelle the look that meant she'd damn well better get over it, and fast.

Michelle pursed her lips and said nothing.

"Michelle, I'm sure these kids are your friends now," Victoria said, waving a hand at the dazed-looking young soldiers from Iron Torr. "So you'll be happy to hear that they're all transferring to Institute headquarters. Brooke told me about the colonel's...excesses."

Brooke sniffled and dabbed at her eyes.

"Oh, you poor thing," Victoria said, handing Brooke a tissue from her purse. "And these young people—just look at them! So horribly taken advantage of. They'll be thrilled for a chance at a proper education."

While her mom chatted with Brooke and a few female soldiers, Michelle scanned the group. A wave of sick horror rose inside her. *Every soldier here looks younger than thirty. They all have enhanced aggression. And they're coming home with us. That's what Colonel Parker meant. The Trojan Horse. That's his fallback plan. Parker will attack headquarters once his wife gets their people inside.*

Michelle felt hopelessly childish, out of her depth against Brooke's age and intellect. *She's got plans inside plans, and none of them end well for us.*

"Mom, we need to talk," Michelle snapped, interrupting the women's conversation.

Victoria looked a little shocked. "Remember your manners, dear. You have been living with Normals, haven't you?" Victoria laughed it off, but gave Michelle a stern look out of the corner of her eye.

"Excuse me, Mom, but this is important."

Michelle stepped over Jensen, who sat on the floor at Victoria's feet, eyes glassy with medication. Blonde hair fell over a thick bandage that wrapped the girl's neck and shoulder.

"Mother! Please."

"Don't interrupt, Michelle." Victoria pulled her daughter down onto the bench beside her. "Have a seat. I was just talking to Britta, here. Britta Jensen, isn't it? Go on, dear. You were saying, about your hopes for the future?"

"Yes, ma'am." Britta nodded politely. "I'm so grateful for the opportunity to transfer to Headquarters. I want to finish college, and then..." Jensen dropped her gaze and smiled shyly. "I really would love to have a baby or two someday."

"I think you already tried that, Jensen! How'd that work out?" Michelle shrieked, leaping to her feet. "Mom, these people are dangerous. We *cannot* take them back to the Institute!"

"Be nice, Michelle." Victoria stared at her daughter like a stranger. "I will not have you making our guests feel unwelcome, after all they've done for you. Without Brooke, you would never have been rescued. She risked her life to tell us where to find you."

"It's all right, Victoria. I know you raised her to have perfectly lovely manners. We can't judge her right now, the poor child is traumatized." Brooke gently took Michelle's hand. "Don't worry. It'll all be over soon, sweetie."

Brooke's mind rolled over hers in an oily wave that smothered Michelle's thoughts. *It'll all be over soon.*

Michelle gazed dully down at her rough-skinned hand, with its torn and dirty nails, lying in Brooke's manicured one. The image wavered, and when it clarified, her hand looked exactly as it would in death, fingers curled and skin mottled with pooled blood. Even this close to the fire, Michelle's body felt cold. She struggled to move, to pull away, but couldn't even scream. Brooke's control was absolute.

Brooke's voice spoke softly in her mind. *You'll keep your mouth shut, if you know what's good for you.*

Michelle slammed up her mental shields. With all her will, she fought back. *Bah!* Michelle screamed the thought, like Stella would, and felt Brooke rock with the impact. A wordless howl erupted from Michelle's mind. She poured all her fear and anger and love into it and used it as a weapon. Brooke shrieked, and then everything went quiet.

The world swam in a stomach-twisting sideways motion, and suddenly Michelle stood on a deserted playground in the shadow of Iron Torr. It took her a minute to realize that she was behind enemy lines, re-living something she'd never experienced.

Snow gleams gray off empty swings. Wind spins the merry-go-round in a slow circle, as if phantom children play there. Long, black hair blows across my face. Not my hair— Brooke's. I...we...wrap our arms across our body and rock in anguish.

A headache began to pound behind her eyes. Michelle clenched her jaw and hung on. *Black hair...this is Brooke's memory, not mine. What's she trying to hide?*

One word leaped clear before Brooke hurled Michelle from her mind.

Sacrificed.

It made no sense.

"Michelle. Michelle! Stop it, you're hurting her." Victoria peeled her daughter's hand off Brooke's. "What has gotten into you?"

Michelle opened her eyes. Brooke took a couple of steps backward, clutching one hand with the other. Her face looked white.

Michelle snapped back to the present. "Mother, if you would just listen to me for five minutes—"

A male nurse in an Iron Torr uniform seized Michelle's arm. He held a naked syringe in his other hand. "Hold still for just a second, miss," he said, in a fake-soothing voice. "This will help you relax."

Victoria gave him the nod. "Go ahead. That's probably a good idea, considering what she's been through."

Michelle yanked her arm out of the man's grip and ran. Brooke and Victoria hurried after her, followed by some green-uniformed teenagers. Despite the tranquilizers, the soldiers from Iron Torr were waking up.

"Would you like us to bring her back, Mrs. Atherton?" one tall boy asked politely, an eager gleam in his eye.

Victoria didn't seem to see it. "Oh, I don't know. I've never seen her like this."

Michelle bolted out the door. She felt like racing for the woods, but saw the Founder first. "G.G.! You can't bring those people home with us! They've got this sick aggression enhancement, and they're dangerous, and I'm sure it's part of Parker's plan to--"

"Michelle!" The old man's voice cracked, cutting her off. "Silence yourself."

The Founder had never turned his anger against her, and for the first time, she saw why people were afraid of him. Power pulsed off him, and even though she recognized it as a ploy, just a simple use of energy, the sheer force of it overwhelmed her.

"You've got to listen to me," Michelle choked out, over an inexplicable compulsion to bow her head and keep silent.

One of the Founder's white eyebrows rose. "You can speak?"

"Stupid question," she hissed over a spasm in her throat.

"Michelle, there's more going on here than you understand," the old man said. "I'll explain what I can later. For now, stay out of it."

"Quit telling me what to do," Michelle cried. "I'm done being your pawn." She turned on her heel and stomped off.

Dillon and Bear hurried toward her. A few seconds later, Brian ducked out of the med tent. They'd all heard her shouting. "What's wrong, Michelle?"

"The soldiers, they're bred to kill," Michelle stammered.

"Aren't you all?" Bear drawled.

"Not like this." Michelle let her shoulders sag. It was a relief to tell an adult who would listen, even if that adult was only a Norm. "Bear, remember when you got sick and then woke up stronger?" She bit her tongue, trying not to blurt, *I did that to you.* "That was an enhancement. Everyone who survived, they all got changed, didn't they?"

Bear glowered. "How do you know about that?"

"You got a few of the genes that make my people the way we are, kind of by accident. Yours are for strength and speed. Wade got a boost to his intellect. He's your tactical man, right?"

"Freeman, did you tell her that?"

Dillon shook his head. Out of the corner of her eye, Michelle spotted the Founder, walking toward her with his long stride. She could tell at a glance he was in no mood to listen.

"Bear, the soldiers from Iron Torr, the young ones, they all got an enhancement that makes them more aggressive. Way more. They're really dangerous."

Bear looked at the placid group of clean-cut young people who had followed Michelle outside. A few smiled back at him. "Really?"

"They're drugged right now," Michelle hissed. "The Conclave doesn't know, and they won't listen to me. My mother thinks those soldiers are lost children or something, and she's taking them home to Headquarters. They'll help Brooke from the inside when Parker invades."

Dillon and Brian looked concerned. They believed her, she could tell.

"If what you say is true, that's good news for us," Bear said. "Load 'em up. Get 'em the hell out o' here."

Michelle swore loud enough to be heard across the clearing.

Great-grandfather marched up and gave her an irate look. "You've clearly expanded your vocabulary during this little expedition. Enough consorting with the Unenhanced. Come, Michelle. You're going home now."

"Wait. Not yet," Michelle begged.

"Two minutes. Say goodbye." The old man turned to Brian. "Mister Halstead, you need to get off that leg. Come with me."

"Yes, sir," Brian said. "But Michelle has a valid concern, and—"

The Founder cut him off. "We will discuss this before the Conclave, back at the Institute. Not here."

"But sir, before we bring those soldiers home with us—"

"*Not here*, Mister Halstead."

"Yes, sir." Brian shot Michelle an apologetic look as he fell into step beside her great-grandfather. The two men walked back to the helicopter together.

Michelle turned back to Dillon. He'd already taken a few steps toward the forest, where his friends stood waiting. With a shock, she realized that he meant to stay. All the life drained out of her.

Dillon put a hand out to her, flashing a free-spirited grin. "Come on, love, run away with me. You know you want to."

Michelle's heart melted, and she followed him a few steps. "I do, but…"

She stared back at the neat array of helicopters. At Victoria's swollen stomach, carrying the baby sister she might never see. At Brian, Jeanette, Todd, and Sylvia, all waiting outside a brand-new luxury helicopter, loaded with food and warm clothes. Michelle suddenly felt cold, weak from hunger, and desperately afraid.

It took Brian a couple of minutes to lose the Founder, and then he began to make his way back across the snowy field. Dillon fixed him with a glare, but Brian kept coming, limping on his hurt leg. Dillon intercepted him before he got to Michelle.

Brian eyed Dillon as if he were betting that his friend wouldn't punch him. "Sorry. Just a word, okay? I'm not going to kidnap her. I just want to tell her something."

Dillon muttered something under his breath that Michelle didn't catch, but the murderous look in his eye was unmistakable.

Brian stopped and looked Dillon in the eye. "If you don't let me talk to her, you'll never know that she chose you, freely."

"Fine." Dillon let out an aggravated breath and whirled, his red-gold ponytail swinging out behind him. He strode off and waited alone, just out of earshot. Bear and a pack of Norms clustered at the edge of the woods, watching him intently.

Brian met Michelle in an open area, where the snow was clean and untrammeled. His brown eyes were lit with love. He began to reach for her hand, but glanced at Dillon and dropped his arms awkwardly to his sides instead. "Michelle... I need to tell you... why I can't let you go. You and me, we fit like we were made for each other. And we were."

At her puzzled look, Brian went on. "About a year ago I started to suspect it. So I hacked our files. You know, to see if we were likely to be matched. We're a perfect cross. Flawless."

"No cross is perfect," Michelle said, bewildered. "That's why Institute kids have more than two parents."

"You're right. This doesn't happen by accident. So I took a risk and asked my mom. She was furious about the hacking, but she told me the truth. When our mothers were young, they thought it would be nice to have our families linked by blood. That made for a powerful political alliance, too. So they created you to complement me in every way, ensuring we'd be matched. We're made to be together."

Brian glanced at Dillon, and then reached out and took her hand anyway. "See?" Their palms meshed perfectly, with his hand just the right size to enclose hers. His touch made her heart pound, and without really meaning to, she entwined her fingers in his.

Dillon bristled and began to walk toward them.

Brian saw him coming and spoke faster. "I know how hard this is, but I'm going to make all this worth it to you, Michelle. I promise. I know you feel it when we touch. No one can ever love you like I do."

As Dillon came closer, Brian let her hand go and dropped his voice to a whisper. "Remember what happened to his father. You can't keep him safe, not if you stay with him."

Dillon stopped a few paces away and stood there in silence for a minute. When he finally spoke, his voice was hoarse. "Michelle, I'm so sorry to do this, when you have, you know, mansions and all that to go back to. But the Conclave will never let me out from under its heel. I can't live like that."

"We could get a place together in the Warren," Michelle said in a small voice.

Dillon quirked his lip in a pained smile. "We could. But think about it. We'd be surrounded by squadrons of your bodyguards. Your friends would feel sorry for you. Enhanced men would come sniffing around all the time, with no respect for me, or our bond." Dillon glanced sharply at Brian, who dropped his eyes. "That's no life."

"Like this is?" Michelle waved a hand at the destruction all around her. Tendrils of smoke still rose from the wreck where Laird died.

"At least we're free here." With an anguished expression, Dillon took a few steps back, holding out his hands to her. "Come with me. I can't live there, and I can't live without you."

Michelle swayed a little on her feet. The world felt unreal, dreamlike and painfully bright all at once.

Dillon stopped. "I can't leave. I have…new responsibilities here. Important ones."

He waited, but Michelle didn't move. She didn't speak. As if in a trance, her mind's eye locked on the deserted playground, sand swirling in the wind. Wind whipped tendrils of hair around her face. Destiny stretched out before her, a billion shining threads of possibility. In a moment of crystalline beauty, time stopped. A single thread gleamed gold. Michelle stared into space, transfixed by the scene in her mind.

That's me. My life is that gold thread, entangled with Dillon's forest green one. And the blue line is Brian's, and the dark, metallic gray—who is that? Oh, Parker.

All her choices, and their consequences, lay before her. Like a massive chess computer, the vision calculated probabilities, playing out the game to all possible ends. Michelle traced each future she had with Dillon. Every one of them gave way to a gold thread that went on alone.

What will happen if I go home to Headquarters with Brian? Their intertwined threads spawned others, silver, burgundy, and palest lavender. *Children? We'll have children, and after that…*

Bundles of multicolored lines gathered around Parker's pewter one. *That's his army, gathering strength.* The bundle overtook her fragile gold thread and severed it. Brian's blue line zigzagged madly across the board, laying waste to hundreds of lives, until his, too, was cut off. Afterward, a lavender snippet swirled alone in the current. Michelle trembled. *I think that means I die first, then Brian. How? In Parker's war? What happens to our children?*

The vision didn't say. Dispassionate as a computer, it laid out her chances. None of them were good.

Michelle bit her lip, trying not to scream. She took a deep breath and went back to the beginning, tracing Parker's destiny through the maze of probability. As Parker's life surged along, it sliced bright Enhanced threads and mowed down whole fields of Normals. Michelle's thin, gold line trailed it. Most paths led to the same outcome—the pair, gold and pewter, coiled together like the head of a snake. Multitudes dragged behind them, towed helplessly through time.

That's…an empire. Led by me and Parker, together! How will he force me to help him? I won't do it. I refuse!

One small path split from the powerful central current, bent like a withered branch. Michelle's breath caught. She scrutinized the low-probability offshoot, a backwater of destiny that would likely never come to pass. Two threads paired up, pewter and gold. They intertwined and moved forward together, brighter than the faint glimmer of the Norms around them. The couple entered a gap, a point in time when few other lives were nearby. The gold line veered abruptly to the right, cut across the pewter, and ended it.

Michelle went cold with horror.

There's only one possible future in which Parker dies. And I kill him. He has to trust me. Even… love me? So I can betray him. Murder him.

She clenched her fists, eyes closed, face to the freezing, gray sky.

I can't do it. But if I don't, he'll kill millions. Is there no other way? No. Only the one path, without Dillon. Without Brian, or our friends. I have to do this alone.

"Michelle? Michelle!" Dillon snapped. "What's wrong with you? I tell you I have new responsibilities, and you don't even bother to ask."

She opened her eyes, confused. "Huh? What?"

Dillon stared past her. "Typical. I have so much to tell you, and you're not even listening."

"I'm sorry. What were you saying, Dillon?"

"Never mind. We can talk later," Dillon sighed. "We've got to go. The clan's waiting. People don't feel safe here anymore."

Michelle stood frozen, her mind still mired in the vision. She tried to speak, to explain, but no words came out.

"Michelle, please come with me," Dillon begged. He opened his arms to her. "I love you. Whatever happens, we'll get through it together."

Michelle didn't answer.

Ever so slowly, Dillon dropped his hands. He stared at her in disbelief. Then, with pain shining from his eyes, he walked away. At the edge of the forest, Norms shifted their feet, eager to be on their way. A line of them started off, single file through the trees. Bear and Elsie hung back, waiting for their son.

"Dillon, wait," Brian cried. His voice broke. Limping rapidly over the snow, he caught up to his best friend.

The two young men wordlessly embraced. Then they turned their backs on each other and walked off in opposite directions. Neither one looked back.

"Come on, Michelle," Sylvia shouted cheerfully, from where she stood outside an Institute helicopter. "You're holding up the show!"

Michelle stood very still, watching both the men she loved leave her at once. Part of her mind analyzed the way they walked, the power in their shoulders, the identical tense lines of their jaws. The rest of her just felt broken.

How can I do this? I love them both.

She stood alone in the snow until Dillon had almost disappeared into the trees. Brian was nearly back to his helicopter. Michelle ached to follow. *One or the other, either or both.*

She closed her eyes and watched empty swings sway hypnotically under a gray sky. Beside an abandoned merry-go-round, a few small footprints remained in the sand. They seemed important, but she didn't know why.

Michelle turned to take one last look at the people she loved. Marking the scar on the horizon that was Iron Torr, she began to run. It felt like her feet didn't quite touch the earth.

The End, until book 3

Acknowledgements

Special thanks to Hank Snider and Tony Katava for plot-line help, inspiration, and line edits. Many thanks also to Kevin Ikenberry and Larry Cope for invaluable input on army and weapons-related scenes.

About the Author

Courtney Farrell escaped from the laboratory where she was genetically engineered by evil scientists. She now lives as a fugitive, penning novels while running from Institute assassins. Contact her at:

Website www.courtneyfarrell.com

Facebook https://www.facebook.com/CourtneyFarrell.author

Twitter https://twitter.com/CAFarrell

Goodreads http://www.goodreads.com/user/show/7894049-courtney-farrell

Amazon http://www.amazon.com/-/e/B001JPBU6S